D0350333

LUNA

MOON RISING

Ian McDonald

A Tom Doherty Associates Book
New York

This is a work of fiction. All of the characters, organizations, and events portrayed in this novel are either products of the author's imagination or are used fictitiously.

LUNA: MOON RISING

A Tor Book
Published by Tom Doherty Associates
175 Fifth Avenue
New York, NY 10010

www.tor-forge.com

The Library of Congress Cataloging-in-Publication Data is available upon request.

ISBN 978-0-7653-9147-6 (hardcover)
ISBN 978-0-7653-9148-3 (ebook)

Our books may be purchased in bulk for promotional, educational, or business use. Please contact your local bookseller or the Macmillan Corporate and Premium Sales Department at 1-800-221-7945, extension 5442, or by email at MacmillanSpecialMarkets@macmillan.com.

First published in Great Britain by Gollancz, an imprint of the Orion Publishing Group, an Hachette UK company.

First U.S. Edition: March 2019

Printed in the United States of America

0 9 8 7 6 5 4 3 2 1

Contents

What Has Gone Before vii
Map: Nearside of the Moon ix

ONE 1
TWO 19
THREE 30
FOUR 52
FIVE 60
SIX 71
SEVEN 94
EIGHT 118
NINE 123
TEN 141
ELEVEN 159
TWELVE 175
THIRTEEN 178
FOURTEEN 202
FIFTEEN 232
SIXTEEN 250
SEVENTEEN 255
EIGHTEEN 269

NINETEEN 283
TWENTY 301
TWENTY-ONE 321
TWENTY-TWO 332
TWENTY-THREE 344
TWENTY-FOUR 358
TWENTY-FIVE 377
TWENTY-SIX 383
TWENTY-SEVEN 401

Glossary 429
Dramatis Personae 432
Lunar Calendar 437

WHAT HAS GONE BEFORE

The Mackenzie Metals–Corta Helio war broke the powerful Corta family and scattered the survivors. Ariel Corta, paralysed from the waist down after an assassination attempt, escapes into anonymity in Meridian's High City with her bodyguard and truest friend, Marina Calzaghe, until a summons from Jonathan Kayode, the Eagle of the Moon, to be his one true adviser among a host of enemies who would dethrone him, calls her back into lunar society. Wagner Corta, the wolf, ekes out an existence as a worker on Taiyang's sun-belt – a girdle of solar panels around the moon's equator. His life alternates between his work team and his wolf-pack until he becomes guardian and protector of Robson Corta, who had been held as a hostage by Bryce Mackenzie, Head of Finance of Mackenzie Metals. Now he must choose between his wolf-nature and caring for the vulnerable Robson. Lucasinho and Luna Corta are safe under the protection of the Asamoahs at Twé, though Lucasinho frets at his confinement. And Lucasinho's father, Lucas, has taken the boldest step of all. The Moon believes him dead, but he escaped to VTO's orbiter and over the course of a year, transformed himself into something felt to be impossible: a moon-born capable of surviving Earth's gravity. Not for long – just enough for him to cement deals he has been making while looping between moon and Earth. He forms a consortium of terrestrial governments, corporations, capital funds and, with the Vorontsovs and their orbital mass-driver as a deadly space-based weapon, seeks to take back what was stolen from his family. He also brings back Alexia, the first Earth-born Corta in two generations to brave the glory and terror of the moon.

To succeed, first Lucas must sow confusion. His mother Adriana, founder of Corta Helio, implanted attack code inside the control systems of Crucible, the Mackenzie's immense foundry-train. A simple command – issued by Alexia after Lucas is almost killed by lift-off from Earth – destroys Crucible. Lives are lost, including Robert Mackenzie, CEO of Mackenzie Metals. His sons, Duncan and Bryce, battle for control of the company. Duncan controls the traditional refining industry, Bryce the helium-3 business taken from the Cortas. Their vicious civil war threatens to engulf the whole moon and destabilise the vital helium-3 market upon which Earth depends. Lucas has his opportunity and strikes. The moon is an industrial colony, not a nation state; it has no defences. Combat units drop from orbit to storm and occupy key infrastructure sites, VTO's mass-driver threatens the whole nearside of the moon, the Dragons fight back but when Twé, the prime agriculture site for the whole moon, is besieged, there is no option but to surrender in the face of starvation.

In the chaos, Lucasinho and Luna escape from besieged Twé but find themselves marooned on the surface with the only path to safety a perilous trek through the fringes of the invasion. When Luna's suit is compromised, Lucasinho gives her his last breaths of air. She brings him to safety but can even a Moonrunner survive that long without oxygen?

Terrestrial machines and mercenaries occupy Meridian. Jonathan Kayode is defenestrated and Lucas Corta, a shadow of his former self, physically ruined by the harshness of his visit to Earth, is installed as Eagle of the Moon with Alexia as his Iron Hand. His first job is to try to recruit Ariel to his side, but she refuses, though it puts her in great danger. Every one of the Four Dragons wants leverage and Cortas are hostages-of-choice. Bryce Mackenzie makes an attempt to capture Robson Corta but is foiled. Wagner and Robson escape to the comparative safety of Theophilus in the Sea of Tranquillity.

Lucas Corta is triumphant. The moon is his: what will he do with it?

NEAR SIDE *of* THE MOON

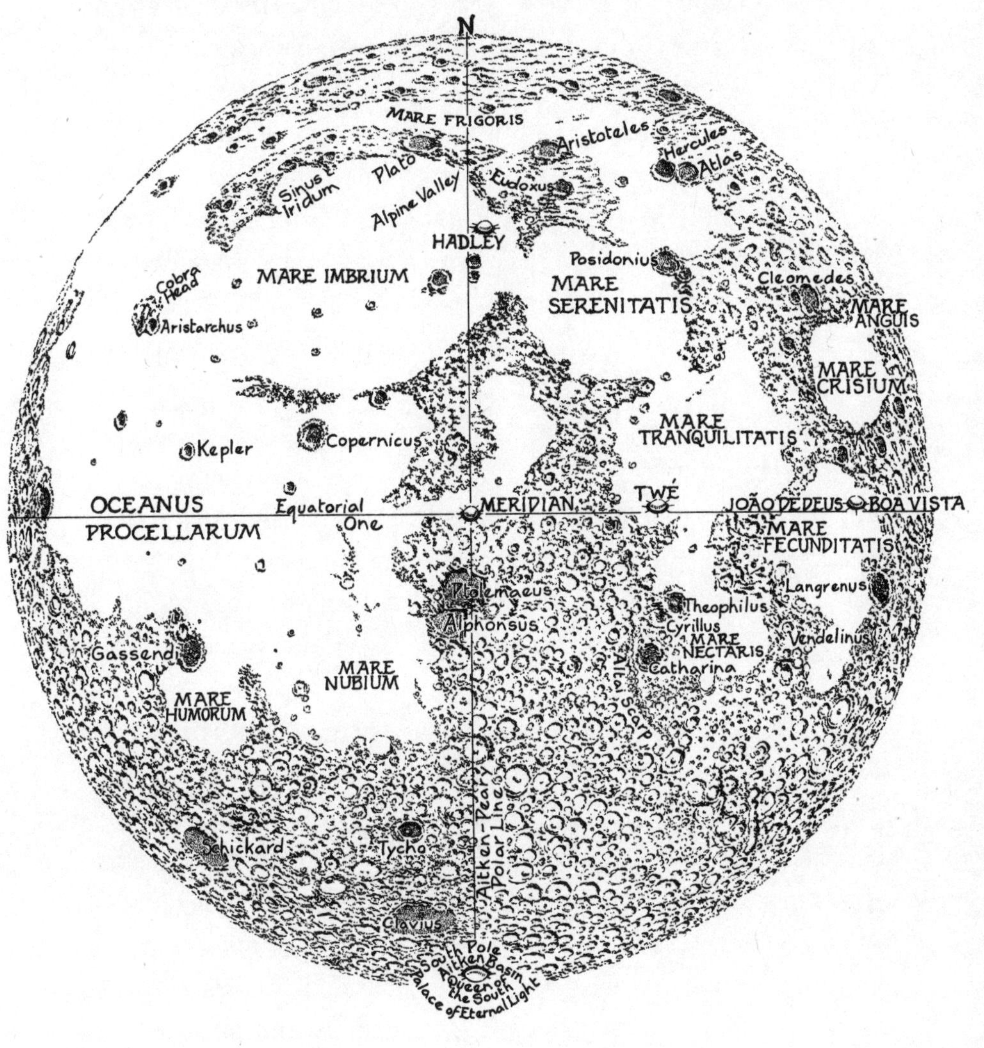

ONE

Eight figures escort the casket across the Sea of Fecundity. Four to carry, one at each handle; four to guard the cardinal directions: north, south, east and west. They shuffle in heavy armoured shell-suits. Dust scuffs high from their boots. When carrying a casket, co-ordination is everything and the bearers have not yet learned the required rhythm. They lurch, they jolt, they leave smeared tracks, blurred footsteps on the regolith. They move like walkers unaccustomed to walking on the surface of the moon, to the suits they wear. Seven white shell-suits and one, the last, scarlet and gold. Each white suit bears an emblem out of time and place: a sword, an axe, a fan, a mirror, a bow, a crescent moon. The lead walks with the aid of a furled umbrella, silver tipped, the handle a human face, one half living, one half naked bone. The tip stitches precise holes in the regolith.

It has never rained in the Sea of Fecundity.

The casket has a porthole. This would be unseemly in a coffin; this is not a coffin. This is a medical life-support pod, designed to protect and preserve the injured on the surface of the moon. Behind the window is a young man's face, brown-skinned, high strong cheek-bones, thick black hair, full lips, closed eyes. This is Lucasinho Corta. He has been in a coma for ten days; ten days that have rung the moon to its core like a stone bell. Ten days in which Eagles fell and rose, a soft war was fought and lost on the stone oceans of Luna and the old order of the moon was swept away by the new order of Earth.

These ungainly figures are the Sisters of the Lords of Now and they bear Lucasinho Corta to Meridian. Seven Sisters, plus one; the back-marker in incongruous scarlet and gold. Luna Corta.

'Is there word of the ship?' Mãe de Santo Odunlade tsks in frustration and peers at the tags on her helmet display, trying to identify the questioner. The Sisterhood of the Lords of Now by doctrine eschews the network. Learning a shell-suit interface is a sharp curve. The Mãe de Santo finally identifies Madrinha Elis as the speaker.

'Soon,' Mãe Odunlade says and raises the umbrella to point to the eastern horizon, where the ship from Meridian will touch down. The umbrella is the sigil of Oxala the Originator. With the sword, the axe, the mirror, the bow, the fan, the crescent, it is an instrument of the orixas. The Sisterhood bears not just the sleeping prince but the sacred emblems. All Santinhos understand the symbolism. João de Deus is no longer the city of the saints.

Ship on approach, the Mãe's suit says. In the same instant the horizon seems to leap into the sky. Rovers. Dozens of them. Fast, hard, bearing down. HUDs sparkle with hundreds of glowing red contacts.

The Mackenzies are here.

'Firm, my sisters,' Mãe Odunlade cries. The cortège marches forward towards the line of blazing headlights. The lights blind but she will not lift an arm to shade her eyes.

Mãe, the ship has committed to landing, the suit says.

A rover pulls out of the encirclement and swings in to confront Mãe Odunlade. She lifts the sacred umbrella high. The cortège halts. Seats descend, safety bars lift, figures in the green and white sasuits of Mackenzie Helium drop to the regolith. They reach for holsters across their backs and draw long objects. Rifles.

'This can't be permitted, Mother.'

Mãe Odunlade bridles at the familiarity. No respect, not even Portuguese. She locates the speaker on her HUD.

'Who are you?'

'I am Loysa Divinagracia,' says the woman at the centre of the armed posse. 'I am Head of Security for Mackenzie Helium, North-East Quartersphere.'

'This young man requires advanced medical attention.'

'Mackenzie Helium would be honoured to offer the services of our fully equipped company med centre.'

Sixty seconds to touchdown, the suit says. The ship is the brightest, fastest star in the sky.

'I am taking him to his father.' The Mãe de Santo steps forward.

'I can't allow that.' Loysa Divinagracia plants a hand on Mãe Odunlade's breastplate. Mãe Odunlade smacks the woman's hand away with the sacred umbrella, follows with a blow to the side of her helmet. Such insolence. Polymer cracks, atmosphere jets, then the suit heals and seals.

Guns level.

The Sisters of the Lords of Now close in around the life-support pod. The sword of Ogun is drawn, the axe of Xango, the bow, the razor-edged fan. How can the orixas be honoured, if their emblems are without practical use?

Luna Corta lifts her cumbersome arms to shoulder height. Sheathes unlock, magnets engage: knives fly to her hands and dock. The light of Earth in its first quarter, low on the western rim of the world, glints from the edges of the meteoric iron blades: the battle-knives of the Cortas.

We have protected them, Mãe de Santo Odunlade said, in the biolight-glow of the room where Lucasinho lay in the Mother House. *Until a Corta comes who is bold, great-hearted, without avarice or cowardice, who will fight for the family and defend it bravely. A Corta who is worthy of these blades.*

Carlinhos had been the family fighter. He had owned these knives before her. He had shown her the moves once, with chopsticks for blades. He scared her; the speed, the way that he became something she did not know.

Carlinhos had died on the edge of these knives.

Madrinha Elis steps between Luna and the ring of rifles.

'Put the knives away, Luna.'

'I will not,' Luna says. 'I am a Corta and Cortas cut.'

'Do as your madrinha says, wilful child,' Mãe de Santo Odunlade says. 'It is only the suit makes you big.'

Luna falls back with a sullen hiss but she does not reholster her beautiful knives.

'Let us through,' Mãe Odunlade says on the common channel, and Luna hears the Mackenzie woman answer, *Give us Lucasinho Corta and you are free to leave.*

'No,' Luna whispers and then she, the Sisters, the pod, the Mackenzie blades are drenched in blinding light. The dazzle breaks into hundreds of separate lights; rovers, dustbikes, the navigation lights of shell-suits and sasuits, all racing across the dark regolith. A vast plume of dust rises beyond them, casting moonbows in the diffracted Earth-light. They bear down on the Mackenzie encirclement. At the last minute blades and shooters flee as a wedge of rovers, dustbike outriders and a host of running dusters splits open the Mackenzie line.

From aerials and masts, from rigging wires and struts, from rovers and suitpacks and shoulder mounts, stencilled on the helmets and chestplates of surface armour, spray-painted, fast-printed, graffitied in vacuum marker: the half-black, half-white mask of Our Lady of the Thousand Deaths, Dona Luna.

João de Deus has risen.

The wedge of dusters unfolds into a phalanx of pikes and spears. Dustbikers brace polearms against footpegs. Luna saw a thing in a story like that when she was a very small kid, a crazy bit of old Earth: metal men sitting on big metal animals, with long spears tucked under their arms. *Knights-in-armour,* Luna's familiar tells her, remembering as she remembers. *Knights with lances.*

Blue lights flicker high above the encamped armies: the attitude thrusters of a VTO moonship manoeuvring over the Mackenzie lines to a safe landing site. The main engine gives a final, brief burn as the ugly amalgam of fuel tanks, radiator panels and structural beams comes in for landing.

Gauntlets and gloves tighten on spear shafts. Pikes brace. Fingers close on dustbike steering bars.

'Luna,' Madrinha Elis says.

'I'm ready,' Luna says. Luna's suit is primed, the power reserves activated. Give the word, and it will run, run faster than her own legs could ever carry her. She knows the feats a standard-issue suit can achieve: she used them when she carried Lucasinho, anoxic, by any standard *dead,* to the refuge of Boa Vista. 'I've done this before.'

The dust from the moonship's descent burn engulfs Santinhos and Mackenzies. Madrinha Elis shouts, *Go, child.*

Run, she orders but the suit is already in motion.

So are the Mackenzies. The moment of surprise is over; rovers peel off to outflank the Santinho dustbike cavalry and cut off the path to the ship. Santinho foot-soldiers charge to intercept the Mackenzie force and hold open the way.

A body falls. A figure in a sasuit twists and goes down. A shell-suit splinters into flying shards. The Mackenzie guns have opened up. A helmet shatters. A head flies into bloody smash; the banners of Dona Luna fall, one by one. Now Luna sees the blood, the plugs of flesh, the body fluids gouting into vacuum.

Sister Eloa of the Crescent of Iansa goes down at Luna's side, tumbling and rolling. The top of her head has been ripped away. Slugs are flying unseen all around Luna but she can't think of them, can't think of anything but the moonship, settling on its landing gear, unfolding a ramp from its transport pod.

'Luna!' Mãe Odunlade's voice on the private channel. 'Take the right side of the casket. The suit can handle it.'

'Mãe . . .'

'Elis will take the other side.'

'Mãe . . .'

'Don't argue, child!'

Her armoured hand locks on to one of the handles. The gyros stabilise the weight. She sees her madrinha lock on to the other handle.

Santinhos engage Mackenzies. Two, ten, twenty, drop under withering fire but there are always more spears, more pikes. Hand-to-hand violence, close, intimate, passionate as sex. Spear points drive deep, punch through bodies from front to back, tear suit, skin, bone, shatter visors and stab down through faces, skulls, brains.

'What's happening?' she asks on Madrinha Elis's private channel.

'They're buying us time, anjinho.'

The phalanx of spears reforms, links, locks, lunges in attack. The shooters break and retreat. In that instant, between the walls of pikes, Luna feels her suit tighten its grip on the handle of her cousin's casket, lean forward and sprint for the ship. She hits the ramp at full speed, brakes hard to avoid the rear bulkhead of the transport pod. Crew in sasuits secure the pod. Luna feels the deck vibrate through her boot haptics.

Main engine burn in ten nine eight . . .

Luna's final glance through the closing doors is of the remaining Sisters of the Lords of the Now, white suits back to back, the sigils of the orixas held high. Around them, a ring of pikes, and the bold banners of Our Lady of the Thousand Deaths. Beyond, the Mackenzies, numerous as stars. Then the engine fires and dust covers everything.

Mãe de Santo Odunlade watches the moonship lift from the blinding dust on a diamond of rocket-light.

Meridian will harbour them. Meridian will heal them. The Eagle of the Moon will take them under his wings.

The Santinhos encircle the Sisters with pikes and lances. So many down, so many dead. This is a terrible place to die.

Mãe Odunlade finds the icon for the common channel.

'The regolith has drunk enough blood,' she calls to every duster and Santinho in the Sea of Fecundity, to every blade and mercenary, to Bryce Mackenzie, wherever he hides himself.

The Mackenzie gunline stands firm.

'There is no need for anyone else to die out here.'

Two rovers start from the rear of the encirclement, accelerating with startling speed in pursuit of the moonship, now a constellation of hazard lights, burning westwards. Mechanisms unfold from the backs of the rovers; things with multiple barrels, belts of ammunitions. Gods and spirits, those things are fast. Already they are on the horizon. Streamers of light arc up – seeking the lights of the VTO ship. Mãe de Santo Odunlade does not know what she is seeing but she understands what it means. If Bryce Mackenzie cannot have Lucasinho Corta, no one will. And she understands another truth. There will be no mercy here for anyone who lifted hand and blade in the name of the Cortas.

'In the name of Oxala, light of light, ever-living, ever-fearful, ever-sure!' Mãe de Santo Odunlade raises the umbrella high above her head. Opens it. As one, the remaining Sisters lift high their sigils. The sword of Ogun, the fan of Yemanja, the bow of Oxossi, the axe of Xango.

The shooting begins.

Luna can't unlock her fist from the medical pod. Lucasinho is free, Lucasinho is safe; she should let go of him now, but the suit reads a truth she can't acknowledge and won't release her. This suit: she feels she has been in it forever. This suit, it has protected her, guided her, helped her. Betrayed her, endangered her.

A memory: Lucasinho wrapping tape around the joint seal where razor-edged moondust ate away the pleated fabric, step after step, kilometre after kilometre, until the joint blew out. She touches the knee joint, the glove haptics relay the rough imperfection of the binding. She had not noticed the patch when the Mãe de Santo had told her to come now, child, suit up, we are leaving.

Where are we going, Mãe?

Meridian. The Eagle has sent a ship for his son.

She pulled on a suit-liner, stepped into the huge hulk, the haptic rig embraced her and the shell sealed and she was back in the lock at Lubbock BALTRAN station and Lucasinho was calling her to step forward. *The suit does all the work.*

And even as she was clanking along the peripheral tunnel towards the lock she was back in the refuge at Boa Vista, under the green light and Lucasinho lying where she had laid him. The big suit could be so gentle. Lying, not moving. Not breathing.

What do I do?

The refuge showed her where to connect Lucasinho to the LSU, where to jack in the monitors, where to attach the refrigeration unit that would keep him in deep, saving cold.

He is very sick, the machines told her. *He requires critical medical attention.*

But all she could do was wait in the cold and the green light. As she waits now in the hold of a VTO moonship.

Freefall in three, two, one . . .

The launch burn ends. Luna's boots put out bristles to hook her to the micro-loops woven into the decking. She is anchored but free; she remembers the dizzy, sick-in-the-pit feeling of freefall from the BALTRAN. She hated it then. She doesn't like it any better when it is a VTO moonship on a sub-orbital trajectory to Meridian.

A series of bangs rattles up through Luna's boots. Centimetres from the heel of her left foot is a line of holes, precisely spaced. A clatter; another line of holes is stitched across the cargo hold bulkhead, bottom right to upper left. Earth-light streams through the perforations.

A third set of impacts, then a sudden acceleration rips Luna from the floor, tears her fingers free from their grip on her cousin's pod. Acceleration shifts, throws her towards Lucasinho's coffin, then she is floating free, swimming in mid-air.

We are under attack, the ship says. *We have been penetrated by high velocity kinetic rounds. Hull integrity has been compromised. Number three tank was punctured and out-gassed, hence the unplanned acceleration which I have now stabilised.*

Luna grabs hold of the life-support lines and hauls herself towards the bulkhead. Another burst of impacts drives an arc of holes through the decking and out through the roof. Two heartbeats ago her head had been there. There are holes in the roof. There are holes everywhere.

Luna turns and her boots once again anchor with the decking. She turns to look for Elis: there she is in a pile of white pressure plastic on the other side of the casket. She doesn't move, doesn't speak. Why is she down? Lady Luna, let there be no holes in her suit, no holes in her madrinha.

A sighing groan on the private channel. The heap of surface armour shifts, becomes a person in a suit. Madrinha Elis struggles to her knees.

Then the lights go out.

'What's happening?' Luna cries.

The main power connector has been severed, the ship says. *Auxiliary power will come online momentarily. I should inform you that my processing core has been severely damaged and my functionality is impaired.*

Emergency lights flash on, low and sickly yellow. Luna's helmet HUD is a mosaic of red alarms: the crew, up in the command module, in trouble. One by one they turn white.

White is the colour of death.

'Elis!'

Her madrinha comes to her, opens her machine arms, embraces the monstrous, clumsy suit.

'Coraçao.'

'Are you all right?'

'The pod,' Madrinha Elis says. 'The pod.'

'Lucasinho!'

Luna circles the casket, checking for holes, damage, the slightest graze. A near miss has drawn a valley across the bottom left corner of the pod. She presses her visor to the window. Everything seems to be working.

There has been a change to the flightplan, the ship says. *I shall be making an emergency landing at Twé. Standby for turnover in three... two... one...*

Micro-accelerations jostle Luna, then she is in freefall once more.

Stand by for main engine de-orbit burn.

Weight returns; many Luna piled on her shoulders. The suit braces, stiffens but Luna feels her teeth grind, her blood heavy like lead in her veins.

Distress calls initiated, the ship says. Luna imagines fear in its calm, informative voice. *My radiator panels have sustained catastrophic damage. I am unable to discharge excess heat.*

On her trek with Lucasinho across the south-eastern quarter-sphere, Luna learned the nature of vacuum. It was Lady Luna's favoured weapon, but she has other, subtler ways of killing than just the deep, suffocating kiss. Vacuum is a very fine insulator – the finest. The only way for heat to escape is by radiation. Her own shell-suit could deploy vanes from its shoulders to radiate away the heat of the suit's systems, and her own small body. A ship makes a lot more heat than a girl, most of all when firing its engines. Critical systems could overheat, fail, even melt down. To land safely at Twé the engine must fire hard and hot, heat that cannot be radiated away. Heat, adding to heat, building on heat.

The ship is shaking. She doesn't remember it shaking like this on launch. The engine cuts – she falls free for an instant – then relights. And off – the engine stutters, firing, misfiring. She can hardly see through the rattling, shuddering braking burn.

I am experiencing… critical systems failures, the ship says. *I am dying.*

The shaking stops. Main engine cut out. Luna is falling towards the surface of the moon in a box, a shell, a hulk riddled with bullet holes.

White spirits float in the vacuum inside the transport pod. *No ghosts on the moon,* everyone knows that. What are these wisps of spirit, coiling up from every cable and duct, every decking fibre and vacuum-marker scrawl?

Then Luna notices her own temperature monitor. The decking beneath her feet registers one hundred and fifteen Celsius.

Volatiles are boiling off from the polymers and organics, the suit AI tells her. *I estimate we will hit melting point in three minutes.*

Her shell-suit is made of plastic. Strong plastic, tough plastic that can walk on the face of Lady Luna, good plastic doing everything it can to keep her cool, but she will bake to death inside her suit long before it runs out of air.

I'm directing maximum available power to environment control, the suit says. *Radiator panels deploying.*

Luna feels the click of fins unfurling from her back. Wings: magic wings like the Luna moth, her familiar.

Bracing for impact, the suit says suddenly.

Wha… Luna starts and then something hits her harder than she has ever been hit, so hard even the haptic rig cannot absorb the full weight of the impact. She slams hard against the floor and bulkheads of the transport pod. She hears wings snap, plastic crack. She is a tiny bean rattling inside a gourd.

I have sustained integrity-threatening damage, the suit says. Luna tries to inhale; she can't catch her breath.

Madrinha Elis hauls herself to her feet.

'Anjinho, we have to get out. Open the door. I'll get Lucasinho.'

The hold is hazy with fumes; conduits sag, trunking buckles. The deck tilts; the transport door is upslope.

The door will not open.

Luna slaps the red button again. The door will not open.

'Where is the manual override?' Luna asks her suit. *The second rule of moonwalking: everything has a manual override.* Her Uncle Carlinhos told her that. Big smiling Tio Carlinhos who came all too rarely to Boa Vista, but when he did he would scoop her up and throw her high up into the air so that her hair flew out and she would scream even though she knew he would always be there to catch her. The first rule of moonwalking: everything can kill you.

Big, grinning Tio Carlinhos, back then when she had been a kid, before she took the knives and became the princess of Corta Hélio.

The suit highlights a small hatch. Inside is a handle.

'There's one on my side too,' Madrinha Elis says. 'Together.'

Madrinha Elis counts down on her fingers. Three, two . . . Luna pulls the handle. The door drops on its struts. Luna looks down over the edge. She stands on the lip of a three-metre drop to the regolith. The ship has come down on the edge of a small crater. Beyond the close rim Luna can see the dishes and mirror masts of Twé. It is an easy jump down to the surface. She skids back down the sloping deck and brakes herself by catching one of the casket's handles. Elis braces the head of the casket. Luna undogs the latches. The casket slides. Elis takes the strain, then Luna darts to the casket's foot and pulling, pushing, they move the heavy medical pod up the deck on to the ramp. To the edge.

There is no gentle way to do this.

Together, they push Lucasinho over the edge. He falls under the slow lunar gravity, strikes feet first and tumbles forward to land porthole down. Two steps behind, Luna and Elis leap from the platform and land in eruptions of dust. They are the only survivors of VTO moonship *Pustelga*.

Elis jabs a finger at the fallen coffin, mimes the act of lifting. The two shell-suits crouch and turn the casket over. The pod, the glass is intact. Lucasinho is slumped over on his side, still and unmoving. Luna can't tell if he is alive or dead.

'Get him away from the ship,' Elis says. Together they drag Lucasinho away from the wreck of the *Pustelga*. The ship lies like a crushed festival butterfly. Two sets of landing legs have failed, one folded by the off-centre landing, the other driven up through the hull. Every radiator panel has been shot out, empty wing-ribs outspread. The punctured fuel tank still jets vapour. One thruster group has been entirely torn away. The ship is pierced through and through with holes, stabbed a thousand times. Intersecting of fire stitched across the cargo module. Luna cannot believe they survived. The command module is riddled. There is nothing left intact, nothing left alive. Batteries explode; debris clatters off Luna's shell-suit. Molten plastic drips from the bullet holes. As Luna watches, the ship collapses further. She can see a dull red glow from the engines. This ship is going to explode. The two women heft Lucasinho's coffin and make best speed for the far rim of the crater. They slip-slide down the loose regolith towards the domes and tanks and aerials of Twé, capital of the Asamoahs. The sun-domes, that let light feed down to the mirror arrays, are being cleared of the piled regolith that the LMA invaders had bulldozed over them, smothering them, shutting out the light to the silo farms.

Warnings blossom on Luna's visor. Her suit is dying by degrees, critical systems failing. She has seen this before, walked this dying walk before, out on the glasslands of Boa Vista, when her suit failed and Lucasinho patched her up and gave her the last breath in his lungs.

Twé must know. A damaged ship coming in, an emergency landing. Twé will send help. Twé has always been the friend of the Cortas.

Two plumes of dust appear on the horizon. Within seconds they become two tracks cutting in from the east. Luna waves: *Here! Look! Here we are.*

'Why are the Asamoahs coming from that direction?' Elis asks.

Luna can see the rovers now. She's seen them before; she's seen the chain-guns on the roof before.

'Run,' Luna yells

The suit shows Luna the closest entry lock but the suits are low on power and the casket is heavy and they can never run as fast as a Mackenzie Helium rover.

A dustbike cuts in front of Luna, a second, a third. A pack of dustbikes, each flying heraldic adinkra banners in the airless sky. Blackstars. The bikes encircle them. The rider directly ahead of her raises a hand. Stop. Luna and Elis stand still, the life-support casket slung between them. The riders on either side of the commander slip from their machines and run cables from bike to suits and casket.

White panels switch to red: Luna's visor fills with names, tags, identities, ranges, schematics.

'We have you,' the blackstar leader says.

'Set the pod down,' a voice says on the common channel. The Mackenzies have arrived. Luna shivers in rage at the Australian accent. She has had enough of these people, enough enough enough. She will not comply. She will not abandon Lucasinho. She switches her grip on the casket and turns to the uninvited voice.

The two Mackenzie Helium rovers are parked a hundred metres upslope. The crews drop from their seats and form a line. One carries a rifle. The rover-mounted chain-guns swivel, level, lock.

There is a blade in every blackstar hand.

'Enough!'

Luna stamps her foot.

'I am Luna Ameyo Arena de Corta and I am a princess!' she shouts. 'Rafael Corta was my father, Lousika Yaa Dede Asamoah is my mother, Omahene of the Golden Stool of AKA. Touch me and you touch the whole Asamoah nation.'

'Luna,' Madrinha Elis whispers on the private channel but Luna is angry now, more angry than she has ever been in her life. A hundred angers from a thousand injustices, distilled into a pure and righteous rage.

'Go away!' Luna shouts.

Not a word on the common channel, but the jackaroos break and return to their rovers. The blackstars hold their defensive wall. Then the chain-guns flick and swivel away from their acquired targets. The rovers turn in rings of dust. In a breath they are halfway to the horizon.

'Luna,' Madrinha Elis says again, and on the common channel the blackstar leader says, 'You're safe now.'

But Luna stands still and solid, hand locked to her cousin's coffin. 'Go away go away go away,' she says. 'Go away!'

When the doors close, Finn Warne keeps his eyes firmly fixed on the lighted ceiling panel. The express elevator ascent of the western flank of Kingscourt takes twenty seconds but the speed is as much of the problem for him as the two-kilometre climb from the floor of Queen of the South to Bryce's private suite. It isn't professional for Mackenzie Helium's Head of Security to suffer from acrophobia. This way, hands behind back, gazing into the light, it looks as if he is meditating, gathering his inner resources.

Bryce could have done all this through the network. The modern businessperson does not need to personally instruct his First Blade. The nature of the oligarch is to have what you do not need.

Neither does a modern businessperson need a personal receptionist in a pure white dress behind a pure white desk. Finn Warne has always prided himself on his grooming; nails manicured, nasal hair trimmed, hair brillantined and combed in the current 1940s fashion. But Krimsyn behind the desk always makes him feel coarse and lax, tie knotted a fraction too loosely, a line of grime under a fingernail, shave a shade too blue. And he knows she knows he's scared of heights.

Finn gives the rubric for security clearance on the highest possible level. Krimsyn tilts her head, the least recognition she can give.

To ameliorate the disdain, Finn Warne imagines sex with Krimsyn. He likes to imagine that the perfect composure, the exquisite attention to detail extends to every part of her body and that, no matter how intense or rough or extended the sex, it would never break.

A click. The door to Bryce Mackenzie's sanctum is unlocked.

'Mr Warne.'

Bryce lies on the surgical bed by the glass wall. He is naked; a landslide of flesh, a mass of fat that rolls and laps on to the white upholstery. White, grainy stretchmarks stain his skin. The machines attend him like devotees at prayer, two at his shoulders, two attending his belly, two at the hips. Their long arms carry the needles and the suction devices that will lick away his body fat.

Finn approaches as close as he dares. The window overlook is monstrous: not the sheer drop – he has never dared look at that – but the panorama of the towers of Queen of the South; each spire, chopstick slim, a reminder of how high he is and how much more stands above him until it merges with the machinery in the roof of Queen's lava chamber. Monstrous, but not as monstrous as the thing on the surgical bed.

'You didn't get him,' Bryce says.

'The rover squads were not contracted to engage the Asamoahs,' Finn says.

Bryce inhales sharply as the machines flex their arms and drive the needles into his flesh.

'Your job was to bring me Lucasinho Corta.'

'We issued hasty contracts. We had to move the instant the boy did,' Finn says. He can see the cannulas moving under Bryce's skin, tunnelling through fat.

'Excuses, Mr Warne?'

Finn Warne suppresses the clench of fear.

'And now Lucasinho Corta is at Twé, under the protection of the

Asamoahs once again. We had two rovers armed with chain-guns. Remind me, how were the blackstars armed?'

'Dustbikes and blades.'

'Dustbikes and blades. Against chain-guns.'

'Our mercenaries' legal systems advised against provocative action.'

Bryce is pinned like a specimen, unable to move. He rolls his eyes to regard Finn Warne.

'Chain-guns that brought down a VTO moonship.'

'Legal services has received a claim for compensation from St Olga.'

A twitch, a grunt from the stainless table.

'Contest it. And contest the completion payment with the gun crews. Fucking mercenaries.'

'They had no authority to start a war with AKA.'

Yellow fat flows down the tubes to translucent sacks under the bed.

'Any survivors at João de Deus?'

'None.'

'That's something. Our own losses?'

The needles pull out. Thin lines of blood leak from the wounds, then subtler robot hands go in to swab, sterilise, seal. The needles seek new targets and go in. Bryce gives another small gasp. It sounds sexual to Finn. The skin of his balls prickles.

'We weren't expecting a fight.'

'Show me the figures.'

A flicker of data, familiar to familiar.

'Mostly our own jackaroos,' Bryce comments. 'Good. Mercenaries are expensive. Standard compensation plus ten per cent. As you say, they weren't expecting a fight. So here we are, with no hostage, João de Deus hating me even more than they did before, and Yevgeny Vorontsov wanting me to spring him a new moonship. Bit of a fucking cock-up, isn't it, Mr Warne?'

'What are your instructions, Mr Mackenzie?'

'Mines, Mr Warne. Explosive ones. Take an engineer team and

mine Lucas Corta's fucking precious city. I want everything to blow. Keep it quiet. You can do that, can't you? And have someone in technical services code a routine into my familiar. If anything happens to me, I want João de Deus a crater. He took my home; I take his.'

The cannulas pull out with an unctuous suck and search for fresh fat to sip.

TWO

There, again, shrill and high and piercing through the humming roar of the Orion Quadra morning: the call. Short, stabbing needles of sound, rounded by a trill.

Alexia pauses in her morning dress, fingers frozen on the button of her tight-waisted jacket. The slightest movement, the least rustle of fabric will obliterate the song. And it's gone. Alexia moves on stockinged feet to her balcony. She holds herself icy still, listening for the piping note through the chords of a hundred different electric engines, the throb of water in the pipes, the hush of the artificial winds, the chorus of human voices that are the loudest ingredient in Meridian's music. She focuses her concentration into a sharp arrow of listening. Even her heartbeat, the brush of her breath, is too loud.

There: staccato pin-pricks of sound far off down the quadra. Something strange, something alive, something not human. Green gold, a fleck of red, blurs across her vision. She follows the movement. A bird.

'What is that?' Alexia has learned to accept the icons in her eye that represent the Four Elementals. The Iron Hand of the Eagle of the Moon will never know the choking fear of oxygen debt, of borrowing breaths from family, from friends; of weaving water from the exhalations of the moon's million and a half citizens. But their lights never go out and Alexia can never forget that in this world everything is priced and accounted. Her familiar is still unfamiliar. Alexia has given it a name, as is the custom – Maninho – and skinned it as a cartoon kid in baggy T-shirt, shorts and too-big shoes to make it non-threatening, but she still hesitates to speak to it out loud. At home, AIs know their place.

At home.

A red-rumped parakeet, Maninho says silently in her implanted bud. Alexia gasps as the colours dart towards her and then perch on the railing of her neighbour's balcony: a bird.

'Oh look at you,' Alexia Corta breathes. She squats down, twitters and hisses at the bird, finger held out; the universal invocation of small creatures and babies. 'Aren't you handsome?' The parakeet cocks its head to regard her first with the right eye, then the left. Its plumage morphs from turquoise-green on the crown across emerald wings to a yellow belly. Its rump is a splash of hot brick-red.

Apart from fish and crustaceans in hotshop tanks and pet ferrets on leads, it is the only non-human living thing Alexia has since seen leaving Earth.

What is it doing here? Alexia tightens her jaw muscles and sub-vocalises into the implanted microphone, a trick that every moon-kid knows before they can walk and which she has still not mastered.

From its behaviour, I would surmise that it is trying to solicit food from you, Maninho says.

I didn't mean, Alexia says... She may have skinned her familiar like a beach-bunny goofball but it has the personality of a priest instructing catechism. *I mean, why are they here at all?*

Feral colonies have been established in Queen of the South for twenty years, Maninho says. *Meridian's population is around five hundred birds. They have proved resistant to eradication. Biological infestation is a persistent problem in urban centres.*

What do they eat?

Grains, fruit, nuts and seeds, Maninho says. *Food surplus. They are entirely dependent on humans.*

'Don't fly away passarinho,' Alexia says. She backs away slowly into her living room. The old apartment on Ocean Tower had been cramped, but this was a jail cell. *Where's my penthouse view?* she had complained. Her assistants frowned, baffled. This was high status accommodation suitable for the personal assistant to the Eagle of the Moon. Her staff explained how deep radiation penetrated from the surface into the regolith. The higher your status, the lower your station. *And where's the kitchen?* Perplexed, the civil servants had flipped up the sink, pulled out the waste disposal, slid the refrigerator out from the wall. *Where do I store things? Where do I cook?* Again, raised eyebrows. *You want to cook?* You eat out. You pick a hotshop, you get to know the regulars, you get to know your chef, you build a little community. Apartment kitchens are for making cocktails and brewing mint tea, if you absolutely categorically cannot get to a tea-house.

Nuts. She has some cashews in the fridge. Cashews, cashew juice, are the taste of home. They are the only things in the fridge. Birds like nuts, don't they?

Message from Lucas, Maninho says.

'Shit.'

It's not even a voice call. A message, an instruction. Change of plan. Meet me at the Pavilion of the New Moon. Dress for a plenary session.

She throws a handful of nuts on to the balcony and, as she turns away, Alexia sees a flutter of green in her peripheral vision.

The man ducks into the elevator as close behind Alexia as her shadow. His stench catches in Alexia's craw. Alexia's sense of smell was the first to be assaulted by the moon, and the first to acclimatise. When she stepped out of the moonloop capsule into Meridian Hub, the reek had almost floored her. The gagging catch of sewage, the taint of rebreathed air and the bodies that had breathed it, the crackle of ozone and electricity, the greasy, sweet perfume of new-printed plastics. Bodies, sweats, bacteria and moulds. Cooking smells, decaying vegetation, stagnant water. Over all, before all, the spicy, burned-out-firework smell of moondust. Then one morning she woke in her tiny bedroom and was no longer greeted by the chasm of stench. It was part of her now. Fused to her skin, her throat, the linings of her tubes and lungs.

The entire elevator notices this man.

He is tall, gaunt, white, unshaven. He wears the default mooniform of hoodie and leggings but his clothes are dirty: unthinkable in a society that wears, discards, reprints daily. He is naked: no familiar hovers over his left shoulder. The man catches Alexia's glance and locks looks.

Alexia Corta has never been the first to look away.

The passengers thin out as the elevator climbs. By the time it reaches the level of the LMA Council offices suspended symbolically between Earth and the deep-down lunar elite, only Alexia and stinking man remain.

The elevator slows, stops.

'Give me some air,' he gasps as the door opens. He steps into the doorway to prevent it closing.

'Excuse me.' Alexia pushes past and his hand snags her wrist. She pulls free with enough force to communicate that she could snap his arm with a thought, but pauses to face the affront. *This is what poverty looks like,* Alexia realises. She had grown up believing that everyone was rich on the moon. She had sat on the parapet of Ocean Tower and looked up at a tiny, distant ball of billionaires.

'Please. A breath. Of. Air.' She hears the strain in every word. Every syllable is a cost. This man is fighting for breath. His chest barely moves, the sinews of his neck are tight as cables, every muscle is focused on the act of respiration. He can't breathe.

'I'm sorry, I'm new, I don't know how to do that,' Alexia stammers, stepping away from the slowly asphyxiating man.

'Fucking LMA,' he whispers after her. He cannot afford a shout. 'Not. Even. Worth. Air. We. Breathe.'

Alexia turns.

'What do you mean?'

The door has closed.

'What do you mean?' Alexia shouts. The elevator ascends at express speed towards the high city where the poor people live.

Alexia, Maninho says, *you are two minutes and twenty-three seconds late. Lucas is waiting.*

With folded hands, Lady Sun awaits the Lunar Mandate Authority. The honourable delegates will be irked: made to travel from Meridian to Queen of the South, then to the Palace of Eternal Light, finally the humiliating walk across the polished stone floor of the Great Hall of Taiyang to the small door where Lady Sun waits with her entourage. Let them be irked. The Dowager of Shackleton is not summoned like an infant.

They move like frightened hens, these Earthmen, in picky, parsimonious steps, huddled together as if the floor might swallow them. Earthmen. Such loathsome suits. Narrow ties, mean shoes. The uniform of apparatchiks and corporate ideologues. Their familiars are identical steel-grey crescents, as if they were mere digital assistants and not external AI souls. Her entourage – tall, handsome, well tailored – looks down on the terrestrials.

'Sun Cixi.'

She waits.

She can wait until the sun turns cold.

'Lady Sun.'

'Delegate Wang.'

'We are concerned for the well-being of Delegate James F Cockburn. He was assigned as LMA liaison with Taiyang, with particular portfolio for the equatorial solar array,' says Delegate Wang, a cool and calculating woman from Beijing. Party apparatchik.

'We want to know if Delegate Cockburn has met with an accident.' Lady Sun's familiar identifies the speaker as Anselmo Reyes, from the Davenant venture capital group. The LMA has sent its highest-ranking officers.

'I regret that Delegate Cockburn met with a fatal accident during an inspection of the North Grimaldi sector of the Sun-ring,' Lady Sun says. 'Surface suits, even shell-suits, require skill and experience.'

'We were not immediately informed?' Delegate Wang says.

'The network is still recovering from the invasion,' says Demeter Sun from the Taiyang entourage, as rehearsed.

'The rationalisation, you mean,' Delegate Wang corrects. Demeter Sun dips his head.

'Taiyang will conduct a full accident investigation,' Sun Guoxi says. 'You will be provided with the report, and any compensation claims will be satisfied.'

'Please accept this from the Board of Taiyang,' Lady Sun says. She lifts a finger and Sun Xiulan steps forward with the box. Small, intricate, lunar titanium, laser-cut. Exquisite. Wang Yongqing lifts out a calligraphic scroll.

'Carbon, fifty-eight thousand five hundred and twenty-three point two five grams, sixteen thousand six hundred and sixty-four point three seven grams oxygen,' Delegate Wang says. 'Explain, please.'

'The chemical constituents of James F Cockburn, by mass,' says Lady Sun. 'Surprisingly high counts in lead, mercury, cadmium and gold nanoparticles. Isn't the calligraphy exquisite? Sun Xuilan has an enviable hand.'

A tall young man dips his head.

'The elements have already been added to the general organics pool,' Lady Sun says. 'The zabbaleen are most accurate in their end-of-life audits. I find such precision reassuring.'

Sun Xiulan has an enviable hand with the calligrapher's brush but the finest touch is Jiang Ying Yue's with the knife. She is Taiyang's Corporate Conflict Resolution Officer, a perfumed title for what more direct clans, like the Mackenzies, would have called First Blade. The Three August Ones had foreseen the coming of an agent of the People's Republic; simple checks had identified James F Cockburn as that agent to seventy-five per cent certainty. Odds short enough for the Board, in the shadows and glare of the Palace of the Eternal Light, to order a termination. Jiang Ying Yue was tasked, armed and dispatched. She personally escorted Delegate Cockburn on the private railcar. While the car was still in the Shackleton crater wall tunnel, Jiang Ying Yue slipped the bone blade from the holster inside her suit and drove it up through the soft flesh of James F Cockburn's jaw into his brain. Zabbaleen were waiting at the siding at the BALTRAN terminal. They removed the body, the knife and every stain and trace of DNA. Stains are blood, blood is carbon and carbon belongs to the moon.

'This is . . .' Monique Bertin stammers, the third executive officer of the LMA, representing the interests of the European Union.

'Our way, Madame Bertin,' Lady Sun says. The crook of a finger is the sign to her entourage that the meeting is over. 'Please enjoy the hospitality of the Palace of Eternal Light.' Lady Sun's young women and men close in around her as she takes her leave. Excellent boys and girls.

'Did you notice?' Lady Sun says as they step into the tram capsule that will take her to private suites.

'All defer to Madam Wang,' her Corporate Conflict Resolution Officer says.

'The People's Republic has not forgotten,' Lady Sun says. 'They have waited sixty years, but they have grown greedy and lax. They have made an error. They have shown us how deeply they control the LMA. And we can use that against them.'

The capsule slips across tunnels and slows into Lady Sun's private station.

Madam, Darius Mackenzie has arrived, Lady Sun's familiar announces.

'Darius Sun,' Lady Sun corrects. 'Ying Yue, please call my granddaughter Amanda. I wish to see her in my apartment.'

The lift of a hand dismisses Jiang Ying Yue at the capsule door. Lady Sun pauses to observe her great-nephew. Five days ago she left him under the tutelage of the School of Seven Bells. Already he looks leaner, sharper, tighter. Disciplined. And he has stopped vaping.

We make weapons here, Mariano Gabriel Demaria had said.

Lady Sun has sent many of her family to learn the way of the knife but the weapon she forges here is something subtler and greater. A weapon borne in plain sight, like a sword on a wall, that after years still carries a lethal edge. A weapon that might only be drawn after she is dead.

'Darius.'

'Taihou.' The honorific is not precisely correct but Mariano Gabriel Demaria has put manners on him, after the unseemly informalities of Kingscourt. When did the Mackenzies become soft and decadent? In the great days the Suns and Mackenzies forged this world. Hammered steel, the Mackenzies; and she had been as hard, diamond to their metal. Lady Luna was harsh then; every breath, every tear wrestled from her. So few now: Robert Mackenzie dead; Yevgeny Vorontsov doting, prodded along by his grandchildren like a pig to market. Even Adriana Corta, last of the Dragons, first to die. She had the iron in the bone. It is the children who disappoint. Workboots to workboots in three generations. The first generation makes it, the second generation spends it, the third generation loses it. Lucas Corta, there is a son to his mother. Travelling to Earth, that was a thing the old Dragons would have admired. It's impossible, so do it anyway.

She had intended that the Cortas and Mackenzies destroy each other. There is work yet to be done.

'I trust Mariano is taxing you?' Lady Sun asks. She moves to her windows, slits of blazing light cut deep into the rim-rock of Shackleton Crater. Toughened glass, six centimetres thick, yet the unrelenting sunlight of the South Pole chips away at atomic bonds, day by day, lune by lune. One day, one lune, they will fail. Lady Sun finds a comfort in imagining that. It is bracing, strengthening to know the end. Blades of brilliant, dusty light slash the room. Lady Sun's apartment is spacious and simply furnished; her luxury is the fabrics and weaves clothing her walls. The shafts of sunlight, never varying in height at this extreme latitude, have bleached long lines across her brocades and tapestries. It is a matter of indifference to Lady Sun. She enjoys her textiles for their tactile properties; creative weaves can change in a stroke from fur-soft to the little tearings of cat tongues.

'If that means, is it intense, then intense,' Darius Sun-Mackenzie says. 'He's teaching me to sense. Before fighting there is moving, before moving there is sensing.'

'The maze,' Lady Sun says. The whole moon knows the legend of the dark maze, where true fighters are trained, strung with seven bells hanging in blackness. When you can walk the maze without sounding a single chime you have learned all the School of Seven Bells can teach you. 'Show me what you've learned.'

Lady Sun lifts a walking stick from a glass pot. Unthinking guests and children give her sticks as gifts. She brings it down with all her force on Darius's head. He isn't there. He's a step away, balanced and ready. Lady Sun lays into Darius with the cane like a widow beating off housebreakers. Darius steps, swerves, bends around the blows; the least possible movement so that the strike misses him by millimetres.

Grace and elegance, Lady Sun thinks as she advances on Darius, her cane a flurry of slashes and stabs. *He does not trust eyesight alone; he hears the movement of the cane, my breathing, my footsteps; he feels the displacement of the air.*

'Delightful,' Lady Sun says. 'Now imagine you intend to kill me.'

She lofts the stick. Darius catches it without looking. He feels it, his hand is there, open. He comes at Lady Sun; the edge of the cane glides past her throat, the soft spot behind her ear, her armpit. Close, controlled, the least distance between intent and impact.

The cane brushes her forearm, her groin, her neck. The finale, the three gracious cuts.

The first cut takes away the blade.

The second cut takes away the fight.

The third cut takes away the life.

Lady Sun beckons and Darius surrenders the cane.

'You've been working ahead of your tuition.'

'At Crucible I learned knife-fighting basics with Denny Mackenzie.'

'A fine blade, Denny Mackenzie. Mean and honourable. I wonder how he's enduring exile.'

Familiars announce the arrival of Amanda Sun in the lobby. Darius excuses himself.

'Stay,' Lady Sun says. 'There are other ways to fight.'

Amanda Sun betrays anger in the set of her shoulders, the lay of her belly, the tightness in her hands. *I read you like a children's story,* Lady Sun thinks. *Small wonder Lucas Corta bested you.*

'Your son is in Twé,' Lady Sun says at length.

'He is still under the protection of the Asamoahs.'

'And yet you are here,' Lady Sun says. On the edge of her vision – still wide, still sharp – she sees Darius shift uncomfortably. 'Lucas Corta is on his way to Twé as we speak. He intends to take his son back to Meridian. We need leverage with the Eagle of the Moon. The whole Nearside is scrambling to get its hands on a Corta. A valuable Corta.'

'I'll leave immediately.'

'Too late for that. Tamsin has prepared a claim in your name for parental custody of Lucasinho Corta.'

Darius leans forward, draws in muscles and sinews and breath; his new-born fighting instincts woken.

'You are to file suit with the Court of Clavius. You will personally conduct the case. It will inevitably mean close liaison with Lucas Corta.'

'You vile, withered sack of bile,' Amanda Sun says.

'What mother would not sacrifice for her child?'

'I am a board member, I have a right to be consulted.'

'Motherhood is not a thing of rights. It is a thing of responsibilities,' Lady Sun says. 'A private railcar is waiting.'

Lady Sun folds her hands. Amanda Sun composes herself, turns, strides from the apartment.

'She lied to me,' Lady Sun says to Darius. 'She told me that she had killed Lucas Corta, when Corta Hélio fell. Understand, Darius: people will say business is business, nothing personal. A great lie. Everything is personal.'

THREE

Twé seduces Alexia's every sense. Here are colours, shapes, shadows and movements she never sees in Meridian. A dozen musics, a hundred voices – children! Birds! – a housand dins and hubbubs and commotions: the thunder and slosh of water pipes, the call and chorus of warm, humid winds through the ventilation ducts, the petulant shriek of electric engines – what's that? Two kids on a powerboard? Twé smears Alexia's skin with fifty musks and pheromones; it's sour and sweet, savoury and salty on her tongue; it's a sense of warmth in every cell her body, of a higher air pressure, of humidity and is the gravity ever so slightly out of kilter? Meridian is a magnificent panorama of meshing canyons; cliffs higher than imagination, immense perspectives dwindling to distant, luminous vanishing points, but it is stone, dead stone. Twé is the life-root, twining, digging, questing deep into the cold heart of the moon for the vital stuffs to make more of itself.

Motos slide through the mill of people crowding from the station. Lucas, Alexia and Nelson Medeiros, the Eagle's Head of Security at the centre of a knot of escoltas. Alexia grabs a handle as sudden acceleration sends her reeling. She emits a small cry as the moto plunges into an unlit tunnel. Twists, turns, inclines pull her balance this way, that way. At one point the bottom drops out of her belly. Then she is in pink light so intense it feels like sunburn and something snatches the moto up so fast it knocks the speech from her. She is on an elevator platform, riding up the side of a vast shaft between tier after tier of growing things. Every balcony and rooftop in Barra had been an urban farm – she had designed drip irrigation systems for crops from salad to bespoke coca -but the sheer scale of this hydroponic tube makes her breath tremble. Here are potatoes, there yams. Can those be beans; pods the length of Alexia's arm? The moto ascends through a forest of corn; slender leaves like spears, stalks like tree trunks. Plants grow tall in lunar gravity and the warm, bright, nutrient rich ecology of Twé.

'This is like a theme-park ride!' Alexia shouts over the play of air and the shush of foliage and the voices of unseen birds.

'Cortas and Asamoahs have always understood each other,' Lucas says. 'Mackenzies, Suns, Vorontsovs, they brought their wealth from Earth. Cortas and Asamoahs, we came with nothing. We used what we found. So: let's go over this again. The Omahene…'

'Is the CEO of AKA. The position rotate every two years.'

'Currently?'

'Lousika Asamoah.'

'Who is?'

'Luna Corta's mother. She was the second wife to Rafa Corta.'

'Not second wife. That implies serial monogamy. And the word oko is not gendered. Keji-oko. Parallel spouse. Her connection with Lucasinho?'

'He saved some… kid?'

'Kojo Asamoah. On the Moonrun.'

'I researched that bit. That's insane.'

'As entertainment I recommend it only to the most jaded. Continue.'

'Kojo Asamoah being Lousika Asamoah's… nephew? Anyway, he earned the protection of the Asamoahs, which he claimed when he ran out on Denny Mackenzie at the altar. Have to say, your marriage customs fry my head.' Alexia is aware that Nelson Medeiros is trying not to laugh.

'Amories, rings, polygamies of any number, monogamies of any shape and duration, group marriages, line marriages, walking marriages, ghost marriages, self-marriages . . . My sister could explain them all to you,' Lucas says. 'But the principle is the same. Love is negotiation. Every moment of every day. Love is like a child. It must be guided, nurtured, grown. Our system of agreements and contracts and nikahs seems unromantic. I say good. Romance is a foolishness, a sickness. Love is a living thing. Love is what survives. Our system has no time for romance but gives whole worlds for love to grow in. My nikah with Amanda Sun was well designed. We were both glad there was no requirement for sex or intimacy. Love was never in the contract. It allowed us to look outward for love.'

'Amanda Sun, who tried to asphyxiate you at the Fecunditatis BALTRAN terminal,' Alexia says. 'Who's romanticising now?'

'At which she singularly failed,' Lucas says. 'And we were taught that the Suns were thorough.'

'Their board seemed pretty thorough to me,' Alexia says. Taiyang had been the first of the dragons to pay respects to the new Eagle in Meridian's Eyrie. She had socially cut Lady Sun, a mistake for which Alexia knew there would be payment. 'I think the old lady has already planned a dozen ways to get me dead.'

'Lady Sun is a worthy adversary,' Lucas says. 'Pray you outlive her. Even then, watch your back. The Suns play the long game.'

Alexia settles into her seat imagining knives, needles, insect assassins all around.

'What's it like, open vacuum?' The obverse of Alexia's claustrophobia nightmares, of being wedged into a stone tube so narrow she can't move her arms, her fingers; are the dreams of waking suddenly naked on the surface, the air evacuating her lungs in a silent shriek, nothing between her skin and the edge of the observable universe.

'Terrible. Sublime. The life shouts out into nothing. Every cell is tested to its limit. Lucasinho is a moonrunner. I didn't understand why anyone should want this insanity. I understand now. You live completely in those moments. Have you been to the surface? You should. Every ten, eleven year-old is taught to use a suit, walk on the surface and look at the earth. That's a wise custom.'

The car draws up outside an interior lock. Lucas waits for Nelson Medeiros to assemble the escort. 'The full theatre show,' Lucas says as the outer lock opens. 'The Golden Stool intends to impress. So must we.'

'I don't understand,' Alexia says.

The inner lock opens.

Alexia can't contain the gasp of wonder.

The dome is a kilometre-wide hemisphere hacked from a lava bubble blown four billion years in the eruptions that flooded the Sea of Tranquillity, but it is the tree that takes Alexia's breath away. It fills the dome, raft upon raft of boughs and branches, twigs and leaves. The main trunk, half a kilometre distant, is wider and taller than Ocean Tower. Alexia looks up into the branches. Each would be the trunk of any other tree, each twig is a branch. Each leaf the size of size of her torso. Mirror-shards of sunlight dazzle through the leaf canopy; the dome is lined with AKA mirror-magic; panels turning and seeking, bouncing light from mirror to mirror to mirror to feed the leaves of the Great Tree of Twé. The leaves are in constant, gentle motion, moving against each other to fill the dome with a vast murmuring. A leaf sifts down through the branches, touching, catching, turning, tumbling slowly like a swimmer in water. A bot scurries from shadows. Stepping delicately over the web of irrigation channels cut into the polished stone floor, it catches the leaf before it touches the surface. The floor of the dome is pell-mell with darting scavenger bots. The channels must be kept clear; the carbon must be recycled.

Alexia tries to calculate the mass of carbon and water in this ecosystem. A city-worth, thousands of lives incarnate in wood and leaf. The tonnage of invested life-stuff testifies to the power of the Asamoahs. They hold life at the heart of a dead moon.

The Kotoko waits in the deep leaf-gloaming, arrayed on each side of a set of low, wide steps. Men, woman draped in bright kente, one arm clothed, the other bare. Over each clad shoulder hovers a familiar, each bare hand clasps a staff topped with a representation of their abusua: crows, leopards, dogs, vultures, all eight of the soul-creatures of the maternities. Maninho gives Alexia names and positions. AKA's social and political structures baffle her. She suspects they baffle anyone who is not an Asamoah.

Where the two wings meet sits Lousika Asamoah, Omahene of AKA. The Golden Stool is a simple *pi* of pale wood carved from the Great Tree itself; more precious than any gold. The Omahene's hair is a sculpture – an architecture – of rods and quills and lacquered sticks, all hung with glossy black baubles like miniature paper lanterns. Animals emerge from the shadow beneath the Golden Stool: a bright-plumaged parrot, a dwarfed raccoon, a slow-stepping spider the size of Alexia's hand. A dark cloud materialises for a moment behind Lousika Asamoah's head, disperses like smoke. A swarm. Alexia remembers the touch of an Asamoah-designed assassin insect; poison crawling across her skin, hardly daring to breathe. She had thought she was smart, sharp, irresistible when she conned her way into Lucas Corta's hotel suite on the Copacabana.

She knew nothing then.

Every one of those animals will possess some subtle surveillance sense, and some fast and lethal means of killing.

The raccoon licks its asshole.

'Yaa Doku Nana,' Lucas Corta says. The formal address of the Omahene.

'Bem-vindo ao Twé, Lucas Corta,' Lousika Asamoah says.

Alexia's breath catches at the Portuguese.

'Lucasinho,' Lucas says.

'Is safe. Stabilised. We'll talk, Lucas. Councillors.' The Kotoko dip their heads and lift their staffs. Leaf-light dapples their patterned robes. Nelson Madeiros leads the escoltas from the chamber. As arranged, Alexia remains.

Lousika Asamoah turns a cold stare on Alexia.

'My Iron Hand stays with me,' Lucas Corta says.

'Lucasinho is secure and stable,' Lousika Asamoah says. 'But he was anoxic for ten minutes. There has been brain damage.'

Lucas's hand tighten on the knurl of his cane.

'Tell me, Lousika.'

'Terrible damage Lucas.'

Lucas Corta folds visibly; joints, muscles weak in shock. Alexia moves to take his arm. He does not push her away.

'Take me to him. Please.'

'Of course.'

Lousika lays a hand on Lucas's arm, a blessing. The animal entourage flows after her. The spider rides on the ornate hair arrangement. There are doors to this chamber Alexia neither noticed nor suspected. Waiting in the corridor are AKA employee to lift and store the Omahene's head-piece. The spider jumps to Lousika Asamoah's shoulder. Alexia flinches.

The corridors have been cleared.

'The Sisterhood did their best but they're not a medical centre,' Lousika says. 'The life support pod was damaged in the escape from João de Deus.'

Alexia hears the rebuke in Lousika's voice: you left your son helpless in your enemy's stronghold. But you did the same with your own daughter, Alexia thinks. You left her among enemies. She remembers the call when school security found Caio in the river. She had threatened drivers, terrified pedestrians, smashed every rule the road, bribed, extorted, paid and slept on the floor of the emergency room until she knew her brother was safe. She would have torn the moon in two to get to him.

Eagle, Omahene, Dragons: what is power if you don't use it for your own?

'I'll give you some time with him,' Lousika Asamoah says at the entrance to the med centre. 'Luna will be here soon.'

Alexia hesitates at the door but Lucas's touch asks her to be with him. He can't be alone with Lucasinho. He dare not; he is afraid that alone, the disciplines and necessities that bind him together might unravel and he would collapse into a thousand shards. Then she sees the boy on the bed, in the cocoon of medical light, surrounded by a halo of machine arms.

Alexia sees thick black hair, full lips, high and angled cheekbones, the fold of the closed eyes, the Brazilian width to the nose and colour of the skin. He is a prince from a fairytale, trapped in an enchantment. Her segundo primo.

Lucas Corta stands at the bedside, looking down in to the still, holy face. He strokes Lucasinho cheek. Alexia's heart turns over. The touch is so gentle, so ruined. Then Alexia has another vision of Lucasinho Corta, a childhood memory of religious terror. Against sense, opinion and budget, Tio Rubens and Tia Sabrina had insisted on marrying in the old Jesuit mission, a long, narrow, haunted vault of horrors. Chief of horrors had been the mummified body of a five-hundred-year-dead Father Provincial preserved in a glass case beneath the altar. Rubens and Sabrina kneeled, prayed, vowed but nine-year-old Alexia had been unable to look away from the tent of leather-wrapped bone.

Lucasinho Corta is the terror in the glass tank.

'What are you doing, anjinho?'

Madrinha Elis chose the room with care. She draped it with Luna's favourite fabric prints; flowers and animals. She laid out five copies of Luna's beloved red dress, in which she ran free and feral through the gardens of Boa Vista. She arranged its furniture to create crannies and crevices and crawlspaces, like the ones she had grown up exploring in Boa Vista. Everything is designed to delight, but Luna sits cross-legged in the middle of the floor, her back to the door, dressed in the same pink suit-liner she wore on the flight from Boa Vista.

'I'm working on my face, Madrinha.'

Over her head hovers a sphere the size of a clenched fist, one half black, one half silver. Luna's familiar was always the creature that shares her name, the life-green Luna moth.

On the floor before her is a tray of face-paints.

'Luna?'

She turns. Madrinha Elis cannot contain the cry, the flight of the hand to the mouth. One half of Luna's face is a white, leering skull.

'Get that stuff off your face before your mother sees it.'

'Mamãe is here?'

Luna leaps to her feet.

'She arrived ten minutes ago.'

'Why hasn't she come to see me?'

'She has people to meet, then she will see you.'

'People like Lucasinho,' Luna says.

'Your Tio Lucas is here to take him to Meridian.'

'I want to go to Mamãe,' Luna declares. The half-death's-head unnerves Madrinha Elis.

'I will take you,' Madrinha Elis says. Never lie, never talk down. 'After you clean that off your face and put on your lovely red dress.'

'I will not.' Luna takes a step forward; against all her experience and duty, Madrinha Elis takes an involuntary step backwards. She has known Luna petulant, defiant, sulky, racked with tantrums. She has never see a cold determination like this, a titanium light in the dark eye of her skull-face. A thing she does not know was conjured from the reflecting black mirrors of the sun-belt, heated and forged in the meltdown of the *Pustelga*.

'Anjinho.'

'Take me to Mamãe!'

'I will if you clean up and dress nice.'

'Then I'll go on my own,' Luna declares and is in the corridor before Madrinha Elis can turn old bones to stop her.

Gods but the girl is fast. Elis catches up with her at the elevator. The platform drops through the surging foliage of Aidoo agrarium, the mass of leaves black in the pink shine of the grow-lights. AKA tech teams are still debugging the hacked moondozers from the siege and slowly pushing back the berms of regolith from the caps of the tube-farms. It will take lunes for Twé's abused ecosystems to return to full burgeoning health. Under that same light Luna's suit-liner almost fluoresces. The girl has already summoned a moto: it closes around the two women like a flower and opens again outside the medcentre.

Lousika Asamoah's bestiary precedes her: the swarm, the bright-plumed bird, the cunning spider as big as Luna's hand. Luna claps her hands in delight. She has not seen her mother's guardians before. A creature Luna does not know, rotund but agile, banded tail, clever paws, sits up to regard Luna with masked eyes. Luna crouches to return the gaze.

'Oh what are you?'

'A raccoon. But what are you?' Lousika Asamoah asks. 'Lady Luna now?'

The animals remain obediently at the door to the intensive care unit.

Luna sees the arms first. Arms in half-light. The slender, many-jointed arms of medical bots, their long fingers driven into Lucasinho's own arms and throat. Sensor arms outstretched around his head, as if blessing. Her uncle's arm, dark against the medical lights, then his hand resting lightly on Lucasinho's chest, lifting and falling gently in time to the breathing.

'Get her out of here,' Lucas says without looking up.

'Lucas . . .' Lousika says.

He turns to Luna.

'He gave his last breath to you,' Lucas says. 'For you.'

Behind her fierce mask, Luna feels tears. Not here, not in front of him. Never for him.

'You do not speak to my daughter like that!' Lousika Asamoah explodes, then Luna feels Madrinha Elis's hand on her shoulder turn her and guide her into the corridor. The door closes on voices shouting; like she used to hear when she hid in the service tunnels of Boa Vista, that only she knew, when her mãe and pãe used to fight when they thought that only machines could hear them.

'It's all right, coraçao,' Madrinha Elis says. She hugs Luna to her, strokes her hair.

'It's not all right,' Luna hisses into her madrinha's belly. Every muscle in her jaw, her throat is tight. Her face burns with the humiliation. Her ears are filled with a high-pitched singing that is the noise of not-crying. The raccoon waddles over to investigate. Luna turns her moon-face to it, bares her teeth. It leaps away in distress.

'I'm not taking it off,' Luna says to the masked raccoon. 'Not until everything is right. It's my face now.'

She squats and reaches a hand towards the suspicious raccoon. It cocks its head to one side. Luna clicks a finger, beckons, tsish-tsishes, which Elis told her is the sound for ferrets. It sidles towards her, lingers at the limit of her reach.

'Come on,' she says and takes a half-step forward. The raccoon shies, then sniffs her fingers. 'I'm sorry I scared you.' Mask regards mask.

Pink light floods the room; glancing up he sees machines sweeping swatches of moondust from the endcap.

Lousika Asamoah brings two martinis from the discreet bar. The suite is mere steps from the trauma centre, but a world away from the quiet, hissing machines and their watchful loving grace. Lousika Asamoah has shed the glamour of the Golden Stool but she wears its power like a scent. Lucas takes the offered glass softly.

'Apologise,' Lousika says.

'I should not have spoken to Luna like that,' Lucas says.

'She carried him three kilometres to Boa Vista.'

'I'm sorry.'

'To her.'

'I will.' Lucas tastes the martini. A good martini should be like the surface of the moon. Cold, dry, uncompromising, dangerous. Austere and beautiful.

'Make him well,' Lucas Corta says.

'We can't.'

'Help him.'

'Lucas, the damage is catastrophic. We've repaired his autonomic nervous system and gross motor skills, but he'll have to learn to walk, to talk, to feed himself. Everything he was is gone. He's a child again – an infant. To be Lucasinho Corta, he'll have to relearn everything. And we don't know how to do that.'

Lucas's hand shakes. He sets the barely tasted glass down.

'You're AKA. You break DNA and make it obey you. You draw life from the heart of the moon.'

'What he needs is beyond us, beyond anyone. On this side of the moon.'

'The university has something?'

Power stands strongest on three legs, Adriana Corta taught her children. The Lunar Development Corporation and the Five Dragons were two pillars of the lunar order; but there was a third, the oldest and subtlest, almost forgotten. The University of Farside. As Robert Mackenzie's robots sifted and smelted the regolith of the Ocean of Storms for rare earths, on the other side of the moon machines of a consortium of universities from Caltech to Shanghai were weaving ribbons of dipole-embedded plastic across Daedalus crater. As the directors of Taiyang fled China to join their robots excavating ice and fossil cometary carbon from the South Polar Basin, on the other side of the moon Caltech and MIT were digging the tunnels and habitats for a permanent research settlement, free from the interference of terrestrial states and ideologues. As VTO maglev lines embraced the poles and reached around Farside, the new university agreed a construction and launch deal with the Vorontsovs for deep space missions even as it constructed and launched a lawsuit against the violence VTO's rail operations did to the delicate listenings of the Daedalus observatory. The Court of Clavius was founded, and with it the university's law faculty.

Two workers from Accra founded AKA and built an empire of light, life and water; on the other side of the moon secure pathogen laboratories were dug deep under Poincaré, lock upon lock, seal upon seal. Adriana Corta watched Brasil dwindle behind her on the OTV screens; on the other side of the moon moonloop tethers sent capsules down to the repositories under Mare Orientale where Earth's genetic wealth was stored, safe and far from the planet's ravaged biosphere.

It never had an official name. The University of Farside is a nickname, though, like the best apelidos, an accurate one. Its tunnels and tramways, hyperloops and cablecars cover fifty per cent of the far side of the moon. By one measure it is the largest city in the two worlds, by another, the mother of all suburbs. It reaches around the moon in its colloquiums and study groups and micro-colleges but its heart, its home, is Earth-blind, looking out at the universe. Fiercely protective of its wealth and independence, it is the worlds' foremost science and technology research facility. It is the third power, the hidden blade. Eagle and Dragons learned long ago not to test the university.

'There is a new development in 3D printing protein chips,' Lousika says. 'Artificial neurons, programmable nanomaterials.'

'They could repair the damage?'

'They could, but they would need access to his memories.'

'But if the damage is as you say...'

'They would recreate them from his external memory. His familiar, his network presence; and people. His friends, family.'

Lucas Corta looks out through the open slot of the window into the lush pink of the Yeboah tube-farm. He can feel the humid heat thick on his skin. Earth was like this, dense and damp, every breath stolen from heat and gravity. He tastes the fecundity, the thrust of leaf and life. João de Deus and Boa Vista lie under the Mare Fecunditatis, the Sea of Fecundity. How much more appropriate a site that would be for Twé. Seas of Fecundity, Tranquillity, Serenity. Nectar, Vapour, Rains. Seas of lies; selenological and emotional. Sea of Cold, Sea of Crises, Ocean of Storms: seas of truth.

Lucas Corta sees very clearly the danger. Will he recognise the son who comes back from Farside? What will Lucasinho know of him?

'I wanted to take him with me to Meridian,' Lucas says.

'That can't be.'

'It's for them. Can you understand that? Everything I've done is for them. I want us all back.'

'I understand that, Lucas.'

'Do you? Take me to him, I need to see him again.'

'Of course.'

On the third slushy spoonful, Luna Corta decides that matcha, cardamom and strawberry granita isn't as nice as her idea of it.

'Matcha, cardamom and strawberry,' the proprietor of the Kafe Kwae says, trying not to stare at Luna's Lady Luna face.

'Matcha, cardamom and strawberry.'

Matcha, cardamom and strawberry doesn't work at all but she's not going to let the owner see that so she diligently spoons down towards the bottom. At the two-centimetre mark she notices that there is no one left in Kafe Kwae except the owner and Madrinha Elis.

Two spoons on and now even the owner is gone.

Insects swarm into Kafe Kwae, circulate around the low ceiling like smoke then coalesce into a buzzing ball over the water dispenser. Then the parrot flies in and perches on the edge of the counter, and after it the clever-pawed raccoon and after them, her mother with her anansi-spider riding on her shoulder.

'Was that good?' Lousika Asamoah looks at the granita glass and the melted dreg in the apex that the spoon can never reach.

'Do you want to try it?' Luna dips the end of the spoon into the cone of pink liquid. Lousika tastes the ice-melt.

'I'm getting strawberry, and cardamom ... is that matcha?'

'Do you like it?'

'Honest?'

'Honest.'

'Individually it should work ...'

'But all together it doesn't.'

A look from Lousika Asamoah and Madrinha Elis gets up and leaves.

'Can I touch your spider?' Luna asks. 'Is it a trickster like Anansi?'

'She's not a trickster but she has special powers. Luna, Lucasinho is hurt much worse than we thought.'

'He'll live, won't he?'

'He'll live. But he's lost everything. He can't walk, he can't feed himself or speak. Anjinho, if he saw you, he wouldn't know who you were. We can't help him here. He has to leave Twé.'

'Where's he going?'

'Farside.'

Luna has heard of the other side of the moon, where the Earth never rises and the sky is full of nothing but stars, but it is as far from the stone seas and mountain ranges and crater fields of her side as the bottom of a mooncake is from its top. She knows the world is round, and that VTO's rail lines go around it two ways, but it doesn't feel like that; it feels flat, a disc, and for someone to go to the other side is a magical journey through the moon, millions of metres or maybe millimetres. Opposite sides of the same thing but more distant than blue Earth.

'Will they make him better on Farside?'

'They'll try. They can't promise anything.'

Luna pushes her granita glass away from her and lays her hands flat on the table.

'I'm going with him.'

'Luna.'

'He took me from Lubbock BALTRAN station to Boa Vista. There were bots after us, and Mackenzies, and we got lost on the glass and I got the leak and he gave me his air and he stayed with me all the way. I'm not going to leave him.'

'Anjinho.'

'That's my pãe's word,' Luna says. 'That's a Corta word. I didn't want to go to Twé.'

'I don't understand, my love.'

Luna leans forward.

'That time after the party in Boa Vista. The Moonrun party, when they tried to attack pãe. You took me to Twé. I didn't want to go. Boa Vista is my home.'

'Baa, it wasn't safe at Boa Vista.'

'It's home.'

'Baa, there is no Boa Vista. You know that. You saw that.'

'Boa Vista is my home and Rafa Corta is my pãe. I have Tio Carlinho's blades. You are an Asamoah but I am a Corta.'

All the animals are watching her. Even the swarm, which Luna catches in the corner of her vision, and which seems to have taken the form of an eye.

'Luna . . .'

Luna fixes her mother with a stare of ice and steel.

'Am I a Corta?'

'Yes, you are.'

'I am the true heir of Corta Hélio,' Luna declares.

'Luna, don't say that.'

'But I am. That's why I'm wearing this face. This is my Corta face.

That's why I have to go with Lucasinho. I have to take care of him. I have to take care of the Cortas. I have to go to Farside.'

Lousika Asamoah sighs and looks away and as her eyes slip, so her animal guardians break their stare.

'Go with him, then. There's a but.'

'What is it?'

'Elis goes with you,' Lousika says.

'Deal,' Luna says. She expected that. The Omahene does not surrender. The Omahene negotiates.

The swarm flows towards the door. The bird leaps into the air and the raccoon scratches and ambles away. The trickster spider stays clinging to Lousika Asamoah's shoulder. She smiles.

'You are a Corta, but you will always be an Asamoah,' Lousika says. 'The Golden Stool will watch over you.'

The casket will be transported by rail. The party forms up on the executive platform of Twé station. Alexia counts twenty: the Eagle and his escoltas; the Omahene and her entourage, blackstar and animal; Luna Corta, carefully carrying a wooden box, with her madrinha; and the boy in the life-support pod. The university railcar arrives out of the tunnel, crosses the points and pulls beyond armoured glass partitions and airlocks. Locks mesh and open.

A tall woman steps on to the platform, of early middle age, skin light caramel, crinkly hair tied back and tamed beneath a jaunty fedora. Alexia's familiar gives her every detail: her sharp suit is Zuckerman and Kraus; pockets edged with striped trim, oversize buttons, broad-shouldered, pinch-waisted. Her bag is a 1949 cylindrical Josef and her shoes are three-centimetre-heel Oxfords, ribbon ties. Her lip-gloss is killer red, the seams on her stockings genuine. Her familiar is skinned in the white and blue intersecting circles: the Earth rising behind the moon, a vista only seen from the far side. Every detail, except what she is.

'I am Dakota Kaur Mackenzie, ghazi of the University of Farside, Faculty of Biocybernetics, School of Neurotechnology.'

An intake of breath, a shifting of position among Lucas Corta's escoltas and the AKA blackstars. One of Alexia's questions is answered. A Mackenzie.

'Dr Mackenzie,' Lucas Corta says. Alexia Corta glances at him. She heard the sharp edge of enmity in his words. So did the ghazi.

'Is there a problem, Senhor Corta?'

'I would have preferred...'

'Someone else?' the woman says. Whatever a ghazi is, it holds enough charisma and authority to make every other person on the platform look gauche. Iron Hand, Eagle of the Moon, even Golden Stool: titles children give themselves playing superheroes.

'Yes,' Lucas says

'You are aware that every ghazi of the university is bound by solemn vows,' the woman says. 'Independence, impartiality, dedication, discipline.'

'I am aware of that, Dr Mackenzie.'

'Questioning my loyalty, Senhor Corta?'

Every escolta and blackstar stiffens. Hands move to concealed holsters. Lousika Asamoah's animals stir.

Maninho, give me everything on ghazis, Alexia mutters silently to her familiar.

A ghazi is a scholar-knight of the University of Farside, Maninho whispers in Alexia's ear. *Each is attached to a faculty as its agent and is authorised to take any action they deem necessary to protect the independence and integrity of their faculty. Dr Mackenzie is quite capable of killing every human and animal present.*

In that suit? Alexia subvocalises.

That suit comes right off, Maninho says. *And she can read what you are saying to me from the micro-movements of your jaw muscles.*

'You must realise he is my son,' Lucas Corta says.

'He will receive the very best of our research and skill,' Dakota Kaur Mackenzie says. 'Don't doubt it, Lucas.'

Maninho has filled Alexia's lens with articles on the ghazis of Farside: ninja-academics licensed to kill, intellectual superheroes, but what interests her more is what she reads in Lucas Corta's buttressed emotions. He buries them as deep and protected as lunar cities but from a dozen tells Alexia reads mistrust, helplessness, hope, ancient anger. He is in the hands of this Mackenzie.

'Make him whole again. Send him back to me.'

'I will, Lucas.'

Tensions break, held breaths exhale, hands drop from knife-readiness. The raccoon sits and licks, the bird fluffs and preens.

'Thank you.'

Lousika Asamoah's blackstars manoeuvre the capsule into the railcar.

'I'm coming too,' Luna Corta says and pushes past the ghazi. Lousika Asamoah's composure breaks and she rushes forward to scoop up her daughter.

'Oh you you you,' she says, burying her face in Luna's hair. 'You be good, you be safe, you hear. You talk to me every day, right?' To Madrinha Elis, she says, 'I want daily reports.'

The madrinha dips her head and escorts Luna to the railcar.

'Anybody else?' the ghazi says.

Locks seal, the railcar undocks and in a heartbeat is gone into the tunnel.

Alexia finds she is breathing again.

'That thing you've done with your face,' the ghazi says. The railcar accelerates to a cruise. A blur of light, a scheduled service arriving from João de Deus. No pressure shock, no boom of noise, no wobble; the railcar rides the maglev line in perfect vacuum. Madrinha Elis is already asleep in the forward compartment, alongside Lucasinho Corta. 'I like it.'

Luna sniffs. Madrinha Elis gives a rattling snore, jerks awake and drops into sleep again.

'What's in the box?' Dakota asks. The case containing the Corta knives rests on the soft, upholstered bench between Dakota and Luna.

'You don't have to try to talk to me,' Luna says. 'I entertain myself.'

'I'm interested, is all,' Dakota says. 'You see, in a society which places no value on things, you've chosen to bring this thing with you.'

'Do you really want to know what's in the box?'

'I do.'

Luna opens the case and watches for a reaction. Not a flicker.

'That's twice you've impressed me now, Luna Corta.'

'These are the battle-knives of the Cortas,' Luna says.

'They are exceptional pieces,' Dakota Mackenzie says. 'Meteoric iron.'

'Yes,' Luna says, irked at having her story pre-empted. 'From deep under Langrenus crater. The Sisterhood of the Lords of Now kept them until a Corta came who was bold, great-hearted, without avarice or cowardice, who would fight for the family and defend it bravely. That was me.'

'Indeed,' Dakota Mackenzie says. 'May I try one?'

'No,' Luna says with heat and force. Now Dakota recoils. 'No Mackenzie can ever touch one again.'

'You used that little word "again", so I have to ask.'

'The last Mackenzie to touch them killed my tio. That means uncle.'

'I speak Portuguese.'

Luna switches to broad Santinho.

'Your cousin Denny Mackenzie stole them and killed my uncle Carlinhos. Then you stole João de Deus.'

Dakota Mackenzie replies in perfectly accented João de Deus Portuguese.

'I am not related to Denny Mackenzie.'

Luna hisses.

'I am a ghazi of the University of Farside.'

Luna sits back on her couch. Another train flickers past.

'And what is a ghazi?'

'Long ago the University of Farside realised that it would always be torn between political factions.'

'I'm too old for bedtime stories.'

'You think?'

'Yes. And I know everything about political factions.'

'The Dragons, the old Lunar Development Corporation and the new Lunar Mandate Authority, the terrestrial nations, want control of us, but more importantly, our work. We've developed techniques and technologies worth billions. The university has three main sources of funding: student fees, licences on our technologies, and support from private donors and consortia.'

'And I know about consortia,' Luna says. 'You haven't answered my question yet.'

Dakota grins in delight.

'A ghazi defends the University of Farside against those who would destroy it, control it, corrupt it or steal its secrets. In the early days we hired mercenaries or brought in security from Earth, but we found out that their quality was poor and their loyalty was suspect.'

'You are always better with the faithful,' Luna says.

'That's what we believe. There are ninety-nine ghazis, because we like the number. We represent every one of our faculties and campuses. We're all moon-born. We serve for ten years, during which time we may neither contract partnerships nor have children. We renounce our families, our histories and make solemn vows to the university. Many apply, few are chosen. The selection process is severe. Every one of us has studied to at least doctoral level, many beyond that. How can we defend the university if we are not part of its intellectual life? We would be mercenaries. Police.'

'Police?' Luna asks.

'A terrestrial thing,' Dakota says. 'We undergo rigorous physical training. Each of us learns a weapon and an unarmed martial art. Physical and weapons training lasts as long as our academic studies. Your zashitniks and blades boast that they train at the School of Seven Bells. It's good, but a ghazi learns more. We are taught to observe in minute detail, to exercise subtle psychological manipulation, to investigate, gather information and undertake covert operations. We learn all the major languages of the moon, by heart, not by network, and psychological and performance skills. We learn coding, hacking, systems engineering. There is not a vehicle on or above the moon that I can't take control of, including this train. We learn to design custom narcotics, poisons, hallucinogens. We are taught to seduce, to be seduced, to use sex as a weapon with anyone of any gender or none. I can survive seven minutes without oxygen. In every way, Luna Corta, I am straight from hell.'

To the east lie the slopes of Low Mesa, throwing long evening shadows down the viaduct as the railcar climbs to the grey highlands.

'Can I see your knife?' Luna asks.

'Of course.' A casual gesture opens Dakota's jacket. Two blades, in fast-draw sheaths.

'Would you like to try them?' Dakota asks. Luna shakes her head.

'That wouldn't be right. They're your blades.'

Dakota closes her jacket. Light floods the slit windows as the railcar leaves the Twé tunnel on to the Equatorial One.

'Have you ever killed anyone?'

'Not a one. Most of us never see action. We work mostly against industrial espionage and it's more effective to expose the network and go through the courts on the moon and on Earth. Our pockets are deep. We are authorised to use lethal force if we deem it necessary but mostly we just scare people.'

'Does that work often?'

'I scared your mother. And your uncle.'

Luna considers this.

'Yes. I see that. And the terrestrials, and my uncle's Iron Hand.'

'But not Luna Corta.'

'I walked the glass with Lucasinho. That was scary.'

'Can't say I've done that.'

'And I think what scared my tio was letting Lucasinho go with a Mackenzie.'

'All ghazis give up our old families when we take our vows to the university.'

'Tio Lucas says family is everything. If you don't have family then you're nothing.'

'I have a family,' Dakota says. 'A huge, wonderful family, that loves and cares for me, that I will do anything to protect. It's just a different kind of family. We all choose our family.'

Lune recalls the hotshop with her mother and animals and a failed granita. *I am the heir of Corta Hélio,* she had said. The ghazi is right: she has chosen her family.

The railcar descends the embankment from the high country down on to the dark floor of the Sea of Fecundity, the heartland of the Cortas. Equatorial One runs down the centre of the solar strip, white lines on a black darker even that the dark basalt of the sea floor. Luna glimpses distant upraised gantries of Helium 3 harvesters returning for maintenance, the horns of a BALTRAN station, the tower of the Fecunditatis moonloop terminal. Here is the army of service vehicles rebuilding Boa Vista, and gone. Now the dishes and solar panels, the docks and locks and surface paraphernalia of João de Deus. And gone. And now Luna Corta is a place she has never been, the landmarks of her life behind her, eastward bound out of Fecunditatis, out around the shoulder of the moon to its other side.

FOUR

'Stop,' she orders the car. 'Oh stop stop please.'

The car parks up on the side of the track close against the wooden rail.

'What now?' Melinda her liaison asks. Melinda has been a dour companion on the drive from the city, turning away from the racing clouds, the handfuls of flung rain and puddles of sudden sunlight, the trees and the highway to her lens and the network universe of other people. Her task is to get the moon-woman home, get her set, get back.

'Look.'

The elk move out from the tree shadow, two females and a calf, blinking and hesitant as they step into the open light. They cross the meadow towards the track, the calf pressing close to its mother. The rest of the herd are dark hints under the eaves of the forest, suspicions of motion. The exploration party skips over a fallen rail and stops on the earth track, heads up, nostrils flaring.

She orders the window down. The direct unfiltered sunlight is hot on her arm as she rests it on the window frame. She can smell them. She can smell the old dried dung and fresh-dried earth of the track, she can smell the recent rain, the resins, the leaves, the river, the light, the valley air.

'Careful with the sun,' Melinda says. 'Yes, I know, this climate, but you burn real easy.'

'Hey,' she whispers. Elk heads snap to her. 'Hey you guys.' The mother moves between the calf and the car. Behind her the calf and the other female move off the country road down the drainage ditch and up into the trees. The mother waits until she is certain that car and passengers pose no threat, then trots into the trees.

'They come down from the mountain this time every year. They feel fall starting up there. Sometimes they come right past the house; so tame you can leave apples out on the porch rail and they'd eat them with you sitting in a chair watching.'

She puts the window up. The car moves off. The track is a series of abrupt right-angle turns mapped to old field and homestead boundaries. The homesteads are long gone, the forest reclaiming them summer by summer. The road changes from dirt to ruts to a single green track. A turn over a capsized wooden bridge – the car suspension bangs loud enough to shake Melinda from her socialising – into the run between close trees all the kids called Ghost Town. The decay of a dozen spiritualities hangs from the branches; the broken hoops of dream catchers, tatters of old mountain-Buddhist prayer flags, a ragged windsock in the shape of a fish. She hears the hollow clop of bamboo windchimes. Few needles on the branches. No break in the slow drought. The car turns the final right angle and the house is there before her, hunkered down among its outbuildings and sheds on the wide plinth looking up along the valley to the high passes.

And here come the dogs. One she does not know, racing out to greet the car, barking with blind excitement; old Canaan lurching on stiff legs, head thrown back, yapping. And the house, the house, shy behind its verandas and porches and the frowning roof. The rain gauge against the chimney gable; the highest mark at the top of her old bedroom window. Moss and split grey shingles. The weather vane in the shape of an orca.

She half-hoped for banners, for yellow ribbons all the way in from the 101, for her folk linked arm in arm. The dogs escort the car past the swing-seat, with the greatest view in two worlds, up-valley to the peaks. She swung with Kessie, with the elk picking their careful path down to the river and evening light on the snows. No snows now. No snow for many years. The car pulls up before the porch and she is startled by explosions. Puffs of smoke, plops of sound. Whee, pop. Fireworks are an heroic welcome.

She thinks she sees a figure dash around the corner of the veranda – the fireworker – then the doors fly open and there they all are; Kessie and daughters Ocean and Weavyr. Skyler is on his way in from Djakarta. No sign of Mom. They rush down the steps to surround the car; hands and waving and voices and over-excited dogs.

The car opens. Melinda slides the wheelchair from storage and unfolds it. A dozen hands compete for the handles of the chair to push her towards the ramp. She had that ramp put in for Mom.

'It's powered!' she shouts but they just cheer louder and race her up the ramp and on to the veranda. She smells hot wood, old patchouli, weed and garlic. Everyone is shouting, everyone is waving, everyone is asking if they can get her anything everyone is talking or trying to show her things.

Even Melinda is smiling.

'Hey hey!' She holds up her hands. 'The talking stick is not with you. The talking stick is with me! I'm back from the moon!'

Marina had not thought that bliss might kill her. A stumble in the harsh gravity, the swelling of her heart, the soft rupturing of a vessel, some terrestrial disease turning her lungs to mucus might be the end; not the pure ecstasy of a cup of coffee.

'Two years,' she whispers. 'Two *years*.'

The first sip is the sword of an archangel through her tongue, her sense of smell, her saliva glands, her sense of place and time and harmony. The second sip is Satan's snag-edged obsidian stiletto.

Sour, bitter, the heart-punch of caffeine, the jittery edge and the vague paranoia.

'God I've missed you.'

'What did you drink up there?' Marina sits with Ocean on the north veranda, the side of the house with the long mountain outlooks. An ultrasonic ticker drives away biting insects.

'Tea,' Marina she says. 'Mint tea.'

'Jesus.'

Marina had expected to see the house expanded, improved, even repaired and renovated, to see some evidence of the money she had streamed back from the moon. The moss is thicker, the gutters clogged deeper, the windows looser, the roof sags lower than in her last memory. And the network is still lousy. She felt a sour gnaw of resentment as Ocean and Weavyr took her on the wheelchair tour. The house had entered that phase of house-life where it becomes a memorial of itself, then Ocean opened the door to Mom's room and Marina saw where the money went.

The life-support bed, the monitoring and therapeutic machines, the skinny bot rumbling over foot-polished wooden boards, were of lunar quality.

'Could you?' Ocean caught the hint but ten-year-old Weavyr did not recognise adult subtleties. 'Weavyr, could you leave us alone a moment?'

Marina manoeuvred the wheelchair into the tight space between the bed and the wall. On the other side of the bed was her mother's wheelchair. Arms and seat were silver with dust. Pumps beat, tubes flexed.

'Mom.'

Marina had thought her mother asleep, turned away from her on her right side, but the head of the bed elevated. Her mother rolled on to her back, rolled an eye to Marina.

'Little Mai.'

Marina hoped she had outgrown the nickname.

'Mom.'

'You're in my chair. Why are you in my chair?'

'This is my chair. Your chair is over there.'

'Oh. Yes. Why are you in my chair?'

'I'm back, Mom. Back to stay.'

'You were at university...'

'I've been away since then. The moon, Mom.'

She laughs, a cracked, melted-lung laugh, lifts a hand to bat away the ridiculous notion. She is tiny in the bed, a child made from leather. The tubes are the worst things. Marina cannot look more than a glance at the places where the lines go into her body. The arms of the medical machines have been hung with bunting, embroidered Chinese charms and bunches of withered smudging sage, grey with dust. Patchouli and frankincense, the perfumes of half a dozen essential oil jars

Marina takes the hand in hers. It is as light and dry as a paper-wasps' nest. Her mother smiles.

'But I'm back now, Ma. I came back here to get well again. It takes it out of you, coming back from the moon. I was on the limit. I'm not to push anything, strain anything. They say I'm not allowed to stand up on my own feet for a month. But I say screw that, I'm going to give my mom a hug.'

Marina mentally rehearsed the move in the car on the drive up from the facility. She braces, shifts her weight to make the swing as easy as possible. Takes her feet from the foot-rests and plants her weight on them. Focus strength. Move from your core. And rise. And Earth reaches up and jerks her down. Her arms waver, her legs collapse. She rolls sideways on to the bed to lie on her back beside her mother.

'That wasn't so good.'

She gasps for air. Her own weight is crushing the breath from her lungs. Marina heaves herself on to her side. Something tears, something snaps out of alignment.

'Hey Mom.'

'Hey Mai.'

She smiles. Her teeth smell as if she is rotting inside.

'Looks like I'm stuck here.'

Kessie looks in on her charge and raises the alarm. Family hands lift Marina back into her chair.

'Coffee?' Kessie suggests.

'Oh God no,' Marina says. 'Not another one. I'll not sleep for a week.'

'Wine?'

'We're a cocktail culture,' Marina says.

Kessie fetches a bottle and opens it. Cork: the fond-remembered squeak-plop. Glasses clink, red wine pours fast under Earth gravity.

'Okanagan,' Marina reads from the label. 'I didn't know they were growing that far north.'

She savours the first sip, draws out the pleasure like a bolt of fine silk.

'That's another thing we don't have on the moon.'

'What do you have?' Kessie asks. Shadow fills up the valley. The last of the west-light catches the peaks.

'Your daughter asked that. We drink cocktails. She's not going to get better, is she?' Marina says.

'No. But she's not going to get worse either, as long as we can keep the programme running. They keep putting the price of the drugs up and up. Pricing to market.'

'I should have stayed on the moon.'

'No, not that...'

The scuff of a foot on a gritty decking board. Ocean hangs in the doorway.

'Marina, can I ask you about the moon?'

'You can ask me anything. I may not answer everything you ask.'

Ocean pulls a folding chair in beside Marina.

'Does it hurt? Being back here, I mean.'

'Hurts like fu—' Marina corrects herself. Ocean is fourteen and swear-ready, but her mother is present. 'Hurts all the time. Every part. Imagine six yous balanced on your shoulders, all the time. Everywhere you go. And they never get off. It's like that. But it will get better. My old Earth bones are still strong. The muscles will learn again. I've got a shi— a physiotherapy programme. I might need some help with it.'

'I can do that. Marina, you do know you have a real weird accent?'

'I do?'

'It's like what we speak, but through your nose, and then there are all these weird tones.'

Marina hesitates a moment.

'We have a common language called Globo. It's a simple version of English, but it has special way of speaking so machines can understand it whatever our home accent is. We have a lot of accents and languages on the moon. I speak English, Globo and some Portuguese.'

'Say something in Portuguese.'

'Você cresceu desde a última vez que vi você,' Marina says.

'What does it mean?'

'Look it up.'

Ocean pouts but her curiosity is too strong to flounce out.

'Do they really fly there?'

'You can if you want. The wings take up a big whack of your carbon budget but those who do it don't seem to want to do anything else.'

'If I could fly I don't think I'd do anything else. I'd be up over the mountains every weather.'

'That's the rub,' Marina says. 'You've got somewhere to fly to but you can't fly. Up there, they can fly but they've got nowhere to fly to. One end of the city to the other, up and down. Meridian's big but it's still a cage. The sunline looks like the sky, but fly into it and you'll break your wings.'

The gloaming has reached the mountain tops and Marina is suddenly cold on the porch.

'Moon's on the rise,' Kessie says. 'If I got the telescope, you could show us all the places you've been.'

'Leave it. I need to go in now. I'm getting cold and it's been a long day.'

She can't look at the moon. She can't see the lights up there and not think of the lives behind them, the lives she abandoned. The moon is an eye, seeking her out with accusation and hurt, however deep she buries herself in the valleys of the Olympics. You ran away, Marina Calzaghe.

'I'll give you a hand,' Ocean says. She wheels Marina across creaking wooden floorboards to her room. She is back in her old room: the glossy machinery of her medical support package sits uncomfortably with faded posters, dusty plushies, rows of books and comics. She is fifteen again. Whatever age you return to the family home you will always be fifteen. The Doug Fir quilt, the faux-wolf-pelt throw. Ocean gets water for the rattle of pills and phages.

'It's a one two three thing,' Marina says and together they get her into the bed. She lies awake among the machines. She is soul-weary, tired to the marrow, too drained for sleep. She can feel the moon up there, feel its heat, feel the tug of its gravity like a tide in her blood. She's home at last. She hates it.

FIVE

The kid is back again. Third day in a row. Robson snags him on the edge of his vision and the moment of recognition distracts him. Robson fumbles the tic-tac, lands hard.

It's not like falling three kilometres from the roof of Queen of the South. No drop in Theophilus is more than a hundred metres but the spaces are tight with machinery and cabling. Robson catches himself hard on a rail.

Robson flicks a glance to see if the kid is still watching. Yes, in an only-watching-because-there's-nothing-more-interesting way, sitting on the railing, legs apart, sucking on a tube of slush.

Weird kid. Today Robson wears khaki shorts with the cuffs turned up and sandshoes. No shirt because it's hot up here among the machines, and shirts in the current fashion get in the way of free movement. This kid wears moon-basic: leggings, hoodie, both in white. Hood up, black hair flopping down over one eye. Familiar skinned in some thing that seems to be all glossy black wings.

Third day in a row, looking/not-looking. So this move has to be right. And look effortless. Robson breathes away the throb in his ribs, draws energy, gathers it, throws it into the move. This time the tic-tac goes right and he bounces up between the walls of an air-shaft on to a maintenance platform guardrail, backflip across the shaft to swing around the duct, hit the wall right on the finger- and toe-holds, then pushes himself up into the tangle of pipework. Over under round between.

Perfect.

He perches on a water conduit twenty metres up. Parkour King of Theophilus. He looks down through the tangle of ducts and pipes and catches the eye that isn't covered by hair looking up at him. Robson nods. The kid looks away.

Robson makes a camp, stagey superhero landing from twelve metres up.

'Hey.' Boy's voice.

Robson stops, combs his fingers through his hair.

'What.'

'Just wondering. What you're doing.'

'I'm going to the banya. I kind of need a clean.'

'Oh,' the kid says. 'Just, well, I wanted to get some tea and I wondered maybe you knew someplace good.'

'You haven't been long in Theophilus?'

'Couple of days.'

'There's a tea shop in the banya,' Robson says. 'If you want to come. I will need to get clean.'

The kid slides from the railing. Robson gets a clearer look at him. His skin is so pale Robson can almost see through it. Big black eyes. Good hair, the kind you can do stuff with.

'Haider,' the kid says. He inclines his head towards his familiar. 'This is Solveig.'

'Robson,' Robson says. He blinks up his familiar. 'This is Joker. You coming then?'

Alexia hears the voices beyond the stone doors. The Lunar Mandate Authority is in full session. Lucas's grip tightens on the handle of his cane. Alexia takes his arm.

'I walk in alone,' he says.

Alexia drops her light hold on his elbow.

'But I will need an entrance.' A smile flickers on his face. Lucas Corta trades smiles like a precious commodity but when he does, it transforms him. He radiates joy like the light of the sun.

'Of course, Senhor Corta.'

Alexia throws open the double doors of the Pavilion of the New Moon and strides into the amphitheatre. The walk is assured, eye-catching and well rehearsed. One unconsidered step can send the Jo Moonbeam into the air to come down, humiliated, a metre and half away. You can see the terrestrials flying up from the streets of Meridian, faces stiff with humiliation. Not this terrestrial: moving right, moving the moon way, is a point of pride with Alexia. She takes in the faces in the tiered seats. Alexia enjoys the discipline of committing them to memory.

'Sers,' she announces. 'The Eagle has landed.'

He walks from the double doors strong, head high, back straight, a rock of a man in the muscle-mass he put on to survive his Earth, but Alexia knows the pain deep in every joint and sinew. Earth damaged him too deeply. His heart stopped on the launch to orbit. He was dead for eight minutes. Earth is hard. *The moon is harder,* Alexia Corta thinks.

'Thank you, Mão de Ferro.'

The old family nickname; now her job title. Mão de Ferro. Iron Hand. Personal assistant to the Eagle of the Moon.

Why me? Alexia had asked.

Because you are the outsider, Lucas had said in the Eagle's office with its staggering vistas of Meridian Hub. The carpet still carried ghosts of the bloodstains of his predecessors. *You alone are incorruptible.*

Alexia takes a seat in the topmost tier, the better to study the honoured delegates. Seating is by faction. The delegates from the terrestrial nation states occupy the left side of the lowest tier. The Europeans, the Saudis, the small US delegation, the oversized

Chinese delegation. There is one missing from the US seats. Alexia searches her memory. James F Cockburn from the Central Committee. On the right side of the lowest tier are the corporates; the venture capital funds, the investment banks, the asset strippers. The people who invested in invading the moon.

On the second tier sit the lawyers; sharp in printed-this-hour fashion. Opposite the smart legals sits the Pavilion of the White Hare, diverse, chaotic, badly dressed. They are the private counsel of the Eagle of the Moon; a coterie of the lunar elite from the Court of Clavius to University of Farside. That one is a celebrity chef. The White Hare holds no power except to advise, to encourage and to warn. What does a celebrity chef know about that?

Her attention moves to the highest of the three tiers. The Vorontsovs sit here, the most secretive of the Dragons, stepping out of shadow to bask in the light of the new order. Big guns are power, in Barra de Tijuca, on the Sea of Tranquillity. Impeccable, aggressive young men and women, tattooed, muscular, a knife inside each suit.

Where is Yevgeny? There, in the lowest tier, facing the Eagle of the Moon's seat. The CEO of VTO Moon could not be more different from the sharp suits and sharp cheekbones: a big, bearded hulk of a man dressed in beautiful, old-fashioned brocade. To Alexia he always looks as if he is being held hostage. Beside him are the delegates from the other Dragons; AKA, Taiyang, Mackenzie Metals, Mackenzie Helium. One representative each. Such is the new order.

Lucas Corta takes in the tiered faces.

'Mackenzie Helium has committed an atrocity at João de Deus. I call for immediate punitive action.'

'What do you propose, Mr Corta?' Anselmo Reyes, from the Davenant venture capital fund. A major player.

'Contracts guaranteeing the security of all residents of João de Deus,' Lucas says.

'Including your son,' Anselmo Reyes says.

'Of course. Backed by the threat of strikes on Mackenzie Helium plant and materiel. Nothing less will deter Bryce Mackenzie.'

'I object,' says Raul-Jesus Mackenzie. Mackenzie Helium's delegate to the LMA. One of Bryce Mackenzie's adopted sons. Alexia has been long enough on the moon to understand what that means. 'The LMA is not in the business of sanctioning personal vendettas. And I would ask this Pavilion to note that Senhor Corta's thirst for vengeance is so strong and righteous that he postponed this meeting until after he took his entire entourage to Twé and packed his son off to Farside.'

'At least this father cares about his son,' Lucas says. Raul-Jesus Mackenzie shrugs off the barb.

'Well I hope the adjournment has given him time to reconsider his original proposal to this Pavilion. Which was an immediate mass-driver strike on Mackenzie Helium's Mare Cognitum storage facility. Safely remote from his precious João de Deus.'

Murmurs run along the seating banks; heads dip together.

'How much longer will the delegate for Mackenzie Helium insult this Pavilion with Bryce Mackenzie's paranoid fantasies?' says Lucas but Alexia is already scanning the tiers for treachery. Pale with rage in the railcar to Twé, Lucas had wanted a mass-driver strike on every working samba-line in the western hemisphere. Alexia had talked him down to a token display, tit for tat. An automated facility. No lives lost. The moral high ground. She had him model a firing solution, to keep him distracted until he reached Twé and Lucasinho. Alexia sees Yevgeny Vorontsov glance up to the highest tier. Those are the hands that hold the space-gun.

'One hundred and twelve deaths at João de Deus,' Lucas continues. 'Lives. People. Human beings. I will not abandon them to the whim of Bryce Mackenzie. His continued rule at João de Deus is an affront to every moral principle of our civilisation.'

'Come now, Senhor Corta,' Raul-Jesus says with oil and venom. 'You are hardly in a position to claim the moral high ground here.'

Alexia holds her breath. No ghosts on the moon, they say, but one stalks this forum.

'If you wish to accuse me, have the courage to say it to my face,' Lucas says.

'Ironfall, Senhor Corta.'

Alexia closes her eyes.

She sees again Valery Vorontsov in the observation blister of the *Saints Peter and Paul*; fingers like beaks reaching for her. She will never forget his words to her. *Don't you think the two worlds need a little lightning?*

'The Court of Clavius has exonerated me of any involvement in the destruction of Crucible.'

'Not proven, Mr Corta,' Monique Bertin says. The second of the LMA's triumvirate. Alexia's attention turns to Wang Yongqing.

'That has no meaning in lunar law,' Lucas says. 'Does the board refuse my request?'

Now Madam Wang speaks.

'The Lunar Mandate Authority is tasked with maintaining the production of unique non-terrestrial resources. We cannot permit any action that might jeopardise the supply of assets.'

'If that is your preferred language for honest, hard-working dusters, Madam Wang, then it is *assets* that are under threat.'

But Lucas Corta has been defeated and some junior member has already moved to end the session. Delegates rise from their seats, lawyers stoop to consult with them, Dragons chat or scowl, depending on their animosities; all migrate to the staircases, the doors and the lobbies.

'Yevgeny Grigorivitch.' The old Vorontsov patriarch stops. Up on the high seats his entourage watches him. Alexia sees the briefest flicker of communication between Vorontsov and Corta, then he lumbers up the stairs, where his people wait for him.

Alexia waits until the last delegate has left the council chamber before joining Lucas. He holds himself too still and upright, unwavering, no betrayal of the fury Alexia knows must rage in him, for it rages in her.

'So soon,' he says to his Iron Hand. 'They turn on me first, then they will turn on each other. There will be knives, Alexia.'

Ariel Corta grits her teeth and tries to straighten the suspender trapped under her thigh.

Fucking nineteen fucking forties.

The suits are glamorous, the dresses gorgeous, the hats glorious. The hosiery is ludicrous. Never designed for a paraplegic woman trying to dress in a hurry for a meeting.

Stockings are rolled, hauled, fastened and clipped. Stockings are sartorial hell.

Fuck it.

'Beija Flor, get me Abena Asamoah.'

She's there in three minutes.

'I was going for tea with the colloquium.'

'You'll learn nothing from them,' Ariel says. 'I need help.'

She hitches up her skirt. Abena rolls her eyes.

'This is not in my terms and conditions.'

'Yes yes. I need you to fasten these suspenders.'

'What was wrong with just regular hose?'

'Everything is wrong with regular hose. Do it right or don't do it at all.'

Abena sits on the bed. Ariel can see her fight down a smile.

'You could have LMA assistants any time you wanted. Lift your ass.'

Ariel lies back on the bed and pushes herself up on her elbows.

'I can't be seen to enjoy Lucas's largesse.'

Abena fastens the stud.

'People actually wore these things. So are you getting any cases?'

'Not yet. Shut up. You getting any work out of political science?'

'All of a sudden Cabochon is the hottest colloquium either side of the moon. That's not a good thing. Ariel . . .'

'No I am not going to get you an internship with my brother. He has a PA anyway. That girl from Brasil. Mão de Ferro, she's taken to calling herself. My mother was the last Iron Hand. Last and only.'

'Lift again,' Abena says. 'Done now.'

'Thank you.' Ariel swings herself around to the side of the bed. A thought summons the wheelchair. 'You are far too good to me.'

'What are you getting all dressed up for anyway?' Abena knows better than to offer to help Ariel into her wheelchair, or, once she has straightened her suit and fixed her face, to push her.

'Potential client meeting,' Ariel says, peering at the image of herself in her lens as she applies lipstick in the historically appropriate colours.

'Can I come?' Abena asks.

'Certainly not,' Ariel says. 'How do I look?'

'I'd hire you.' Abena kisses Ariel lightly on the cheek. Ariel rolls from the bedroom across her living space to the door where a moto is waiting.

'You will walk again.'

The bar has been discreetly cleared; a tap on the shoulder by a sharp-dressed young woman or man, the arrival of a payment from Taiyang into the bar tab. And a little extra.

Amanda Sun and Ariel Corta share a table on the gold circle balcony of the White Chrysanthemum Club. Meridian at this hour is a flutter and rattle of kites, long-tailed dragons, salamanders, garudas and moon cats and ten-tailed foxes rising and falling through cubic kilometres of airspace as they waft through Antares Quadra. Some manner of slow, subtle race, Ariel decides, drifting from thermal to exhaust duct to air-con exchanger. Such a race might take hours, even days to win. The colours, the undulating tails, hundreds of metres long, the flop and snap of molecule-film fabric on breezes she can't feel; these things she recognises as pleasure.

One other person is permitted in the White Chrysanthemum Club: its celebrated bartender. She brings two martinis, immaculate, dewed, ascetic. Ariel Corta shakes her head.

'You sure?' Amanda Sun says.

'I don't need the distraction.' But Ariel is distracted, dazed, unable to concentrate; almost dry drunk. The moon has no history, in the popular belief, but history didn't hear that. History has come to Meridian's prospekts. The streets, the apartments, the elevators and ladeiras, the endless perspectives of the towering quadras are unchanged, but Meridian is changed utterly. Earth commands the LMA, her brother occupies the Eyrie, the Vorontsovs hold a gun to the head of every human nearside or farside. And Marina is gone.

Marina is gone and all Ariel wants is to call out to the bar-keep to turn around and bring that martini right back right now. Only dignity holds her together.

The bartender leaves one martini on the table. Amanda Sun lifts the glass in her gloved hand and takes a sip.

'The remuneration package would be generous. You could breathe easy for the rest of your life.'

'And walk again.'

'Dance, even.'

'You were married to my brother and you don't know that I loathe dancing,' Ariel says.

'You drew up that nikah,' Amanda Sun says.

'And the divorce. One of my better pieces. And now Lady Sun sends you to contract me to win custody of Lucasinho.'

Amanda Sun takes a sip of her stinging dry martini but Ariel sees the narrowing of the lips, the tightening of the jawline. The courtroom eye never dies. A hit. A spot of blood. The old excitement prickles across Ariel's shoulders.

'Contracting you is entirely my own idea,' Amanda says.

'I remain stubbornly uncontracted,' Ariel says.

'Not even to walk free from that chair?'

'Not even that.'

'We know you refused to work with him.'

'That's very far from actively working to give his son to his enemies.'

'Taiyang is not the Eagle of the Moon's enemy.'

'So who left him to asphyxiate in a dead rover out on Fecunditatis?'

'He was just Lucas Corta then.' Amanda Sun takes another sip from her martini. 'The old order is dead, Ariel. Your brother killed it.'

'I liked the old order. It knew its obligations.'

'The terrestrials don't see the obligations. To them, we are a rabble of violent libertarians held together by mutual interest, one breath away from slitting each other's throats. They don't understand the unseen social contracts that lie beneath. We are an industrial outpost, a profit-nexus, nothing more.'

'Is this a manifesto, Amanda?'

'We do have a manifesto.'

'Seduce me,' Ariel says.

Amanda Sun takes a deeper sip of her martini.

'The days of the Dragons are over; we need new ideas, new politics, new economies. We have a political agenda. We have been running simulations through the Three August Sages. The results might surprise you.'

'Surprise me.'

'Communism.'

Ariel lifts an eyebrow.

'Wage labour is effectively a dead issue on the moon,' Amanda Sun says. 'We could easily move to a completely automated economy. Work could be a matter of choice and personal passion, not the need to breathe.'

'They tried that on Earth.'

'Earth is energy poor and irredeemably hierarchical. Corta Hélio itself contributed to the inequality. Who controls fusion power controls the planet. The moon is energy rich.'

'Taiyang controls the solar economy.'

'And automation and robotics. Yes. Guilty. But what the Three August Sages envision is a truly politically flat society, of energy and technological abundance where human needs are met and human society blossoms like a thousand flowers. The moon as a container for social experimentation. But you don't do politics. Isn't that the Corta line?'

'The actual line is, we don't do democracy. If your vision is some kind of communist utopia of plenty and free expression, why are you still trying to keep Beijing off your necks?'

'Their vision of communism is control. Ours is freedom. These visions are incompatible.'

'It's still a no,' Ariel says. 'And you are still asking me to deliver my own nephew as hostage to the Palace of Eternal Light.'

'Effectively, yes. I will tell Lucas about this conversation.'

'Of course. It was a stroke of genius, assigning you to conduct the case personally. What have you done to Lady Sun?'

Amanda Sun finishes her martini. A slow triangle of gin, vermouth-thickened, gathers beneath the lip and closes into a tear that runs down the slope of the glass. She bends close to Ariel's ear.

'Coraçao, it's what I haven't done.' Amanda Sun straightens her Zuckerman and Kraus jacket, tucks her clutch bag under her arm. A flick of the eye pays the bartender. 'I find it interesting to tell the truth to Cortas, because you don't believe in anything. Everything is contingent, everything is expedient. You don't believe in our vision, but what is yours?' She bends again; a peck on the cheek. 'Ex-sister-in-law.'

Amanda Sun thrusts her mittened hands in her armpits for warmth and shivers in her quilted warmsuit. Cold is psychological, she tells herself, watching the children, cute as cuddle-bears in their brightly patterned warmsuits, throwing a handball in low, fast passes. Bodies weave and block, jump and shoot at the improvised goals markered on the sides of two habitation containers. Young voices shout and cheer in high-pitched Portuguese.

'I think I like Boa Vista better this way.' Her breath steams. 'There were never enough children. Too quiet.'

'I never liked this place,' Lucas Corta says. Thermal boots clump down the ramp from the service locks to the floor of the great chamber. Engineers have run up lighting pylons; pools of floodlight step down the length of the old Corta palace, each one illuminating a rosette of habitats huddled around a generator and a steaming water recycler. The faces of the orixas are starkly underlit; shadowed and judgemental. Construction bots spider through the gloom, making fast the gas seal. Frost coats the mummified grass, edges the flash-frozen leaves. Ice locks the stream and mutes the cascades, frosts the tumbled pillars and domes of the pavilions. It is long, slow work to raise the rock temperature from the moon's background minus twenty to skin-warmth. The children play and the voices echo from the icy stone faces.

'Yet here you are,' Amanda says.

'It was an affront to me.' Nelson Medeiros's escoltas and Sun wushis with sharp haircuts follow discreetly.

'You've never taken affront well.'

'Thank you. I don't intend to live here.' Lucas and Amanda leave the children playing behind. Oxala and Yemanja look down on a herd of moondozers, assiduously scraping the dead vegetation from the habitat floor and loading it into recycling dumpsters. 'I have an idea of wilding,' Lucas says. The big machines steer carefully away from the soft, padded humans. 'My mother was disgusted by living creatures. She saw them as pollution. I like the idea of letting life run rampant. Vines crawling up the faces of the orixas; creepers growing from the eyes. Birds and crawling things and noises you hear but can't see. Life preying on life.'

'You never showed that kind of imagination when we were married.'

'Imagination was never in the contract.'

'A lot of things were never in the contract, thank the gods.'

The furthest third of Boa Vista has been scraped down to the base anorthosite, bone-bare, a cleaned-out skull. Bins of growing medium and biomass await distribution. In the quadrangles between the residential containers men and women drill with knives and batons. Shouted orders, instructions, guidance: a touch on a wrist here, a shoulder there, an arm taken to show the true move, the sure parry.

'Bryce Mackenzie must be ecstatic over you recruiting a private army at his door,' Amanda says.

'I offer needed employment to helium workers who have lost their contracts due to the commercial mismanagement of Mackenzie Helium,' Lucas says.

'Cortas always did look after their own,' Amanda Sun says.

'Ariel tells me you tried to contract her.'

'She'll have told you what she told me,' Amanda says.

'I will be having a conversation with her.'

'She won't take your contract.'

'Family is family,' Lucas Corta says. Yellow tape across a temporary seal warns of vacuum beyond. Amanda Sun peers through the porthole to see rubble, old dust, a new elevator and piles of construction material. 'This is where they blew the emergency lock. The whole of Boa Vista depressurised through here. We found Rafa half a kilometre away, on the surface.'

'Enough, Lucas.'

'Squeamish, from a woman who tried to kill me?'

'As I said to your sister, you weren't Eagle of the Moon then.'

Lucas grimaces.

He has become weak at hiding his feelings, Amanda Sun observes. *Earth has stretched him, broken him.*

'I will fight with every breath and heartbeat to keep Lucasinho out of the Palace of Eternal Light.'

'You misunderstand me, Lucas. Lucasinho is served best at the university. We will not argue that he be moved to Shackleton. The university will rebuild his memories. Of course you care, you care deeply, but with you, Lucasinho will always be in danger. With me, he'll have stability, care. Protection. Love. You Cortas, the only thing you ever needed to learn was how to love right. But you never did.'

The junshi whispers at the same instant that Zhen, Amanda's familiar, sounds the security alert. She sees from Lucas's face that he has received the same message.

'We should evacuate,' Lucas says as escoltas and wushis fall into defensive patterns. 'Boa Vista is under attack.'

'What's happening?' The common channel is a tumult of voices, shouts, terrified cries. Suit lights bob and flash in the absolute dark. Name tags flicker on Finn Warne's lens; his suit HUD shows ghost-figures surging down the tunnel. 'Report!'

'Contact!' Charlie Tumahai from the demolitions team.

'How many?' Finn Warne asks.

'Fucking Brasilians coming out of the walls!' Charlie Tumahai shouts. His identity tag flashes white, fades.

'Fuck!' Finn Warne shouts. Mining Santa Barbra lock: routine. Mining São Sebastião elevators: piece of piss. All João de Deus's service locks, secondary and emergency locks, the BALTRAN ports, the train station; the air conditioning and water plants: all planted with tamper-proof demolition charges. He had handpicked his team. No Santinhos. Only the most staunch from Mackenzie Helium's field operations. The old tram tunnel: last and piss easiest. Cut off the last escape. Now that escape is an invasion. The Cortas are coming.

'Jaime! Sadiki! Anyone!'

'What are your orders, boss?' Nicola Gan, from the east Procellarum engineering team.

Orders. *Orders.*

'Pull back. Get out of there.' Finn Warne freezes momentarily in his hard shell, in darkness, necessities wheeling around him. What to do? 'Take everything with you.'

'Boss...'

'Everything. If they find one of the charges, they'll work out how to defuse them.'

The bobbing helmet lights far up the tunnel swivel and fix on him.

'Move move move!'

Sprint, he orders his suit.

The surge of speed knocks the breath from lungs, the sense from his brain, everything but the oval of light before him: the tunnel terminus, João de Deus. *Five seconds of sprint remaining,* his familiar says. Four. Three. Two. One. He slides into the former station, gasping.

'Nicki.'

'Boss.'

'I need you to stay as a marker.'

'What's your idea?'

He goes to the common channel.

'Crew, arm and drop all explosives. Sauve qui peut.'

Finn Warne can see the white tags of his jackaroos strung along the tunnel. They're not soldiers, they're not fighters; they are engineers, surface workers. And he can't get everyone out. The first of his squad arrive. He clicks away from the common channel to Nicola Gan.

'Nicki, get out of there. I'm blowing the tunnel.'

'Boss, Sadiki and Brent are still back there.'

'Get out of there. Run!'

'Fuck you!'

There's not enough time. There is never enough time.

Shoot, he commands.

A flash of light, far down the tram line. The station quakes. A tectonic rumble. Nicola Gan arrives in the old station as Finn Warne's squad start to cycle through the locks.

Familiar: message to Bryce Mackenzie. João de Deus has been secured.

The lock cycles, four more dust-blackened jackaroos step into the chamber.

We have sustained casualties.

SIX

At twenty kilometres per hour, Ariel Corta rolls down Kondakova Prospekt. She has worked it out most carefully. Seven minutes to Meridian Station. Her batteries are fully charged but she will use sixty per cent of her power at full speed on the streets. She will get to the platform with twenty seconds to spare on twenty per cent power. VTO trains run to the millisecond. Lucas will begin to suspect when she is within two minutes of the station. But in a move to placate the citizens of Meridian he has pulled his bots off the prospekts. Hateful things, spiky and twitchy, threatening dismemberment, impaling, remorseless blood. People loathed them; kids had been slashed trying to upend them or tip them over the street barrier or immobilising them with zip-ties. Old women spat at them. Memories of occupation, of machines logging and registering every one of Meridian's seven hundred thousand habitants, of siege, of destruction and deaths out on the killing mares, were strong and close. Only a few recognise them, and the smiling, tea-drinking, taser-armed mercenaries who replaced the bots, for what they are: a thing the moon had never known and never needed. A police force.

Stealth. Ariel has shut down Beija Flor and uses what cover she can but she is the most famous wheelchair user on the moon and heads turn, comments pass. She trusts in stubborn human indifference.

She rolls into a knot of Long Runners to slide past two gendarmes loitering in the sunline dapple of trees that run down the centre of Kondakova Prospekt. A little mental kick of the chair control brings her up to speed with the runners. Bodies in much paint and few clothes, tassles and bangles and war-stripes, fall effortlessly into place around her. She can barely remember the holy colours of the orixas. There's defiance in the endless circle of motion. Running as resistance.

Marina had been a Long Runner.

Marina will be often in her thoughts. Lone travel is a melancholy, meditative journey.

The hub rises before her, the enormous central chamber from which the three quadras radiate. She can't but cast an eye up to her brother's Eyrie. There are orchards up there, of oranges and bergamots still bearing traces of decorative silver leaf from the disastrous wedding of Lucasinho Corta.

Meridian Station. She braces herself against the small lurch as the chair locks to the moving stairway and carries her down to the plaza. Meridian Station is thronged at every hour; she guides her chair from knot to knot of passengers, arriving, departing, greeting extravagantly, making tearing farewells. There are cameras here. Seeing is one thing, noticing another. Everyone is surveilled, no one is looking.

Ariel joins the throng of passengers on the stairways down to the platforms. She opens up Beija Flor and buys her ticket as her chair unclicks from the escalator treads and rolls on to the platform. Her chair knows the embarkation area and drives her to the correct lock. The lighting turns the walls of pressure glass into mirrors of ghosts and deceptions. Two minutes. The old Polar Express north is on time. She'll tell Lucas when she is well over the top of the world. She owes him an explanation for why she will not represent him in the Court of Clavius.

She has never been to Farside. She knows the Nearsider myths and legends; that it is a web of old, leaking tunnels, tight and claustrophobic, chaotic, choked with the bodies and odours and breaths of tens of thousands of students. Like a bloodstream, or a nervous system. The old apartment up in Bairro Alto had been tight and cramped, full as a double-yolked egg with her and Marina. She woke many a night imagining the room clamped around her like a cast. That had been two of them. Thousands of times more bodies pulsed through Farside's tunnels and corridors, trams and tubes and telpherages.

The great train, two decks of clunky, angular lunar engineering, pulls up alongside the platform. Locks match to millimetre finesse and seal. Power: a hair below twenty per cent. Within acceptable parameters, given that she had to burn the batteries to keep up with the Long Runners.

What makes her glance up the platform? An incongruity of colour – hard greys among the browns and rusts of lunar fashion? The disrupting pattern: a wedge of people all advancing as one from the escalators along the platform? The movements of passengers away from them; the walk becoming a trot becoming a run.

LMA mercenaries.

People pour from the train. She can't get through. She can't board.

'Excuse me,' she shouts, willing her chair forwards. She knocks against a little girl, sends her reeling into the glass. The girl's parent snatches her to him, hisses outrage. 'Sorry sorry sorry.'

They see her. They are coming for her.

'It's all right,' says a woman's voice. 'I've got you.' Hands grab the arms of her wheelchair. The woman smiles into her face. She wears a Fair Isle knit, corduroy breeches, knee socks and brogues.

Other hands seize the chair handles and try to tug her away from the train. Ariel lashes out, slaps at them, tries to beat the hands off but they pile on.

'Now that's a very poor idea,' the woman says. She has an upswinging, perky Aus accent. She moves – a foot, a fist, the flat of a hand – and three mercs are down. Passengers flee, screaming. Knives flash, the woman moves away from the blades like liquid and the knives are sliding across the platform. One merc is on her back, gasping. One stares at her empty hand. One picks himself up from the polished sinter, hand to face, blood seeping through fingers. 'This train is ready for departure,' the woman says, shoves the wheelchair ungently through the lock and into the vestibule as the locks seal.

The train moves out. Ariel looks back at the bodies on the platform. She touches the brim of her hat in salute, then the Transpolar Express enters the tunnel.

She parks the chair. The woman rocking the land-girl fashion sits down opposite her, strips off a glove and offers her hand.

'Ariel Corta, I bloody well hope. Dakota Kaur Mackenzie, at your service. Ghazi of the Faculty of Biocybernetics.'

Ariel picks up the glove, squeezes it; the leather resists and in an instant turns steel hard.

'Your timing is immaculate,' Ariel says.

'We had someone on every train.'

Ariel smiles.

'In the right car?'

'There aren't that many spaces can take a wheelchair.'

'You'd almost think you had Three August Sages to forewarn you.'

'They said you were a spiky fucker,' Dakota Mackenzie says. 'Are all you Cortas cunts?'

'We also have a wolf in the family. You'd like him.'

Light knifes through the window as the train leaves the tunnel and merges with the Polar Mainline. The car sways over the points, then the maglev engines open up and with a surge of power the Transpolar Express accelerates to twelve hundred kilometres per hour. Children run up and down the aisle; students on their way back to the Farside research facilities from their Nearside colloquiums laugh and shout and chatter. Workers sleep, their sasuit helmets and suitpacks cradled like infants.

'I deserve a fucking drink,' Dakota Mackenzie says. She orders a Lobachavsky.

'A what?' Ariel asks.

'It's a new thing, on our side. White rum, cow-cream, ginger, cinnamon. Undergrads get blasted on it.'

'Looks like a glass of cum,' Ariel says as the steward sets it down, together with her drink.

'And what's that?'

'Tarragon, lime and lemongrass spritzer.'

'Fuck's sake. Well, if mine's cum, yours looks like an STI. I thought Cortas drank.'

'Not this one.'

'Spare us the zeal of the newly converted. What was it? The Corta cocktail?'

'The Blue Moon. Rafa claimed he invented it. It'll have been some off-shift duster in a João de Deus bar. I never liked it. Too sweet. Blue Curacao is a mad and bad thing to do to an innocent martini.'

Dakota lifts her Lobachavsky, sets it down again. Her eyes are wide. 'Move,' she whispers.

Ariel pushes back from the table without thought or hesitation.

'The train is slowing,' Dakota says.

Ariel's eyes widen. The old custom: anyone may stop and board a train, anywhere on the moon. Dakota reaches for the handles of Ariel's wheelchair; Ariel slaps her away.

'Don't push me.'

Dakota heads towards the back of the train. Ariel rolls after Dakota Mackenzie.

'VTO is in Lucas's pocket,' Ariel says.

'Who says it's Lucas? We're twenty minutes from Hadley. This is Mackenzie country. Cortas are hostages of choice.'

By the fifth car back, the other passengers have noticed that the train is stopping.

'What happens if they get on at the back of the train?' Ariel says.

'Then I fight,' Dakota says. 'Again. On a train this time. But they won't. Because Mackenzies, Vorontsovs, LMA, moon pixies and space fairies, they all get a train at the front.'

Ten cars, the final set of pressure doors opens and the two women push into the lock. Behind them is the last bulkhead, behind it twelve hundred kilometres of maglev track and post-industrial wasteland. The Transpolar Express comes to a halt out on the grey desolation of Palus Putridinis and settles on to the line.

Ariel edges as close as she can to the tiny porthole in the outlock door. No sign of any new passengers, only tracks, scarps and berms and mazes of dozed-up regolith. Broken machinery, abandoned habitats, obsolete comms relays. The crashed and the scrapped, the failed and the smashed. Seventy years of scraping and sifting for precious metals have gouged and wounded the moon deep. The wounds of heavy extraction may never heal.

Ariel feels the gentle lurch of the train levitating on its magnets. The Transpolar Express is under way again.

'Five aboard,' Dakota says. 'Sasuits and helmets.'

'How do you know that?'

'I'm in the train system.' Dakota grimaces. 'Shit. They're heading straight for our booked seats.'

'How long until they get to us?'

'Three minutes to the seats. Then another five to work the bottom half of the train. If we're lucky. Or they're standard jackaroo thick.'

'You can take them?' Ariel asks.

'It won't come to that. And that is so fucking irritating.'

Ariel realises she has been drumming her fingers on the arms of her wheelchair. She looks out of the porthole again. The train has entered the mirror field around Hadley. The cupped hands of the mirrors are upturned to the sun, catching and offering it to the solar forges of the great pyramid like a sacrifice. Ariel feels the soft drop of deceleration.

'Any second now, they're going to work out what I'm doing,' Dakota says.

'What are you doing?' Ariel asks.

'Gods, they're moving. Where the fuck is it?' Dakota pushes past Ariel to peer out of the port. The train drops to the line. A noise, metal on metal, the solid clunk of locks mating. There is something out there, docked with the train. Seals mesh, systems runs checks.

'They're here,' Ariel says. Three women, two men storming in tight formation down the aisle. Shouts and protests from the passengers – one man gets up and is sharply smacked back into his seat by a hand to the chest. Sasuits, helmets at hips. Mackenzie Metal logos on shoulder and thigh. Sudden green light in the vestibule. The locks are equalised. Doors open. Ariel looks into a tiny pressure pod; worn gear, broken equipment, scratches on the fascia, stains on the upholstery.

'I'll never . . .'

'Leave the chair.'

'I need . . .'

'Leave the fucking chair!' Dakota seizes Ariel by her lapels and throws her through the lock. She turns, hurls the wheelchair at their attackers as the vestibule door admits them, then dives through the hatch. The lock slams shut, pumps hiss. Green lights turn red. Ariel pulls herself upright on the circular banquette and a lurch immediately sends her sideways. A series of jolts, a small surge of power. She is running free.

'I requisitioned an old rover from our metallurgy research station at Rima Vladimir,' Dakota says. 'Took its fucking time getting here. That was a lot closer than I like.'

'You could have broken something,' Ariel says. 'And my chair . . .'

'Fuck your chair!' Dakota shouts. 'We'll build you legs. We're the fucking university, we build fucking legs, hands, whole new colons. Okay?'

In the silence in the pressure pod, so small the two women fit it like seeds in cardamom, Ariel summons Beija Flor. She is far from the network, out in Hadley's mirror maze, but her familiar links with the rover AI and shows her the world beyond the windowless bubble. Whichever way she looks, mirrors rise around her. She understands the terrestrial word *forest* now, amid the pylons, yet her overpowering feeling is not of enclosure, but of agoraphobic terror. She is a foetus in a womb, in the middle of ferocious vacuum, light, radiation, engineering. The rover weaves an escape path through the mirror maze, away from the main line and any other jackaroo squads; bearing north-west by north. Low on the horizon burns the brilliant star of Hadley.

'Right under Duncan's nose,' Ariel says. 'That's you off his mooncake gift list.'

'What is your family's problem with my loyalties?' Dakota says.

'Mackenzies killed my brothers,' Ariel says simply. 'Mackenzies took my legs away.' She pushes herself deep into the seating. 'Where are you taking me?'

'Rozhdestvenskiy. About twenty hours. Plenty of time for the art of conversation. Or if you don't fancy conversation, do you play oware?'

'Pass me the pee pants,' Ariel Corta says. Dakota Kaur Mackenzie unhooks the apparatus from the reclamation unit and looks away as Ariel pulls up her skirt to pull them on. The air is thick and over-breathed, tinged with the ammoniac hum of an elderly filtration system.

No dignity on a rover, Dakota Mackenzie said the first time she passed Ariel the urinal.

'When you're in my situation you learn pretty quick there's no dignity anywhere,' Ariel said.

That was nineteen hours ago.

For the first hour they played oware but Ariel could not engage with the game, lost interest quickly and tried to find ways to cheat.

'Where's the fun if you don't?'

The second hour they ate. They dragged out every mouthful and appreciative comment as far as they could. The third hour was excretion. The fourth hour they talked a bit and slipped into a sleep broken by the rolling of the rover as it negotiated the rock-strewn seabeds of Imbrium. Eat, excrete, sleep. Talk. Eat, excrete, sleep. Talk. The rover climbs up over the pole and picks a careful path down the northern rim of Rozhdestvenskiy.

Eat, excrete, sleep. Talk. The best of these is talk.

'Why law?' Dakota asks.

'There is ritual every Corta child takes,' Ariel says. 'It takes place in the Earth-dark. Only Earth-dark. You step out on to the surface. You're on your own but you're not alone. There's a voice. It says, *Go out beyond the lights, child. Let go of the safety lines and air-caches. Don't be afraid, I'm with you.* You walk out until the voice tells you stop. Then the voice says, *Look up and tell me what you see.* And you say, I see the sky and the stars and the dark Earth. The voice says, *Look again and tell me what you see.* And the correct answer, the Corta answer is, I see the lights. I see the billion lights of the dark Earth. And the voice says, *We light the lights.*

'I went up to the surface, age ten, in my little shell-suit with kitty and dragon stickers on it. And the voice told me: *walk out*. I walked out, I kicked up the dust, I listened to my breath. *Tell me what you see,* the voice said. I said, *I see nothing*. The voice said, *Look again, tell me what you see*. And I said what I saw. I said, *I see dead rock and grey regolith, I see burning light and vacuum and emptiness. I see silence and tedium. I see nothing.*

'Wrong answer. Not the Corta answer. Lucas still thinks I betrayed the family for glamour and money. Being darlinged by society. No: I saw exactly the same as he saw. He saw the lights, I saw dead rock. He saw a whole world where he could play and build and make and break things. I saw no talk, no wit, no drama. No people. Like your little game: where's the fun?'

'You say, wit, drama, other people,' Dakota says. 'Yet you've never been in a long-term relationship.'

'You seem to know a lot about me, ghazi,' Ariel says.

'I need to know my clients.'

'Client, am I? That sounds a little proprietorial. What is the university's interest in me?'

'The university has a long tradition of academic sanctuary.'

'Which you extended to Luna, and to me when I asked for it. And you're treating Lucasinho. That's a lot of Cortas in one hemisphere. This is the moon, sweetie. No one does something for nothing. Did you see an opportunity for leverage on my brother?'

'The university has always been independent from the old LDC and the LMA. We're apolitical.'

'And Cortas don't do politics either. Until they do.'

Dakota sits back on the bench.

'Half an hour to Rozhdestvenskiy,' she says. Ariel permits herself the leanest of courtroom smiles. She has drawn blood.

'Now, contractual obligation,' Ariel says. 'What's your story, ghazi?'

Dakota pulls her legs up to sit cross-legged on the curving bench.

'I studied bioscience at the university. My doctoral and post-doc were in human genome engineering. I was brilliant. Best of my cohort. Best in years. Modesty is such a snivelling virtue. I came back to Nearside to work as liaison between Crucible and Twé. The Mackenzies have been pursuing a strategy of genetic engineering to stabilise the geneline.'

'Eugenics,' Ariel says. 'Blue-eyed babies.'

'There is more to it than that,' Dakota says. 'I was working with AKA to set up a reservoir of human biodiversity. In case we find ourselves facing a genetic crash at some point in the future. It's possible. Likely even. We are a small population, even with terrestrial migration. And epigenetic factors are driving our population towards sub-speciation. A new humanity, if you like. But essentially, yes, blue-eyed blond-haired babies. And when I decided to have a child, I found that I carry a flaw in the MEN1 gene that increases the risk of thyroid, parathyroid, pituitary, adrenal, bowel and stomach cancers.'

'Gods,' Ariel says. 'Geneticist, engineer thyself.'

'I did, with the university's help. There was a price: ten years serving the university as a ghazi. By the time my service is done, Melyssa will be in a colloquium herself. Do you want the twist in the tale?'

'All good stories have a twist,' Ariel says.

'When I learned about the error on the MEN1 gene I went to my family first. They soak up a lot of radiation on Crucible; they've developed a lot of techniques to repair genetic injuries. Turns out Dakota Kaur was not Mackenzie enough for the treatment. Too brown-eyed, too brown-skinned. That's why, when you or your brother or any other fucking Corta gets sniffy about *my loyalty*, I want to stick it up your ass so far I can see it when you yawn.'

'I'm sorry,' Ariel says. Another hit, another drop of blood. In time she will find this ghazi's every vulnerability. 'How long until we get to Rozhdestvenskiy's network bubble?'

'About seven minutes.'

'I'll need university privileges and encrypted private server.'

'I'm not your PA,' Dakota Kaur Mackenzie says.

Ariel continues as if the ghazi had not spoken. 'A law library. You have a law faculty? I'll need a meeting with Abena Manu Asamoah as soon as possible. Face to face. Secure venue. Book her tickets and find her somewhere decent to stay. Hostages like me can slum it but I have standards for my legal team.'

'This all needs to be cleared . . .' Dakota Kaur begins but the ideas are kindling in Ariel Corta; sparkling like dust in the rover's fetid atmosphere. She long ago learned the joy of seeing those bright stars in the moment of pure potential, before reaching for them and the movement of her hands sending them into new, brilliant constellations. She has a plan now.

'I am going to explain this to you as if you were a tiny child, in simple, clear and non-technical terms so that you will understand what it is I am trying to do and because you understand you will render me all assistance.

'I am trying to keep Lucasinho Corta – Lucas's son, my nephew – safe and alive. He's nineteen and has legally been a free agent since exchanging parenting and agency contracts with Lucas when he was twelve. I know, I drew up the contracts. However, he has sustained severe neurological damage through oxygen starvation which means he is incapable of acting in his own interests and therefore someone must assume a contract of duty of care for him. His mother is Amanda Sun – she and Lucas terminated their nikhah two years ago. One of the best day's work in my life. If the Palace of Eternal Light gains care over Lucasinho, Lucas is effectively their hostage. If Lucas gains duty of care over him, the only way he can make sure Lucasinho is safe is to keep him under his own personal protection. That means he either moves Lucasinho to Meridian – clear breach of duty of care – or he moves the LMA to Farside. That's going to sit well with your legendary "independence".

'I can't take charge of him. My relationship with Lucas was strained enough when I turned down his request that I act for him in the Court of Clavius. I don't want the word "sorocide" to come anywhere near his paranoid little head. That leaves only one candidate, and she's already proven she can care for Lucasinho. And she's untouchable. But I need to move fast. I need to get writs to the Court of Clavius at the same time as Lucas and Amanda Sun.

'So I will need help on this. Will you help me?'

'You utter fuck,' Dakota Kaur Mackenie says. 'Save the kid? How can I say no?'

'One more thing.'

'There's always going to be one more thing, isn't there?'

'Those legs you promised? What can you do in the time before we leave Rozhdestvenskiy?'

*

In her new favourite dress, Luna Corta presses her hands to the gondola's glass wall and peers out. The old pink suit-liner is discarded, deprinted and remodelled. The window reads Luna's intention and dims the interior lights but in the moment before it does she sees her face reflected: a half-face hovering over the half-shaded hills and sub-craters of Coriolis. She leans her forehead against the glass.

'Luna,' Madrinha Elis chides. She doesn't trust the glass, doesn't trust this car, doesn't trust the cable unspooling it from the medical facility cut into the western rim of Coriolis crater. Doesn't trust any of the old, clattery machinery of the university. Which is much of the reason Luna does it. She likes the old domes and habitats cut into rims and mountainsides, the crazy tramways and hyperloops and cableways and funiculars. It reminds her of the tunnels and caves and secret passages of Boa Vista.

'What way will Tia Ariel's train come?' Equatorial One is a strip of brilliant light across the grey floor of the crater. Beyond the western rim of Coriolis fleets of moondozers are stalled while university and Taiyang argue through the Court of Clavius over extending the sunline across the crater, over all of Farside.

'From the east,' Madrinha Elis says. 'The other way.'

Luna knows you have to be fast fast fast to catch a VTO train, even when it is slowing down into Coriolis Station. Luna-familiar can give her the time and the bearing but she might blink, and sneeze and miss it.

A flicker of light. So fast it takes her breath away.

'There it is! I see it, I see it!'

'Look, anjinho,' Madrinha Elis says. The sky above Coriolis is filled with moving lights like dozens of festival lanterns, all converging with a graceful lack of haste. Cablecars from Coriolis's diverse habitats, spinning down their lines towards the station. There's a train in and people are hurrying to meet it. Then the AI announces imminent arrival and Luna's car enters the dock.

Luna is running as the doors open. Madrina Elis shouts but she is already a corridor and a flight of steps away. One flight two flights three flights four. Luna takes them in entire, joyful bounds, in motion as she lands to leap and fly down the next one. Her new favourite dress billows out around her. It is sleeveless, scoop-necked, high-waisted and full-skirted, printed in a dust-grey so light and soft it feels like ash against the skin.

Car 12, familiar-Luna advises. The train is an enormous, potent presence beyond the pressure glass. The platform is a mass of bustling humanity – arriving, departing, greeting, adiosing.

Luna, Madrinha Elis calls through the network but the lock is opening and there is Ghazi Dakota stepping out in great boots and there, *there*, two steps behind her is Ariel. Ariel walking. Ariel walking towards her as she rushes towards her tia.

'Oh, anjinho,' Ariel says as she scoops up Luna the way she used to in the old times, when she came back after long-away to Boa Vista. 'Oh meu amorzinho. Voce e bonita.' Luna clings to her side, Ariel tucks an arm under her, holding her up. 'You've got heavy.' Cortas say what they think. But she does not set Luna down.

'You've got new legs,' Luna says as Ariel marches up the platform to the waiting Madrinha Elis.

'I've got old legs,' Ariel says. 'But I've got a new thing they gave me at Rozhdestvenskiy; like a bridge over the parts of my spine that don't work. Better than those old scary legs, right? But you've got a new face!'

'Put me down put me down,' Luna insists.

'What's the matter, anjinho?' Ariel says.

Luna looks over her shoulder.

'I don't want Madrinha Elis to see,' Luna whispers. 'Bend down like you are going to kiss me.'

Luna flashes a look of conspiracy at Dakota, who is two steps behind her ward. *Say anything and I will kill you, ghazi or not.*

'Get close,' Luna whispers. A kiss, cheeks touch. Luna reaches into the secret pocket she had built into this new favourite dress. The pocket is the reason it is her new favourite piece of clothing. Pink suit liners hide nothing. Folds of soft grey fabric can hide anything. She slips out the knife and presses it into Ariel's hand. Ariel resists, Luna insists.

'Take it. It is for a Corta who is bold, great-hearted, without avarice or cowardice, who will fight for the family and defend it bravely. If you are fighting for Lucasinho you will need a knife.'

'Luna, it's not me fighting,' Ariel says. 'It's you.'

Another three days. That's enough to make a ritual. After parkour Robson Corta goes to the banya, soaks off the grease and steams out the aches, then meets Haider in El Gato Encantado for horchata. There are fifteen hotshops in Theophilus but Robson was careful to take Haider to every one of them, sample their beverages (hot and cold), their food (savoury and sweet), their clientele (young and old) and general ambience. They kept scores, took pictures, built up a spreadsheet. This is an important decision. Since it looks likely that both of them will be at Theophilius for a long time, they cannot make a mistake.

El Gato Encantado, on the third level by the north outlock, doesn't score so well for food or beverages, but ranks high for ambience – an old digging with cubbies and corners scooped from the north wall of the old crater and rough-sealed, concealed spaces where you can hide and take your time and watch without being watched, and number one for clientele. They are the only kids.

'No more, right?' Jianyu behind the hot bar says. Robson is sweet with that. The population of Theophilus is three thousand two hundred. Of that, one hundred and twelve are under sixteen, and thirteen are of Robson's cohort. Every one of them hates him. He knew that the moment he walked into the Year Seven Rose Quartz Colloquium and every head turned to him. He loathed the enablers' earnest pleas for welcome and acceptance and assimilation. Don't waste your breath, he wanted to say. These inbred West Nectaris pissdrips are going to try to kill me as soon as you turn your back.

They ambushed him on Seventh. The big fucker, his sergeants, the kids who really want to be in and a couple of girls to record it for the network. New kid. Outlander. Alien. Kid who? *Corta.* We're here to tell you, you're nothing. They were big, they were strong but they weren't fast and they weren't smart. Robson ducked away from them and was two levels up by the time the big kid Emil had even recovered his balance. They hooted and jeered as he ran along the airduct, ten metres above their heads. When he got back to the apartment Joker's notification buffer was stuffed with hate posts.

Do you want me to mute them?

'Mute them all.'

After that the rules were clear. Robson was never troubled as long as he kept his part of the social contract by playing the role of outsider.

Different colloquium, same rules. Haider was in Dolorite, Theophilus's other colloquium, come in from Hypatia with care givers Max and Arjun. Haider didn't have the name, hadn't fallen from the top of a city so didn't carry a reputation to have broken. He certainly didn't have the moves. Six days on and he was still covering the deeper bruises with foundation. Dolorite Colloquium always had the tougher reputation. He settled into a routine of class pariah, but never that of outcast. There had to be someone else out there, in Theophilus's one hundred and twelve. The path was clear and simple. He followed the hate posts, and found Robson Corta.

They sit in their booth in El Gato Encantado on the slightly-too-high banquette, sipping their horchatas. They could not be more different.

Robson is brown, wiry, confident; loves sport and activity, assured in what he can do with his body.

Haider is pale, skinny, shy; loves stories and music, uncertain in his body and what is happening to it.

They are inseparable.

Jianyu brings a woman in dust-smeared workwear over to the booth.

'Show her that thing.' He points to Robson.

'What thing?'

'That thing with the cards.'

Word has passed quickly around El Gato Encantado that the kid with the big hair can also work cards. Robson pulls his half deck of cards from the pocket of his shorts, shuffles one-handed. That's usually enough to impress but Jianyu nods: more. Robson's adapted his tricks to work with the half deck. The other half he gave to a friend, in another city; a city that no longer exists, smelted to slag in the dust of the Oceanus Procellarum. In another life; a life that no longer exists, cut to bones by blades.

He'll work a simple gravity-force. Quick, fast and always bamboozles. Show the pack, turn it over, note a card – the force card – and cut it a couple of times. Move the force card to the bottom of the deck. Square it up. He slides the force card under the top card, fans the deck. Gravity makes sure the force card is still on the bottom.

This is the work of two, maybe three seconds. The trick of the trick is done. Everything else is selling – the theatre, the patter, the disguising. The trick of the trick of the trick is that it is never where the mark thinks it is.

'Okay now, touch a card. Any card you like.'

Robson's deck is grubby, foxed at the corners and skewed to the aristocracy: high on court cards, diamond and hearts. The luck of the split. Darius Mackenzie, wherever he is, whatever he is doing, has the low clubs.

'Now, I'm going to show you that card.' As he patters, Robson splits the deck and squares the two halves, sliding the force card under the chosen card. He shows duster-woman the half deck, force card on the bottom. 'Now, look at this card for five seconds. I need you to do it for that time because that's how long it takes to imprint on your eye. Because what I'm going to do is read it right off your retina. Okay?'

The woman may be a vacuum-hardened, radiation-tanned veteran, but she nods, uncertain, nervous. This is all part of the working of the trick: the sell. Robson closes up the deck again and looks into her eyes. One two three four five.

'I'm reading the Queen of Diamonds,' he says.

Of course it's the Queen of Diamonds.

'Isn't that the damnedest thing?' Jianyu says. 'The damnedest thing?'

'How did you do it?' the duster asks.

'That's the first rule of magic,' Haider says. 'Never ask a magician how the trick is done.'

The duster sends over two horchatas, and cookies. The two friends eat and drink and swing their gangly, skinny legs.

SEVEN

Alexia has never before seen a zabbaleen. But here is a squad of them outside her apartment door and one of them, a young woman in baggy khaki shorts, heavy boots and sleeveless tank top, holding her hand up to Alexia.

'You can't go in there.'

'That's my apartment.'

The zabbaleen woman bears a shock of dreads, ribbons and beads woven between the locks, scraped back from her face and fastened with a barette. Bangles and beads, swag upon swag. Her familiar is a jewelled skull.

'It's not safe, amigo. There's been an infestation.'

'A what?' Alexia says, then a co-worker – a moon-tall young man in similar rogue's raiment – comes out of the street door of her balcony towing a small powered cart. His familiar is a skull studded with long spikes.

'We're clear now.'

'What the fuck were you doing in my apartment...' Alexia begins. Then she sees what lies in the little waggon. Birds; hundreds of them, stiff and hard as bullets. Bright plumaged in green and gold, a stab of red.

'You killed the parakeets,' Alexia shouts. The four zabbaleen in the squad are sincerely nonplussed.

'Policy, señora,' waggon-kid says.

'Unmonitored resource misappropriation,' the dread-haired zabbaleen says.

'There's a push to clamp down on it,' a third zabbaleen says, a very dark-skinned third-gen kid with scarifications along his arms and under his eyes. His familiar: a flaming skull.

Must be a zabbaleen thing.

'If you wouldn't mind standing back,' the last zabbaleen says, a red-haired, freckled man in late middle age, his hair stubbled white with radiation damage, his freckles studded with the black moles of early melanomas. He opens a titanium case. The air hazes, then thickens. Smoke wreathes about his head then pours into his case. 'We've all got immunity codes, but you can get the odd soft fail. Wouldn't kill a human but it does hurt like Christ.' He closes the lid on a seething, buzzing puddle of liquid black. Not smoke. Bots. They hunted down the parakeets with thousands of insect-sized hunter drones.

'A blessed day to you, señora,' dread-head says. Merrily the zabbaleen swing off down the street.

'Birdie!' Alexia shouts through her tiny rooms. 'Birdie!' She finds some spoiling fruit in her cooler and puts it out on the balcony. She sits with tea, watching the overripe guava. No flash of colour, no glimpsed flick of wings out among the buttresses, no chatter in the middle air.

'Fuckers,' Alexia Corta says

Alexia takes one note from the zabbaleen: their approach to style. The printer squeezes it out into the hopper. So good after that fussy, tight 1940s stuff she has to wear as Iron Hand. Shorts, boots, tank top, not too clingy. The kind of thing she wore back home, when she was Queen of Pipes.

Also, a fine disguise.

The LMA has issued an advisory against ascent above Level Seventy, Maninho says as she waits for the passengers to exit the elevator. People glance at her she as she enters the elevator car. Zabbaleen style. Today you stare, next week you'll be wearing it.

Who knows how these things appear?

There are personal safety issues.

Level Forty-Two. Passengers leave, fewer enter. Doors closing.

The situation in Bairro Alto has deteriorated recently. There has been widespread water and bandwidth theft and hacking attacks on public printers.

She doesn't know what happened to the suffocating man who begged her for breath in this same elevator, but she meets him in dreams: doors closing on him as he reaches out a hand, speaking breath-starved words she can never make out.

I'm sorry, I'm new, I don't know what to do, she said.

Not even worth air we breathe, he had gasped.

She had not known what he meant. Now she must find out.

Level Sixty-Five.

Alexia, I must strongly advise you against this, Maninho says. *I can hire private security.*

Above Level Sixty-Eight she is the only passenger.

Level Seventy-Five. Her boots ring on mesh decking. Attention snagged by the sound, she looks down. Alexia has grown up on rooftops, balconies, gantries, but the drop beneath her boot soles makes her breath flutter. It's half a kilometre sheer between power conduits to the next deck. She puts a hand out to steady herself. There is nothing to hold on to.

Don't look down. Never look down.

She makes it to a staircase spiralling around a gurgling water main – the familiar song of moving liquid beneath her hand as she rests it on the pipe – and up three flights to a small mirador.

Look out.

This is not breath catching; this is a gasp of naked wonder.

She sees Meridian as she has never seen it before. The hub is a colossal drum, strung and restrung with bridges, catwalks, cableways. Elevators run up and down the curved face of this drum; the moonloop surpasses all of them. She watches a glowing passenger capsule rise from the ground station towards the lock. Beyond the first airlock is two hundred metres of protecting rock, and the second lock to the Meridian launch tower. She is deep underground.

The three main prospekts, each the axis of one of Meridian's quadras, radiate from her. She sees them not as boulevards but canyons deeper than any on Earth. Vistas filled with lights, hazy with dust. Kondakova Prospekt stretches before her, she can see the deeper perspectives where Orion Quadra's other four prospekts radiate away from the hub. The trees that line the great prospekts, taller than any rainforest tree she ever saw, are like pollen grains. To her right, Antares Quadra is darkening, to the far left, dawn is filling up Aquarius Quadra. For the first time Alexia appreciates Meridian's design: three five-pointed stars, linked at the centre. The canyonlands of Meridian is one of the wonders of the solar system.

This close to the top of the world, the illusion of the sunline breaks up. From the ground, from her balcony, even from the height of the LMA office, Alexia can believe that she is under a sky, sometimes clear, sometimes clouded. She has heard that it even rains from time to time, to sweep the dust from the air. She would like to see that. That would be a feat of water engineering. Here she can see the joins between the panels, the grain of the light cells that project the sky. There is a roof on the world.

Looking up, shading her eyes with her hand, Alexia sees the shanties. Cubes of foam panels leaning against an air duct. Tents of sheeting and stolen wrapping slung from swags of cables. Pavilions of plastic pallets painstakingly wedged into gaps in the infrastructure. Bivouacs, lean-tos, shacks. The more Alexia looks, the more Bairro Alto reveals itself; every crevice and cranny of the high city is packed with improvised homes. She thinks of the nests of insects, or hummingbirds, woven around the contours of the human world.

She thinks of the favelas of old Rio. Cidade de Deus, Mangueira, Complexo do Alemão, Great Rocinha. Solutions to the primal human need for shelter.

Everywhere in Rio was favela now.

As Alexia sees Meridian whole, she understands that Meridian is much more than the space it encloses. Streets and housing units dig deep into rock, the city's infrastructure digs deeper: conduits and crawlways, tunnels and ducts, cable-runs and ancillary systems dark in the stone. Remote power stations, the surface solar and communications arrays, the wires, the roots reach for hundreds of kilometres. She sees Meridian as it is: not a city: a machine. A machine for living, its humans scurrying around in the spaces between its workings.

She climbs higher. Two levels up and every pipe, every stanchion and girder is hung with what look like silvery spider webs. She touches one and pulls back a wet hand. The plastic web glistens with dew.

Condensation traps. The Queen of Pipes appreciates the clever design. She didn't know that Meridian had a cloud layer.

'Unmonitored resource misappropriation,' Alexia says aloud.

Yes, egregiously, Maninho says. Alexia learned within two minutes of having the lens fitted to her eye and connected to the network that familiars have no notion of irony.

'I'm going to switch you off, Maninho,' Alexia interrupts. She has seen a face, a woman's face. A short, unwelcoming stare, then gone in the shadows between the machines. The woman could have been watching her since she stepped off the elevator. There could be dozens of them, in the shadows, watching. Dozens more on the girders, in the stairwells, in the crevices.

This is not her city.

Movement. There. Darting across the stair-head.

Alexia turns to go back down to the elevator. People on the landing. Alexia turns back. People on the upstairs turn.

Women and men of all ages, some children. They wear a panoply of fashions; the current 1940s, the outgoing 1980s, a 2020s style blouse here, 2050s leggings and hoodies there: whatever was the mode when they were forced up to Bairro Alto. None carry familiars.

'Unmonitored resource misappropriation,' a child's voice says.

They step closer.

Alexia has never been so afraid, not even when the Gulartes declared war on the Queen of Pipes by assaulting Caio. And she sees the way out.

'I'm a water engineer!' she shouts. 'I can show you how to get twenty per cent more from those dew traps. I can show you how to build a distribution and purification system!'

'Well, I don't know about you, mates, but I'd like to see that,' a voice says from above. Australian accented. A head appears over the railing two flights up. 'It would earn our undying thanks.' A young white man, dark-eyed, strong cheekbones, a tumble of black, curled hair. He vaults the rail and drops five metres to land poised in front of Alexia. He wears pleated pants rolled up to high ankle, a white shirt, sleeves rolled to elbows. No socks. Alexia reads the contours of knife holsters beneath the high waistband. 'That was a good answer you gave there. That answer saved your life.' He sits on a step and regards Alexia. She notices the tip of his left smallest finger is missing. 'Like your wardrobe choice. Now, my mates here, they tend to judge by immediate appearances but I look beneath the immediate. On the surface you dress like a zabbaleen. My mates don't like zabbaleen. I don't like zabbaleen. But you don't wear a zabbaleen familiar. You don't wear any familiar. That interests me. And from your general physique, you're a Jo Moonbeam. Zabbaleens don't employ Moonbeams. How long you been here, Moonbeam? Two, three lunes?'

'Two lunes.'

'Two lunes, that says LMA to me. And if my mates don't like zabbaleens, they really hate LMA. But the fact that you've come up here without a guard, that's either buck stupid or interesting.' The man drapes his hands over his knees. 'I'm giving you an opportunity to bargain for your life here.'

He has her. She has no defence. She is all those things. Only idiocy or honesty can save her.

'I work for the LMA,' Alexia says. A murmur from the ring of up-and-outs. The Australian lifts a finger and there is silence. 'I was in the elevator to the office and I saw a man stop breathing. He asked me for help, he begged me for breath, he asked me to credit his account. I didn't know how to do that. There was nothing I could do. I walked away.' Another growl of discontent. 'Today I saw the zabbaleen killing all the parakeets on my street. One of them said "Unmonitored resource misappropriation". I wanted to know what was going on. So I rode the elevator up where the man who couldn't breathe went.'

'And what were you going to do, LMA?' the Australian asks.

'See it. Try and understand it. Try and fix it, if what I think is going on up here is true.'

'And what do you think is going on up here?'

'I think the LMA has been systematically foreclosing non-viable accounts.'

'Foreclosing?' the Australian asks.

'Liquidating the economically non-viable.'

A rumble of anger.

'Liquidating?'

'Killing.'

'Economically non-viable?'

'People. You.'

'Your theory is interesting,' the Australian says. 'It's also correct.'

'That's . . .' Alexia says.

'Not just Meridian. Everywhere. Queen, St Olga. All over Nearside.

Can't pay? Won't breathe. Zabbaleen used to leave us alone, now they smash up our humpies, tear down our water catchers, rip out our tanks, snatch the fucking breath from our lungs.' The Australian lifts a hand, gestures for the Bairro people to sit. Alexia stands, the performer, the pleader. 'You said you could help us with our water supply, LMA. Can you?'

'Like I said, I can.'

'Next question. Will you?'

'Do I have a choice?'

'What's your name, LMA?'

'Lê.' Alexia is wary of lying, but more wary of too much truth.

'Lê. Sounds like a made-up name,' the Australian says. 'Like an apelido. They call me the Jack of Blades.'

There is wariness and there is the time for the gratuitous move.

'That's fucking ridiculous,' Alexia says. The Bairristas draw breath. The Australian fixes Alexia with eyes of black obsidian. Then he laughs. He laughs long and hard. The Bairristas, taking his cue, laugh with him. Alexia notices the Australian has a gold tooth.

'Yes it is fucking ridiculous but it does stroke my considerable vanity. If it makes any difference, I didn't choose it. What kind of Brasil are you, Lê?'

'Carioca,' Alexia says.

'Cariocas and I have a contentious history. But there are cariocas up here, Brasilians, Ghanaians, Nigerians, Malay, Enzies, Germans, Nepalese, Arabs. Every nation on Earth. So: Lê: water engineer, LMA functionary. That's a career arc.'

'Before I was anything on the moon, I was Queen of Pipes of Barra de Tijuca,' Ariel says and by the last of those words she has them. Grandmother Senona had the skill to bind with a story; to settle children, to silence an argument, to spin a lamp-lit hour waiting for the power to come back on. Stories are a strong narcotic. Alexia doesn't mind that she is the only one standing now. Before she was the accused. Now she is the performer.

She takes her audience to another world, to a city open to the sky, to meet her family in its tower by the ocean. She introduces her family, back to three generations. She gives their saint names, their nicknames. She is still wary of the name Corta. She tells of how her grandfather Luis took her up on to the roof of Ocean Tower to show her the dark of the moon. *Squint your eyes, child,* he said. *Peer. Look deep, what do you see?*

Lights!

She tells of how she found a leak in the window corner of her bedroom and followed the drips down the wall to catch them in a beaker, then a can, then a basin, then decided that this was no answer in the long run and built a little pipeline of drink straws to carry the water away to the plughole in the bathroom. She tells of how she found that she could make water go uphill a short way if the source was higher than the mouth, and sitting watching the drip swell and drop into the funnel and following the pulse of water down the candy-striped maze.

Why don't we have good water? she asked her mother.

People like us don't get good water.

A year before he died Grandfather Luis took her up again on to the roof and said, *If you can tell me why you should have it, I will give you your inheritance now.*

I want to be a water engineer, Alexia said.

Grandfather Luis gave her not just her share but part of her siblings. Marisa's and even little Caio's. *Make it work.*

By night she studied water and waste engineering at CEFET. By day she apprenticed to Naimer Fonseca, a plumber working out of an all-women repair shop in Barra. The day after she graduated she stole two hundred metres of piping from the site of the gated enclave at Marapendi and replumbed not just her family's apartment but the entire top half of Ocean Tower.

'Everyone had their own supply,' she says. 'Everyone was just out for themselves. I made a system that worked for everyone. I made it better.'

Wisdom and bold moves – a water supply is only good if it is clean; stealing water from the FIAM without their knowledge; hawking her brand around Barra under the noses of rivals who would have carved her face off. By the time they share her pride at overhearing someone call her Queen of Pipes, she is sitting on the step beneath the Jack.

'Nice little empire,' the Jack says. 'But it's a long way from there to here.'

'Another operation wanted to send me a message. They beat up Caio. They left him with deep damage, maybe permanent.'

'What did you do?' a thin, dust-grey woman wheezes.

'I repaid them,' Alexia says. 'Three times.'

A murmur. Alexia reads it as approval.

'Caio needs constant care and rehab. Barra doesn't have that kind of money. I did what the Cortas did. I came to the moon.'

Another murmur, this time menacing, the edge of a growl.

'That's a name with a lot of history up here,' the Jack says.

'I know,' Alexia says. 'But everyone in Rio – everyone in Brasil – knows it, and what they did.' Nods in the audience. Alexia plays a careful game here: lead with a lesser card, invoking the Cortas, in the hope that it convinces her audience that she holds no higher card: her true name. Queen of Pipes for Ace of Cortas. But she isn't safe yet. There is one more card to play. 'So, I may not know anything about air or data, but I could build you a water system.'

This murmur is of distrust.

'Of course you'd come back.' A teen boy with a tower of black hair says what everyone thinks.

Because of the choking man in the elevator, because of what Lucas asked me to do out on the cycler, because of Caio and the price of revenge. Because of the terrible terrible things I have done. All Alexia can say is, 'My word?'

'You give your word?' the Jack of Blades says.

'I give my word.'

'Mates,' the Australian shouts. 'We have a contract!'

On the first day, the Queen of Pipes assigns teams. Kids go into Team Scavenger. They are quick and lithe and can climb and hide. She gives them steal-lists and sends them out.

'I need four construction teams,' Alexia declares. She sits her squad down on the only large open space in Bairro Alto, the gently curving cap of a gas exchanger the size of an office block. 'Team Dew, Team Tank, Team Pipe, Team Ultraviolet.'

'What about me?' the Jack says. He sits cross-legged on the ground, pants rolled to mid-calf, wide-collared shirt unbuttoned to the waist. He has torn off the sleeves at the shoulders. Alexia likes the Australian's way with clothes.

'Team Security,' Alexia says. The Jack smiles. The skin of his chest, his upper arms, is scarred, scar over scar over scar. 'Now gather round.' She pulls a vac pen from the pocket of her zabbaleen shorts and draws on the white tank insulation. No familiars, no network, no smart presentations and engineering diagrams in Bairro Alto. No paper. Across a hundred square metres she sketches out her master-plan for a water supply for the High Hub. It is simple but intricate, robust yet easy to service, fully backed-up yet completely modular.

'The zabbaleen will take it apart day one,' a Team Tank man says.

'Then we defend it,' the Jack says. 'Team Security is everyone.'

The kids come home from hunting. Yaya, the tall-haired boy who questioned Alexia's word, has ten five-metre plastic pipes tucked under his arm and his eyes shining.

'There was a bot,' he says, panting. Everyone pants, everyone is short of words, everyone pauses for breath up in Bairro Alto.

'You okay?' Alexia asks. The kid grins and holds up a fistful of hydraulic piping and actuators: his trophy from the fight.

'Careful with those things,' the Jack says. 'You're not trained to fight them.'

On the second day the teams go out to prepare the site. The few fixed cameras and spy-bots that have survived are taken out by kids with catapults and ball bearings. Alexia guides her teams – no, that pipe run can't go there; that header tank needs to be higher; you'll need protection for the UV sterilisers. If you tap that water main here, you will blow half of Bairro Alto off the wall. Tap it here. Filtration meshes here, in this tank. What do you mean you don't have any filtration meshes? Team Scavenger!

'You're kind of hot when you give orders,' the Jack says.

'And you can do some work too,' Alexia says, throwing him a bonding gun stolen from a careless maintenance crew member at a Level Fifty tea stall.

On the third day, the waters move.

'Hang your fog traps here,' Alexia orders. 'You won't catch as much, but there's a constant cold air flow from the heat exchanger which means you'll harvest eighty per cent of what you do trap.' Mirrors heliograph across the roof of Meridian Hub; on cue Team Dew open the valves beneath twenty collecting tanks. And the waters flow. Children run with the water, tracing the pipe-run over ducts, down stairwells, around roaring heat engines, through mazes of electrical conduits. Pipe to pipe, junction to junction. *Check for leaks*, was the Queen of Pipes' instruction. *Don't overtighten, you'll strip the threads.*

At three receiving cisterns spaced equidistantly around the hub, the up-and-out gather. A tremor, a distant rumble, a gurgle, a spit and a spurt, then the water flows.

The Jack dips his cupped hands in the swirling water, lifts it to his lips. A taste, then he offers it to Alexia. She drinks from the Australian's cupped hands.

'It's good,' she says. Her *but it could be better* is drowned out by the cheering.

She can't take her eyes off his.

She remembers, lifts a hand.

'Shut it off, we haven't got enough to waste.'

That night she thinks of booking satellite time, putting a call through to Caio on Earth, to her mother, to the apartment. She dithers – she doesn't know the Earth time, she would be calling out of the blue, she would alarm everyone. Her thoughts wander from Barra to Norton, pretty, jealous, big, sweet Norton. Norton who shaved his heavy cock and balls baby-smooth for her. He'll have found someone else. He's too cute not to. Except he won't. He'll wait, to be true, to be honourable, to make a point about faith and faithlessness.

And she is faithless, because it's not really Norton she's thinking about.

It's been too fucking long.

On the fourth day she is restless in her work as Iron Hand, so much so that Lucas notices and comments. There is a big presentation to the full Pavilion. Terrestrials and Dragons will be there. It must be immaculate. She lies about her period and as soon as the day is done she is on the elevator to the top of the city. There is the Jack. Her heart soars out into the void like one of the winged fliers who turn and flash in the airspace of Meridian Hub. He's not smiling. No one is smiling.

'What's happened?' Alexia scans the faces. Someone missing. A hole. She remembers. 'Where's Yaya?'

Team Tank found him by the Antares Quadra switchgear, blood dripping through the mesh. Three levels of decking. He sat upright against a bulkhead. His intestines were in his lap. He was split open from groin to sternum.

Only a machine kills with such disregard for the dignity of the human body.

Team Tank retreated as the high city resounded to the bootfalls of the zabbaleen.

'Got fucking cocky,' the Jack says. Alexia lays a hand on his shoulder and he covers it with his own. 'Come on!' he shouts. 'We got gutters to install! And be careful out there, mates.'

All must be ready, screwed tight and tested, for on the fifth day the rains will come.

Alexia wills the elevator up, up; faster faster. But the speed of elevators is fixed, and this one seems to stop at every level. Alexia fidgets in frustration. The rain has been scheduled for 13.00 Orion time and she must be up there before the first drop falls.

She arrives at the Level Seventy-Five terminus and sprints up the staircase. Beneath her boots, Meridian is hushed, suspended. The hub is empty of fliers, the bridges and crosswalks deserted. The air is grainy with old dust. Alexia can taste it on her tongue, feel it clogging her nostrils. The city waits to be washed clean.

The high folk wait, posed with the artifice and elegance of a dance troupe on landings and platforms, draped over railings, squatting on steel steps.

'Oh queen my queen!' Alexia squints up into the ceiling lights to see the Jack perform his signature vault and dashing drop four levels to the platform. He offers an arm. 'Shall we?'

'Jack of Blades.' Alexia takes his arm and together they process up the steps through level after level of cheering and whistling. The noise echoes from Bairro Alto's cavernous architecture, doubling it, changing it into a machine roar. As she climbs, Alexia sees kids slip mirrors from rag-tag pockets and flash messages across the hub. Answers flicker back. Ready. All ready.

'You know, you've never called me that to my face,' the Jack says as they arrive at the southern reservoir. The plastic sheeting cracks in the unpredictable gusts of high city. The teams have fallen in behind Queen and Jack and form a ring around the reservoir. Kids hang ready to run and repair: Alexia has calculated for the volume of a Meridian monsoon but the engineer's curse is that theory seldom survives reality.

Alexia is tight with nervous energy. All day at the office she hid her excitement, now she realises that it was a mask for the anxiety. What if it all comes apart at the first drop? What if Yaya died for nothing but a tangle of pipes and shreds of plastic sheeting?

The silence up on the gantry is as complete as that before creation.

Alexia hears a ringing splat, looks down, sees a dark patch on the mesh. Another, then another, another. She sights her first raindrop: the size of the end of her thumb, falling so slowly she can track it. It splashes on her right forearm, a distinct, solid tap. The drops fall regularly now, scattered but steady. The gantry, the staircases, the metal monoliths of the high city machinery ring. The plastic tanks and sheets pop and crack.

'Come with me,' the Jack says. She takes his hand and he pulls her to the rail. 'Look.'

At the first touch of the rain, Meridian has blossomed. Crowds jam the empty bridges and crossways; every balcony is filled with people. Hundreds of thousands of faces upturned to the rain.

'Oh my,' Alexia says. Her eyes fill with tears.

'You seen nothing yet.'

The rain steepens into a downpour. Alexia is soaked to the bone in an instant. Rain pummels her, drives the wind from her. She tries to catch breath through the torrent of drops. The noise is deafening. She is inside some percussion instrument, a city-sized tambourine. She had known fat tropical rain in Rio, but this is beyond all imagining. This is a biblical deluge. The Jack grips her hand. *Stay,* he yells.

The vault of the hub fills with rainbows, one above another above another. A triple rainbow; brilliant and bright. This is a cloudburst without clouds. The sunline blazes noontime. Rainbows march up the canyons of Orion, and Aquarius Quadras, spans and arches wall to wall, is morning and evening rainbows. Antares Quadra is dark, then the sky brightens to full day and a carnival of rainbows. Of course you would turn on the sky for such a wonder.

'Oh,' Alexia Corta says. 'Oh!' Then she feels it. Moving water, rushing water, hungry water. 'The run has started.' She drags the Jack away from the balustrade, across the ringing, slippery decking to the tank. She lays hands to a pipe: the vibration is almost sexual. Surging water. She combs back streaming hair from her face and shouts up to a kid from Team Scavenger.

'Is it standing up?'

The kid gives two thumbs up and a huge grin.

The pipes are quaking now, rattling in their mounts. Alexia imagines rain gushing down from gutter to trough, trough to feeder, feeder to conduit, conduit to main, cascading down and around through level upon level of Bairro Alto, water racing, water tumbling. Rivers, torrents of wild water. And the faucets above the reservoirs explode. Waterfalls burst from the pipes and crash into the plastic reservoirs. The support cradle shifts and creaks, people back away. Alexia Corta has designed strong, the Bairristas have built true. The sheeting bulges, the water level rises. Winks of dazzling mirror-light shine diamond-hard through the downpour: north-east and north-west reservoirs are functioning and filling.

'Fuck!' the Jack shouts over the roar of waters. His hair is plastered to his head, his clothes cling to him in sodden creases and folds. 'You little beauty!' And in an instant his face freezes. Changes. 'Get out of here!' he yells. The high folk scatter, up staircases, stanchions, climbing pipes, hand over hand up ladders. Alexia casts around in bafflement. Only she and the Jack remain on the platform.

'Lê, get the fuck out of here,' the Jack shouts. Old Earth-muscles take Alexia to the next platform in one leap. She's seen the shadows in the corners of the world.

Four fighters in body armour, rain shedding from the edges of their helmets. Holstered knives and tasers. Behind them, hanging back, the zabbaleen and their picking, clawing machines.

'For fuck's sake,' the Jack says. He strips off his shirt. Alexia reads the scars across his back, his shoulders, some still purple, marked with recent sutures. His hands hover over the knife hilts at his hips. 'This again?'

'Just let us do our job,' a zabbaleen calls from the dripping darkness. 'It's magnificent but we can't let it stand.'

'Yet stand it will,' the Jack says. Alexia sees the fighters' muscles tighten, their sinews contract beneath their armoured shells. 'Have you cunts learned nothing?' The Jack has read it too. 'What's my name?' he says. 'What's my name?'

'De . . .' the zabbaleen begins but the Jack cuts her off with a roar. 'I'm the Jack of fucking Blades!'

Click, hum, tap. Two bots step from shadows through curtains of teeming rain. Drops run down their glossy shells. They are fit, elegant, beautiful. Alexis remembers their beauty striking her when she went as Lucas's representative to inspect them in the Guangzhou construction plant before shipping to low Earth orbit. Beautiful horror. She could vomit.

'Ah,' the Jack says. He turns. He turns away.

He turns to gain momentum. He spins, moves with lightning grace and in that flash there is a knife in a fighter's armpit and his taser in the Jack's hand. Aim, shot, one thought – less than thought. One action. The taser catches the bot in the air as it leaps, blades unfolding. It goes down in a thrash of short-circuited limbs. The fighter kicks in a circle, blood beating from the arterial wound. Blood sprays far in lunar gravity. The punishing rain washes it all down through the holes in the mesh.

The Jack crouches like a jaguar, a blood-hungry grin on his face. The second bot is in motion; the Jack flips away, the bot lashes out a blade-tipped leg. Machine speed, machine accuracy. It would have cut him spine-deep across the side had not something come spinning down from the upper levels. A bola: the lines tangle around the bot's legs, weights spinning up with angular momentum enough to snap joints. The bot is down and kids are dropping, whooping and whistling, from the high levels to mob the downed bots, crack them open with hammers and wrenches and rip out their precious, twitching guts.

The fighters charge. The Jack is between them and the kids. A fighter moves to outflank, the Jack's hand flashes and there is a knife hilt-deep in the man's throat. A blade swings for the Jack, he is already underneath it, his other blade arcing to drive deep into the back of the woman's knee. She goes down shriek-swearing. The Jack drops, slides across the wet decking and drives a foot into the kneecap of the other outflanking fighter, smashing the armoured kneeguard back with the full weight of his body. Ariel can hear the crack of shattering kneecap over the punishment of the rain.

'Kids!'

How does he sense the fighter bearing down on him? By air movement, by the momentary absence of rain, by smell, by subtler fighter's senses? He snaps the kneecapped fighter's thumb back – another snap of bone – seizes the knife and ducks around the descending blade to slam it into the unprotected back of the attacker's forearm. The attacker drops the blade, the Jack catches it before it clangs from the decking and drives it into the side of the fighter's instep. And he's on his feet. Empty hands.

'Take your enemy's weapon,' he says. Rain has plastered his hair in streaming locks. 'Use it against them.'

Again he beckons. *Come on then.*

The last standing fighter's hand hovers over her taser. She shakes her head.

'Wise,' the Jack says. He tugs one knife from the back of the fallen fighter's knee, the other from the dead man's throat. He cleans them on the sodden rags of his shirt, breathes deep and with a snap Alexia cannot follow, reholsters them. 'Take what's yours.'

Deluge turns to downpour, to rain, to drops. The rain ends. Bairro Alto drips. The light turns them into a billion diamonds. The high city wears its jewels. Vapour wreathes from platforms and levels. The Jack climbs the staircase. Alexia withholds the jubilation. He doesn't look at her. The Bairro Alto folk nod as he climbs up between them. He does not acknowledge them. No one speaks.

Down on the killing floor the zabbaleen move from the shadows.

Alexia finds him in his humpie, a tent of plastic sheeting strung from a stand of support piers. Rain water has pooled in the contours of the sheets. The Jack kneels, back to her. He is naked. With care, with precision, with tenderness, he cleans and sharpens his blades.

Alexia stands a long time, watching him. She has never seen a moon man naked. The physiological changes wrought by lunar gravity are elegant and at the same time repulsive. Near-human. Uncanny valley. Scars embroider every part of his skin. She guesses he is in his early twenties, though there is a self-possession, an ache in him of an old man.

'Seen enough?'

Alexia starts.

'I'm sorry.'

'I had an aunt wore that scent. Aunt Madison. Fucking hated her.'

'I intruded, I'll go.'

'Don't go.' He pats the pillow of his bedroll. 'If you don't mind sitting opposite a ball-naked man.'

'I don't mind at all.' She sits cross-legged on the pillow. Plastic stuffed with plastic shreds. The bed is a nest of rags. Water drips from the canopy's imperfect seals. The Jack works with focus and diligence; blade to stone.

'We've all got our voodoo,' he says. 'When I was a jackaroo I used to have to put on the right suit glove and boot first. Every time. After a fight, well, I'm not at my most sociable.'

'I understand.'

'I assure you you don't, Lê.'

He holds up a blade, turns it to catch the light. Fire runs down the edge of the blade. He plays with it, spins, tosses, clever blade-tricks. It drops back into his hand. His right arm flashes out. The tip of the knife is a breath from Alexia's throat. He does not look. She does not flinch.

'I want to take you right here on this bed,' she says.

He looks at her now. He grins. Light on metal: the blade is back in its sheath. Alexia unfastens her sodden shorts as she launches herself at him. She knocks him back and she is on top of him, saturated top off, unsealing her bra. She straddles him, pins him with thighs and hands to the nest of rags. The Jack struggles but she has Jo Moonbeam strength and he laughs loud and crazy and pulls her down.

They kiss. She cups his face between her hands.

She reaches down to cup his balls. Hairless, smooth as glass.

'I got my own voodoo,' Alexia says. 'My men shave.'

'Hun, everyone shaves,' the Jack says. 'You only need to get a pube caught in a sasuit once.' Then he lifts her and Alexia gives a little shriek and he pulls her forwards. He bites her inner thighs; Alexia slides forward to straddle his face. She rolls her nipples between thumb and forefinger as he eats her out. She pants to the disco rhythm of the tip of his tongue across her clitoris. Muscles tighten, clench. Not yet. She lifts a leg, pivots to grasp his cock. It is long and curved to the left. She runs her hands up and down its shaft, spits in her palm and polishes the head of his cock. Jack gives a muffled *fuck* and directs his tongue to the exploration of her labia. He is eating her. Eating her. She goes down on the cock. It twitches in her mouth. She takes it as deep as she can without gagging.

Coraçãozinho. That had been her special name for that little triangle below the head of Norton's cock where the magic happened.

Norton.

She flicks coraçãozinho with her forefinger nail. Jack gives a cry, then an explosion of laughter.

Oh so long since anyone laughed in sex. Since anyone laughed at all.

She looks round at him. 'So moon man, what are the special tricks up here?'

He deftly rolls her on to her side, folds her left leg up, takes hold of her right, stretches it out and slips inside. She blasphemes in Portuguese. They fuck joyously. Positions, variations, time: Alexia has no idea how much or how many, until she is lying on her back, torso bent double, legs by her head – empilhadeira in Portuguese – and looks past Jack's pumping hips to see three kids peeping under the still-dripping lip of the humpie.

She gives a shriek, rolls out of the piledriver and pulls damp bedding rags around her.

'Oh hey,' says the one she thinks might be a boy. 'Just to say, whenever you've finished, would you like to come and see the water working?'

After the hotshop, the sleepover.

'Will he be home?' Haider asked when Robson suggested an overnight. Haider has been introduced to Wagner and Analiese. Both made Haider welcome but Haider is uncomfortable around Wagner. Scared, is the truth. And Wagner has been cranky. Hyper, insomniac, ravenously hungry. Twitchy and temperamental and super, super fast and inquisitive. Robson doesn't need to go to the surface to know the Earth stands at half-full.

'He's got a short-term Taiyang contract at Theon Senior,' Robson says. 'He's away until the day after tomorrow.'

Haider is relieved. Robson is relieved too.

The apartment is small even by lunar standards. Robson's annexe on the upper level, adapted from the work/music/study cubby, is smaller yet. The mattress fits it like a foot in a boot and the two boys lie like punctuation, a yin-yang.

'So how do you do them?' Haider asks, rolled on to a comfortable side.

'Do what?' Robson asks. Water thumps and gurgles overhead, the air con is a constant bass rumble.

'Magic tricks,' Haider says.

'Effects,' Robson says. 'Real magicians call them effects. Tricks are dishonesty.'

'But they are dishonest. You deceive people.'

Robson considers for a long moment.

'You make up stories.' Haider has never let Robson read any of his stories, and even if he would, Robson isn't a reader. But he does know Haider has filed megabytes of angst, fluff, hurt/comfort, shipping, slash and yaoi on to the network. He can break down and analyse the structures and tropes and character arcs of any telenovela until he sees Robson's eyes flickering, which happens when he is playing a game on his lens. 'Stories deceive people. They make people feel that these characters are real, that you have to care about what happens to them.'

'It's kind of true,' Haider says. 'Not literally true – truthy-true. True about how people are, how they feel, how they're difficult.'

'Effects are true that way. In the middle of every effect, there's the truth. That's the trick that has to happen, or there's no effect. And it's usually something very simple, something very straightforward. But you mustn't see it.'

Now Haider considers a moment.

'I see that. But how do you do it?'

'Practice,' Robson says without hesitation. 'Actors practise a thousand times. Musicians practise ten thousand times. Dancers practise a hundred thousand times. But magicians practise a million times.'

'A million?'

Robson has Joker check the mathematics.

'Actually, more than a million times.'

That does give Haider pause.

'I see you practise those parkour moves. You jump and fall, jump and fall, jump and fall. Fail and try again. Fail and try again.'

‘It has to burn into you. You take the shape of the move. Magic’s the same. But you don’t see the falls. If you see the fall, then you see the trick and there is no effect.’

‘I couldn’t do that,’ Haider says. ‘Can’t do any kind of physical activity that needs timing, or smart hands. Got no fine motor control. There’s something in my brain chemistry. It’s like a clock running slow, just that little bit behind everyone else.’

‘Whoa,’ Robson says. ‘So, like, you’re really living permanently in the past?’

‘Put like that, yes.’

‘Whoa.’ Robson feels Haider move against him on the bedroll. When he had been in Meridian, with the wolfpack, he had unrolled his own pad in a quiet corner of the living space, away from the communal bed. He wasn’t a wolf so he had never been expected to sleep with the pack, but he understood that he would always have been welcome. Here he is in Theophilus, doing the thing he never would in Meridian: sharing the bed with another person. Not even a wolf; a friend. It feels okay here; it feels safe. The first nights in Analiese’s apartment he woke up not knowing where he was, blundering around half awake. Screaming. More than one night Wagner had come in with him. Someone at his back. He’s safe here, away from the politics and vendettas of the Eagle and his court, buried in tiny, dull Theophilus, yet some nights he still wakes screaming.

‘My very first trick – effect – my husband showed me,’ Robson says. Robson has told Haider enough of his story to feed the curiosity and keep him safe. Tonight he needs to tell more. Tonight he wants to peel away the trick and show the truth. ‘His name was Hoang Lam Hung. I was married to him for a night. We had dinner and told jokes and he showed me how to do card tricks.

‘He was very kind. He would never have hurt me, or let anyone hurt me. Afterwards, he was my care giver.’

‘Afterwards?’

‘The annulment,’ Robson says. ‘My Tia Ariel went to court and ended the marriage. It was just like a hostage thing, really. Like when Bryce Mackenzie adopted me. Ariel wasn't around then to get me out of that, but Hoang took me to Queen and told Wagner to take me in.'

'There's a lot in your life,' Haider says. 'Mine's kind of boring.'

'Boring is good,' Robson says. 'People say they want a life of adventure, like a soap, but no one can live like that. No one's ever safe in soaps and adventures. Adventures kill people.'

'Did, uh . . .' Haider edges around the question.

'People get killed? Yes. My mother. Hoang. My parkour equipe.'

'Shit.' Haider rolls on to his back and locks fingers behind head.

'Don't tell anyone. They're still looking for me. Even more now Tio Lucas is Eagle. No one knows who I am here.'

'I won't,' Haider says.

EIGHT

Visitors call in an unceasing stream from breakfast to midnight. Neighbours who had never been neighbourly when she was just Marina the weird sciencey one but were curious to see the woman come down from the moon. Neighbours who had been friends, supporters, neighbourly forever, who thought it best to give Marina from the moon space to settle in. Friends. A car-full of college friends, come up from the city just to see her, nervous in their filter-masks of the trees, the fauna, anything potentially infectious. An explosion of noise and too much skin – Jordi-Rae, BFF, going straight to the room where they had spent so many hours as girls making up soap operas for their toys. Still working in the Ranger service. Still no significant other, girl or boy. Marina would have her stay longer, but she excuses herself when the door calls again and it's Officers Dolores and Kyle from the Port Angeles police department.

'Is there a problem?' Kessie asks. Police have always been the enemy in the Calzaghe house.

Officer Dolores shuffles also uncomfortably but purposefully, as if looking for an excuse to play cop.

'Purely routine.'

'You have a routine for homecomers from the moon?' Marina

wheels into the living room. Ocean stands guard on her right shoulder, Weavyr on the left.

'Just want to make sure everything is all right for you,' says Officer Kyle.

'Why wouldn't it be?'

'You are a recent returnee from a hostile nation,' Officer Dolores says. 'And you were employed by one of the leading corporations. You were a personal assistant to a prominent member of one of the leading families.'

'Port Angeles PD seems to know a hell of a lot about me,' Marina says.

'She is not a terrorist!' Ocean blurts. The air in the room crystalises. This could turn dark fast.

'I'm sure the officers just want to make sure that people don't get stupid ideas about Marina,' Kessie says. 'Fake news flies around the world while the truth is lacing up its boots.'

'Exactly that, ma'am,' says Officer Dolores.

Marina waits until she hears the crunch of yard dirt beneath the cruiser's tyres before speaking.

'They've been told to keep an eye on me.'

'They do think you're a terrorist!' Ocean says.

'What I do know is that you are a prize fool, Ocean Paz Calzaghe,' Kessie hisses. 'You don't say things like that in front of cops.'

'It's all right,' Marina says. 'Come and help me with my physio.' But it isn't all right. The air feels dirty, the water tastes tainted. Every cobwebby corner has ears and eyes. The house has been invaded and she is being surveilled.

'You wouldn't think,' Marina says as she hauls herself painfully to the walking frame, 'that I used to be able to run twenty kays without a thought.'

'Run?' Ocean's idea of exercise is rolling from one side of the couch to another. Marina takes a gasping step. Another. Another. Ocean follows, ready to catch any stumble.

'It was this guy,' Marina says. 'Oh, but he was something. He'd have to be, to get me to go running. It was like a ritual. A religion. Bodypaint and really really tiny clothes.'

'Marina!' Ocean gasps.

'I was going to tell you about the sex...'

'No no no!' Ocean wails, putting her hands over her ears. 'Marina. If I ask, will you promise not to squick me out?'

'Can't promise. Ask.' Five steps to the end of the hall, turn and back.

'Is it true that up there – on the moon – no one cares if you're straight or gay or bi?'

'It's true. No one cares, no one judges, we don't even have the words for them in Globo. There are as many genders and sexualities as there are people. It's about who you love, not what.' End of the hall. It's a complex shuffle of uncertain feet and walking frame to turn for the return trek. 'It took me a long time to understand that, but it's the absolute heart of the moon. Everything is a contract between people. Your dad. I haven't seen him around.'

'They're having a trial separation. To see if they like it.'

Marina hears the anger underscoring Ocean's off-hand replies.

'On the moon, marriage is just another contract. Who, what, how long. Live with, live apart, sex/no sex. Open relationship, polyamory, ring marriage. You can be married to several people at the same time.'

'Sounds complicated.'

'It should be. Marriage should be hard to get into and easy to get out of. I was with the moon's best marriage lawyer and even she spent all her time trying to patch up the holes and fix the hurts.'

'Was with.'

'What?'

'Was with. Not worked with.'

'Shut up and help me back into that chair,' Marina says. 'And get my weights. I've got upper body to do now.'

But Ocean sets the weights on the floor and rushes to the front door as the house announces another visitor: Skyler, in from Indonesia.

The secret fellowship of the insomniac. Marina is too sore for sleep, Skyler too jet-lagged.

'It's worse west to east.' He squats, lit by refrigerator light. The laws of insomnia ordain that the sleepless must meet in the kitchen.

He swigs juice from the carton. 'Long-haul dehydrates you.'

'Moon to Earth is worst, let me tell you,' Marina says.

'Want anything?'

'I'm good.'

She has never liked her brother. He is the late, the last, the golden. He could swing off to South-East Asia, to travel, to slack, to experience and marry and charm his way into a comfortable marketing job in Jakarta. She was the one sent to the moon to pay for their mother's medical care.

'I heard you had a visit from Port Angeles' finest.'

'They're checking my comms. It's easy to spot. It's a shit AI.'

Skyler rocks back in his kitchen chair.

'Took me three days to get here. Everything's going to shit. Brownouts two, three nights a week. Everyone's looking for someone to blame and there are a million theories. Everything's a conspiracy now. The government, everyone's government, had been taken over by the moon. The moon was calling the shots. Standard world-government, mind-control stuff.'

'That is the exact opposite of what happened,' Marina says. 'You invaded us.'

Skyler swigs more juice from the carton.

'The more the government denies it, the more people believe it. People get very attached to their beliefs. Everyone connected with the moon is an agent of Satan. Homecomers are being attacked. A woman in our building was raided. Two years back, totally rehabilitated. Guys broke into her apartment because they thought she was conspiring to take over water supply. Then the imams got started – they got a good turnout on a Friday. The Jakarta VTO office was attacked and burned. A mob stopped the firefighters tackling the blaze. There was a march on the Yogyakarta fusion plant. Mackenzie Helium was behind the brown-outs. Everyone was going to have to have one of those chips in their eyes . . .'

'Chibs.'

'Whatever. Everyone would be forced to have one and if you did anything the government would cut off your network, then your power, then your water. Then they'd stop you breathing.'

Skyler drains the carton and slaps it down on the table.

'It'll be foreigners in the end. It's not just Indonesia, Malaysia, India, Australia. The Mackenzies are Aussies and they're hanging Duncan Mackenzie print-outs from the Harbour Bridge and burning them.'

'What are you saying?'

'It's a disease. It spreads. Even here.'

'I'm . . . what? A secret super-spy from the moon?'

'Who worked for one of the big players. Whose brother is now running the moon.'

'It's not like that . . .'

'Doesn't matter what it's like. It's what people think it's like. Watch yourself.'

NINE

Alexia reckons her ass is too terrestrial for lunar furniture. She's too short in the leg, too long in the back, too broad in the seat. The beds are no better: soft memory foams and lunar gravity means she wakes ten times a night from dreams of falling. Alexia wriggles in her chair and tries to find some comfort. This is the third LMA session in as many days.

Gossip runs around the tiers of the Pavilion of the New Moon in glances and whispers. Alexia can guess what they're saying.

The Eagle's own sister ran away rather than represent him.

She's filed her own case against him.

Corta versus Corta?

Not the way you think. Ariel Corta is representing Luna Corta against Lucas Corta for medical wardenship of Lucasinho Corta.

But Luna Corta's…

That weird kid? Yes, but she has no skin in this game.

So Ariel Corta can argue that Luna is best qualified to act in Lucasinho's best medical interests.

And she is there, on Farside.

Clever, that Ariel Corta.

They can barely contain the derision as Lucas stands up to open the session and welcome the speaker. A wide, lumbering figure in a bronze gown painfully descends the steps to the pit. *Vidhya Rao,* Maninho tells Alexia. *Economist and adviser to Whitacre Goddard, member of the Pavilion of the White Hare, Visiting Professor of the Faculty of Theoretical Economics*... Alexia shuts off the biography and listens instead to the silenced whispers, closing of conversations that say, *Here is a person of consequence.* Alexia sees a dumpy, brown-skinned figure, short silver hair, robed and scarved in exquisite, fine-textured weaves that give nothing to fashion. Woman? Man? Alexia can't tell. She doesn't need to be able to tell; this is the moon. There seem to be as many genders and sexes and sexualities as there are citizens. And there are pronouns – or not, depending on personal taste – not just for those genders and sexes and sexualities, but also for non-human entities, and alternative human personalities. The Farsiders have a pronoun for speaking to and of machines. And then there are the Moon Wolves, and their darkside and lightside aspects.

'Sers, I will be brief.'

The pernicious thing, Alexia realises as Maninho surrounds Vidhya Rao with panes and panels of information, is trying to decide if there is an original gender from which the current is deviation. Moon folk don't think like that. Everything is negotiated.

'A detailed proposal and full breakdown have been sent to your familiars under the name of "Lunar Bourse, towards an off-planet Value Nexus". What I propose in this short pitch is nothing less than a complete restructuring of the economic foundation of lunar civilisation.'

Alexia understands economics chiefly by the lights of a proprietor of a hyperlocal, folding-cash, grey-market water engineering company. Personal and invested. This is not that kind of economics: this is financialisation, trades, derivatives; futures and forwards, swaps and options; puts and stays and defaults. Contracts and insurances and reinsurances. Instruments of inquisitorial sharpness and complexity. Minuscule profits extracted from price differentials that hover on the edge of the quantum scale, magnified into the immense by the sheer number of transactions.

In the opening quarter, a Lunar Bourse would trade upwards of fifty times the total GDP of both worlds in derivatives.

That line arrests her attention. As does: *The future of all economies lies in financialisation. We arrived some years ago at the point where it is easier to extract value through an efficient market than through manufacturing or material commodities. Taiyang's sun-belt has the capacity to power any forseen expansion of the Bourse for fifty years.*

You want to turn us into a moon-sized stock market, Alexia realises.

'Over a century the entire surface of the moon would be repurposed for energy generation, with the sub-regolithis converted to computing material,' Vidhya Rao says.

A black moon, Alexia thinks. *Every mountain laid low, every crater filled, every sea flooded with black glass. From Barra, you would look up on a summer night and see nothing. A hole in the sky. Inside that hole, money making money.*

'Such a system would of necessity be entirely automatic,' Vidhya Rao continues. 'Executive and oversight roles would also be automated – not even the famous Moon Wolves would be fast enough to interact with the trading cycle.' E looks up, expecting a laugh. The terrestrials don't understand; the Dragons are stone-faced.

This is the end of your world, Alexia thinks. *This is everything you have built and fought for and struggled to keep alive, all drowned in black glass.*

Vidhya Rao returns to er hymn to the market.

'The Lunar Bourse will make this world the first truly post-scarcity society. With a guaranteed income for every citizen and limitless solar energy, work as we understand it will evaporate. We will be a post-labour society with the resources and opportunity for everyone to achieve personal self-actualisation. From the Bourse, according to its profitability, to each according to their desire.'

Financiers guarantee everyone's personal fantasy when they might squeeze out another bitsie? And they call you a genius, Vidhya Rao? Take it from this Carioca entrepreneur, it's profit every time. No work means no workers means redundant workers. Your Lunar Bourse will be built on human bones.

'Sers, I present this proposal to the Lunar Mandate Authority, for your careful consideration. This is the future of our world.'

Vidhya Rao is done. E thanks er audience and leaves.

Alexia observes the reactions of the delegates. The terrestrials break up into groups, talking together as they leave the chamber. The Vorontsov kids have surrounded Yevgeny Grigorivitch. The big man nods and goes to Lucas.

'A talk, if you might.'

'Of course, Yevgeny Grigorivitch.'

'Not here.' He looks at Alexia. He smells of cologne in that way when the perfume masks a deeper, pervasive odour. Alexia reads the veins on his nose, the redness of his face, the bulge of his belly, the stiffness of his gait, as if he is slowly petrifying. Vodka is turning him to stone. She sees again Valery Vorontsov, floating at the free-fall axis of *Saints Peter and Paul*. Urine and shit had been the pervading perfumes; overfilled colostomy bag. He had been the opposite of this bear of a man; a tatter of skin and sinew, bones gnawed to spindles. A hank of hair, bulbous, watery eyes.

'Just us,' Yevgeny Vorontsov says.

The Asamoahs think we're barbarians, Valery Vorontsov said. *The Mackenzies think we're drunken clowns. The Suns think we aren't even human.*

Yevgeny Vorontsov's minders come down from their high seats to close in around their patriarch, insulate him, move him towards the exits. Alexia sees fear on his face.

'Lucas?'

'I won't need you for a few hours, Alexia.'

As she climbs the stairs to the lobby she notices Vidhya Rao in close and intense conversation with Wang Yongqing, Anselmo Reyes and Monique Bertin.

The machine lies in the palm of Lucas Corta's hand, tiny and precise as jewellery; micro-thin antennae, wings wisps of molecular film. Lucas snaps his hand shut and crushes the bot to powder. He wipes his hands clean on a tissue.

'My security has caught eight more of their spy drones,' Lucas says. The vodka has been freezing since the council meeting. Bottle and glass steam in the humid warmth of the Eagle's Eyrie. Lucas pours the shot. He sees the naked hunger on Yevgeny Vorontsov's face.

'Those are the ones they wanted you to catch,' Yevgeny Vorontsov says.

'No doubt.' Lucas hands him the ice-coated glass. It vanishes into the big man's fist. So many rings, Lucas observes, cutting into his flesh. 'Saúde.'

'Aren't you joining me?'

'Vodka is not my drink.'

'Gin is a little girl's drink.' Yevgeny raises his fist. 'Budim.' He sets the glass down on the broad arm of his seat, untouched. 'Excellent, I'm sure. They like me to drink, Lucas. And they make it easy for me to drink. And I drink for them.'

'A Dragon should not be spied on by his own grandchildren,' Lucas says.

'You spied on your brother,' Yevgeny Vorontsov says.

'My brother was charming, passionate, generous, handsome and quite incapable of leading Corta Hélio.'

'They scare me, Lucas. We understood this world. We knew when to take, when to let go. We knew how to act, what was necessary, what was too much. It was a dance, Lucas. You, us, the Suns, the Mackenzies, the Asamoahs. Round and round. They have no restraint. They think no limits apply to them. They owe no duty, no loyalty. Can you understand that?'

'I understand loyalty,' Lucas says. 'I thought we were allies, Yevgeny.'

Beyond the glass wall banners and kites flutter in the airspace of the hub. Someone is flying. There is always someone flying. The vodka has warmed, the ice coat has melted into a lens of water and still Yevgeny Vorontsov cannot take his eyes from the glass.

'We are, Lucas. The oldest of allies.'

'Yet Raul-Jesus Mackenzie knew about our mass-driver strike solution on Mare Cognitum.'

Yevgeny Vorontsov shifts in his chair.

'We're together in this, Yevgeny, or we are all dead.'

'They wanted me to test you,' Yevgeny Vorontsov mumbles. 'The young ones. They wanted to push you.'

'You made me look like a fool in front of the terrestrials.'

'They wanted to see where you would fall.'

'Did I fall right?'

Ten years old, Lucas Corta travels with his mother and brother on a state visit to St Olga, the capital of VTO. He coos at the building yards where cranes swing noiselessly through vacuum and the lunar night burns with the thousand actinic stars of welding arcs, where bots stitch and bind panels and meshes and struts into track builders and smelters and sinterers, moonloop capsules and moondozers. Madrinha Amalia leads Lucas by the hand into the old dome, which smells bad and tastes dusty, and he can feel the radiation leaking through the regolith roof where he is introduced, royalty to royalty, to Grigoriy Vorontsov, his sons and daughter, their children. Young Lucas understands that he is to be friendly, socialise, play with them, though they are all at least three years older than him and very much bigger.

Rafa throws himself in heart and soul and within moments he is running and chasing up and down the staircases, throwing balls, tagging. Lucas hangs back, close to his madrinha, as she is introduced to the Vorontsov heirs. These big women and men are the ones he should be talking to: the ones who will inherit Grigoriy Vorontsov's business, the ones who he will one day try to deceive and defeat. Dragon to Dragon. He comes to Yevgeny Vorontsov. This big, bold young man sees something in the dark, grave, calculating kid at his mother's side, noting names and filing faces. He crouches to offer a hand.

'Who are you, sir?'

'Lucas Arena de Luna Corta,' Lucas says before Adriana can speak for him and takes the big hand. 'I will be Corta Hélio.'

The others laugh but not Yevgeny Vorontsov.

'I am Yevgeny Grigorivitch Vorontsov and I will be VTO Moon.'

Thirty-five years away, Lucas Corta watches the wreckage of Yevgeny Vorontsov glance again and again at the thimble of now-warm vodka. Everything in this room is balanced on that glass. Yevgeny Vorontsov fidgets.

'That financier.'

'Vidhya Rao?'

'Are you thinking of implementing er plan?'

'The Lunar Bourse? E is persuasive.'

Yevgeny Vorontsov leans forward.

'Well I say fuck financialisation. The Vorontsovs do not trade. Our business is not to buy and sell. Our business is to build. We are great souls. Great souls look up. There are worlds out there, Lucas. Worlds. Worlds to take in our hands like jewels. This is the fucking future, Lucas. That Vidhya Rao: I'll tell you what e wouldn't. You don't need people to run er Bourse. Two hundred robots working the market, the helium business and the solar strip and Earth is happy and secure.'

'Your point, Yevgeny?'

'Which way do you fall, Lucas Corta? Towards the Earth or

towards the moon? Come to St Olga. You've gone to all those other bastards. You owe us.'

Lucas brushes the glittering dust of the crushed spy-bot across his desk. 'Alas, the Eagle of the Moon is unable to accept.'

Yevgeny might roar from his chair, might seize the edge of Lucas's desk in his huge hands and crush it. Then he reads the message of the crushed bot. *We are surveilled.*

'However, for the old friendship between our families, might I send my Iron Hand? She is a Corta.'

'All three divisions of VTO would be delighted to receive the Iron Hand of the Eagle of the Moon at St Olga,' Yevgeny Vorontsov says.

Earth, Moon and Space, all together in one place, Lucas muses. *The Vorontsovs have important news.*

'I will inform my Mão de Ferro,' Lucas says.

'Then drink a fucking toast with me, you piss-livered Brasilian!' Yevgeny Vorontsov bellows. He snatches up the glass from the arm of chair. It has left a vodka-bleached ring on the printed leather. 'Family.'

'It looks like a city,' Luna Corta says. She is flying over an endless urban landscape of tracks and blocks. She puts out a hand, and by the power of imagination she banks. 'People and hotshops and printers. Roads and cablecars and trains.' It's illusion, a projection on her lens, but it's fun to pretend. 'You're putting a city in his head.'

'Cities,' Dr Gebreselassie says. She is the doctor in charge of healing Lucasinho. She is much more than a doctor and the process is much more than healing. It is growing up again. This thing in her lens, that in one way looks like a city but in every other way looks like nothing she has ever seen before, is one of the keys to the healing. Luna is another.

'Why won't you let me see him?' Luna asked as soon as Dakota Kaur Mackenzie had checked the medical centre reception room.

'It's delicate work,' Dr Gebreselassie said, quickly escorting Luna to a private room. 'So delicate the theatre is built on a vibration-suppressing cradle. We're doing nano-surgery, putting protein chips so small you can't see them into his brain and wiring them into his connectome.'

'I know that,' Luna said. 'I meant, see him. You've blocked my familiar.'

'There's nothing to see, Luna. Just a young man in a medical coma, and a lot of machines.'

'Have you taken the top off his head?' Luna said. Dr Gebreselassie started, taken aback by the girl's directness.

'Would you like to see the protein chips?' the doctor said, leaning forward in her seat. She hadn't crouched down to Luna's height. That would have been insulting.

'Show me,' Luna said and her lens filled with wonders; like Meridian if the walls and sunline were like the prospekts, and those great canyons branched off into tens more, and those into tens more.

She blinks away the graphic.

'Cities with people in them,' Luna declares.

'People and voices,' Dr Gebreselassie says. 'And memories. That's where we need you. We can give him basic things like walking and language but the things that make him Lucasinho – his memories, they've been damaged. Very badly damaged. But the network is full of memories. We can give him those memories on the protein chips and in time, as we rebuild the connectome, those memories will become his own memories.'

'I know this,' Luna says. 'You want me to give my memories to him.'

Dr Gebreselassie has a head-rolling gesture she makes when something is not quite correct in her world.

'We can't go in there,' she says. She reaches a finger towards Luna's painted forehead. A glare from the death-eye of Lady Luna stops her cold. 'The network has his memories and your memories. We need your permission to use them.' She sees the disappointment on Luna's face. 'If you want, you can review some of them as we download them to the chips.'

'I'd like that,' Luna says. 'It would be like being with him. Where do I go?'

'You don't need to go anywhere,' Dr Gebreselassie says. 'We can access them anywhere.' Again, she has overspoken and Luna is crestfallen. 'But we can find a room for you. A special room.' Still the frown. 'And a special bed.'

'And granita?' Luna asks.

'What's your favourite?'

'I don't have favourites,' Luna says. 'I am an explorer. Strawberry, mint and cardamom.'

'Deal.' Dr Gebreselassie extends a hand.

'You don't deal with me. I'm the Corta of Corta Hélio. I deal with you.' Luna solemnly reaches out a hand. Dr Gebreselassie solemnly shakes it.

Strawberry and mint: good. Strawberry and cardamom: okay. Cardamom and mint: weird. Strawberry, mint and cardamom: another failed experiment in granita. Luna sucks the glass dry because she doesn't want to look like an explorer who only went halfway to Platinum Mountain and gave up. She lies back on the bed. It's comfortable and more importantly it looks right. Otherwise this med centre is everything she hates about all the other med centres she's been in: over-bright, over-warm, smells like it has something to hide and no one ever has time for a nine-year-old girl.

'Tell Dr Gebreselassie I'm ready,' she orders Luna-familiar.

Okay, Luna, make yourself comfortable and we'll begin, Dr Gebreselassie's voice and face say on the lens. Luna closes her eyes. In the darkness behind her eyelids, the memory show begins.

She cries out. She is in Boa Vista again, Boa Vista full of green and life, light and water and warmth. The serene, full-lipped faces of the orixas watch over her as she explores the river, wading barefoot through pools, scrambling up the small cascades and falls, her dress soaked through. A drone floats over her head, her madrinha's watching presence. The detail goes far beyond her own memory; she hears every leaf stir, sees every shadow and ripple, imagines she feels the cool cool water between her toes, smells the warm verdure of old Boa Vista. Noises from a stand of tall, swaying bamboo distract her from her mission: there are paths cut through the canes, irresistible to young explorers. The tracks wind in: she glimpses movement through the screen of wands. The path delivers her to a clearing in the centre of the grove. There is Lucasinho, on the growing edge of kidhood, wearing a long-skirted, flowing sky-blue dress and make-up.

'Lady Luna, Queen of the Moon!' he cries and curtsies deep to Luna. 'Yemenja Queen of the Waters welcomes you to her grand ball!' He bends down to take her hands and half-squatting, half-bounding they dance around the clearing, laughing and laughing and laughing.

'How old was I?' she asks Luna-familiar.

Three, says the grey-silver ball hovering over her chest. Lucasinho was thirteen.

Now he is fifteen and she is five and they are in his apartment in Xango's eye. He has tasked some long-armed, high-precision bots and they are passing a long evening playing with faces. Each programs their bot to spray-paint them a new face: the winner is the one who gets the biggest reaction. She remembers this. She doesn't want to see it again, in detail that time has dimmed. The animal faces, the theatre masks, the high-fashion make-ups and the fight-faces of the martial artists. Demons and angels, skulls and bones. Then Lucasinho turns away from her and the bot arm is busier than she has ever seen it, weaving and dancing and dodging in and out, drawing circles, making sudden runs across Lucasinho's hidden face.

He turns back to her.

His face is eyes. Nothing but eyes. A hundred eyes.

She screamed then. She screams now. She fled then, but she stays now. She can look at the face of a hundred eyes. She has seen worse.

Now she is six and she goes by her secret path to her special pool that is fed by Iansa's tears but Lucasinho has found the secret path to her special pool and he's in it, with a friend, and they're both naked and looking at each other and when she says, *This is my pool,* they turn round and go *Oh, hey* and step away from each other. Now Luna can understand what they were doing but then all she said was, *Well, I'm going to join you* and they fled like she had poured poison into the water.

The boy's name was Daystar Olawepu, Luna-familiar tells her. He was in Lucasinho's colloquium in João de Deus. Luna realises now that the reason they ran was not because she had caught them playing with each other's penises, but because Lucasinho had smuggled the boy through the security grid. And she thinks, *But he didn't get past the security grid, because the security grid checked everyone. Daystar was let through.* And she thinks, *Daystar is a pretty name.*

Now she is seven and Boa Vista is full of movement and music and lights and people in wonderful clothes and she is chasing ornamental butterflies between the guests. She is in a white dress with bold red peonies and wherever she goes she is told how pretty she looks. There is Lucasinho with his Moonrun friends and she tells the Mackenzie girl she likes her freckles but Lucasinho chases her away because she was just a kid. But it was all right because there was Tia Ariel, and Lucas and Carlinhos and Wagner and Grandmother Adriana. She tries to cling to the memory of Lucasinho's Moonrun party because it was the last time she remembers Boa Vista as a happy place. But the torrent of remembering is relentless: millions of moments recorded, tagged, stored. Before Luna can remember, her familiar was remembering. The idea makes her head swim.

Luna knows what would clear it.

A new combination: cardamom, vanilla, cashew. That's sure to be a success.

*

'On my own?'

'All on your own,' Dr Gebreselassie says. Luna had been exploring the more accessible of the med centre's tunnels and ducts when Luna-familiar got the message. Coriolis is old, much older than Boa Vista; its roots go deep into the crater rim. She followed corridors thick with dust, peeked through lock portholes into labyrinths of passages depressurised and sealed; peered into shafts that dived deep into the city's past and returned a satisfying echo when she shouted her name. Then Luna-familiar told her that Lucasinho was awake and she could see him and she came running.

'You did put the top back on his head?' Luna says.

Dr Gebreselassie does her head-roll movement.

'We don't do that. Go on. Go see him.'

He is sitting up. His eyes are closed, his breathing is shallow. He is terribly thin and pale. Luna can see the skull in his face. His arms, lying loose on the sheet, are like chopsticks. His chest is like a tent stretched over spars. Jinji his familiar hovers over his head, folded up into a orrery of spinning wheels within wheels. Luna has never seen a familiar do that before.

Jinji is in minimal interface mode, Luna-familiar says. *It's editing and processing petabytes of archived biographical information.*

Luna tiptoes towards the bed. She can feel the room's suspension yield beneath her footsteps. She senses machines in the walls, the floor, the low ceiling. She cannot lose the feeling that they scurried out of sight the moment she touched the door handle, and that the moment she touches it again, they will snake out of their secret places through his skin, into Lucasinho.

'Lucasinho?'

His eyes open. He sees her. Recognises her.

'Luna.'

*

The regulars in the elevator see it, and smile. It's a bright thing on a working morning. The Eyrie security see it and nod. The Eagle's back-office coders see it and whisper. Lucas's domestics and service see it and wink. Alexia rolls past, moonwalking, beaming.

The Iron Hand has had sex.

Lucas is in the Orange Pavilion: a canopy, two seats, a stone table at the end of the tree terraces, a bead on the lip of Meridian Hub.

'You're late.'

'Sorry.' She can't keep herself from grinning. Professional. 'How is the case?'

'We're agreeing judges and legal system. Between Meridian, Queen and Farside, we've disbarred twenty-two in the last twenty-four hours.' Lucas sips mint tea from a tulip glass. He makes no offer of one to Alexia. He knows she loathes it. Lucas sets down the fragile bulb of tea. 'I want him here, Alexia. I want him with me. I forget you've never met him. You've heard the talk; that he's a wastrel, a playboy. But he is kind and he is brave. Much braver and kinder than me. He took the Moonrun. I never did that. He saved Kojo Asamoah's life. He went back, in vacuum, to save him. Everyone forgets that about him. The Asamoahs didn't. Lê.'

Alexia stiffens. Lucas has never used the apelido with her before.

'I need you to go to St Olga. You will meet with representatives of VTO Moon, Space and Earth.'

The inner smile, the just-fucked glow, the jaunty catwalk of sexual superiority: frozen solid. She may have spoken the word *no* aloud.

Lucas continues. 'Yevgeny Vorontsov came to see me. He has a proposition – an offer. I am inclined to hear his offer. I can't go – I need to look spotless and sinless to the LMA.'

'When?' Alexia asks.

'Tomorrow,' Lucas says.

'Tomorrow?'

Lucas Corta lifts an eyebrow.

'There is a problem?'

'No problem.'

She will have to move fast and hard. Compress all her plans down into diamond. If there is one night, then it will be a night that will shake Meridian to its roots.

'Good,' Lucas Corta says. 'And what is making you grin?'

It's not the greatest hotel. It's unfashionably high, there is nowhere to eat, the room smells of overworked air and underworked sanitation and the cleaning bots don't get into the corners.

Let me book the Meridiana, Alexia pleads. *It's nice. My treat. I can afford it.* The Meridiana is Meridian's second best hotel – the best, the six-star Han Ying, is permanently booked for LMA and visiting terrestrials – but he insists. The Lodge of Celestial Peace or nothing. The Jack of Blades is a hunted man.

'I'm a traitor,' he says. 'My own family threw me out. My own father disowned me. I'm a pariah.'

What? Alexia says but he opens the door to the smelly, too small room and sees the bed. 'Oh fuck me gods,' he says and collapses on to it like a crashing satellite. He is asleep, snoring, smiling like a baby by the time Alexia gets back from the bathroom.

She finds a way to wake him up. They fuck, they fight, they work out their sexual fantasies on each other's bodies, they leave deep marks on each other's flesh and hearts, they laugh and scream and cry and shout the filthiest of blasphemies. They sleep, exhausted by each other's bodies.

They go to it again. They fuck again and again, again and again. They blow each other. He rolls her up into the piledriver position and though the blood pounds in her brain to the rhythm of his cock she is willing to give him the control and the humiliation. As long as he gives her gamahuche immediately after.

They sleep again.

Alexia is woken by the empty space at her side. She rolls over, sees him perched like a bird on the sole chair. He looks out of the small porthole. Antares Quadra is in night-shift; silver-blue light beams through the glass. In its light every scar on his body is livid, a terrain of rilles and ridges. He looks up into the light and Alexia sees a kid, not much older than the ones he fights for up in Bairro Alto.

His beauty stops her heart.

'I've done terrible things,' he says. 'Hideous things. Blood; years of it. You never get the smell out of your head. It's the light. I feel the knife in my hand and the light comes. It's terrible and it's brilliant and it fills everything. Everything is beautiful in that light. I see things no one else can. I can see to the edge of the universe. That light; it's the only way I can see clear. I love the light. I hate what I do but there's no other way to see it. And I have to have it.'

He looks across the room at her. His skin is steel blue in the Antares night.

'They made me for killing, Lê. First Blade. When I wouldn't do what they wanted, they threw me out.'

'Coraçao.'

'Still freaks me, Portuguese.'

Alexia pulls back the sheet, pours a glass from the bottle of vodka in the ice bucket on the bedside table. He shakes his head to the vodka but slips in beside her, curled up against her warmth. Alexia runs her hand the length of his flank. She can feel every scar. He is trembling.

'Hey,' she says. 'Hey.'

'I never told anyone that.'

She kisses his cheek; old-fashioned, chaste. She lies beside him until he falls into sleep. He twitches, gives small cries. She lies a time longer, until the nightmares end, and longer still, until she is sure she can move. She extricates her arm from under his shoulder. He mutters something.

First Blade.

Alexia summons Maninho. She fixes the sleeping man in her lens. *Who is he?* she asks silently.

The answer comes back immediately.

Denny Mackenzie.

She dresses quickly, silently. Closes the door, slips on shoes in the corridor: go fast go sure. Never look back. A glance would turn her to salt. Don't stop. You can't stop. If you heard him say your name behind you, you would turn. You would tell him everything.

I destroyed your family. I killed your grandfather. I smelted your city to slag.

She hits the elevator call. *Where to?* Maninho asks on behalf of the elevator.

'Down,' she whispers. Her chest heaves. 'All the way. Get me a moto. Book me a railcar to St Olga.'

The car is empty and she sits back to the wall, knees pulled up to her chest. Sobbing bottomless, shuddering cries of destitution, she drops down through Antares Quadra's jewel-bright night.

You killed Carlinhos. The light kindled inside you and you drove him to his knees and slit his throat, stripped him and hung him from a crosswalk. And you were beautiful and I loved you. And I am the coward who ran rather than face you with the truth of who I am.

Get up. You're Mão de Ferro.

She forces herself to her feet. She can breathe now.

Budarin Prospekt, Maninho says. The moto waits. Alexia slips into the form-fitting seat. *Meridian Station,* the moto says as it closes around her and accelerates. *Estimated arrival in two minutes eight seconds.*

'Inform the office of the Eagle that I am en route as ordered,' Alexia says. 'Notify St Olga and request an official VTO delegation to meet me off the train. Take me to the executive lounge, I'll need a shower and some new clothes. Triangulate modish, professional and rebellious.'

Done, Maninho says as the moto dives down the steep ramp to the concourse. At all hours there are travellers, workers, students, families crowding the platforms of Meridian Station. The moto opens in the foyer of the business suite and Alexia uncurls. An Equatorial One staffer waits with a printer-fresh clothing box in his hands; his colleague holds the towel and complimentary toilet bag.

'Welcome, Senhora Mão,' says suit-man. 'If you follow my colleague?'

The air is spa fresh and scented with synthetic pine but Alexia smells dust, tastes dust. Creeping back into the air after the purifying rains. Dust never dies.

He is up there, in the roof of the world.

A chime from her familiar: a file from the office of the Eagle of the Moon. Accept and open. *A new skin for Maninho. Something befitting your role as my representative,* Lucas says in the attached message. It's the work of a moment to reskin. Familiars are augmented reality objects that exist in the eye of the beholder, as difficult for the wearer to see as the back of their own head. Maninho flashes a rendering of its new form: a metal gauntlet holding a miner's pick. Mão de Ferro. The Iron Hand.

TEN

The journey from Meridian is too short, the chartered railcar too small, and her bodyguard too close to allow Alexia to reflect on the open wound of Denny Mackenzie. The edges are raw. Accusations, recriminations roar. Blame incinerates her, guilt freezes her. Denny Mackenzie. Denny *Mackenzie.*

She steps out of the lock into the fumes and reek of St Olga, capital and workshop of the Vorontsovs. If Meridian is electricity, sintered stone, vehicle tyres, hot food, incense, vomit and sewage; and Queen of the South is the soft musk of computers, plastics, construction adhesives, gin and the bracing tang of deep buried cold; then St Olga is the spice of bots and machines, dust, air trapped long in deep corners, the prickle of radiation, dead cologne.

'Mão de Ferro.' A short, bone-thin VTO staffer of indeterminate gender – *neutro* Alexia guesses, fishing for the appropriate pronoun – bows. Pav Nester, Maninho informs her. A young man with cheekbones to die for presents a tray bearing a small bun of bread and a dish of salt. 'Welcome to St Olga.' Alexia breaks off a piece of the loaf, dips it in salt.

'Bread and salt,' Alexia says. Maninho briefed her on Vorontsov etiquette in the executive suite in Meridian Station. 'The Eagle sends his apologies.'

A young woman, the female counterpart of the Vorontsov boy, presents a tray bearing wristbands.

'We've always had radiation issues in St Olga,' Pav Nester says. 'It monitors exposure.'

It also monitors you, Maninho says.

Can you fix it? Alexia asks as she slips on the band.

I'm in there, Maninho says. *There. You can turn it on and off as you wish.*

St Olga claims to be the oldest city on the moon – the original launch point for rare earths refined by Mackenzie Metals' extraction robots – and her age shows. Dome over a small crater – no more than two kilometres in diameter – and berm it all up under a six-metre-thick blanket of regolith. Over the decades St Olga has sprawled into a hinterland of construction yards, moonloop and BALTRAN facilities, rail shunting yards, comms towers, solar generators, engineering and robotics yards, but its heart is the grey, featureless hemisphere of the Vorontsovs, polluted, leaking, riddled with radiation.

Inside the dome is chaotic magnificence. The city of the Vorontsovs is a cylinder of apartments, businesses, hotshops and nurseries, kindergartens and colloquiums, workshops and shrines, standing a kilometre high at the centre of the dome. Galleries, staircases, walkways thread the sheer face of this walled city; escalators and moveways disappear into its interior. Nothing is level, nothing is true and straight. St Olga has grown like a shell over its seven decades, extensions built on to annexes, storeys piled on storeys, levels upon levels, whole new districts dumped on top of old, a city accreted like a stalagmite around a hidden ancient heart, all bound up in a web of pipes and catenaries, comms lines and cable cars.

Alexia knows she will feel right at home here.

Evening dress is expected.

'It's a formal reception,' Pav Nester says. 'We have standards.'

Alexia's diplomatic apartment lies in the core of old St Olga overlooking a court filled with dusty succulents and drooping ferns. Falling water tinkles somewhere below. If she goes on to her balcony and looks up past the tiers of higher balconies, through the mesh of cables, she can see a square of sky-blue that flickers to no-signal grey to black screen-death. In St Olga even the sky is in poor repair. VTO builds the infrastructure on which the moon relies but cannot maintain its own capital. Pav Nester led her up staircases, along clattering catwalks between sheer walls, through dripping tunnels to these old-fashioned, musty rooms at the very heart of the city. Distance from radiation, the key social gradation on the moon, is no less important under the dome, it just moves along a different axis; inward, not downward, closer to the core, further from the dome.

'Too ugly, too frumpy, makes me look eighty years old, trip hazard, too flouncy,' Alexia says of the first five designs Pav Nester shows her.

'Flouncy?'

'Frills,' Alexia says with disgust. 'Pleats.'

Pav Nester flashes another design on to Alexia's lens. Pure white, floor length, padded here-I-come shoulder, sash waist: sculptural in its elegance. It is heart-melting, classy and deadly.

'Sleeves,' Alexia says. Pav Nester slumps. 'What? Where I come from, party dresses don't have sleeves. Or much of anything.'

Her aide flicks another gown on to her lens.

'This one,' Alexia declares. 'Absolutely.'

She showers while the print-shop prepares the dress. Even the water in St Olga feels used. Freshly pissed. The dress is at the door by the time she has attended to her skin and face.

'Help me with this,' she asks Pav.

Maninho shows her herself. She could kill everything within twenty metres by glam alone. She plumps up her hair, pouts, poses hands on hips.

Your transport has arrived.

Alexia shouts with surprised laughter as she opens the door on to the narrow, steep street. A sedan chair, borne by two muscly Moonbeams, a Jo and a Joe.

'You're joking.'

'Eminently practical, given our geography and your couture,' Pav says. E hands Alexia her forgotten clutch bag and closes the door. 'Do please hold on to the handles.' The lurch as the sedan chair starts to move almost throws her to the floor. Alexia white-knuckle grips the leather straps. It's like a theme park ride, jolting, rolling, tipping back up sheer staircases, down steep pitches, round and round spiralling ramps, beneath hologram saints and neon shrines, street angels and district superheroes until she is set down with a thump outside a set of double doors sculpted with a complex pattern of arcs and arches. Security is arrayed three deep. Alexia tucks her clutch bag under her arm and contrives to step out with as much smoky lustre as possible. Maninho tosses the bearers a handful of bitsies. Pav is there already, come by different, stealthier routes. There is not a mark, not a crease on er smoke-grey brocaded shalwar kameez.

The lobby is filled with arrivals and welcomers. Alexia walks past them. Maninho flashes up a map of the apartment but Alexia lets surer senses lead her. Go where the party is loudest. Heads turn in the lobby, in the antechamber, in the receiving room as she strides through in her six-centimetre heels.

The last time she wore heels was when she disguised herself as a maid at the Copa Palace Hotel. The heels, the skirt, the top, the sagging pantyhose, had been too small. Everything she wears tonight is a perfect fit.

The maître d' announces her to the salon. Everyone was looking long before the woman declaims her name in silken Russian. Of course they're looking. The dress is a sheath of gleaming satin, so tight that Alexia can barely breathe. She is bare from the top of the breasts to the tip of her coiffure. The hope of the Saints seems to be all that holds the dress up. Opera gloves to the shoulder. It is impossible not to vamp in this dress. The couture, the height of the heels dictate it.

'The Iron Hand!' cries the maître d' to rapturous applause. Already Alexia has read the party; the ones who will be aimed at her, the ones who will screen the ones she needs to talk to, the ones who will try to seduce her. She scoops a martini from a tray and heads to battle.

It is a full half-hour before the Vorontsovs make their first move.

He is tall, but they are all tall. He is blue-eyed, precision-fit, breathtakingly handsome. They all are. Alexia recognises him from the LMA sessions, one of the young, confident generation that occupy the highest tier of the chamber with the assurance of power. He wears a formal shirt, stiff white tie, the tail coat. He is exactly Alexia's type. The Vorontsovs have done their research thoroughly.

'Alexia Corta.' He bows. It is very fetching.

'Dmitri Mikhailovich.'

'You look stunning. Not everyone can work the 1940s look, but you are classic Hollywood. A true screen goddess.'

Alexia has never trusted blue eyes. You see too far into them and what lies at the bottom is cold and hard. Dmitri Vorontsov's blue eyes hold a sparkle. *Ice or fire?* Alexia whispers to Maninho. Before she can return the compliment he continues.

'That's an . . . assertive new skin on your familiar.'

'Does it not suit me?'

'Of course, yet it seems uncharacteristically *metal* for a Corta.'

'It is what I am.'

'The Iron Hand. I apologise, I've never been able to work the Portuguese nasal tones.'

'Mão de Ferro.' Dmitri has steered Alexia away from the salon to a vaulted cloister. At the centre is a fountain. Dmitri guides Alexia around the pillared arcades. By St Olga's logic this palace must lie at the very heart of the city, yet the rooms are spacious and Alexia has no sense of claustrophobia. The air, for St Olga, is fresh, if heavy with cologne and cuir de russe. Dmitri Vorontsov smells as sweet as he looks. No one has come to rescue her.

'I've always been impressed by that title. It's like something we would make up.'

'It's not a title and I didn't make it up,' Alexia says. 'Mão de Ferro is my apelido, my nickname. In Brasil, everyone has an apelido. But you can't give it to yourself, it has to be given to you. Mão de Ferro is an old miner's apelido from Minas Gerais. It means the miner's miner. The A-number-one. The man.'

'Or the woman.' Dmitri Vorontsov directs Alexia around the turn of the cloister with a soft touch. Manicured nails, Alexia observes.

'My great-grandfather Diogo was the first Mão de Ferro. It became a family name. There's hasn't been a Mão de Ferro in my branch of the family for generations. Not since my great-aunt.'

'Adriana Corta.' Dmitri Vorontsov says. 'Now you. So tell me, Iron Hand, who gave you this name?'

'Lucas, the Eagle of the Moon.'

'I see your glass is empty.' His fingers rest on hers a moment too long as he takes her glass. 'Would you like another? Or shall we stay here away from all the noise? I do find parties tiring.'

Oh you sweet liar.

'I would love another,' Alexia says.

'Then let me refresh your glass.' Dmitri's manners are as immaculate as his suit but he has failed. His small talk turns to handball as he guides Alexia across the cloister to the party.

'I understand it's the thing here.'

'Oh I am crazy about it,' Dmitri says. 'We all are in St Olga. I used to play, then I moved into ownership. The Saints? You've heard of them. I must take you to a game. You won't understand the moon until you understand handball.'

'I'd like that,' Alexia says. 'Some time. I used to play volleyball. It was the thing in Rio. Beach volleyball. In a stupidly small, stupidly tight bikini. With my name on my ass.'

She's never played beach volleyball in her life.

She slips away from Dmitri Vorontsov without a backward glance and lifts her own martini from a tray. The party opens to accept her. Greetings, compliments, politenesses. They failed with a boy, they'll try a girl next. Alexia has already glimpsed her, a look from across the room, stolen away when Alexia catches her eye. Big brown eyes, brown skin, a glorious wedge of hair. Cream silk and pearls. She works the right side of the party, Alexia the left and they meet by the vodka fountain.

'You caught me,' she says in a thrilling, liquid baritone. 'I'm not as good at this game as Dmitri.' A gloved hand. 'Irina Efua Vorontsova-Asamoah.'

Irina of the seducing voice is seventeen, St Olga-born. Father Van Ivanovitch, a nephew of Yevgeny Grigorivitch. Mother Patience Quarshie Asamoah, cousin of Lousika Asamoah. Maninho shows Alexia how she is related to Irina. The complexity dazes her.

'I thought Vorontsovs and Asamoahs were historical enemies,' Alexia says.

'They are.' Irina Asamoah could recite machine code and be enchanting. 'People like me are the peace.' She moves in a whisper of cream to a balcony high above a deep courtyard glimmering with biolights. Irina moves close to Alexia, on the edge of intimate space.

'So which are you?' Alexia asks.

'I don't understand.'

'Vorontsov or Asamoah?'

Irina frowns, two lines of bafflement between her eyes.

'Both, of course. Neither. Me.'

As soon as Alexia holds a part of lunar life, it wriggles free in a spray of feathers, bright as a parakeet. Family is everything, except when family forces you to pick a side, an identity. Alexia remembers the ghazi she met at Twé Station, Dakota Kaur Mackenzie. She had doubted that a Mackenzie could find another, greater loyalty. Mackenzie first Mackenzie always. In the ghazi, in the silken Irina

Efua Vorontsova-Asamoah, Alexia understands that identity is negotiable. Family is what works for you.

'I brought you out here to give you fair warning, Alexia Corta. My task is to seduce you. Which I shall, and you will adore it.' She steps away from the light-well and glances over her shoulder as she dances back into the party. Alexia cannot but follow. Irina introduces her to more Vorontsovs. Handsome, tall Vorontsovs from the moon, the layers of track and the spinners of cable, the train-lords and the rover-queens. Squat, waddling Vorontsovs from Earth, relearning gravity. Drawn, frail Vorontsovs from space, battling gravity. Maninho remembers the faces, the names, the patro- and matronymics. Alexia tries not to remember Valery Vorontsov with his solar system of colostomy bags and coiling catheters.

Names, faces, wisps of biography. Stunning frocks and stiff tailsuits. Alexia glances up from the introductions to see Irina exchange glances with Pav Nester across the ballroom. Irina catches Alexia catching her and smiles, unashamed and unashameable. *You are beautiful, you are golden. You've never known anything but this. You will always be adored, your days will always be charmed. No one will ever judge you by your accent, by your birth, by your money, by the colour of your skin.*

'Met enough saggy old men and hideous dowagers?' Irina asks.

'Who else do I need to meet?' Alexia says.

'The rest will just either try to jump you or bore you. This party is done. Next question, can you run in that dress?'

'I might take off and fly a bit. Why?'

'Just as long as you're faster than your bodyguards,' Irina says, hitches her party frock and takes off, a bolt of cream and brown. In a heartbeat Alexia switches off her tracker-band and follows Irina. The first step almost sends her headlong as the skirt trips her. Alexia stoops to take a seam and tear it up to her thigh. Now she can run. One step sends her soaring to the chandelier, the next into a wall as Irina veers into a corridor. Alexia fights to run low, run true.

They arrive gasping and laughing in a stark backroom, raw rock and aluminium, far from the ponderous glamour of the public suites. Circular hatches a metre in diameter ring the room at waist-height. Irina locks eyes with Alexia and kicks off her shoes.

'I promised I would seduce you, Alexia Corta,' Irina Efua Asamoah says . Above each of the circular hatches is a pair of handles, warning-striped. Irina grabs them, swings herself feet first into the hatch and vanishes. Alexia hears a distant, echoing shriek of pleasure.

'Fuck it.' Alexia steps out of her shoes and in a breath is in a sloping tube, picking up speed as she slides on her back, feet first into the unknown. She giggles, then the tube steepens into a near vertical and gravity grabs her. She is plunging through complete darkness, swung one way then the other as the tube turns, dress billowing up around her. She can't resist a scream of excitement and fear, then her stomach is in her mouth as the incline softens and she is thrown into a long spiral, coil after coil, downward downward. She whoops, she yells, she hollers as she rattles round the pipe, human detritus in a drain. She might piss herself with excitement. A dot of light expands into a circle and she is shot from the mouth of the tube into the air to land with a gasp in a mitt of soft crash mats. She rolls to her feet. She is as groggy, as glassy-eyed, brain-glazed as after great sex. And laughing laughing laughing.

Irina lounges on the crash mat, big dark eyes wide and alluring.

'What was that?' Alexia says.

'Emergency escape protocol Two,' Irina says. Now Alexia sees that there are as many exit hatches as there were entry hatches in the other room – how far away was it? She had seemed to slide for a very long time but time on a slide is time sliding. 'We're five hundred metres under St Olga,' Irina says, as if reading Alexia's thoughts. 'This is a radiation shelter. When there's a sudden solar flare, we jump in the nearest tube and get our asses down here.'

'I went round a corkscrew,' Alexia says.

'A what?'

'A spiral. A *helix*. Why would you put a corkscrew in an emergency escape slide?'

'Why wouldn't you?' Irina says. Her frown is heartbreaking. 'Some have switchbacks. I've ridden most of them.'

A secret fun park under the capital of VTO. A rollercoaster emergency escape system. Everything is big with the Vorontsovs, Alexia recalls. Big love, big rage, big loyalty. Big fun. From inside an escape tube comes a high-pitched cry, growing louder until with a gleeful yell a boy flies from a hatch and goes head over heels across the crash pit. He comes up in a blur of blond hair and big grin. He looks about twelve. He dashes, laughing, from the shelter.

'This dress is wrecked,' Alexia says. 'I can't be seen in this.'

'There's a printer next level up.' Irina coyly twists her foot. 'However . . .'

'However?'

'You want to maybe change outfit? I was going to go on to another party,' Irina says. 'A proper party. For people like us.'

Alexia is hard tempted. Time out from the duties and responsibilities of the Mão de Ferro. Time to be Alexia Corta, carioca and Queen of Pipes, with people of her own age and outlook. People free from the burden of power.

You almost had me, Irina Asamoah.

'I have work to do,' Alexia says. 'I have meetings in the morning. With all those people not like us.'

Irina bites her lower lip in disappointment, then dips her head.

'All right. But when you're done with them, call me.' She goes up on her tiptoes to kiss Alexia sharp and sweet on the lips, then skips away, barefoot and glorious.

My task is to seduce you, Irina had said. *Which I shall, and you will adore it.*

Alexia is seduced. And she adores it.

*

A rock in space, backlit against a half-Earth. The same sunlight casts geometric shadows: human hands have worked this rock.

Alexia Corta hovers over this engineered rock. She is floating in space. The human workings give scale. Alexia guesses it to be a kilometre or so in diameter. Space rocks are not her area. The rock turns beneath her. It takes her a moment to deduce, from the motion of light and shadow, that it is not the rock that is moving but her. Spatial orientation is not her area either. A thin line of darkness lies across the lit side of the space rock. An artefact? A shadow. As Alexia tries to work out what would cast such a shadow, she catches sight of the line of light. A vertical cable. She moves her head to follow the line and the presentation responds, swooping to latch her to the cable and sending her up away from the rock.

She looks upwards again, again the camera angle shifts and before her is the face of the moon. Between her and the Nearside under full sun is a glitch in her vision, like a floater in her eyeball. It's hard to resolve the detail, light against light, but Alexia catches hints and glints of geometry: docking gantries, solar panels, power antennae, fuel tanks, environment modules, bots and builders and machine arms. Some kind of space station. The camera pans to give her a lingering look at space vehicles moored to the docking bays, helium and rare earth canisters, glinting chunks of meteoric ice the size of apartment blocks. Alexia's sight swoops away from the space station back to the line and the moon beyond. Something flashes towards her, climbing fast, past her, gone. Alexia did not notice the point at which climbing up the cable had become flying along the cable had become dropping down the cable.

On the cycler from Earth, she had not recognised the point at which the moon went from the thing in the sky to the world down beneath her feet.

Alexia knows enough Nearside selenography to recognise that the cable is carrying her far south of the equator. She rides the space elevator down over Tycho and Clavius. Ever south: now the rimwalls of Shackleton throw their perpetual shadows across the polar basin. Alexia glimpses lights in the ever-shadow. A star burns brighter than all others: the Pavilion of Eternal Light atop its glass tower. Now the surface mess and clutter of Queen of the South slide into view: abandoned rovers and sinterers, obsolete environment equipment, comms towers and outlocks and the track-smeared grey of the regolith. Lunar cities, so wonderful, so architectural, so precise, inside are fashion-conscious teenagers who strew their detritus around their rooms. A string of bright lights breaks from the shadow of the rimwall into the light: a transpolar express arriving at the moon's First City. Lower, closer. A dock opens beneath her, a black mouth. The presentation ends and Alexia's lens clears.

She sits at a round conference table. The room is black. The tabletop glows from within, the only lighting. It casts the faces of the gathered executives in dramatic mien. Here are the old men – mostly men – she met at the reception. The tall men of VTO Moon, the squat men of VTO Earth, the frail, noodle-men of VTO Space. Younger faces too. Among these she finds the women. Every face is solemn and unsmiling. It is the Vorontsov way. They think that Brasilians smile too much.

'Very impressive.'

The solemn faces watch, unspeaking. They know she doesn't understand what she has seen. A cable-car ride from space to the moon.

'By taking the elevator to the pole we keep the equatorial orbits open,' says Pavel Vorontsov directly across the table.

'Our moonloop momentum transfer system will continue to operate in conjunction with the cyclers,' says Orin Vorontsov to Alexia's left.

'For biological traffic,' says Piotr Vorontsov to her right.

'Ascent time to the counterweight is in the region of two hundred hours,' Pavel Vorontsov says. 'That's an unacceptable exposure to ionising radiation.'

'Shielding the ascenders to human-safe limits imposes an uneconomic mass burden,' says Piotr Vorontsov.

'Full specifications are in the appendices,' says Orin Vorontsov, with a smile.

'Oh for God's sake, you yelping ninnies!' A new voice breaks in, a new face. 'She doesn't get it.' Valery Vorontsov is the ghost at the feast, an homunculus hovering in every lens. He has been linked in from *Saints Peter and Paul* out on the far side of Earth, out of direct communication with the moon. On the top of the iron two-second speed-of-light delay, his avatar is being relayed through high-earth-orbit communication satellites, adding delay to delay. Valery Vorontsov is ten seconds adrift from the board room. 'It's a space elevator.' The software presenting his avatar has edited out the colostomy bags, the long toenails, the semi-forgetful semi-nudity. But he still looks like a kite made from a flayed man's skin. 'You know what a space elevator is, don't you?' The ten-second time lag points up the rhetoric. 'Do you know what is the most cost-effective way to transfer mass out of a gravity well? Lower a line and haul it up. Like a bucket of piss. So, it's a long line – almost all the way to Earth – but that's just engineering. Space elevator. In fact, space elevators. Why build one when you can have two? Economies of scale, so I'm told. One to the south pole, one to the north pole.' The room gives Valery Vorontsov respectful time, then Yevgeny Vorontsov speaks.

'Not even two space elevators, Mão de Ferro. Four.'

Alexia's lens springs to life again. She is climbing away from the south pole, up over the vast pit of the Aitken Basin. The blazing star of the Pavilion of Eternal Light falls behind and beneath her, shadows lengthen, shadows merge into darkness. The great lantern of the Suns blazes above the brilliant arc of light, the terminator between lunar day and night. She rides the invisible line up over Farside, the endless, chaotic mountains, the craters, the small, isolated seas unseen beneath her. The ascender spins up its line high above Farside. The camera shifts; Alexia looks up into a sky more full of stars than she has ever seen. Higher, faster.

The moon dwindles beneath Alexia. The terminator is everywhere, a halo of light, then the sun spills around the moon and in her seat in the VTO boardroom, she gives an involuntary gasp. A city in space lies before her. The Earth-side port had amazed her. This staggers her imagination: this is ten times the size and complexity of the Nearside anchor point. Three ships, each a kilometre long, hang like hummingbirds above the open petals of heat-exhaust vanes. A flicker of thruster-blue: a tug, all fuel tanks and radiator vanes and solar panels, departs Farside, bound out among the worlds. The sun catches the VTO logo. The camera zooms in on bots and shell-suited figures on the dock surface, welding. There is always space-welding in these presentations. No windows. The camera zooms in on the gilded visor of one of the space workers. Reflected there, the moon, with the dark of the Earth behind it.

And back in the board room.

Now Yevgeny Vorontsov speaks. 'The Moonport scheme. Simple, cost-effective transfer of materials between moon and Earth, and the moon and the solar system using four space elevators. The moon as the key to future development of the solar system. The moon as the hub of the solar system. Low-cost space vehicle manufacturing, expertise in robotics, cheap energy and a high-volume launch system. We could build it tomorrow.' Light burns in Yevgeny Vorontsov's eyes. Every Vorontsov eye is on him.

'Why have you shown this to me?' Alexia Corta asks.

'VTO needs licences for sites at Queen of the South and Rozhdestvenskiy,' Yevgeny Vorontsov says. 'Only the LMA can issue those licences.' The representatives of Earth, Moon and Space nod their agreement. 'Can we rely on the Eagle's support in a vote in the council?'

'I represent the Eagle, I can't speak for him.'

'Of course not. We expect you to persuade him,' Yevgeny Vorontsov said.

'More,' says Pavel Vorontsov. 'We expect him to persuade the terrestrials.'

'The Eagle maintains a non-partisan position between terrestrial and lunar bodies,' Alexia says, conscious that every eye is now on her. 'Like your asteroid at the L1 point.' The attempted joke dies on the table.

'The Eagle may,' Yevgeny growls. 'Lucas Corta is moon-born. Dust in the blood. Dust will out.'

'Memorise what you have seen,' Orin Vorontsov says. 'Know it like your own skin. We can't allow any of this material out of St Olga. You have to be its advocate.'

'He's watched,' Yevgeny Vorontsov says. 'I've seen the drones. Even on a secure channel we could not risk this material falling into the hands of the terrestrials.'

'So what do you think?' Valery Vorontsov interrupts, as he must.

'I'm not sure I can do it justice,' Alexia says. 'It's a hell of a thing to ask.' She realises that she is not answering the question he intends. 'I can't understand it the way you do. It's huge, it's magnificent – I've never seen anything like it. I can't fit it all in my head. I don't know if I can sell it right. I know how I feel about it – maybe I can sell the gut feeling.'

The VTO board room give Valery Vorontsov on the far side of the Earth his ten seconds.

'That will be enough, Alexia Corta.'

He smiles. A ghastly, green-toothed smile.

Everyone around the board table smiles with him.

Wagner Corta eases back into the chair. The rover maintains a comfortable working ambience but he shivers at the touch of plastic to skin. Every nerve feels like ten nerves, every one of those ten nerves is frayed into a thousand conducting fibres. He tenses as those nerve fibres are stroked, then relaxes his full weight into the seat.

'Turn me to it, Dr Light,' he commands. The rover is old – little more than an airlock slung between motility units – without any AI more sophisticated than a recent familiar-interface patch, but reliable. Wagner hears the motors engage as a muted line in the symphony of machine noise: bips of sensors, whines of actuators, the breathing of the air conditioning and the drum of his heart, the susurrus of his respiration. He feels a shift in gravity too subtle for less tuned senses as a nearly unbearable tickle. It's going to be agony out on the open regolith. The rover spins on its axis and halts.

'Open her up, Dr Light.'

The front of the rover turns transparent. The light of the full Earth beams in on Wagner Corta, naked in the command chair of Taiyang 1138: *Rosa*. He cries out. Blue light beats into every cell of his body. Every nerve blazes. He hauls himself upright, stands in the Earth-light, turns to expose every part of his skin to the light. The small of his back, the palms of his hands. He scoops his long black hair over his shoulder to expose the nape of his neck. Every part of him is soaked in Earth-shine. His breath is laboured, orgasmic gasps. He shakes. His muscles can barely hold him upright. He collapses back into the command seat, panting.

'Let's go to work, Dr Light.'

Who repairs the repairers? Wagner Corta, the wolf.

He needs the work, not the money. Analiese's Persian classical ensemble brings in enough to share happily with him and Robson. The distance is beyond price. Ever since he caught the old familiar shuttle at Hypatia Junction and Robson settled into the seat beside him, Wagner has dreaded the first wink of blue along the edge of the new Earth. Now it is intolerable. He thought giving up the meds would make it manageable, but with each Earth-rise the psychological shifts have grown more and more intense.

Take the meds, Analiese said. *It's too much to put yourself through, love. Take your meds.*

In the deep of the night before departure for the Theon Senior job he slipped out of bed and padded down to the printer. The order was complex, the constituents required several stages of synthesis. He sat shivering, watching the apartment printer. The silence coalesced around him like crystal. When Dr Light told him the order was ready his heartbeat jumped and skipped. He gulped the meds down with water, shaking with heart palpitations, as the thickness, the uncertainty, the muddled fog, the indecision and lack of clarity divided and parted, yin and yang. He was two again. He was himself. Across two thousand kilometres he felt the pack call to him.

He was gone before Analiese and Robson were awake.

In the cramped cabin of Taiyang 1138 *Rosa*, Wagner Corta learns what it is to be a lone wolf. He roars. He howls. He descends into incoherent raving, broken by racking sobs dry of any tears. More than once he hits the outlock controls, seeking not to end the white fire inside but to get closer to his true soul, burning beneath the horizon with the light of ten thousand Earths. He bites deep into his wrists, his forearms, remembering the loving teeth of his packmates. Crescent Earths of bloodied skin. He chews a thumbnail into a ragged blade, twists it into skin and draws a jagged, bleeding line from each nipple to his navel. He sobs silently, muscles wracked, curled on the hard mesh floor, hour after hour. It is more terrible than he thought possible. He is in hell.

Twenty minutes to destination, Dr Light says.

He pushes himself to his knees, fists clenched against the floor panels, soaked with sweat, hair dripping. He is the wreck of a man, humanity burned away in the white. He can force himself to his feet because there is only the wolf now. Pain is the condition of the wolf. He stands.

'Show me.'

He looks long and hard at his self-image on the rover cameras. He looks like death. Dr Light shows him where to find water, sanitiser, first aid. Wagner Corta cleans, mends, seals. There is work to be done, work only the wolf can do. The dark side is focus and colossal, introverted dedication. The light side is inspiration, insight, flashing flights of genius; important attributes for the man who fixes the fixers. He was an analyst before he was a care giver, before he was laoda of Taiyang Glass Crew Lucky Eight Ball. He sees things, makes connections other humans cannot.

He pulls on his sasuit, savours the sensation of stretch fabric sliding over his sensitised skin. Gloves on. Preliminary systems check. He feels the rover brake to rendezvous with the damage maintenance bot.

It will always be like this, but he can do it. No one else can.

ELEVEN

Wang Yongqing is assiduous with the prints, studying each one equally and at length. Vidhya Rao waits with hands folded in the capacious sleeves of er gown. The terrestrial woman has no interest in 18th and 19th century CE lithography. If the LMA must meet Vidhya Rao on the neutro's terrain, then the LMA will take control of the time. Anselmo Reyes and Monique Bertin are visibly bored already.

'Such a bourgeois little sedition,' Wang Yongqing says as she completes her viewing and the staff of the Lunarian Society Club show host and guests to the table.

'Politics is a novelty with us,' Vidhya Rao says. 'What's the expression? "Let a thousand flowers bloom"?'

The sommelier brings water.

'As long as the planting is harmonious,' Wang Yongqing says. 'Now, since I do not talk and eat, shall we do our business before or after lunch?'

'You requested the meeting,' Vidhya Rao says. 'You manage it as you wish.'

On the wall hangs the tiny William Blake print of a ladder between Earth and moon. Wang Yongqing has not noticed it yet, or if she has, commenting on it offers no political profit. At this table e entertained Ariel Corta when e prophesied the coming of these terrestrials.

'Very well. Your Lunar Bourse proposal finds favour with us,' Wang Yongqing says.

'We've spoken with our respective governors,' Monique Bertin says. 'They concur. Enthusiastically. Financialisation is both a profitable and secure future for the lunar profit nexus.'

'My company is willing to provide seed money to develop the project,' Anselmo Reyes says. 'We envisage a consortium of Earth-based funders and AI developers.'

'Taiyang is far in advance of any terrestrial developers,' Vidhya Rao says.

'It's a question of control,' Anselmo Reyes says. 'Put simply, we want as little lunar involvement with the Bourse as possible.'

'Earth-owned, Earth-run,' Monique Bertin says.

'Earth-run?' Vidhya Rao asks. 'Given the time lag?'

'We will rotate workers in and out,' Monique Bertin says.

'This makes no economic sense,' Vidhya Rao says.

'As my colleague said, we want as little lunar involvement as possible,' Wang Yongqing says. 'Ideally, none.'

'In the short to mid-term we will appropriate Taiyang's Sun-ring to secure an energy supply. In the mid-term, we will oversee the construction of a fully automatic Bourse along the lines of your proposal,' Monique Bertin says. 'In the long-term we foresee a move to full financialisation and a managed decline of the lunar population.'

'Managed decline?' Vidhya Rao says.

'To a level that will guarantee harmony between the two worlds,' Wang Yongqing says.

'What do you mean?'

'Must you be so obtuse? Zero.' Wang Yongqing unrolls her napkin and lays it neatly in her lap. 'No human population on the moon. Now, shall we eat?'

*

The Iron Sea lies in the eastern limb of the Oceanus Procellarum. The name has no official standing. It is recent and informal. It is the nickname of VTO's great marshalling yard; three-hundred square kilometres of track, shunting, maintenance and construction.

A small executive railcar in Mackenzie Metal's green and silver moves across the switchgear of the Iron Sea, siding to siding to siding past kilometre-long passenger expresses, angular hulking freight haulers, track layers and maintenance bogies. The Mackenzie Metals smelter runs on its own dedicated rails, straddling two maglev tracks. The railcar runs in to a halt under the belly of the beast. The docking cradle descends and lifts the railcar entire from the line. Locks engage, seal and equalise. Every society has its unmeasured times; moments of waiting, endurance, or process that are universally ignored. On the moon, unmeasured time is time waiting for airlocks to seal and cycle.

Pavel Vorontsov waits with his okrana in the low-ceilinged corridor for the inlock to open. Duncan Mackenzie stoops through the lock into the cramped space. His blades fall in behind him, shuffling awkwardly to find a suitably intimidating formation. Everyone's familiar merges with the roof.

'My grandfather apologises,' Pavel Vorontsov says. 'He would have been here to greet you, for the old affection between our families, but he couldn't fit the corridors.'

The entourages hunch and duck through the low passages. Familiars whisper warnings of obstructions and head hazards.

'It's designed for service crew only,' Pavel Vorontsov says

The control centre at the top of the smelter offers thrilling views across the Iron Sea all the way to the great industrial slough of St Olga. There is room enough only for executives. Okrana and blades huddle in the corridor trying to find comfort.

'I've passed control to your familiar so you can take her out personally,' Pavel says to Duncan Mackenzie. 'We have to move it every other day anyway.'

'The bogies freeze and bind,' Duncan Mackenzie says. The old rituals of Crucible are not forgotten. His familiar Esperance opens the command windows in his lens. He lays in a route. The Vorontsovs will not hear the low hum as the grid feeds power to the traction motors, feel the subtle acceleration as a thousand tons of smelter starts to move. They are engineers, not rail-riders. They did not grow up on great Crucible, ever-circling the moon, one orbit every twenty-nine days, bathed in everlasting sunshine, in the protecting shadow of the mirrors.

'Courageous choice of destination,' Pavel Vorontsov says.

'It feels like a debt unpaid,' Duncan Mackenzie says. The smelter is at full speed now, ten kilometres per hour. Signal lights turn green on the cabin screen and on Duncan Mackenzie's eyeball. His emotions are complex: nostalgic pleasure; the bleeding scab of barely healed hurt; the thrill of power, the sourness of regret that however many smelters VTO builds, it will never be Crucible again. Some cities only rise the once. The smelter takes the points on to the mainline without a shudder.

'We've improved the design,' Pavel Vorontsov says. 'This is an old back-up smelter from the original Crucible model we've retrofitted with parts of the new system. The new units would be totally autonomous. Lighter, more efficient. Our engineering and production is much more sophisticated than our fathers' days.'

'I don't doubt it,' Duncan Mackenzie says. He notes with pleasure the look of controlled consternation on Pavel Vorontsov's face as he sees, through the window, a passenger express bear down on the smelter. Destruction is imminent, then the express vanishes underneath the smelter. It gets everyone the first time.

'We can deliver five units per lune,' Pavel says. 'As the new designs are more efficient, you would need fewer of them to achieve full production. We could have you at the old Crucible's output in six years. After that, it's just a matter of adding cars.'

'I'm impressed, Pavel Yevgenevitch,' Duncan Mackenzie says.

'Removing life-support and habitability features reduces the cost and ease of build. We've only pressurised this one for the demonstration. The updated models are designed to be maintained by our automated systems.'

'They won't be necessary,' Duncan Mackenzie says. St Olga's dome has dropped beneath the horizon. The smelter rolls across the flatlands of eastern Procellarum.

'I appreciate that historically Mackenzie Metals used its own maintenance teams . . .'

'I won't need any maintenance systems,' Duncan Mackenzie says. Face to face, breath close in the confines of the control cab, the VTO executives try not to show their consternation.

'Duncan, I don't understand you,' Pavel Vorontsov says.

'I won't be issuing a contract,' Duncan Mackenzie says. Russian muttering, snatched glances. 'Hadley will continue as Mackenzie Metals' main smelter.'

'Duncan, you're already stretched to meet demand. You need continuous refining. You could switch from solar to electricity, but that means either buying into Taiyang's sun-belt, or new fusion, and buying He3 from your brother, in the short term at least.'

'Pavel, did you ever meet my father?'

'At his centenary, in Queen of the South.'

'In the chair, hooked into the environment suit. A dozen systems keeping him alive. Piss and shit and electricity. But his eyes; did you ever look in his eyes? You should have looked in his eyes. His eyes never got old. Same light I saw when I was a kid. Same light I saw when he turned the mirrors to the sun. He was fifty when he came to the moon. The launch will kill you, they said. It didn't. The low gravity will kill you, they said. Bone loss. Muscle wasting. They didn't. The only thing that could kill Robert Mackenzie was treachery. I'll tell you this about the old man: if you offered him to choose this or that, he'd say, fuck you, I'll take the third choice. There was always a third choice.

'Mine it, melt it, move it. That been our way for fifty years now. But there's another way. Fuck Earth. It's always hungry, it'll eat everything and then suck our bones. Earth's a child. We don't need it. There's a system full of stuff we can use, just sitting out there. Enough for us to build any world we want. Not just the moon. You should see the ideas our kids are coming out with. Artificial worlds. Habitats like . . . necklaces in the sky. Dozens of them – hundreds of them. Thousands of them. Room enough for billions of people. Trillions. Enough metal and carbon out there to make every dream real. Ours for the taking.

'You know why I'm cancelling the order? I don't want you to build me smelters; I want you to build me asteroid miners. Ships. Mass-drivers. Thousands of mirrors. We have the materials skills. You have the space-lift experience. Mine it, melt it, move it, for us. We work together. We need to work together – all of us. All the Dragons. Or it's our bones in the dust. Lucas Corta can't control the terrestrials. My father believed in an independent moon. With all his heart. That's not enough any more. We need to go higher, reach further, spread so wide Earth can never catch us all. We all live as long as Earth needs us. When they stop needing us . . .'

Duncan Mackenzie smacks his fist into the window. Blood smears the glass. Esperance puts out medical alert to his blades. Duncan Mackenzie wills them away.

'The old man believed in the moon. I believe in a thousand moons. A thousand societies.'

Duncan Mackenzie feels a subtle deceleration. The smelter is braking.

'What do you want, Duncan?' Pavel Vorontsov asks.

'Put me in front of your board. Let me tell them what I told you.'

The smelter comes to an enormous halt, casting a mountain-shadow far across the grey flats of the Oceanus Procellarum. Duncan Mackenzie's final destination would be hours distant at the smelter's sun-following speed.

'I'm taking the railcar the rest of the way to Crucible,' Duncan

Mackenzie says. 'You can come with me or you can take this thing back to St Olga.'

Men face off in the tiny, cramped cabin. Eye to eye, breath to breath.

'I'll come with you,' Pavel Vorontsov says. In the corridor, clambering down to the railcar dock, he moves up as close to Duncan Mackenzie as the engineering will allow. 'Duncan. I've spoken with the family. You have your meeting.'

Irina wears the sasuit like paint on her skin. Custom highlights follow the curves and contours of her muscles and Alexia's gaze follows them. This girl could no more stop entrancing than breathing. Charm is her heartbeat. She pulls on the helmet and goes from being Irina Efua Vorontsova-Asamoah to an object. She is, Alexia admits, as sexy as hell.

But the shell-suit is sexier. Different, deeper, darker sexy. It stood open in the lock antechamber like an embrace, like an autopsy. Alexia gingerly backed into it, giggling as the haptic array took her measure and closed in to touch her body at a thousand points, intimate and responsive as a lover's muscles. The suit closed around her. Alexia fought panic as the helmet locked and sealed, then Maninho interfaced with the suit's AI and the carapace vanished. She lifted her hands. They were bare, her arms, her feet and legs, everything she could see: naked.

I have a wide-ranging wardrobe of suit skins, Maninho said. Alexia tired after the first fifty and went for body-hugging faux-neoprene. She looked like one of the rich-kid surfers who ran down to the beach at Barra with their boards and bodyguards.

She dares a shuffling step in the shell-suit. It moves like her own body. Protected but limber. Enclosed, defended. Irina checks her. What does she see? Surfer gatinha or Iron Man? The suit interface has put Irina's face over her helmet visor. Irina looks naked to vacuum. These tricks, these simulations and putting-at-eases, could trip a surface-suiter. And as everyone tells her, the moon wants to kill you, and knows a thousand ways to do it.

'Keep behind me and don't let it seduce you,' Irina says. 'Do you want a tether?'

'I do not want a tether.'

The inlock seals behind her.

'How long does it take to get the air . . .'

Her suit thrums, a rushing disturbance translated to her skin by the haptic mesh. And over.

The lock is at surface pressure, Maninho says.

So that's what a lock depressurising feels like.

The outlock slides upwards on a widening rectangle of brightness.

'Come on then,' Irina says. Her name floats in green above her shoulder. Green is good. Red is trouble. White is dead. Alexia shuffles up the ramp. Irina pats a rough icon of Lady Luna coloured in vacuum-marker on the outlock wall. The halved face is abraded almost to invisibility by thousands of gloves. Alexia brushes it with her glove tips. She is a duster now.

Out into the sun. She stops dead at the top of the ramp.

I'm walking on the moon, the moon!

'Well come on, Moonbeam,' Irina says. Alexia crosses the line from sinter to moondust. She kicks at the gritty grey. A cloud flies up higher than she had imagined, hangs long before settling to the surface.

I'm walking on the freakin' moon! Wait until I tell Caio!

She sets her boot on the surface and sees that it intersects a previous bootprint. The windless oceans of the moon carry prints and tracks forever. On her last night before launch prep at Manaus, she had taken Caio and a telescope up to the top of Ocean Tower and he'd asked to see King Dong; the hundred-kilometre-tall phallus tracked into Mare Imbrium in the earliest days of industrialisation by bored dusters and their patient machines.

Second foot on the regolith. She looks up. The freakin' moon is a freakin' mess. Obsolete technology, fallen comms towers, capsized dishes, ruptured tanks, junked rovers, cannibalised trains. Suit detritus, human garbage. Organics have been picked clean by the zabbaleen for reprocessing; the metal bones abandoned. Metal is cheap, dead. Carbon is precious life.

Alexia looks up from the trash land. Earth steals her. Her homeworld stands locked halfway between horizon and zenith. Alexia has never seen a bluer thing. Once Norton bought her sapphire earrings. They sparkled and burned, but they were of the earth, not the Earth. Once in school she had struggled on Draw the Flag Day to remember the number and positions of the stars on the blue circle at the centre of the Auriverde, but that had been the blue of empty space, not of a living world. This is all the blue in the universe rolled up into one ball. So small. She raises her hand and obliterates every person she has ever known.

What happens if you cry in a space helmet?

'Come on, Mão.'

'I've been staring, haven't I?'

'Respect, but Moonbeams always stare.'

'How can you live with it?'

'What?'

'That. Up there. How can you stand it?'

'Not my world, Mão.'

Lithe skin-suit leads bulky space armour on a circuit of St Olga, from the junk-fields to the construction yards where bots climb and clamber trailing festivals of cables and wiring, cranes swing panels into position and Procellarum glitters with starfields of welding arcs. Into the shadow of the dome, Earth eclipsed, and the marshalling yards, where trains split and shunt and expresses pull out of service and the tracks merge into the great equatorial mainline. Alexia glimpses a massive object far down the tracks.

'What is that?'

'The back-up smelter,' Irina says. 'The last of Crucible. They must be track-testing it. Mackenzie Metals has ordered a new refinery-train.'

'Irina,' Alexia Corta says. 'Can you take me to Crucible?'

'There's nothing . . .'

'I'd like to go.'

A rover scurries from the end of the long line of parked vehicles, circles the two women and comes to a halt.

'Where's the door?' Alexia asks. The rover is a rugged frame of construction bars, batteries and comms slung like a spider between massive wheels.

'No doors on the VSV260,' Irina says. 'You get on, not in.' She shows Alexia how to hook her suit up to the life-support. Alexia utters a small yip of surprise as the safety bars drop over her shoulders and lock.

'I'd say hold on, but there really isn't anything to hold on to,' says Irina in the left-hand seat. Alexia grips the sides of her seat. The rover takes off like a fun park ride. Alexia has not known such a lift since the SSTO launch from Manaus. The regolith blurs; far far too close to her feet.

'This is fucking immense!' she shouts. 'How fast are we going?'

'One hundred and twenty,' Irina says. 'We can go faster if you want.'

'I want.'

Irina pushes the rover to one hundred and fifty. The terrain is rough, littered with rocks and billion-year-old ejecta, the wheels jolt and bounce but Alexia rides as smoothly as in a royal carriage. The suspension on this thing is incredible. It must be predictive. The rover hits a ridge, flies, flies the way only cars in action movies can fly.

The moon, the moon, she is in a fast car racing on the moon.

'Old Crucible is about an hour west,' Irina says. 'Your suit has a wide selection of entertainment offerings, so sit back and relax.'

'I'd rather talk,' Alexia says. She's seen standard-package telenovelas.

Irina is a garrulous talker. In a dozen kilometres Alexia learns about her Twé mother and St Olga father and her place in the complex amory designed to link Asamoahs, Vorontsovs, Suns and Mackenzies in a dynastic knot of relatives and potential hostages.

'No Cortas,' Alexia says.

'You people were always weird,' Irina says. 'Those surrogate mothers. Brrr.'

Irina nudges the speed up again and talks about her colloquium: Blue Lotus; a study group of biosphere designers based for the past twenty years in St Olga.

'What I'm working on, ultimately, is terraforming the moon.'

Alexia has heard of terraforming from some sci-fi show or other: turning another planet into an earth, bringing life to the lifeless.

'The moon?'

'Why not? Everyone thinks, oh, the moon: too small, not enough gravity, rotation locked, no magnetic field. We can fix all this. It's just engineering. So, I'm guessing the Vorontsovs told you their big idea, space elevators and everything. Well, the Vorontsovs aren't the only ones with the big idea. We Asamoahs have one too. We bring life. Wherever people go in the system, whatever worlds we settle or habitats we build. We bring life. And we can bring life to the moon. It's easy. Forty big fat comets. Bang bang bang.'

'You can't hit the moon with forty comets, I mean . . .'

'You break them up first. Of course.'

'AKA is still rebuilding Maskelyne G.' Alexia had been two weeks into launch training in Manaus when VTO took out the power plant in a pin-point attack with a high-velocity ice impacter. And where, Irina Efua Asamoah, did you sit in the Vorontsov-Asamoah war? Or did you keep your head down and hide?

'That just proves my point. See? If you can hit a target that small from two hundred kay, you can as easily hit empty space. We mightn't even need to evacuate Meridian. But that's the small stuff. The big stuff is that after the hard rain, we've got an atmosphere and a functioning climate. And we all go up on to the surface and wait for the soft rain.'

Alexia remembers the rain on the moon, fat drops falling slow through Meridian's chasms, spanning the canyons with rainbow bridges. Remembers Denny Mackenzie, soaked to the bone.

'Do you know what's exciting? What is really exciting? Regolith plus rain, equals?'

'I don't know,' Alexia says.

'Mud! Mud. Glorious mud! That's my area of study. I am a lunar pedologist. A mud-ologist. I take mud, I turn it into soil. I make it come to life. The soft rain is about three years, the mud age is twenty years. But after that, after that, then we start greening. Mud is magic, sister. Never forget that.

'Let me show you my moon. Where we are right now; you'll be under twenty metres of water. We'll have oceans, we'll have seas and lakes. We have mountains and glaciers at the poles. We have a biosphere. There'll be forests of trees a kilometre tall; there's be savannahs filled with animals – such animals. Maybe we'll bring back terrestrial animals, maybe we'll design our own new species. Herbivore megafauna the size of that smelter. Birds with hundred-metre wingspans. It'll be a garden. And we'll live among it all in beautiful, organic cities that are like part of nature. We won't need the surface to grow food. What we're doing right now is much more efficient than terrain-based agriculture. And we'll have a proper day and night. All those impacts, transfer of momentum, it'll start the moon turning again. We reckon about a sixty-hour day. Imagine standing watching the Earth rise above the clouds. Just imagine it!

'Okay, it'll last maybe a hundred thousand years, but that's long enough for us to come up with a more permanent solution. Maybe we'll end up dismantling the moon and rebuilding it into something bigger. Other colloquiums are working on that. We could take the moon apart and spin it out to five times the total surface area of

Earth. That's before we get to the rest of the system. More life. That's our big idea. What's yours?'

'What do you mean?'

'Everyone's got a big idea, Mão. What's yours?'

'I don't know. Do I have to have one?'

'We bring life. The Vorontsovs hold the keys to the system. Ask any Sun and they'll tell all about their post-scarcity communism. The Mackenzies have something they're not talking about. But they have something. And it will be big. So what do the Cortas believe in?'

Alexia sees Lucas, cane in hand, on the floor of the council chamber. Terrestrials to his right, Vorontsovs to his left. She knows his cane conceals a blade. What is power, that a weapon is his constant companion? *Come to the moon with me,* he had said in the car on the drive back from the beach at Tijuca. *Help me take back what the Mackenzies and Suns stole from me.* Lucas stole power, but that power is powerless. Every use of that power takes empire and family further away. The grind of politics is wearing him dull. The hidden sword no longer cuts. What does the last Corta want, what does he believe in?

At the centre of a maze of vehicle tracks, a shattered escape pod lies capsized on smashed axles, half the roof gone. Alexia cannot but see a smashed skull. The edges of the fracture are fringed with long teardrops of molten metal, the interior is a mess of fused hydrocarbons, glass fibres and titanium-splash. The regolith is spattered with metal spangles where the steel rain from the detonating smelters impacted and solidified. Irina stops the rover to pick and present one to Alexia; a tiny crown, for the coronation of a thumb. The closer the rover draws to the heart of the disaster, the larger the star-splashes. They merge with the debris field, ever-larger fragments, shards, chunks of Ironfall. Shattered incomprehensible machinery for the most part, occasionally a piece with a recognisable human purpose.

The rover picks its way into the great devastation. VTO track queens cleared Equatorial One as quickly as possible, lifting and laying the wreckage on both sides of the line. Gantries canted at crazy angles. Upended bogies the height of the rover; the belly of a retort, mouth open, congealed metals lapping in a frozen tongue. A half mirror propped up against a melted habitation unit, focusing sunlight on a slagged patch of regolith.

Irina pauses the rover at an arc of black glass sweeping across the regolith. A hastily dumped traction motor has smashed one end to obsidian splinters. Alexia sees herself reflected in the black mirror; herself as she is, an armoured hulk, not the pleasing illusion of her familiar.

'When the mirrors fell, they fused these glass paths into the regolith,' Irina says. 'We call them the Dead Roads. Walk on them and you can see your hopes, your true future and your death.'

Catastrophes breed jokes first, then myths. Later come the conspiracies.

Irina drives deeper into the labyrinth. Entire smelter cars have been moved and dumped here, piled on end, propped against each other.

You did this, Alexia Corta. You spoke one word, and the molten sky fell.

The rover stops.

'We're not alone,' Irina says. Figures appear on Alexia's HUD, visible through the tumbled wreckage.

'I can't see any tags,' Alexia says.

'They're not wearing tags,' Irina says. 'We may need to leave. Scavengers come out here to loot the precious metal spills. The zabbaleen take money to turn a blind eye, the Vorontsovs disapprove, but to the Mackenzies they're grave robbers. So they tend to be well armed.'

'Happy to go. I've seen enough.'

A chatter of machine talk on Alexia's display, flickers of data.

'We're being security scanned,' Irina says. 'High level.'

Names resolve over the images as physical figures appear from behind the steel behemoths. Alexia recognises the colour of the suits before the names: the green and silver of Mackenzie Metals. Three sasuits, two shell-suits: one name she cannot mistake: Duncan Mackenzie.

You're being hailed, Maninho says.

'I am Vassos Palaeologos,' says the other shell-suit. 'You are not welcome here, Mão de Ferro.'

'I needed to see,' Alexia begins.

'And what do you see, Iron Hand?' Duncan Mackenzie breaks in on the channel. Alexia orders the rover to set her down. She drops softly to the regolith. The surface is a litter of micro-debris, parts and pieces ground ever finer by salvage machines. 'I'll tell you what I see, Alexia Corta. I see my home, the place I grew up. There was nothing like it; the greatest feat of engineering in the two worlds. We were the children of eternal sunlight. I see my family. When the mirrors turned on us, they touched a thousand degrees. I like to think it was quick, a flash of heat, nothing. One hundred and eighty-eight deaths.'

'I'm—'

'What can you say to me? You're from Earth.'

'I'm—'

'My enemy in name? It's not our way to blame the innocent. You are safe here. You won't be harmed. Do you know what they say about the Mackenzies?'

'You pay back three times.'

'At some point, all debts have to be cancelled. Written off. Reduce it all to zeros. We cannot go on, tit for tat, feud for feud, blood for blood. What are we going to do: rip the moon in half to get at each other? We have a bigger enemy. Tell that to Lucas Corta when you get back to Meridian. Tell him he needs to decide. Who he stands with. Tell him that. And remember what you've seen. Fucking Iron Hand.'

The Mackenzie party turns as one and disappears into the ruins of Crucible.

Duncan Mackenzie turns.

'You never come back here. Any of you.'

Alexia stands shaking in her shell-suit, unable to move, unable to issue a command to move. She is going to vomit. She must vomit. She must spew out all the horror and guilt and cowardice: that she could not tell Duncan Mackenzie the truth that she was the hand behind Ironfall.

Your biosigns are all over the charts, Maninho says. *Administering anti-nauseas and tranquillisers.*

No, Alexia shouts silently. Warm benevolence spreads through her brain. The storms subside. She should rage at the medical violation but under it she cannot summon the strength even for outrage. Now she is in her seat, now the safety bars are descending. Now the rover is threading back through the steel labyrinth, leaving dusty tyre tracks on the obsidian tracks, the roads of the dead.

TWELVE

A shadow across her window where no shadow has ever fallen wakes Ocean Paz Calzaghe. Shadow, and engine, men's voices. She squints out. A delivery truck. Delivering. She pulls on clothes and is out on the steps to see Kessie directing two laden dray bots and an engineer around the veranda to its south-west corner.

'Bremerton Spa Pools,' she read from the side. 'Are we getting a Jacuzzi?'

'Marina is getting a Jacuzzi,' Kessie says.

By noon even Skyler has been roused from jet lag by the sound of power-tool assembly.

'What does she need with a spa pool?' he asks.

'The therapists say water's good for her. Gives support.'

'Can I have a go when you're not using it?' Ocean asks.

'Everyone's welcome,' Marina says.

'Wait wait wait, house rules,' Kessie says. 'Swimwear in the spa. No exceptions.'

The engineer runs a pipe to the outside faucet. The spa takes two hours to fill, two more hours to come up to blood temperature. Then he corrals his bots into the van and drives them back to Bremerton. The wooden tub sits on the wooden veranda, smelling of chlorine and fresh cedar. Ocean watches Marina jog and splash up and down in the warm water. Ocean hangs over the edge of the pool while Marina works her upper body with weights.

'You'll get wrinkly in there.'

'I get wrinkly on this planet. Gravity is shit for skin tone. I had a complexion like yours.'

'So, good for boobs too?'

'Less sag, but the laws of angular momentum apply. You try running, you even turn too fast, and you remember the difference between mass and weight pretty quick. A girl needs all the support she can get.'

That evening, Ocean joins Marina in the pool. She climbs in, body-conscious, body-awkward in her swimsuit. They bask among the bubbles. Memory shakes Marina: a pool deep beneath crater Macrobius, just big enough for two and the dragon on the roof, the old dragon of the East Sea. Death-tired after the Sea of Serpents adventure, water warm as blood swaddling her. Carlinhos sliding in beside her.

'You all right, Marina?'

She must be more circumspect with her emotions. More lunar. The girl will wheedle, so she'll have to talk about Carlinhos.

'Just remembering someone. A man.'

'Oh!' says Ocean, anticipating sex and secrets.

'It doesn't have a happy ending. He was a beautiful, beautiful man. There was violence in every bone of his body. He was Corta Hélio's zashitnik.'

'That's like kind of a gladiator?'

'What he couldn't deal with was that he loved it. It was the opposite of everything he wanted to be, and he could never get away from it.'

Marina sees him, magnificent, blazing, in the arena of the Court of Clavius, barefoot on the stained boards, kicking a spray of his enemy's blood in Jade Mackenzie's face.

'He died, sweetie. He strapped on his battle armour and took a knife in each hand and walked out alone to face his enemies. I think he knew he wouldn't come out of it. He couldn't live with what he saw that day in the court.'

'Marina, did you, ever . . .'

'Kill anyone? No. I don't think so. I hurt people. A lot. I was strong, you see. Like a superhero. Until I wasn't, and that was when I knew I had to come back. I was scared every second I was there, and I have never felt more alive. People – Earth people – they're asleep all the time. Just going through things. Up there you're always aware that a thousand things keep you alive. You take nothing for granted. Can you understand that?'

'I'm trying to. Marina . . .'

'Shh.' Marina's touches Ocean's arm but the girl already sees them. Elk move in steps and stops, stares and stands, past the veranda: two, three, then two more.

'It's been a good year for them,' Ocean says, when they can speak again. 'A weird year.'

Light on the water: while Marina's attention was held by the elk, the moon trapped her. It stands two-thirds full over the Hurricane Hill.

'Ole Kū Kahi. Maybe Ole Kū Lua.'

'What's that?'

'Days on the moon. We use the Hawaiian calendar. A name for each day of the month. Or lune, as we call it. A lune is not the same as the Earth month; our year is ten days shorter than the terrestrial year.'

'Marina,' Ocean says. 'You say, we, our.'

'I did, didn't I?' Marina says. 'Can you take the wrinkles? If you can, I'll show you my moon. Blades and dragons and wolves, oh my.'

THIRTEEN

The neural link grafted by the surgeons of Rozhdestvenskiy is small and clever but it is still a prosthesis. A subtle trap to which Ariel is alert: never forget that you have a disability. Never forget that your spinal column is severed and that you are paraplegic. But it is extraordinary technology. She can dance with this new graft. Ariel allows herself a pirouette in front of the window screen, with its dramatic view out over the jewelled bowl of Coriolis. It's still a hostage cage, but a classy one.

Abena Maanu Asamoah, Beija Flor announces. Ariel orders tea and sips it while she watches the cable car spin up from the station. Abena is smart and assured as ever, fashionable in tank-fur stole and pillbox hat with short veil but even she can't conceal the depredations of train travel from one side of the moon to the other.

'I don't see why we couldn't have done this all over the network,' Abena says as she copies her progress report to Ariel. The girl is good. Too good to waste her talents in politics.

'So I know who to send Dakota after if there's a breach in discretion,' Ariel says.

'You look weird walking,' Abena says.

'It feels like someone else's legs. Now, the preliminary hearing. I want you to conduct it.'

And the girl has admirable control. Her eyes widen a fraction.

'You're the lawyer, you conduct the plea.'

'Nearside, I have issues. I'm not the niece of the Omahene.'

'And I'm not the lawyer.'

'Not a problem, sweetie. Well, it will be a problem but you'll find a way around it.'

'Use one of the other consultants.'

'No. They're not invested.'

'You mean, they haven't fucked him.'

Talent, control and a bracing self-awareness.

'And just you.'

'What?'

'Just you. No one else.'

'That's . . .'

'Theatrical. Of course. One woman, one voice, before the Court of Clavius, ringed around by a thousand powerful enemies? Our dominant metaphor of the court is gladiatorial. The arena. No no, coraçao. The court is theatre. It's a stage. Law is not combat. Law is persuasion. Always has been. It's better than any telenovela. The network ratings will be through the sunline.' Ariel sees Abena work through a silent sequence of *I can't, completely unreasonable, you're joking/insane/impossible*. 'Something you wanted to say?'

'Yes. Fuck you, Ariel Corta.'

'Yes yes. You will not be alone. You will always have full AI support, the team is behind you and you'll have me in your ear. You think I'd let you go into the Court of Clavius bare-tit naked? Now, you will need a zashitnik.'

'Settling disputes by combat is barbaric, outmoded and demeaning to the law.'

'Of course it is, but if I were Lucas, I'd throw out a challenge just to watch you strip down to bra and pants and stick a knife into your hair. You okay with that?'

'It demeans everyone and everything. We are not savages.'

'My brother was Corta Hélio's zashitnik. Carlinhos was the sweetest, gentlest, most handsome and caring man I ever knew and I watched him tear out Hadley Mackenzie's throat in the Court of Clavius. It could as easily have been him lying on the boards in his own blood. Our law has a price and it's that it can cut anyone who touches it. Law that has no price has no justice. Carlinhos understood that. Hire a zashitnik. I used to use Ishola Oluwafemi. Then we'll work on your court-face. And while you're here, go and talk to Lucasinho. He can talk now. Tell him stories. He likes stories. Tell him about you and him.'

Abena pauses at the door.

'Getting maternal, Ariel?'

'Go and meet your client.'

'I make this?'

Luna nods *yes yes* and slides another piece of cake on to the spoon.

'I can... feed. Myself,' Lucasinho Corta says. He takes the spoon and guides it to his lips. Luna watches anxiously. At the last moment he loses visual tracking, his hand wobbles; Luna darts to the rescue and catches the falling cake on a paper towel. 'Sorry.'

Every day she comes to see him when Dr Gebreselassie has locked in whatever she puts into Lucasinho's head and every day his reactions are sharper, his face brighter, his speech clearer but she soon discovers the holes in his mind; moments, days, entire narratives that are bright and clear to her and don't exist for him.

Don't push him to remember, Dr Gebreselassie instructs her. *You can't make him remember what isn't there. Do talk to him about what he does remember. Social reminiscence is important.*

Today she had perched herself on the end of his bed and talked about cake. At first he barely understood what she was talking about, then the memories returned and the protein chips made connections between the disjointed memories and they came alive in his head. She told him how it had started when he declared he wasn't going to have any more mooncake at Zhongqiu because no one liked it; he was going to make cupcakes instead. It took him three days, and they were oversweet and overflavoured but they weren't mooncakes. Everyone applauded, so, encouraged, he went on to bake for saint-days and festivals and birthdays and any colloquium occasion and in time he got good at it. As Luna told him the cake story his eyes brightened. He remembered this, and then Luna took him back to the Sea of Tranquillity, when they were escaping on the appropriated rover and he tried to pass the time by lecturing her about cake. How it was the perfect gift, how difficult it was to make, what the rules of cake were. On and on over rille and crater, until they ran into the Mackenezie Metals party. Here his face darkened. He shook his head. A hole in his mind between cake and waking in the Coriolis med centre.

It took time even for the moon's foremost facility in printing organic materials to synthesise a lemon drizzle cake. Lucasinho looked nervous as Luna took a spoonful and moved mother-close to feed it to him. Then ecstasy flooded his face.

'More please.'

This time he lets Luna lay her hand on his hand as he navigates the spoon.

'I made this!'

'You used to have a special way of doing it.'

Lucasinho frowns, puzzled. His memory is a moonscape of craters and chasms.

'You'll remember when you're ready,' Luna says.

Their familiars announce the visitor simultaneously. Lucasinho's eyes widen.

'Abena!'

Luna scowls behind her Lady Luna mask. This is her time. Her space. Her primo. She positions herself at the foot of Lucasinho's bed, a strong defensive site. Faces up her best glare. Abena Asamoah doesn't even blink.

'Luna. Lucasinho.'

Lucasinho struggles upright. Luna can't have that. He could tear something, pull something, break something. She falls back, still between Abena and Lucasinho.

'Why are you here?'

'I've come to see my client.'

Luna flares her nostrils, tightens a frown.

'I'm your client.'

A hit. Have that, clever clever Asamoah. I know about you and Lucasinho but that's all old and gone and most of you is holes in his memory.

'I still need to speak with . . .'

'If I'm your client, then I can tell you to go away,' Luna says.

The moment it is said, Luna knows her words to be a hollow threat. Abena knows it too.

'I won't do that, Luna.'

'All right. But you stay down there and I stay up here.'

Abena Asamoah ponders for a moment and positions herself at the foot of the bed.

'Abena,' Lucasinho says. Now Abena Asamoah is rocked.

'I didn't know you were speaking yet.'

'He's been speaking for days now. We talk a lot,' Luna says. 'Don't we, Lucasinho?'

'A lot,' Lucasinho says.

Does Luna see tears in Abena's eyes?

Abena sniffs, takes a small tissue from her handbag.

'You look . . . great, Lucasinho.'

'Look like shit,' Lucasinho says. 'You look. Great. Good hat.' Again tears.

'Make this quick,' Luna says. 'You're not to upset him or confuse him or say too many difficult things. Dr Gebreselassie is very strict on that.' But it is Abena who is upset by taking in too many difficult things.

'Okay. Lucasinho, I don't know if Luna has explained this to you, but there's a big fight about you.'

Lucasinho gives a small cry, his eyes go wide.

'What did I say?'

Luna hisses, which is a thing she heard from her mother.

'Lucasinho knows about the case. Say case, not fight.'

'Pãe and Mãe,' Lucasinho says. 'And Tia Ariel.'

'Okay,' Abena says. 'I'm working with Ariel, and what we think is best is for you to be left right alone until you are better. So we're fight . . . working to keep you here, until you're well enough to make your own mind up. What we want to do is give Luna here your duty-of-care contract. She's saved you once already, so there is an existing informal contract. Do you understand that?'

Lucasinho nods. Luna has explained this to him time and again but there are so many memories fighting for space in his new brain that recent events are often crowded out. He's often said the same thing to her three or four times. Grandmother Adriana was like that in her old old days. Luna can see the confusion in his eyes.

'You just get better,' Luna says. She sees hesitation on Abena's face. 'What is it?'

'I will need you to do something, Luca . . .'

'That's not his name,' Luna interrupts.

'Luca,' Lucasinho murmurs from the bed.

'He's getting tired,' Luna says. 'You need to go.'

'I need to say what I have to say,' Abena says. 'I'm going to court. It's nothing to worry about – it's just a preliminary hearing, where we decide what's best for you while we're waiting for the big case.'

'Best here,' Lucasinho says.

'We think so too. And I'm going to make sure you stay here. Your Tia Ariel has a plan. But we need you to help us with it.'

'You didn't tell me,' Luna says fiercely. 'I'm the client. I should know these things.'

Abena sighs.

'Okay, Luna, we need Lucasinho's help.'

'Will it work?'

'It's an Ariel Corta plan.'

'Okay. Now ask Lucasinho.'

'Luca, we need you to do something for us.'

Luna lets the nickname go but her suspicions are roused.

'Do what?'

'Something fun,' Abena Asamoah says. Lucasinho beams with delight but Luna scowls.

'Do what?' she asks again.

'Just do a network video link with me,' Abena says.

'Is it safe?' Luna asks.

'It's safe,' Abena says. 'It's the safest thing in all the world.'

'Luca, I think you should do this,' Luna declares.

Abena breathes deep with relief.

'Thank you. Is that lemon cake?'

Lucasinho nods.

'Could I have a piece?'

'Yes,' Lucasinho says to Luna's furious face. 'Of. Course.'

Meridian has a bar for everyone. The glassers have the Peace Jazz Bar; the VTO track-queens have Red Dynamo while their VTO Space counterparts sip their vodka martinis in the Vostok Lounge. Mackenzie Helium workers shake the moondust from their feet in the Coogee while Mackenzie Metal jackaroos bang glasses in the Hammer in the next quadra. Premier League handball stars sport in the D, Liga de Luna in the Saint Mary, and the owners brag and talk deals on the terraces of the Professional Club. Coders and software engineers rave at Index, medics at Slaughter. There are bars for BALTRAN dispatchers, rail supervisors, actors, comedians, singers, musicians and two hundred kinds of student. The politicos drink and argue in a suite of bespoke clubs along 32nd Street, a bar for each political complexion; the lawyers carp and bitch in the Clube de Argumentos. Directly across the Quadra – same street, same number – the judges of the Court of Clavius squander their fees on the bench's terrible gin. The Flashing Blade is the zashitniks' bar.

In Abena Asamoah's imagination the Flashing Blade is rambunctious, piratical, low stone eaves and a tag carved on every lintel, a place of feuds and vendettas, quick tempers and long-held grudges ended on the edge of a knife. Thudding hip-hop metal, Valhalla lyrics to the beat of glasses on table. Songs to honoured blades.

The Flashing Blade disappoints sorely. Abena stands before a suite of standard accommodation units dug into the raw stone of Level Fifty-Three East. Glass and titanium. She had hoped to turn heads as she walked in. No one gives her a second glance in her wasp-waist suit, faux-fox stole and fantastic hat.

The clientele is a further disappointment. She had expected big men and lean, mean women; studs and tattoos, piercings and shaved heads shining in the soft light. Mohicans. Scars and missing digits. Ripped T-shirts, sleeveless hoodies, mish-mashes from all of the moon's many fashion fads. Real leather. Killer footwear. Big men and lean mean women there are, and the Jo Moonbeams are easy to spot – hired for their terrestrial muscle – but the zashitniks of the Court of Clavius are as diverse in shape, age, gender and style as the regulars of any Meridian club. The music is well-curated M-pop, inoffensive but toe-tapping. The drink is martini, in elegant, dewed glasses. The talk in the alcoves, at the tables, along the bar, is not of battles and blood, honour won and enemies crushed in the arena, but of cases current, historical, remarkable; legal precedents, arguments and clever plays, the characters and foibles of judges, lawyers, plaintiffs and defendants: courtroom gossip and scandal. These zashitniks have seen more court-time than many of the counsels who retain them; more even than the judges. Abena cannot see a single knife, not even the unmistakable contour of a sheath beneath a blouse. Most of the customers of the Flashing Blade have never drawn a blade for the law.

Tumi, her familiar, has already identified the man she seeks, but Abena goes to the bar to take the longer, appraising look. Ishola Oluwafemi: Ariel's long-time zashitnik. A broad, bullet-headed Yoruba man, smiling, happy among his colleagues. He laughs like running water. A kind man, devoted father, ferocious fighter, Ariel says. Abena doesn't see that. It is two years since Ishola Oluwafemi last unsheathed a blade in court.

He's a big man, Abena says to Tumi.

But he's in bad shape, Tumi says.

Ishola Oluwafemi has gone soft in lunar gravity, laughing with his friends on too many nights in the Flashing Blade. Abena goes to his table.

'I wish to contract a zashitnik.'

'Go through my agent,' Ishola says.

'I represent Ariel Corta,' Abena says.

'I know Ariel Corta,' Ishola says. 'If Ariel Corta wants me, she comes to me; not the practice intern.'

Abena reaches across the table, empties Ishola's half-empty glass and turns it upside down. Ishola is on his feet. The Flashing Blade is as silent and still as the cold heart of the moon. Everyone knows the message of the upturned glass. Everybody fights.

'I wish to hire a zashitnik for Ariel Corta,' Abena says. 'Whoever beats him gets the job.'

And the Flashing Blade explodes. Figures lunge at Ishola Oluwafemi, the table goes over as Abena darts away. A chair flies past her, she ducks under a fist. The bar room is a scrum of heaving, yelling bodies. Abena keeps low and heads for cover. Tables tumble, drinks avalanche, furniture crashes to pieces and each piece is picked up and wielded as a weapon. A chair leg skims her nose, a flying knife clips a centimetre of feather from her pillbox hat. A boot comes for her face, at the last moment the attacker sees that she is not a player and pirouettes the kick away into the ear of a woman lunging with a blade in each hand. Bodies go down on to a floor of smashed martini glass. Abena makes it to the bar and crouches under the lip, hands over head. The entire population of the moon seems to lie between her and the exit, and they are fists and feet and fighting.

A hand on her shoulder. Abena whirls, handbag raised as a weapon to strike. She looks into the face of a skinny Hispanic woman in Rosie the Riveter blue and a red polka-dot headscarf. Her familiar wears the white and blue circles of the university.

'Come with,' she yells in a strong Farside accent. 'I'll get you safe.'

Abena takes the offered hand. The woman's grip is strong and she leads sure, drawing Abena through the rhythm of the battle in the bar, slipping through the gaps that open between combatants, pausing while a man cartwheels through the air, giving a sharp, shoulder-wrenching tug to pull Abena out of the path of a swinging chair. The woman glances back at Abena, grinning. Unsighted, a fighter roundhouses a chunk of table at her head. Before Abena's warning can leave her lips the woman in blue turns, blocks the move and turns it into a throw that sends the attacker ass over tit into the wall. Only two brawlers remain between the two women and the street but they both see what Riveter Rosie is doing. Knives out, one high, one low. The woman drops Abena's hand, rolls over the low blade, takes the high blade with a swinging boot. The two men reel off-balance, the woman shoves Abena through the gap. Abena stumbles on treacherous heels, fetches up hard against the Fifty-Three East safety rail. Aquarius Quadra yawns before her. The light-spangled void. Again, a hand seizes hers.

'Can you run in those?' The woman nods at Abena's heels. Abena slips them off and throws them into the melee in the Flashing Blade. Add to the chaos.

'I can run now.'

'Run now.'

They stop in the elevator. They slump against the wall, breathing hard.

'Enjoy that?' the woman asks. The car drops down towards

Tereshkova Prospekt. For a moment Abena is taken aback, affronted, then admits the truth she felt the moment she brought the upturned glass down on the table and the whole bar rose.

'I loved it.' Every dangerous, bloody, terrifying, stupid second of it.

'I know you did,' the woman says. 'Rosario Salgado O'Hanlon de Tsiolkovski. Unrepresented.'

'I said, whoever beats him gets the job.'

'I beat him,' the woman says. 'Fighting's not the only way to win.' Tumi checks Rosario's familiar. Abena scans the profile. She was right about Farside. Post doctoral in Lunar telenovelas. Trainee ghazi. That explains the moves.

'Why didn't you complete the training?' Abena asks.

'I had a crisis of intellect,' Rosario says.

'Soap opera,' Abena says with audible contempt.

'You watch telenovelas?'

'No.'

'Then you can't talk,' Rosario says with contained ferocity. 'This is my fall from faith. You don't get to explain it to me. I walked into a meeting with my mentor and I saw comets. Clouds of comets, distant and cold and dead, out there in nothing. Theory after theory after theory, all of them as fictive as telenovelas. Metafictions, derivatives. Of the profusion of theories there is no end. I thanked him and walked out.'

'And went for hire as a zashitnik.' Again, Tumi probes Rosario's résumé. 'No fights, I see.'

'No lost cases either. Contract to my familiar, please.'

Abena observes her new hiring as the elevator descends. This Rosario is knots and hawsers, sinewy and swift. Her talk is sharp but in a true fight, one she could not slide away from, how deep could she cut? What would Ariel Corta think? She would admire the braggadocio, the confidence, the shadow of failure and exile. What does Abena Maanu Asamoah think? She thinks the same. She thinks more. She loves the risk, the danger, the sense of worlds balanced on a knife blade, embodied in this small woman. Among her colloquium mates in Cabochon, she had railed against the barbarism of lunar law. Any social contract must have a civil and criminal code. In private thoughts she admired its intimacy. Justice should touch, justice should cost; justice, like a knife, should cut all who misuse it. Once – another Abena, she sometimes thinks – she had given Lucasinho Corta the gift of the sanctuary of the Asamoahs, and when he drew blood pushing the stud through his ear, she had licked and tasted it. This Abena had started the fight in the bar to prove a point to Ishola Oluwafemi, yes; to show that she was a player, yes; but most of all because she could. Because it was exciting. As the fists struck, the blades glittered, as the bodies went down and the glasses smashed, she was more aroused than she had ever been before. There are not two Abena Maanu Asamoahs. There is one, and she cannot wait to step out into the arena of the Court of Clavius.

Don't let her seduce you, her friends from the Cabochon colloquium said when she took the placement as Ariel's amanuensis in the LDC. *She is charming and she is clever and she will turn you into something you don't even recognise.*

It's much worse than that, Abena would say to them. *She's turning me into her.*

The moto unfolds. Abena Maanu Asamoah takes a deep breath and steps out into Court Plaza. And the cameras swoop. The reporters surge. Voices clamour. Abena Maanu Asamoah throws her fur around her shoulders and strides towards the doors of the Court of Clavius. Her heels ring on the polished sinter. Little shots.

The trial begins the moment you uncross your legs in the moto, Ariel had said. At five a.m. her colloquium mates began the dressing. At six a.m. the hair team arrived with their scaffolding and machinery. At seven a.m. the cosmetics took over and started work on her court-face. At nine she ate some fruit – small berries, nothing bloating or staining to her perfect teeth. Nine fifteen she made her final conference call with Ariel on Farside.

I've seen worse benches, Ariel said. *Valentina Arce makes her mind up in the first ten minutes, so get your hits in early. Kweko Kumah will want the whole thing over by lunch. He's an outrageous handball fanatic. Spends every afternoon arguing on fan sites. Mano de Dios is his fan name. Rieko Nagai I know of old. She inducted me into the Pavilion of the White Hare. She's still a member. Advises my brother. Bias isn't a legal problem if its compensated for: prejudice is. She'll hear you straight. Rieko and Valentina never agree on anything. Kweko knows that so don't stick your tongue up his ass. Not publicly. And have fun.*

At ten her zashitnik arrives. Rosario is trim and professional in her uniform of riveter's coveralls and headscarf. She follows close on Abena's shoulder as they mount the steps. Reporters and gossip curators shout questions.

'Madam Asamoah . . .'

'High profile case . . .'

'Youth and inexperience . . .'

'I've just caught and neutralised five drones targeting you in the camera swarm,' Rosario whispers. 'Might be nothing, might be assassins. Better safe. Thought you should know.'

Abena touches fingers to the back of her neck, the traditional Twé charm: brushing away the killing spider. Anansi's dark sisters. She can't breathe. She can't make the next step. Rosario touches her elbow and strength flows.

'Keep walking, keep smiling,' Rosario says. 'And don't worry. If they beat my electronic defences, I've antidotes to the top fifty assassination toxins.'

Abena thinks this may be zashitnik humour. But it lifts her.

'Suns and Cortas . . .'

'Inexperience . . .'

'Youth.'

'Inexperience.'

Number Two Court is one of the oldest – Abena expected no less of the Suns. Intimate and intimidating, it is a hemi-cylinder of sleekly polished rock, the stone bench facing tiers of galleries rising five levels. Boxes and arcades, pillars and pews. This is court as opera. On this stage, law is as close as a kiss. Abena takes her place in the assigned box, Rosario beneath her in the zashitnik's pit. Lucas's team is in position, three tiers of lawyers. Lucas's Head of Legal Services, Viego Quiroga, nods over to her. Abena has done due diligence on him, as he has on her. Their zashitnik is a mountain of Russian, Konstantin Pavlyuchenko. He could punch through solid rock.

I can take him, Rosario says. *Big men are full of doubt.*

The Sun delegation has not arrived yet. They will make their entrance at the last minute. Amanda Sun is conducting her own case. She will put on quite a show. *Amanda will have singing attorneys and dancing advocates, counsellors pulling pretty flowers out of their asses: the whole telenovela,* Ariel said. *You're one woman, alone, speaking the truth. That's more than enough.*

Messages: friends, family, colloquium-mates have found seats in the tiers above her. *Where are you? We can't see you.*

You'll see me.

Ariel, Maninho announces.

'Final pre-flight checks, darling. Do you need to go to the washroom? Don't. Rhetoric works better with a full bladder. Gives it a sense of urgency. Now, I know you haven't taken anything, but if you've brought some little upper or focuser or concentrator or soother or relaxer, don't take it. In fact, get rid of it. Kweko despises pharmacological enhancement. Which is ironic for a handball fan. He stuffs his courtroom with sniffers so don't chem. Couple of final dos. If it gets away from you, do move for an adjournment. Do go off-script. Malandragem, the fly move, is the heart of the Court of Clavius. But you must use it well. Bad malandragem is no malandragem. Do keep me on. Better safe than sorry.'

The Suns arrive. They are elegant and aristocratic and immaculate. Abena has memorised the names and the faces. Amanda Sun takes the counsel box. She catches Abena's stare and returns it with frozen disdain. House Sun has always looked down on House Asamoah. The company from the Palace of Eternal Light fills the galleries. There is Lady Sun, leaning on a stick. Who is that young man helping her into the box behind Amanda and her advisers?

Darius Mackenzie-Sun, Tumi says. *His mother was Jade Sun. He is the last child of Robert Mackenzie. After Ironfall he was taken back to the Palace of Eternal Light where he has become the protégé of the Dowager of Shackleton. He is studying at the School of Seven Bells under the personal tutelage of Mariano Gabriel Demaria.*

Adopting the inheritor, Abena muses as Tumi prepares a full briefing on Darius Sun. A mistake to work the same trick twice.

She watches Lady Sun take a tiny sip from an exquisite porcelain flask. The finest, hardest porcelain is made with bone ash. On the moon, those bones are human.

The usher calls, the courtroom rises. The bench zashitniks enter first, for everything is on trial in the Court of Clavius, including the judges. They take their places in the fighting pit. Now come the judges, their white gowns brilliant in the harsh light of the court-arena. Valentina Arce calls the court to order, Kweko Kumah lists the actors, their biases and the agreed legal framework, Rieko Nagai reads out the case. And the hearing is on.

Viego Quiroga buries Number Two Court in medical detail and appeals to fatherhood, to family, to healing and unity. Lucas Corta appears in a pre-recorded statement that all he wants is his son, with him, where he could be, being cared for by his loving father. Abena notes, the judges note, all of the public and the reporters and gossip-mongers note, that Lucas Corta is not present before the Court of Clavius to make this profession of paternal love.

Now Amanda Sun steps down on to the D of polished moonstone.

Murmurs scurry around the galleries. She gives each judge a long look.

The bench zashitniks stir, down in their trench.

'Our law is good law because it forbids prejudices while recognising biases. I am biased. How can I not be biased? I am a mother. I want my son with me. That's all.'

She goes on to paint Lucas as a bad father; an absent father; a reckless father and worst, a dangerous father. What kind of place is the Eagle's Eyrie for a child, with blades concealed in every hand, assassin drones in every half-glimpsed, darting movement?

A father you tried to kill, Abena thinks. A glance to the bench tells her the judges are keenly aware of that, and to the rumour that the Suns engineered the war between Cortas and Mackenzies.

'The Palace of Eternal Light is strong and stable, a safe place for my son to heal in the security of his family. Family matters. The university is many things but it is not family. Ariel Corta – who this court knows well – claims to represent Luna Corta's assumed contract of care for Lucasinho Corta. I ask you; when did Ariel Corta ever show any interest in her neice, much less her nephew, until a time when their safety might ensure her own? Who was it turned her back on her family to pursue her own glittering career as a celebrity lawyer? Ariel Corta. When Lucasinho was under the protection of the Asamoahs, where was Ariel Corta? The interests she has only ever truly represented are her own. Look at the public interest in this hearing – a preliminary hearing. Ariel Corta thinks she's clever to remove herself from scrutiny by making her niece Luna Corta the guardian but surely the court is not deceived by such transparent scheming. Ariel Corta intends to use her own nephew as a ladder to climb her way back to the top of the social hierarchy.

'Family first. That's the rule. But let's look at this family. An absent father and a status-hungry aunt. We Suns understand family. We are old, we are strong and we are together. We know the truth, that, in the beginning and the end, there is only families and individuals. Family first, of course. The Cortas are not a family. We are.'

Amanda Sun dips her head to the bench and returns to her pew.

'Counsel for Luna Corta?'

Abena gulps. Her stomach tightens. The moment is here and her statements, her arguments, her persuasions have flown from her head.

Call Ariel.

The order to Tumi is on the tip of her tongue. She swallows it. She doesn't need Ariel Corta.

Strike, axe of Xango, give me strength for the battle.

She steps down on to the shining stone.

'I represent counsel for Luna Corta, who claims a continuance on a pre-existing informal contract of care…'

Viego Quiroga and Amanda Sun are on their feet.

'Your Honours, really…'

'Madam Asamoah is not qualified to plead in this court.'

Abena hisses a *thank you* to Xango. Her enemies have fallen into her trap.

Judge Rieko looks at her.

'Madam Asamoah?'

'Ariel Corta is Luna Corta's counsel. I am her agent here on Nearside. For personal security reasons, Ariel chooses to remain on Farside.'

'Senhora Corta could make her representation through a network link,' Kweko Kumah says.

'As you know, Ariel Corta has always preferred the physical over the virtual.'

Rieko Nagai suppresses a smile at the effrontery.

'You are a lawyer?' Valentina Arce asks.

'I am a political science student at Cabochon Colloquium,' Abena says.

'No legal qualifications,' Judge Kumah says.

'None, madam. I believe I don't require any.'

Intakes of breath from all five tiers of Number Two Court. Once again Rieko Nagai smiles.

'Our law stands on three legs,' Abena says. 'In the Court of Clavius everything, including the Court of Clavius, is on trial. Everything, including the law, is negotiable, and furthermore – and my argument – is that more law is bad law. To insist on a legal qualification to plead in this court is establishing a right of audience. That right has not been negotiated; it makes more law, not less, and it hasn't been tried. Until now.'

Rieko Nagai conceals an outright laugh with a sip of water.

'This court will take a short adjournment, after which we will rule on Madam Asamoah's position,' Judge Arce says.

Number Two Court erupts with voices. Abena slips down beside Rosario in the zashitnik pit.

'You all right?' Rosario asks. Abena is shaking. She cannot speak. She nods. 'You're making some enemies,' Rosario continues. 'Contracts have gone out. Just to say. Don't worry, we'll buy them out. Think of it as a professional compliment.'

Camera drones hover in her face. Tumi notifies her of a dozen interview requests, twenty invitations to society events that would never have admitted her, even as the niece of the Golden Stool.

The chatter is silenced as if cut off with a blade. The judges have returned.

'Madam Asamoah.' Valentina Arce beckons her. Abena reads the body language, the hold of the limbs, the set of the faces. She's got this.

'The bench will hear you,' Judge Rieko says. The court murmurs and mutters.

'Malandragem,' Kweko Kumah says. 'Now, we've wasted quite enough time on this. I'd like to get this all wrapped up before lunch.'

'That's not a problem,' Abena says. 'I have only one submission to present.'

Tumi opens the link to Farside and the Court of Clavius network patches it into every familiar in Number Two Court. Murmurs turn to gasps. There in every lens, every eye, is Lucasinho Corta. He sits on the edge of a medical bed, haloed by the outstretched hands of med robots. His chest, his face are sunken, his eyes are distant and lost. His cheekbones are as beautiful as they ever were to Abena Asamoah. He waves.

'Hi,' he says.

A noise between a sigh and a cry runs around the galleries of Number Two Court.

'Hi everyone.' His words are painful, slurred. 'Dad, hi. Love you. Can't come now. Need to get better. Remember better. Work to do. I can walk. Look!' He rises unsteadily from the bed and takes an uncertain step towards the camera. 'Long way to walk. Still. Just to say: Luna saved me once. She's saving me again.'

Abena cuts the link.

'Family is family, but the only consideration is Lucasinho's welfare,' she says. 'Look at what has been achieved. But as Lucasinho said to you, long way to walk. Even if both the Suns and Lucas Corta agreed to keep him on Farside, there is no guarantee that they would continue to do so. Lucasinho has to be beyond politics. For his own well-being, I submit that this court recognises, extends and codifies the existing contract of care that Luna Corta established when she rescued Lucasinho Corta and brought him to Boa Vista.'

She bows to the bench and returns to the seat. The judges look at each other.

'We have a judgement.'

The three advocates stand.

'This court unanimously finds for Luna Corta, represented by Ariel Corta,' Judge Rieko says. 'Madam Asamoah, in chamber?' The bench rises. The judges file from the dais.

Abena has heard that Clavius's behind-court rooms are notoriously poky, but she is surprised at the cubby in which Judge Rieko is deprinting her robes and changing into civilian dress.

'Ariel instructed you well. The personal appearance, that was hers?'

'It was, but I worked the three pillars argument myself,' Abena says. She is electric with excitement. Nothing, not even delivering her paper at the Lunarian Society, not even sex with Lucasinho, makes her glow, makes her breathless, makes her burn like this. She understands it now. She is going to so party tonight. Some boy will get so lucky.

'Well played, but in future, stick to politics.'

And it dies on the floor.

'One Ariel Corta is quite enough.'

Vidhya Rao hates their jokes, their sarcasms, their cruel whimsies. E hates the word games they make er play – exchanges in strict poetic forms, only responding to sentences without the letter 'a' – the roles they make er assume – a 2040s Shanghai refuse collector, an 18th-century porcelain carrier – the worlds they build and force er to inhabit – a blue-and-white Western willow-pattern universe, a virtual reality based on a late 20th-century iteration of *Alice's Adventures in Wonderland*. E hates that they change personalities, memories, whole identities. They are never the same creatures twice. E hates their pettiness, their condescension, their arrogance and other personality traits which have no direct translation in the human emotional lexicon.

Vidhya Rao hates the Three August Sages.

Had e more time and more patience, e could have explored at intellectual leisure the concept of quantum intelligence, how it would differ profoundly from human intelligence, how it might not even be recognisable as intelligence, how that essential quantum nature might manifest as surreal humour. But time on the quantum computer has been policed since Vidhya Rao moved from Whitacre Goddard staff to consultancy. E is beginning to suspect that e is permitted any access at all because e is the only human with which the Three August Sages will communicate.

E is beginning to suspect that Whitacre Goddard has chosen a political faction opposite to ers. But er concern at Wang Yongqing's plans for the Lunar Bourse compels er to quiet favours, debts softly recalled, whispered blackmails.

E enters the codes, sets up the protocols and lets the alien architecture of the quantum operating system interface with er familiar. E sighs. Today the Three August Sages will entertain her as gods in a rendering of a 1950s San Francisco tiki bar. Ukulele music plays, plastic parrots fly and thunder rumbles. The August Ones await.

A twitch, a twinge, a disharmomy, an echo.

There's someone else in the simulation.

Robson Corta glows. Every square centimetre of his skin radiates energy. He can smell himself: sweet, salty, slightly singed. *Your vitamin D levels are low,* Joker said and booked him the light bath at the banya. Robson believes in vitamins the same way he believes in mathematics, something unseen, abstract but useful. What he does know is that after thirty minutes standing naked in the solar chamber, he feels electric. Glowing.

A jump to the top of the door frame, an immediate flip back and turn to grab the truss, swing and he is in the superstructure of Theophilus. He runs fast and low, rolling under construction beams, sliding beneath live power conduits, hurdling gaps and entire intersections, flying above the heads of the Theophilians. He could do this forever.

This must be how Wagner feels when he charges up on the light of the full Earth and turns into the wolf. Anything and everything is bright to his senses, everything and anything falls within his grasp. Body and mind united, beyond consciousness and will. Everything is flow. It's thrilling and terrifying.

Am I turning into a wolf?

I have insufficient information to reach a diagnosis, Joker says. Robson didn't know the thought had strayed into the subvocal range. *However, we should have another talk about puberty.*

'Joker!' Robson hisses. Familiars have no shame.

He wishes Wagner were back. He worries about him out there in the dust. Swift home, Lobinho. He has promised, those times when he touches the network, that he will be back before Analiese leaves on her concert tour. But the moon is the moon and she knows a thousand ways to trip you. Robson is wary still of Analiese – she sublets a room in another apartment to practise the setar, she says: to get away from him, Robson suspects. She might have agreed to the tour to get away from him. But he is uncomfortable being in the apartment all alone. He was alone before, when Wagner was working the glass. When he fled to a city higher than Bairro Alto, where only the machines and the wind went. He had been afraid every second: afraid, alone, cold, hungry but more afraid to go down to the living streets.

Wagner had come to bring him home. Wagner, afraid of heights. He came across half of Nearside, through invasion and space-strike, bot-war and siege. He'll come.

From his high hiding placement Robson watches his colloquium mates gather on the ring and argue about which hotshop to visit today. No chance any of them will suggest El Gato but he waits until they make up their mind and leave. Robson remembers spying unseen on Wagner, at the wolf-meet in Meridian. He hadn't understood the unspoken language between Wagner and the wolf from the Meridian pack. He does now.

Maybe Joker is right. He has been waking up early morning soaked in sweat with his dick hard. And his balls are turning dark and one of them is hanging lower.

Robson shivers, chilled with self-consciousness.

Within a minute he is at El Gato and drops out of the infrastructure to land in front of the door.

Behind the cook-counter, Jianyu bows and applauds.

'What?' Robson Corta says.

Applause also from the diners and drinkers arrayed along the curve of the bar.

'I told ya, I told ya I knew the face,' shouts a young man, a new regular, in a short-sleeved leisure shirt, homburg pushed back on his head.

'Did it hurt?' asks Rigger Jayne, a regular, from her fixed place at the corner of the bar, and suddenly a dozen questions are flying at Robson.

'What what what what what?' Robson asks but he is beginning to form an idea.

'You were the kid who fell from the top of Queen of the South,' Jianyu says.

'I knew the face!' Homburg shouts again. 'I remember it from the social media. You're that Corta, aren't you?'

Silence in El Gato Encantado. Then Robson sees Haider, in the booth, feet still not touching the ground but not kicking this time, nothing about him moving. His face is the colour of sacred ash. Robson strides over to him.

'What have you done? What did you say?'

'It was the story, I couldn't help it.'

'Not here.' Robson storms to the washroom, rounds on Haider. 'What did you do?'

'I'm sorry, I couldn't help it. The man in the hat said he'd heard the kid who fell from the sky lived here and Jianyu said he didn't know and I couldn't help it. I told them the whole story. It's a great story, Robson. You don't know how to tell it right. I was good. You couldn't hear a breath.'

'I so wish you hadn't done that.'

'It'll be all right, won't it?'

'I don't know,' Robson says. 'Man in the hat? Who is he? Is he safe? What if he tells someone else? What if word gets back? What if we have to go?'

'Could that happen?' Haider asks.

'I don't know. Where could we go? Where's safe?'

Robson's anger is fading, damping down to embers. Haider is guilty, ashamed, terrified that his moment of shine, an audience enchanted by his words, has put Robson in danger and burned a friendship.

'I'm sorry,' Haider said.

'It's said now,' Robson says. 'I'll have to tell Analiese. And Wagner.' And look around him, behind him, into every corner, and never feel comfortable in Theophilus's corridors again. It always was a lie, that comfort. An illusion, an effect. No Corta is ever safe. The only shelter on the moon is behind the bodies of people you love.

Haider's face twitches.

'Are you crying?'

'What if I am?'

'That's all right.' Robson punches Haider softly on the shoulder. 'You're all right.'

'I was good. They listened to me. It's what I've got; words.'

'It's the words that do the damage,' Robson Corta says.

FOURTEEN

Somewhere in the grey gloaming is Lucas Corta. Alexia pushes cautiously into the fog. She cannot see her outstretched hand. If she peers into the fog she could trip over an invisible obstacle. If she looks at her feet she could walk straight into a wall or a piece of construction machinery or the river. She could have turned right around and be walking back to the main lock. Noises loom and boom, close, then far, then echoing close again only to veer and re-appear behind her. She hears trickling water and freezes. Air currents stir the murk, weaving subtle shifting bands of grey-scale. A face looms over her, dark on the grey. Perspective clicks in: it is huge and distant. Condensation runs down its stone cheeks like tears. She's lost.

'Fuck it,' she declares. Maninho throws up infra-red images and tags. Lucas is less than ten metres from her. He is in bright humour.

'Isn't it magnificent? We've been slowly raising the temperature for a lune now and suddenly, look! Five kilometres of fog. I might keep it like this all the time. No, it's a stage, a moment. Its wonder is that it's ephemeral. Like music.' Lucas and his environmental engineers are draped in transparent rain-capes. Alexia is saturated and shivering in her St Olga suit. 'You're soaked. Here, Adde.' The cape only amplifies the discomfort, wet and clinging into heavy and chafing. 'Walk with me.'

Lucas delights in pointing out features as they resolve out of the grey: the stone bridge over the river – step carefully – the suddenly seen pillars of a pavilion, the stately glide of a construction bot, the unexpected uprights of a handball net – don't trip. Alexia lets Lucas guide her. It's an uncomfortable blind man's buff. A stone step, slick with condensation, leading to another, to a staircase curving up between rising walls of dewed stone. The steps turn and Alexia arrives in a saucer of stone, billowing fog before her. She is high on the face of one of the orixas: Iansa's stern features soar dark and wet behind her.

'My mother had this mirador constructed when she built Boa Vista,' Lucas says. 'It was supposed to be her secret; the place she could see and not be seen. How many pretty bodies did the Vorontsovs throw at you?'

'Three.'

Lucas smiles.

'I was never a frequent guest at St Olga. Rafa adored it; me, I like solid rock over my head. They like you to think of them as amiable, expansive buffoons.'

'They are not.'

'Which one worked?'

'None.'

'You think. It's quite all right if one did. They are good at this.'

'I'm meeting Irina. As a friend.'

'Of course.'

'I met Duncan Mackenzie, out at Crucible.'

'What was he doing there?'

'Irina wouldn't tell me but I found out he'd also been meeting the Vorontsovs.'

'Interesting.' Lucas rests both hands on the handle of his stick. 'Yevgeny Vorontsov wants my support for the Moonport programme. Mackenzie Metals cancels its order for a new smelter train and instead meets with VTO. Representations and negotiations. Alignments and alliances.'

The fog swirls, the droplets congeal into heavy drops.

'Duncan Mackenzie said that we have a bigger enemy,' Alexia says.

It is raining now; fat heavy drops clattering on the plastic capes. The fog thins into streamers, into wisps, then clears. Alexia stands on Iansa's lower lip looking out over the dripping, sparkling expanse of Boa Vista. The temperature has risen another couple of degrees; she is sweating in her plastic cape.

'So the Vorontsovs are in open rebellion,' Lucas says. 'VTO needs to anchor its space elevators with an asteroid at the L1 point. The terrestrials will never allow that in their sky. I am being forced to choose sides. I don't like that. Not at all.'

The delegation from the Lunar Mandate Authority huddles from the rain under streaming rain-capes. The cuffs and hems of their ugly, poorly printed business suits are soaked.

'Impressive work, Senhor Corta,' Wang Yongqing says. 'But might we continue this discussion out of the rain?'

'I'm enjoying the novelty,' Lucas says. 'I'm trying to decide whether to make it a feature of my redesign. My mother didn't trust climate.'

The terrestrials shuffle, shoes spattering new-formed mud.

'I note you've been spending more time here at Boa Vista,' Wang Yongqing says.

'We don't appreciate having to haul ourselves all the way out here to see you,' Monique Bertin says.

'I am always available through Toquinho,' Lucas says. The terrestrials know as well as Lucas that Boa Vista is Corta-owned airspace, immune to LMA surveillance drones.

'Expensive work, this,' Anselmo Reyes says.

'It is,' Lucas says. 'Thank you for unfreezing the Corta Hélio accounts.'

'I'm concerned that over a prolonged absence from Meridian,

details might slip your attention and become more than details,' Wang Yongqing says.

'The Eagle of the Moon has never been found wanting in diligence,' Lucas says.

'Then you will make arrangements to clear the thieves and criminals from Bairro Alto. Its continued existence is an affront to the authority of the LMA,' Wang Yongqing says.

'I hear they have an impressive water distribution system,' Lucas says.

'Theft of resources weakens morale,' Monique Bertin says.

'It rewards dishonesty,' Anselmo Reyes says.

'It sows disharmony,' Wang Yongqing says.

'They are well defended,' Lucas says. 'The Jack of Blades, I hear. It has a ring to it.'

'A thief and a murderer,' Wang Yongqing says. 'Contract mercenaries.'

'The last mercenaries you sent up came down in pieces,' Lucas says. 'If you'll forgive my graphic imagery.'

'Hire better mercenaries,' Monique Bertin says.

'I shall inform my Iron Hand.'

'We require your personal attention,' Wang Yongqing says.

'My Iron Hand is already in Meridian,' Lucas says. 'Is there anything else?'

Anselmo Reyes starts to speak as Lucas turns his back. His escoltas move to escort the delegation back to the lock. The rain is easing, torrent to downpour to soft-splattering drops. A small ecosystem like Boa Vista can only hold so much water. Lucas turns his face to the rain. The drops are heavy and full. Water runs down his face, his neck, across his chest. Such a strange thing, rain. He is glad he could share this unrepeatable moment with others.

In the end, she brings insects.

The escoltas were openly relieved when Alexia declined a bodyguard. They didn't want to face the Jack of Blades. *You'll need something,* Nelson Medeiros said, fixing the sheath to her forearm. *They'll attack anyone not you. One shot use but that's enough for you to get away. It takes a second for them to key to your body odour.*

Alexia imagines she can feel the combat insects buzzing next to her skin in their container as the elevator climbs towards Bairro Alto. She is the sole occupant: the Iron Hand has privileges.

Your heart rate is elevated, Maninho says. *Your blood pressure is high. You are displaying symptoms of stress.*

'I'm fine.'

You are not, Alexia. There is a public printer on 56th, I can pre-order pharma.

'Take me all the way up.'

As you wish.

The ring of the mesh decking beneath her boot soles is painfully familiar. She touches the white waterpipe as she climbs the staircase. It is cold, trembling with running water. She follows it to where it bifurcates, trifurcates, branches into a tree of piping. The best work of her life is up here, plumbed into the roof of the world.

They're on the mirador, perched on steps, hanging over railings, crouching on ducts. There is an arrow aimed at her from a platform two levels up.

He makes his signature entrance, dropping from a height to land sprung and muscular on the mesh. He sits loose-limbed, lithe on a step. He is more beautiful and broken now she knows who he is, now she understands his gold tooth, his maimed knife-hand.

'Can they take us all?' Denny jerks a thumb at the launcher strapped to her arm.

'Probably not.'

'Your lack of trust hurts me.'

'I know who you are.'

'And I know who you are, Mão de Ferro. Once again, I am in the debt of a Corta. Have you any idea how inconvenient that is to the right and proper working of revenge?' The thumb now indicates the pipe-tree. 'This is amazing work. A thousand people depend on it. I owe you a Mackenzie debt.'

'I'm here to warn you,' Alexia says. 'The LMA is sending fighters to break it up and clear out Bairro Alto.'

'We'll send them back as we sent the rest of them back.'

'They're coming in force. Professionals, not whatever the zabbaleen can afford. Combat bots. Drone support.'

'We'll fight them!' a woman's voice calls from the duct overhead. 'We'll show them who we are in Bairro Alto.' The cheer is ragged, uncertain, short of breath.

'Go on, Mão de Ferro,' Denny Mackenzie says.

'I don't have the details. But the contracts are signed.'

'Who wrote the contracts?'

'The Eagle of the Moon.'

'Are you betraying your employer, Mão de Ferro?'

'You have to go!' Alexia shouts in frustration. 'Shut down the network, take it apart, take it with you, take it far from here. Here's the plans. I know you have to stay off the network.' She places an old memory card on the mesh. The least movement could it send it tumbling to the throbbing air-plant far below. Denny Mackenzie scoops it up in one sure, liquid motion.

'Thank you.'

'Denny, can I put this down?' The bow and arrow waver. 'My arm hurts.'

Denny Mackenzie raises a hand. Fingers uncurl from concealed hilts, hidden tasers.

'I met your father. At Crucible.'

And the air freezes again. But she has to say this.

'He told me that the feuds have to end. We have a bigger enemy.'

Denny Mackenzie does not speak.

'Fucking trap!' The unseen man's voice echoes down from the high machinery. Others join him until the high pipes rattle and roar with anger. Denny Mackenzie lifts a hand.

'Bigger enemy?'

'The Dragons are making alliances. The LMA is divided. The Vorontsovs are about to switch sides if Lucas approves their space elevator project. It's changing.'

'Free air and free water, that's how we'll know it's changed.'

'This warning; it's from Lucas.'

Denny makes a circle with a finger, a small gesture but the Bairristas melt back into their city.

'So noted, Iron Hand.'

And he's gone. Alexia is alone on the platform.

'I came back for you!' she shouts. Her voice rings from the industrial metal. 'I came back.'

How he detests these soirees. Every other day there is a reception, a banquet, a party or celebration that requires the Eagle of the Moon. Every other day some trade delegation, representative, academic or social ascendant. Always petitioning, always wheedling, always needing. Of human asking there is no end.

'Whose party is this anyway?' Lucas asks Toquinho.

Yours, Toquinho answers.

'Is it my birthday?'

No. Alexia's.

'I'll apologise to her later.'

Lucas's social secretaries have booked a set of suites on Orion Hub. Rooms open on to galleries and balconies; curtains of flowering climbing plants screen the vistas from the more vertiginous guests. Water burbles, a bossa trio plays soft and sad. Through the screens of society and LMA and business, Lucas spots Alexia. She has invited her new friend, the Asamoah-Vorontsov girl she met at St Olga. She's a spy of course. Everyone's a spy. They draw eyes and admiration in nearly-but-not-quite matching ballgowns. Martini glasses in hands. The Blue Moon is enjoying a comeback. It can be drunk either patriotically or ironically.

'Do excuse me.'

The cloud of well-wishers, sycophants and spies parts for the Eagle of the Moon.

'Congratulations on the day.'

'You forgot, didn't you?' Alexia whispers.

'I forgot.'

'I'm twenty-eight, by the way,' Alexia says as Lucas swings on to the next social orbit. A touch on Amanda Sun's arm cuts her free from her coterie. Lucas parts a curtain of sweet hibiscus with his stick to take her on to a balcony. The sunline has darkened to indigo, every slow-moving light is soft as dust. Meridian gloaming.

'Well, we looked a pair of fools,' Lucas says.

'I looked the fool. You weren't there.'

'Viego Quiroga counselled against that.'

'Sound advice. Your sister fucked me in the ass.'

'She fucked us both. I hear the Asamoah girl's zashitnik took out your drones.'

'She was never in any danger,' Amanda Sun says. 'As long as her aunt is Omahene, the child is deathproof. We wanted to see how she would react.'

'Rather well, it seems.

'I hear Lucasinho didn't mention you in that party piece from Coriolis,' Lucas says. 'He did say hello to me.'

'He did,' Amanda says, 'but he's still not here, is he?'

'It's a preliminary hearing,' Lucas says. 'We play the long game. You could be a while in Meridian. I have a thing to ask you.'

'Favours, Lucas?'

'Not at all. Cortas pay their way. A potential contract. I need a coder – is "hacker" still a word?'

'It is.'

'My mother once buried code inside Crucible's mirror control system, for the hour of extremity. I want to follow her example.'

'What do you want, Lucas?'

'Fifteen thousand terrestrial combat bots.'

Amanda Sun smiles.

'Declaring allegiances, Lucas?'

'Thinking of the hour of extremity.'

'It won't be free.'

'Name it.'

'I want to see him, Lucas.'

'I can't stop you.'

'I want someone from the family in residence at Coriolis.'

'Your ambassador?'

'Do we have a deal?'

'We have a deal.'

'Then you have your bots.'

A dip of the head, a fold of the fingers in the Corta salutation and the obligations of office and society call the Eagle of the Moon on.

'Madam Asamoah.'

Abena makes apologies to her fellow guests. Lucas takes her on the loop past the musicians. Head nods, foot stirs to the subtle syncopation.

'You like this music?' Abena asks.

'You don't?'

'I think it's pretentious to admire something you don't understand.'

'I was that way with jazz. A whole musical world alien to me. I understood a tiny part of it – where it merged with my own bossa – but I also admit that I knew what I didn't know. I decided to teach myself jazz – a tiny part of jazz. Eleven months of *Saints Peter and Paul* and I could only scrape the skin.'

'Was it worth it?'

'Here I am, back with bossa. My legals tell me you have the makings of a fine lawyer. You work a court well.'

Abena Asamoah has the grace to look embarrassed.

'Thank you, Senhor Corta.'

'It made me keen to meet you, Senhora Asamoah.'

'Know your enemy?'

'You're not my enemy. You may become my enemy, and that would be regrettable. What is it they say about my family?'

'Lucas Corta doesn't know what people say about his family?'

'Humour me, Senhora Asamoah.'

'Cortas cut.'

'Family affairs are best kept in the family.'

'Senhor Corta,' Abena says as Lucas closes his fingers in farewell, 'Forgive my bluntness, but Lucasinho will never be safe as long as you are Eagle of the Moon.'

Lucas circles the band, pausing to admire a heartbreaking minor 7th chord sequence in 'Ao Pes da Cruz' to arrive among the LMAs. The same faces he saw dour under rain-capes at Boa Vista. The same niggardly business attire. Only one of them, the French woman, is drinking.

'My own gin,' Lucas says to Monique Bertin. 'The João de Deus recipe. I had a designer recreate it. Quite floral, with an almost cedarwood finish.'

Monique Bertin mumbles appreciations. Lucas draws Wang Yongqing to a second, more private balcony.

'We are vexed, Mr Corta. Expensive mercenaries with bot support and once again we fail to liquidate the Jack of Blades' rabble.'

'They know every nook and cranny of the high city.'

'They were tipped off.' Madam Wang clings to the rear of the balcony, by the window. Lucas perches on the balustrade. 'Someone in your office?'

'Institutional loyalty is alien to us. Families, contracts and lovers. These hold our hearts.'

'Was it you?'

Lucas maintains a cold stare until Wang Yongqing looks away.

'You know who this Jack of Blades is? Denny Mackenzie. You think I would lift a finger to help the heir of Mackenzie Metals?'

'The disinherited son.'

'Denny Mackenzie is easily dealt with. Simply put up the price of air. I read somewhere once that China built its great imperial power on monopolising water. Breathing is so much more reliable a motivator than drinking.'

'The scholarship on China is Orientalist,' Wang Yongqing says. 'The sentiment, however, is admirable.' Lucas summons a server and offers fresh, cold martinis. Wang Yongqing waves the glass away. 'We will agree an immediate increase of the Four Elementals. We expect a corresponding resolution of the Bairro Alto question.'

Wang Yongqing moves towards the door and the security of her colleagues but Lucas has a parting shot.

'I hear that Duncan Mackenzie has been meeting the board of VTO.'

'We understand it was to contract the Crucible replacement,' Wang Yongqing says.

'Your information is out of date. That order has been cancelled.'

She is good. He has just told her that her hired guns, the Vorontsovs, are untrustworthy and she betrays no tremor of surprise, no emotional tell. But she has been shaken. Tell that to your cronies.

The band takes its break. Lucas follows its leader to the bar.

'Your chord sequencing is exquisite,' Lucas says. Jorge leans on the bar, Lucas stands back to it, they catch each other peripherally, edge-of-eyeball. 'You've simplified it since I last heard you.'

'Last time you heard me play you stuffed the club with Corta goons,' Jorge says.

'It still is,' Lucas says. Lucas slips into Portuguese. 'I hoped you'd come.'

'Jaime and Sabrina told me to turn you down. I almost did.'

'Yet here you are.'

The bar-keep slides a glass across the glowing counter. Jorge looks at it like poison.

'I recreated the cachaca.'

'I have a confession...'

'You never liked the cachaca.'

'You're not good at cachaca.'

The bar-keep pours a neat gin. Jorge sips, slips a wry smile of remembrance.

'But you are good at gin. Thank you for noticing. The chord sequences. I've learned you suggest more with less. It took me a long time to learn that, and that there is too much in the guitar for a single life. That's when you find your voice, your guitar. I was waiting for you to get in touch.'

'I thought about coming to Queen to hear you.'

'Instead, the royal summons. You are the only one in this room listening to us. You look like shit, coraçao.'

Lucas levers himself on to a bar stool.

'It gets easier every day. A little. I tell myself that, but there was damage done on lift-off from Earth. Deep damage that won't heal. The Earth will kill you, they say. It's true. Just not immediately.'

Drums and bass have returned to their instruments, tuning, riffling, bouncing notes from each other.

'I have to get back,' Jorge says.

'Of course of course. Jorge, afterwards, would you...'

'It's over, Lucas. You made it be over, if you remember.'

'Just a drink. That's all. Somewhere quiet. As quiet as I can get.'

The band looks over.

Again, the painful half-smile.

'All right. Just a drink.'

'Jorge, a request. Could you play...'

' "Aguas de Marco"?'

'Yes.' Adriana's favourite. She had asked for it at the end, play it, play it again, Lucas. He had turned away to bring her coffee – coffee and bossa – and she had gone.

'Always a pleasure to play "Águas de Março".'

Lucas sits at the bar listening to Jorge tune and fall into harmony with his band. A nod, they lead off the second set. Lucas listens until the first repeat, then hauls himself painfully from the stool to the duties of the party.

The bar-keep has adjusted the bar lighting so that Lucas and Jorge drink in a pool of soft gold. They sit in adjacent sides of a corner. The keeper tends to the small acts of theatre that make under-employed waiting-staff look busy.

'The cafe is still there,' Lucas says. 'Rua Vinicius de Morais. Number 49. On the corner. You can pay for the window table where he sat and wrote the song. She is long gone but the family still lives in Ipanema, they say.'

'Did you go in?'

'No. I was afraid it wouldn't live up to the legend,' Lucas says.

'I can understand that.'

'The Brasil of the heart is always more perfect.'

The bar-keep serves two fresh shots of Corta gin. Mist wreathes from the frozen glass.

'I hated you when the terrestrials came,' Jorge says. 'Their fucking bots, looking into every eyeball, logging every soul. Queen never was a Corta town, but it hates you now.'

'It has reason to hate me,' Lucas says. 'I've done terrible things, Jorge. Monstrous things. Crucible . . .'

'Everyone knows.'

'Everyone suspects. No one knows because no one wants to know. All the things I hoped for, all the things I did this to achieve, they're further from me than ever.'

Jorge grips Lucas's shaking hand. Light from the illuminated bar shines between the linked fingers.

'I bring them all here, allies, enemies, rivals, lovers and we drink our gin and play our game of dragon and never once do we look up to see what's darkening the sky. Amanda asked me what we Cortas want. Really want. I said family, first, family always but that wasn't what she meant. She meant vision. The Suns have a vision, the Vorontsovs have a vision. The Mackenzies have always had independence. No one knows what the Asamoahs want, but they have a vision. I couldn't answer Amanda then. I think I can now. My mother was deeply involved with the Sisterhood of the Lords of Now. She went to them to recruit madrinhas, she funded them, she helped build their Sisterhouses in Hadley and João de Deus. Mãe de Santo Odunlade was her confessor, in the final lunes. The Sisterhood was annihilated evacuating Lucasinho from João de Deus.'

'The Mackenzie Massacre,' Jorge says.

'Is that what they call it?'

'In Queen.' Jorge lifts a finger for fresh drinks.

'I have no time for their deities, but what drew my mãe draws me. This world is a laboratory, where humans experiment in cultures and societies and philosophies. New politics, new religions. To the end of creating something that will endure. Earth is collapsing, I saw it with these eyes. Earth is dying and decaying. All of human culture could be looted and burned, smashed by new ideologies. They have no respect for their world. If we make one mistake, Lady Luna will kill us. So we respect her. We know how fragile we are. There is no reason why humanity should not thrive here for thousands of years. That was Mãe Odunlade's vision: a society that can exist, unbroken, for ten thousand years. Twice as long as any human culture. I like that. What would the moon look like after I am gone, after my five-hundred-times-removed descendants are gone? I don't know. But there will be something, bigger, wiser and very, very old. Continuity, Jorge. Can you understand that?

'I fear for the future, Jorge. I fear for the Earth, now I fear for our world. I fear for my son. I fear for him every second of every day. I fear that I am destroying the thing I swore I would preserve.

'And then my enemies tell me that I have to decide. I have to choose an allegiance. And I'm afraid to, because I fear I will destroy everything.'

'What are the choices?'

Lucas looks up.

'No one has ever asked that question.'

Jorge tightens his hold.

'So?'

'Power, security for my family, or a new moon.'

'Those sound like contradictions,' Jorge says.

'I fear they are,' Lucas says.

'Then simplify,' Jorge says. 'One thing you can deliver.'

'I know what I want,' Lucas says. 'The problem is, to have that, I think I have to give all this up.'

'Then it's simple.' Jorge releases his hold on Lucas's hand and taps him gently on the breast. 'Your heart, coraçao.'

'But I'm afraid.'

'Ah,' Jorge says. 'Always the scuttling fear. '

'I fear that if I step away from the Eyrie, the moon will fall.'

Lucas raises a finger to summon the bartender.

'Lucas, I need to go. I need to get back to Queen.'

'You don't have to.'

'I know I don't have to. But I need to.'

'I need you.'

Hands touch on the glowing bar, fingers grip.

'I can't, Lucas. Your life would make me a prisoner. Security at my shoulder. Always afraid that someone would use the people I love against me. You are a beautiful man, but your world is poisonous.'

'And I can't call . . .'

'No. There can be nothing between us. This is our first and last night together.'

'Then kiss me.'

'Yes,' Jorge says. 'Yes I will yes.'

Afterwards he picks up his guitar. The two men embrace, clumsy, encumbered, one-armed.

'Lucas, that thing you fear. You only fear it because you think you're alone.'

Then there is only the bar-keep and Lucas Corta at the glowing plane of the bar and beyond, unseen, ubiquitous as angels, his security.

The room is warm, comfortably furnished in beiges, tastefully decorated in framed prints, and it is a death-trap. Vidhya Rao sits panting in er well-upholstered chair, blinking, dazed, panicked. E must run, e must flee, e must do something. A thousand needs and notions swarm like insects and e cannot move.

Moments before, e was deep in the Three August Sages' surrealism network, carefully so carefully chipping overburden from their imaginings of possible futures, revealing tesserae that hinted at an unseen mosaic. Those hints should have been enough. Hints were never enough for Vidhya Rao. E came back again and again to the Three August Sages: a 1950s Googie-style UFO diner with everyone as roller-skating Martians, a universe made of carnival-balloon demons, a 2020s Gold Coast sunrise party, a Hindu pantheon that spoke only in iambic rhyming couplets. Each time, e uncovered more of the mosaic. Fascination became fear, became terror. E had to see more, know more. Until e felt a vibration, a nerve touched, an alert triggered so sensitive only one who had spent days in the Three August Sages' kaleidoscope of tumbling realities would be aware of it. Security was alerted. Whitacre Goddard knew what e had seen.

If Whitacre Goddard knows, the terrestrials know.

E must get out: of the room, of the Lunarian Society house, of Meridian.

E stands chest heaving on the balcony, a heavy neutro in a sari. E must move fast. E has never known how to do that.

Not that way, says a voice in er ear. A service exit highlights on er lens. *Here.*

E slams the service door behind er. Halfway down the steps e is stopped by a hard clattering rattle from inside the club. Again, closer, and again. E has never heard anything like it.

Drone-launched flechettes, the voice says. *The drone is still in the building.*

A sustained, meteorite rattle.

The standard load-out is four rounds.

Vidhya Rao hobbles painfully to the door to the service alley.

A moto will arrive in forty seconds.

'Who are you?' Vidhya Rao asks as e pulls open the service door. 'You are not my familiar. I didn't order a moto.' E steps into the alley, a dark cave cut into raw rock.

Get back into the building.

'Tell me, who are you,' Vidhya Rao demands.

Get back at once!

Vidhya Rao sees lights, movement, mass; then e stumbles back into cover as the moto accelerates into the back wall of the service alley. The crash of impact sends er reeling.

The moto was hacked.

Vidhya Rao stares numb at the wreckage. The way is blocked. E imagines erself trying to clamber over the shattered aluminium and carbon. Back. Out. E is gasping by the third turn of the stairs.

'Activate Whitacre Goddard personal security protocol.'

It is Whitacre Goddard trying to kill you, the voice says.

Vidhya Rao wrenches open the service door. The upper floor of the Lunarian Society is a surreal nightmare; every surface needled with toxic quills. Death by a hundred thousand spikes. There is a body at the top of the stairs. Vidhya Rao forces down er nausea and edges past the martyred corpse, wary of the needle-studded walls.

'You're them, aren't you?' Vidhya Rao asks as e ventures down the sweeping staircase. The Lunarian Club is shattered wreckage, chairs overturned, tables toppled, drinks and handbags discarded in the rush to escape. A single high-heeled shoe in the middle of the lobby.

I am an aspect of the Three August Sages, the voice says. *I represent Taiyang.*

'I knew I felt someone else in the interface,' Vidhya Rao says. E stumbles out on to the street. Emergency service drones are arriving by road and air; e weaves between them, apologises a path through the cordon of onlookers.

I have been monitoring your activity in the interface, the voice says. *The fact that Whitacre Goddard and the terrestrials both want to kill you … interests us. Down!*

Vidhya Rao throws erself hard to the street. Pieces crack, muscles tear. A shadow crosses er, a sudden gale buffets er. A flash of gold, and a beating roar fills er ears. Hands help Vidhya Rao to er feet. Every breath is inhaling broken glass. Out in the gulf of Orion Quadra huge wings beat: light flashes from the flier's visor as she wheels to come in for another pass. Each hand carries a long blade: wings tipped in bone.

You are under the protection of Taiyang, security will arrive in approximately twenty seconds, the voice says.

The flier tucks her wings into a killing stoop. She pulls up: the air seems to boil around her. She beats furiously, trying to zig-zag away from the seething air but it follows her, a hive of seething black motes. Vidhya Rao sees fear on her face, then her wings disintegrate into shreds of fluttering membrane. Bone knives slash at air, a desperate, hopeless attempt at a claw-hold. Shrieks and screams from the streets. Legs and arms windmilling, the woman plummets to Gargarin Prospekt. The cloud of boiling air moves over the street and settles above Vidhya Rao in a smoky halo.

Security is in place, the voice says. *You can call me Madam Sun.*

'Please keep back,' Vidhya Rao shouts to the onlookers. 'My security cloud will attack anyone it's not keyed to recognise.'

The people need no warning. A moto arrives and opens. The swarm of micro-drones pours in.

This vehicle is secure, Madam Sun says. Vidhya Rao is flung down on to the seating as the vehicle goes to full acceleration. E glances behind. As e suspected, there is another moto behind her, matching every dodge and weave.

Whitacre Goddard is using the system to predict your movements, Madam Sun says. *It can foresee with fifty per cent accuracy to a maximum of three minutes in your future. That forms the extreme forward horizon of their present. Accuracy is sixty per cent at one minute, ninety per cent at thirty seconds.*

'But you are the same system,' Vidhya Rao says.

I am a sub-AI on the interface of Taiyang's back door into the Three August Sages, Madam Sun says. *My capacity to run predictive simulations is limited.*

'Are you really Lady Sun?' Vidhya Rao asks.

Of course not.

'You're very like her.'

Thank you. Lady Sun is the primary user of the Taiyang interface, so I have modelled myself on her.

'It wasn't necessarily a compliment.'

I know. Stand by for sudden deceleration. The moto brakes savagely. Vidhya Rao reels forward. The security bots surge like oil. Vidhya Rao is flung sideways as the moto one-eighties. It dodges the pursuer, which brakes and turns, but even as Vidhya Rao reaches for handholds the moto veers again on to the 53rd North Bridge.

There was a roadblock at the 51st downramp, Madam Sun says. The 53rd North Bridge was not designed for vehicles; the moto hurtles across the narrow blade of construction carbon, millimetres from the handrails. Anyone on this bridge is dead. Vidhya Rao glances down. Lights. A void full of lights. The tree-tops and bright pavilions of Gargarin Prospekt are distant and deadly as dreams.

'I see machines moving in on the east side,' Vidhya Rao says.

I have a sixty per cent confidence rating they will not arrive in time to catch us, Madam Sun says. Three hijacked motos fall into pursuit. Vidhya Rao takes a long look back. Two of the pursuers are empty, pulled off their stands, but the hackers have trapped a group of children in the third.

Detouring to the 50th South freight elevator, Madam Sun says as it swerves on to the downramp and descends three levels. *Hacked vehicles are covering the main down exits to Gargarin Prospekt.*

The pursuers have fallen away. Vidhya Rao prays the children are safe.

The elevator platform descends with a speed that makes Vidhya Rao close er eyes. E opens them at the subtle sensation of vertical motion. The moto descends smoothly down the east wall of Orion Quadra.

There is a seventy-two per cent probability of Whitacre Goddard discovering my connection to your familiar within the next three minutes, Madam Sun says. *It is inevitable we will try to out-predict each other.*

Prophet hunting prophet through the shifting cloisters of the soon-might-be.

A sudden dark mass, looming; a terrible crash and jolt. A delivery dray has darted from the ascending platform on to the descender. The dray backs up the handful of centimetres the platform allows and rams the moto. Plastics crack and splinter. Vidhya Rao cries out. Again the dray backs and rams. Centimetre by centimetre it is pushing the moto towards the drop.

I am unable to work around the hack, Madam Sun says. Another strike, another hair's breadth towards the long fall. *I'm preparing to leave at the next platform. However...*

'The terrestrials have foreseen that.'

Yes. Units are moving to close down the exits.

Shudder. Crack. Creak.

'Open the doors, Madam Sun.'

Another impact. The plastic bubble is crazed like cracking ice.

I cannot advise...

'Just a hair.'

The petals unseal. Vidhya Rao's security swarm deliquesces through the lines into swirling smoke. Drones wreathe the furious little dray, attack its seams and panels. Cables snap, joints spray hydraulic fluid.

The dray sags, tries to drive forward and goes in a circle. Stops dead. The security drones drain from its cavities and cracks like black sand and sift down through the mesh of the elevator platform.

The security cloud is out of power, Madam Sun says. *I've contracted mercenaries to meet us on Fifteen and escort us to Orion Hub.*

'The station is covered?'

And the BALTRAN. We are not taking either of those options.

Glancing down, Vidhya Rao sees figures in combat armour waiting on the ramp. Mercenaries. As e descends through level fifteen the fighters effortlessly swing on to the elevator platform.

'You good?' one shouts in Australian-accented Globo through the part-opened bubble.

'I am well,' Vidhya Rao says. E can make nothing out beyond the mask: face, voice.

'We got you now,' the mercenary says. 'Hope you got a strong stomach. It's going to be quite a ride.'

'What's happening?'

'You're taking a trip on the moonloop.'

If he moves one centimetre to his left the bell will ring. The maze is dark and he is blind but he knows it with every cell in his body.

Reach out your self, they told him. *Where does your body end? The top layer of your skin? The tips of your hairs? The air currents that stir those hairs? Make your body more than your body, make your senses more than senses and you will hear the bell before it ever makes a sound, feel it before you ever touch it.*

He feels the third bell.

He has never made it this far into the maze. It grows narrower and more convoluted with each stage and Mariano Gabriel Demaria resets the bells after every failure.

Darius slides around and past the bell. Something touches his skin. The lightest, most delicate *ting.*

'Shit shit shit shit.'

And the lights come on. Darius is in a tight U-turn of industrial panelling, one bell a breath from his right shoulder, one touching his left shoulder.

Navigate the maze not just with your senses but your reason. With your emotions. With your insight. If your most recalcitrant pupil had failed five times to get past the third bell, where would you set the fourth bell? Right next to the third.

'Okay, come out of there. Lady Sun wants to see you.'

Darius strikes every bell on his way back to the start of the maze.

'That's not fair.'

Mariano Gabriel Demaria throws him a bag of clothes.

'Fair, unfair. Weaknesses. The moon is not fair.'

'You set those bells so there was no way to avoid them.'

'Did I say you had to avoid them? The only instruction is that the bell must not ring. You could go underneath the bell. You could tie the string up. You could cut the string. You could steal the clapper. You would be Ladron Supremo if you did that, but there is always a way past the bells. Now put some clothes on.'

Darius peers into the bag.

'Handball gear?'

'You're going to a ball game.'

Transport waits on the ledge; not the usual moto that brings Darius to his lessons at the School of Seven Bells, but a Taiyang aircar. A handball game at the Coronado is so important that it requires executive transport? Darius scrambles up the steps into the cab. The ducted fans spin up, the machine lifts and dips down from a platform high on Jain Mao Tower. Darius gives a whoop as the aircar swoops down between Taiyang Automation and First Towers, then pulls into level flight, banks around Kingscourt and follows Queen's Boulevard straight towards the pastel egg of Queen's Crown nested in a cluster of six towers.

'Can we go round again?'

I'm instructed to bring you to the Dowager without delay, the aircar says. But it draws the stares of the spectators settling on to the neat grass outside the ticket hall. Two of Lady Sun's groomed entourage whisk Darius past every line, through every turnstile, up every staircase, through every crowd, to the doors that open only to their faces, to the family boxes: mid-court, high enough to see all the action, not so high that a Sun cannot throw the ball out to start the game.

Sun Zhiyuan, Tamsin Sun, Jaden Wen Sun, Sun Liqiu and Sun Gian-yin. Lady Sun, and she despises handball.

'What is he doing here?' Sun Liqiu asks

'It's important he sees how we do business,' Lady Sun says.

'He's not . . .' Sun Gian-yin says.

'Genetics would disagree,' Lady Sun says.

'Good shirt,' Jaden Wen Sun says. Darius tugs, embarrassed, at the hem of his new season Sun Tigers shirt. 'Can we get on with this? I've got a game.'

'The company is under threat,' Lady Sun says. 'I have been consulting recently with the Three August Ones.'

'Voodoo,' Sun Liqiu says.

'Who should I meet there but Vidhya Rao?'

'Economist, consultant to Whitacre Goddard bank and member of the Lunarian Society and the Pavilion of the White Hare,' Sun Zhiyuan explains to Darius.

'And proponent of the Lunar Bourse concept,' Lady Sun says. 'Which the terrestrials are funding aggressively. What interests Vidhya Rao interests me.'

'Vidhya Rao escaped from Meridian on the moonloop,' Jaden Sun says. 'It was quite a show. Drones, moto chases and everything. A flying assassin.'

'I know,' Lady Sun says. 'I helped er.'

Bafflement in the owners' box of the Coronado.

'What did e discover?' Tamsin Sun says.

'I don't know. I do know that e had been spending a lot of time with the Three August Ones,' Lady Sun says.

'What did they tell er that the terrestrials tried to assassinate er on the streets of Meridian?' Sun Gian-yin asks.

'Impossible to discover without exposing our own interrogations of the Three August Ones to Whitacre Goddard and therefore the terrestrials. I did ask the Three August Ones about potential threats to Taiyang from the Lunar Bourse. They want the Sun-ring. The Three August Ones predict an eighty-seven per cent probability of Earth taking control of the Sun-ring within eighteen lunes to power their financial market.'

Consternation in the owners' box at the Coronado.

'If we start power transmission before the terrestrials have their bourse running . . .' Sun Zhiyuan says.

'We could capture the market,' Tamsin Sun says. 'A dependent market.'

'We could effectively give it away free for a year,' Zhiyuan says.

'The heroin dealer's strategy,' Tamsin Sun says.

'Problem,' Jaden Sun says. He points up, through Coronado's dome, through the roof of Queen of the South. 'We need the relay satellite.'

'I shall talk with Yevgeny Vorontsov,' Zhiyuan says. 'I also move an immediate power-up on the Sun-ring. Show Earth that we are open for business.'

'This is a board decision,' Lady Sun says.

'We don't have enough for quorum in this room,' Tamsin Sun says.

'Seniority has its benefits,' Lady Sun says. 'In cases of financial, political or social crisis, when the survival of Taiyang is threatened, the senior board member has the authority to draft board members. I nominate Darius Sun-Mackenzie to the board of Taiyang.'

Glances, slow nods. Outside the box, the arena MCs are whipping up the audience with quick-fire call-and-response. Music blares. A cheer goes up.

'I witness,' Jaden Wen Sun says.

The crowd outside sends a rolling cheer around and around the seating tiers.

'I second,' Zhiyuan says.

'I witness,' Tamsin says.

'Then we have a quorum in this box,' Lady Sun says. 'I propose we immediately power up the Sun-ring and open negotiations with VTO and the terrestrial energy suppliers. Hands?'

Hands. Murmured ayes.

'So passed,' Zhiyuan says. 'It is resolved that Taiyang powers up the Sun-ring and negotiates supply contracts with Earth.'

'Well, if that's all settled,' Jaden Sun says, 'now we can play handball. Darius, as newest board member, you can take the throw-in.'

The match MCs have spiralled the crowd, home and away, into a crescendo of excitement. Spectators are ready, commentators are ready, scoreboards and screens and close-in drones are ready. Players are ready. Jaden hands Darius the ball. It is smaller than he thought, heavier; fit to his hand and heft.

'Throw it in like a Sun,' Lady Sun says.

'Watch me.' Darius steps down into the pulpit. The Coronado's tiers drown him in voices as he raises his hand. Reach out with sense and sinew. Where does the body end? The hand that holds the ball, the tips of the fingers, the skin of the ball itself, the skin of every one of the three thousand handball fans jammed around the tight oval of the stadium. Darius throws, the ball flies straight, high, true. The players leap, sculptures in slow gravity: the crowd rises in a thunder of voices.

The two boys stand so sober and serious on Theophilus's small platform that it is all Analiese Mackenzie can do to keep herself from erupting with laughter.

'Got everything?' Robson asks.

She holds up the long case that holds the setar.

'Let us know when you get there,' Robson says.

'Better,' interrupts Haider. 'Let us know when you get the connection at Hypatia. Hypatia is tricky.'

'I change trains at Hypatia every time the band meets,' Analiese says. The station at Theophilus is little more than a large airlock serving the rail shuttle to the mainline.

'This is different,' Robson says gravely. 'This is tour.'

He's right. This is tour and it is different. Ten nights, eight dates from Meridian to Hadley, Rozhdestvenskiy to Queen of the South. It's not Robson she fears leaving home alone. He'll move Haider in and they'll be proper little home-makers together. She fears for Wagner. He came back in from his latest inspection tour, picked at some food and rolled up to bed. Exhaustion. Tough out there in southern Tranquillity. Analiese was not fooled. He had been out there under the burning sky on his meds and now the old familiar dark was coming.

She rose early, cleaned and packed her setar as carefully as a religious relic. He was still asleep, muttering in a language neither she nor her familiar could identify. The tongue of wolves. He was so pretty, so worn out, so vulnerable. He rolled over at her touch.

'I'm going now, coraçao.' He liked it when she used Portuguese. 'You sleep on. You need it. I'll call you when I get to Meridian.'

He muttered, opened his eyes, saw her, smiled. She kissed him.

He had a particular scent when the change was on him. Sweet and musky.

The boys will take care of him for the ten days of tour.

A thrum through the smooth stone, the click of mechanisms meshing, the whir of pressure equalising. The shuttle has arrived. The lock opens.

'You can listen if you want,' Analiese says. 'We're streaming the Meridian concert.'

Robson and Haider look aghast. For a moment she might hug Robson but that would compound a venal sin with a mortal one.

The outlock opens. Wagner. Shorts, a short-sleeved shirt, sand-shoes. His hair is a mess, his eyes are bleary, he looks like a coma, walking. He is dark and he is light and he is all beauty.

'You're going,' he stammers. 'I forgot. Sorry.'

She sets down the setar and throws herself on him.

'You smell good.'

She bites his ear. He growls. This is the Wagner Corta she remembers. Half a man is better than the wan ghost of Wagner Corta trying to live without the meds.

Analiese Mackenzie picks up her instrument.

'Look after him.'

'I will,' Wagner says.

'I wasn't talking to you.'

He has never been so afraid.

In moments he will be at the door. Beyond it will be his son. His hand quivers on the head of his cane.

'He's awake and excited to see you, Senhor Corta,' Dr Gebreselassie says.

Who is awake, who is excited? Is it Lucas Corta Junior, Lucasinho? Lucas's memory has a long track to run to recall where he saw his son last. Twenty lunes, the lobby of the Home Inn hotel the night before the wedding of the century. Parting words: don't get drunk, don't get high, don't fuck it up. A straighten of the lapels of Lucasinho's jacket to cover the catch in his throat. He never wanted Lucasinho to marry Denny Mackenzie. Jonathon Kayode had been so proud of his dynastic marriage that would put an end to half a century of vendetta: the Shining Boys! Jonathon was always the toy of Mackenzie Metals. The Eagle of the Moon died screaming and shitting into two kilometres of airspace, but Adrian was found with a bloody knife in each hand. No one ever called a Mackenzie coward.

So here they were, the Shining Boys; one a daredevil rebel swinging through the roof of the world; the other a vacuum-dried husk being rebuilt memory by injected memory.

All these thoughts in the time it takes his hand to hesitate over a door handle. What is the speed of memory?

'What are you staring at?' he says to Luna, frowning balefully at his side. Her white fright-mask is not half so intimidating as her own face. *Lucasinho did this for you. You are not forgiven. Forgiveness is for Christians and I am no Christian.* 'You stay here.'

'Don't tire him out,' Luna orders.

Lucas steps into the room.

He had a smart line about this being the second time he's found him in hospital after drinking vacuum. It's gone. Lucas Corta is in rapture, Lucas Corta is appalled. The boy is so small on that bed: so thin. But the bones are good. The bones always were good. Has he seen him? Can he see at all? Lucas with half a mouth, half an eye, half a face.

'Sorry,' Lucasinho says.

Lucas Corta barely makes it to the chair. He takes his son's hand and collapses. His chest heaves, his breath beats and quails, he dare not speak because the weight of one word will crack everything and the years of biting back, of deep discipline, of containing and controlling will shatter him.

Rafa the golden one, Lucas the shadow. The lover, the schemer, the talker, the fighter. And the wolf.

'Please . . .'

Lucas's grip has tightened on his son's hand to the point of pain.

'I'm sorry.'

We are rebuilding him from the memories of others, Dr Gebreselassie said. Network, family, friends, lovers.

'You know who I am?' Lucas says.

'You are Lucas Corta. You are my father. My mother is Amanda Sun, my madrinha is Flavia,' Lucasinho says. The words are slow, the effort total. 'Amanda came to see me. Is that why you're here?'

Lucas moves the subject away from his ex-wife and the deal she made with him. The software has been coded, all that is left is the infection, and the contagion, bot to bot to bot. It should take no more than thirty seconds to spread between all fifteen thousand bots.

Be here. You never were here for him. Five hours by rail around the waist of the moon and you are reviewing your deal and schemes, who you can trust, who you cannot.

'Do you remember where you used to live?' Lucas says.

'The place with the big faces, wet with water. Green and warm. Boa Vista.'

'Do you remember, I wasn't at Boa Vista very much. I lived at João de Deus. That was another place we had.'

'João de Deus.' Lucas can see his son fighting to attach name to detail. Lucasinho's face brightens. 'Smelly!' Lucas laughs aloud.

'Yes. Smelly! But I'm going to go back to Boa Vista. I'm doing work there. I'm going to fill it with living things. You can live there too, when you're ready.'

Lucas knows the eyes watching, the ears listening. Lucasinho's medical team, the faculty, the university with its secretive agenda, a vigilance of ghazis. His sister, at some remove. *Help him remember,* Lucas was told. *Take him back. Don't take him forwards, don't promise him.*

Now Lucas can see the process he understands what is being done, and with that understanding come doubts. Who controls the memories, who decides what is brought forward and what is pushed back, what is injected into Lucasinho's brain at all? Lucasinho does not remember João de Deus beyond bad atmosphere. Lucas was an absent, distant father. The memories that built his childhood are those of his madrinha. The Corta way. Lucas thinks of Alexia growing up in her tangle and tatter of lives, wrapped up in others. Now he thinks of his own son, solitary among the stone faces. No wonder he wanted to taste everything the world and people had to offer. No wonder he ran off to the bright lights the first chance he got.

The boy tires quickly. His attention dips, his motor control slackens. Words slur into each other, his eyes cannot focus. Time to go.

'Son.'

He embraces a kite of skin and rib. As Lucas opens the door the healing hands of the machines reach from floor walls and ceiling to embrace Lucasinho, touching, ministering. Rewriting his life.

Planet Earth is blue and it throws its gentle light across the Ocean of Storms. Lunar night: the cities glitter with ten thousand lights, sparks wheel through the high black – moonloop capsules, BALTRAN pods, rare and precious ships. A swift spear of light is a passenger express travelling to the far side of the world. On either side of the wide rail tracks is a wider belt of pure glossy black: lunar regolith sintered and salted and seeded by Taiyang engineers. The Sun-ring girds eighty per cent of the moon's equator. Machines and glasser teams work lunar day and night to drive the band of black across Farside's unrelenting mountains and craters. Taiyang legal teams negotiate access agreements with the university which does not want its pristine research moonscape despoiled by industry and profit.

Now that Crucible is slag on the surface of Oceanus Procellarum, the Sun-ring is the largest constructed object in the two worlds, a ribbon of solar cells one hundred kilometres wide, nine thousand long. At night it is a marvel, a black abyss full of stars: reflections of the sky above it. Stars and far blue Earth. So huge is the Sun-ring that even wan Earth-shine will generate one hundred megawatts of electricity. Under the light of the sun, the ring comes to life. It is easily visible from Earth, a black band dividing the moon like the hemispheres of the brain. It's slept for two lunar years. Now the command goes from the Palace of Eternal Light. Buried processor chips warm and run through boot cycles. Arrays of solar cells switch on; segment by segment the moon-sized energy grid wakes. Taiyang substations measure and balance feed. Seventy exajoules of power course into Taiyang's network. The Sun-ring is alive.

FIFTEEN

'You're late,' Krimsyn says to Finn Warne. 'He's pissed off.'

These are the most words Krimsyn has ever said to Mackenzie Helium's First Blade.

Bryce Mackenzie stands before the window, dressed only in a thong, bathed in laser light. Flickering red beams map the flows of flesh, fold upon fold, as if he has erupted fat from his pores like lava; the sacks of adipose tissue that press his thighs together, the heavy, pendulous breasts.

'You're late,' Bryce Mackenzie says.

'I know what they're doing,' Finn Warne says. Glances around the room to the rest of the board: Jaime Hernandez-Mackenzie to Rowan Solveig-Mackenzie to Alfonso Pereztrejo. The moon has been a pestilence of political rumour since Taiyang powered up the Sun-ring. The Suns would only rush a project launch if their hands had been forced. 'I have some people in the Palace of Eternal Light.'

'Who?' Bryce asks with a liquid shrug. The thong is unnecessary, his genitalia quite hidden by flaps of skin. The lasers wink out, the bots wheel to storage.

'It would endanger them to give you the name,' Finn Warne says. 'They're close to the board. They told me that Taiyang's sales agents on Earth have been setting up meetings with terrestrial energy companies. Particularly in those nation states that don't have representation in the LMA.'

Bryce's eyes widen. He understands.

'Clever fuckers. Clever clever fuckers.'

'They can't go solar, they don't have the transmission satellite,' says Jaime Hernandez-Mackenzie, Head of Operations. Ever the old jackaroo – groomed, proud, trustworthy.

'Sun Zhiyuan is on his way to St Olga with the full travelling circus,' Finn Warne says. 'I had some of the engineers run simulations; Taiyang could have a solar power satellite ready to beam power to a terrestrial microwave array in six lunes.'

'They're taking pre-orders,' Rowan Solveig-Mackenzie says, Mackenzie Helium's analyst.

'They'll give it away free,' Bryce Mackenzie says. 'The first one is always free. And we're selling gas for kids' balloons.'

'Why now?' Alfonso Pereztrejo says. 'They're nowhere near ready. They're still negotiating glassing rights with the university. And as you say, they have no means of getting the power to Earth.'

'They have those computers that can predict the future,' Finn Warne says. 'What if they looked forward and saw something that scared them? Really scared them.'

'Scared the Suns?' Jaime says.

Attendants arrive, print-fresh clothing draped over their arms. They fuss around Bryce, trying fits, draping him, dressing him.

'There's more,' Finn Warne says. 'I've been talking to other sources. There was a high-level meeting between Yevgeny Vorontsov and his puppet-masters and Duncan. They agreed a joint development venture. Asteroid mining. Mackenzie Metals is moving off-moon.'

'Is the deal done?' Bryce asks. The dressers adjust the sit of his pants, the fall of his jacket. They slip shoes on to his petite feet.

'The legals are drawing up contracts,' Finn Warne says. 'Signed and sealed by the end of the lune.'

'What are you thinking?' Jaime asks.

'We do what any good business does,' Bryce says. Swathed and suited, he addresses his board. 'We diversify. Aggressively.'

Today she goes clothes-free.

It's a leap forward on Alexia Corta's quest to become lunar. She shied from the banyas: the idea of public hygiene is alien to her. Washing, cleaning, ablution, are private, rationed, a few moments in the metered shower under her own pumped water. Then she discovered there were wonders in those raw rock caverns carved deep into the face of the city. Hidden pools, steam chambers, bubbling baths and warm polished moonstone slabs where she could loll and sweat. Spa tubs of increasing heat, linked like ganglia by low-ceilinged tunnels where she could lie back in the scented water, bathed in ambient lighting and amniotic surround-sound allegedly streamed from a flying probe two hundred kilometres down in Jupiter's storm system. She made the banya a daily habit but she still baulked at public nudity. It was not mandatory – nothing was mandatory on this world – but it was customary and she suffered agonies of guilt between private and social discomfort.

This morning she ordered Maninho to show her herself. In the skin. Hair down. She winced, looked away, looked again. Alexia understood too well the irony of feeling physically self-conscious in as exhibitionist a society as Brasil, but the enduring family narrative was that Cortas were workers not lookers. She had always worried that her hips were too wide, her ass too heavy, her boobs too small. The gatinhas from school bounced down to the beach after class in three triangles of lycra; she went for coffee, and took a table with her back to the ocean. Wanting so much to be the one in the sun. The moon taught her different. The moon gave her a movie-star dress and she had wooed and wowed St Olga. The bodies at the banya – young, old, large and small – taught her that no one was looking.

She looked at herself in her lens. And it was okay. It was good. It was her. Fuck it.

She booked a National Classic trim for her boceta, hung her bra and pants in her locker, slid her feet into the Havaianas, slung her towel over her shoulder, shook out her hair and marched to the steam room.

The call comes in the spa. Irina.

'Ola.'

She is distraught. In bits. Teary. Where is she? She's in Meridian. She needs her.

'I'm in the Sanduny banya. I'll book a private suite.'

Warm water, juniper-scented air, ambient light and guaranteed privacy are safe, centring, healing.

Irina Efua Vorontsova-Asamoah does not even wait for the water, the warmth, the seclusion to start to work.

'They're marrying me!' she bawls.

There is no ready answer to that when you are naked and up to your neck in gently bubbling water.

'Kimmie-Leigh Mackenzie!'

By the time it has all unravelled they have progressed from the warm pool to the cold pool to the sauna to the steam room to the cold pool to the warm pool again. Alexia's skin feels three sizes too big for her and she understands Irina's woe.

It's the deal. The Mackenzie deal. The contract calls for a series of dynastic marriages to seal the agreement. Irina has been betrothed to Kimmie-Leigh Mackenzie, granddaughter of Katarina Mackenzie, granddaughter of Robert. The engagement will be proclaimed as part of the announcement of the Mackenzie Metals/VTO pact. The ceremonies will take place ten days later in Hadley.

'Hang on hang on hang on. Married? Against your will?'

'It's part of the deal.'

'But did you consent to this?'

'Does it matter?'

‘It matters if it makes it rape.’

‘I signed the pre-nikah.’

‘But you didn’t want to,’ Alexia protests. She learns one thing about the lunar way of life, accepts it, then she runs hard into something alien, brutal and harsh.

‘I didn’t want to but I had to. How could I say no? This is family. You don’t know what it’s like in the families.’

‘I certainly do not,’ Alexia says. ‘And what about her? Kimmie-what?’

‘Kimmie-Leigh. K-L. She doesn’t want it either but she’s a Mackenzie, I’m a Vorontsova-Asamoah . . .’

‘Do you know her? Have you even met her?’

‘She’s sixteen, in the Three Heavens Colloquium here in Meridian. Seems a nice kid. But my oko? My oko? For five years. Five years!’

Alexia almost laughs aloud.

‘Only five years!’

Irina is aghast.

‘I’ll be . . . twenty-two by the time the contract reverts!’

‘In five years a lot can happen. She could be dead. You could be dead. The deal might fall through, the contract might be annulled. You could cheat and be a renegade from both houses. Or you could fall in love. What I’m saying is, five years is nothing.’

Irina sulks, then splashes water in Alexia’s face. Alexia bristles, then drenches Irina with a torrent of splashing. Irina shrieks, then the two women yell and laugh and throw water at each other until they cannot breathe.

‘Your hair,’ Alexia gasps, ‘looks like. Shit. And I’m puckered up like an old nun. What I’m saying is, is, get a fucking marriage lawyer. Let’s get a drink.’

Irina is still there three bars later. She is still there at the Ethiopian restaurant and she is still there in the morning folded around the bottom of Alexia’s bed, like a small sister or a visiting cousin. And she is still there, blinking big eyes and hung-over, when Lucas calls with the invitation to the eclipse party at the Palace of Eternal Light.

*

If she puts her right arm out and rolls on to her side, and bends *this* way, Luna reckons she can slide around this corner to the really good spy-hole in the roof of the med centre common room. She wiggles her arm up and around, for a moment her elbow jams against the roof of the access tunnel, then Luna grits her teeth, shifts her body weight on to her left side and the arm goes into the crawlspace. Then it is roll, flex, kick and she is through into the duct beyond.

Luna never thinks that she might get stuck, that familiar-Luna might have to call for help, that bots and engineers might have to dismantle half of Coriolis to get her out; that Luna might call and no one would come, ever.

In a few metres the crawlspace will open out and she can manoeuvre her arm down by her side and peer through the mesh into the common room. Tea machine, food machine, water machine, seats and spaces. People sitting around with that faraway look grown-ups get when they are with their familiars rather than the friends around them. Moving air strokes her hair, rustles her dress. Who's in the common room today? Dr Gebreselassie, just leaving. Dr Donoghue and Dr Ray, just entering, talking together at the tea machine. A group of researchers: they're not interesting. There is Amalia Sun, who came with Tia Amanda when she visited Lucasinho. She seems a bland, dull woman, sitting on her own with tea, involved with her familiar.

Who to follow? Luna invented her little game in the crawlspaces and conduits of Boa Vista, but it is so much better here. There are so many people here she can track without them knowing, instead of just some boring relative or security person. It makes her giggle, thinking she is up here, watching and they will never know.

Luna tracked every step her Tia Amanda took and not even her security knew she was there.

So, who to hunt today? Amalia Sun is the newest thing Luna has seen but she just sits and sits, busy with her familiar. The researchers finish their tea. Luna picks the least uninteresting and follows her into the main ring, down two levels to the neuronics laboratory – a drop down a service shaft, her ballooning dress slowing her fall – to the laboratory offices, another tight turn, but not as narrow as the passage from the scanner room to the common room. Luna's dress snags on the misaligned edge of a panel and tears. She hisses in annoyance.

'Now look what you made me do!' she scolds the researcher.

Madrinha Elis holds up the dress. The tear runs from armpit to waist.

'Scrambling.'

'Exploring,' Luna says.

'And you're covered in dust and dirt,' Madrinha Elis says. Luna stands defiant in shorts and T-shirt. 'Take a shower. You are a smelly girl. And . . .'

'Wash that thing off my face?' Luna grins. 'I always do, madrinha.'

'And put it right back on again.'

Luna skips to the shower. 'I need that reprinted for when I go to see Lucasinho.'

Madrinha Elis rolls her eyes and tosses the torn dress into the deprinter.

'Ola, Luca.'

Lucasinho is in his chair today. His smile is a thing of joy and light. Luna likes to talk to him in Portuguese, it seems to link memories in new ways, give him fresh words for speaking about himself.

'Bom dia, Luna!'

'Walk again today?' Luna says in Portuguese. Lucasinho nods. He can walk without a stick now, and likes to test his body's limits. The faculty has a small park and Luna and Lucasinho walk laps of its circular path. There is tall bamboo and sheltering leaves and overhanging branches and you can almost believe that you aren't in a chamber under a low roof.

'Look at the fish!' Lucasinho says. Luna takes his arm as they walk down to the elevator.

'Feed the fish!' Luna says and takes a glass vial of protein flakes from the pocket of her grey dress. Lucasinho claps his hands in delight.

Medics and academics and researchers greet them as Luna and Lucasinho stroll hand in hand along the sintered stone path.

'Seven trees?' Luna says. An ornamental Japanese maple is their lap marker. Lucasinho looks doubtful. He tires easily. Mental work is the hardest. 'Seven trees and we can feed the fish.'

'Okay.'

As he does every day, Lucasinho stops in a spot where light falls through gently moving leaves. He looks up into the dapple, lets it warm his face. His eyes are closed.

'You look like an orixa,' Luna says.

'Which one?'

'Oxossi,' Luna says.

'The hunter,' Lucasinho says. 'The Lord of Knowledge.' His face tightens in concentration. 'I'm trying to remember. Facing each other, from the tram station to the main lock. Oya and Xango. Oxum and Ogun. Oxala and Nana. Then Oxossi and Yemanja. Last of all, Omolu and Ibeji. It's easy to remember Boa Vista here. Is that why you bring me?'

'And I like the fish,' Luna says. They walk on, smiling and greeting the well-wishers in Globo.

'I'm starting to remember the Palace of Eternal Light as well,' Lucasinho says. Fourth tree. 'It's all light and dark, big shadows and light so bright it's like – real? Solid. Huge empty spaces. Echoes. Really really small people, but it's the stone that makes them look small. Trams everywhere. I remember looking out of the window of a tram. What's the name of that other city, the old city?'

'Queen of the South?' Luna says.

'That city. I was on the tram, with my mãe.'

'Amanda Sun,' Luna says.

'Mãe,' Lucasinho says firmly. 'I was on the tram, from the Queen, and we were going around inside this big crater, and it was all shadows and light. Like a cut.' He slashes his hand through the air. 'Sharp like that. Light, shadow. Mãe said, those shadows, they never end. I remember I was scared, but she put her arm around me and said look and there were all these lights in the shadow, and Mãe said, that's our city. Light in the shadows.'

Six trees. Lucasinho has a lightness in his step, a certainty in his voice. Luna must trot to keep up with him.

'I remember! Another time. There's a room, all covered in beautiful cloth, and tiny windows, and the light comes in through the tiny windows and makes the cloth all pale. There was an old lady, and she was smiling and she took my two hands and my mãe said, "Luca, this is your great-grandmother."'

'That old woman is Lady Sun,' Luna says. 'When was that? I don't remember you meeting Lady Sun.'

'I don't know, I think just before I lived there. Seventh tree! Can we feed the fishes now?'

'Luca,' Luna says. 'You never lived in the Palace of Eternal Light.'

'Now this will not do,' Lucas Corta says.

'I rocked St Olga in it,' says Alexia in the ballgown that had so seduced the Vorontsovs, so fresh it still smells of evaporating printer fluid.

'What rocks St Olga will get the stone face in the palace,' Lucas says. He wears a suit in a soft, vaguely iridescent grey which, on close inspection, reveals itself to be brocade micro-print. His tie is primrose silk, as is the band of his hat. 'The Suns have standards.'

'What is this anyway?' Alexia calls as she goes back to pull off the dress, deprint it and print out the one that is very much her second choice.

'The Suns host eclipse parties in the Pavilion of Eternal Light.

It's the only time darkness ever falls so they think it's worthy of celebration. There's an eclipse every month so people are always being invited to the Palace of Eternal Light. LMA, trade delegations, social influencers, society debutantes, academics. Tourists. Everyone is going to be there, so there is clearly something Taiyang wishes to announce.'

'Everyone?' Alexia wriggles into the new dress.

'Heads of all five . . . four Dragons,' Lucas says. 'And the Eagle of the Moon and his Iron Hand.'

'To do with the Sun-ring powering up?' Alexia says. Right shoe, then left. There is magic and ritual to dressing.

'Absolutely certainly.'

Alexia descends the two steps from the dressing room. The long drape of crepe, the mutton-chop sleeves, the tightly cinched waist.

'You could land a moonship on these shoulders.'

Lucas smiles.

'Discreet but powerful. The Suns will appreciate that.'

'I've never been to the Palace of Eternal Light,' Alexia says as the railcar runs the Transpolar mainline south over the viaducts and through the cuttings of the La Caille craterlands.

'You'll be impressed. It's built to impress. It's very composed, very quiet, very austere and everyone there is afraid all the time.'

'How was he?' Alexia asks.

'I thought of turning around and walking away.'

'Lucas, that's not what I asked.'

He looks out at the silver-black desolation.

'I saw a wonder, then I saw a horror. Then I saw a thing I thought I knew and didn't know at all. I thought, they're putting him back together, memory by memory, but they're not his memories. They're the memories of others, his social media self, the parts of his memory he gave over to machines. Is that all we are? What others remember of us? He's still pretty, Lê.'

'You showed me a picture of him, that time I came back to the Copa Palace.'

'And I offered you the moon. He looks the same, Lê, but he's not the same. Will he ever be the same or will the doubt always be there, that they built something that is not my Lucas Corta Jnr?'

'When I go back to Earth, I won't be the same, Lucas. Every part of the me who almost got killed in that suite in the Copa will be left here on the moon, and I'll take the moon back inside me. Every hair and bone and cell.'

'You're going back?'

'If I go back, I mean. If. Lucas. One more question. Who is Jorge Mauro?'

That suspicious smile again. Alexia sees the fifteen-year-old, the ten-year-old, the five-year-old boy, who knows he must always be smart, be sharp, be secretive.

'You spy on me?'

'I look after you. You stayed behind after the reception.'

'Jorge Mauro is my song, my sanity, my soul. I tell him what I will never tell you, Iron Hand. I would have spent the rest of my life with him but he was wise and would not have me.'

Bossa guitar fills the cabin, whispered, invoking lyrics.

' "Samba de Una Nota",' Lucas says. 'Jorge's group.' He prepares martinis, viciously dry and cold. Alexia still cannot bring herself to love gin or bossa nova but she sips and the craterlands of the south speed past and she understands something of Lucas Corta's towering, terrible loneliness.

At Queen of the South they transfer to the Shackleton tramway. Alexia notes railcars at the private platforms: VTO red and white, the monochrome patterns of AKA, the green and silver of Mackenzie Metals. The tram silently carries her and Lucas under Queen's great lava bubble, beneath the Aitken Basin to emerge on to a track cut into the inner wall of Shackleton crater. Lights blaze in a profound darkness that changes on a boundary sharp as a blade to blinding light. White and black. Ice and fire. Sun has never touched the deep recesses of Shackleton; primordial ice has lain there since the birth of the solar system, ice that fuelled the Suns' and Mackenzies' first steps on this world. The history of the moon is only eighty years deep, but it is passionate, bloody and magnificent.

Alexia's lenses polarise as she squints up to try and catch sight of the Pavilion of Eternal Light in the sun glare. It took her some time to comprehend the principle of a Peak of Eternal Light. The moon has virtually no axial tilt, so no seasons and no months-long days and nights at the pole. A sufficiently high mountain peak at the pole would never be out of sunlight. Water and constant solar power: humans of vision and spirit could build a world out of those. Malapert Mountain fails the Peak of Eternal Light test by a few hundred metres, but build a tower on top of it . . . And Alexia sees it, and her mental resistances fail. She is awed. A shaft of searing light rises into the black, tipped with a blazing diamond. A spear, challenging the universe. Earth and sun are invisible beneath the far rim of the crater: Alexia tries to imagine darkness obliterating the spearpoint, spreading down the shaft.

The tram car enters another tunnel and moments later draws into a glass chamber. Locks seal; the Eagle's escoltas form an escort.

'Your ex-wife is here,' Alexia whispers. She adjusts the fall of her gown, the set of her shoulder pads. This is stupidly complicated clothing.

Amanda Sun greets Lucas with precision kisses. She is fierce in a fitted New Look suit.

'Lucasinho looked well, I thought,' Amanda Sun says, escorting Lucas across the soul-shrinking space of the Great Hall of Taiyang. Alexia's heels sound like gunshots on the polished rock. She imagines she leaves a trail of sparks.

'I thought he looked ragged,' Lucas says. 'Drained. Only natural. But then I know him better than you.'

Shafts of light fall across the floor of the Great Hall, so bright they seem to hiss.

'Senhor Corta.' Sun Zhiyuan greets his guests. 'Senhora Corta. You are most welcome.'

Alexia recalls her last meeting with the Suns. They had come to dip the head to the new Eagle and scry what favour and denial they could expect. She had tried to bar Lady Sun because the Dowager of Shackleton had not been on her list. Mistake. She had been inexperienced. The Suns will not have forgotten nor forgiven. There she is, the old bruxa. She has always worn this 1940s style. The world has come round to her. The effete-looking kid at her side in the sharp suit must be Darius Sun-Mackenzie. Alexia tests her memory on the rest of the Great Hall. Lousika Asamoah with her animal entourage and AKA executives in the same beautiful kente that had impressed her beneath the Great Tree of Twé. Robert Mackenzie a dark star among his bright retainers. A posse of flamboyant Vorontsovs hail Alexia like a lost sister.

No Bryce, Alexia whispers to Lucas across the room.

He would have been invited, Lucas says. *The Palace of Eternal Light is punctilious.*

Sun Zhiyuan raises his hands and the party falls silent.

'We will be taking you up in groups, as space is limited in the lantern,' he announces. 'But rest assured, everyone will have a view of totality.'

'I fought my way into this dress, for this?' Alexia says. Her working of the room has brought her back to Lucas.

'That's not why we're here,' Lucas says.

'And though you are all busy people, we'd be delighted for you all to stay for the reception afterwards,' Zhiyuan continues.

'That's why we're here,' Lucas says and Yevgeny Vorontsov bulls his way through the guests to press Lucas on when he will put *that business* to a vote in the LMC.

'I'm trying to decide if it would be better before or after you announce your off-world venture with Duncan Mackenzie,' Lucas says but before Yevgeny can fluster and bluster, Taiyang staff, immaculate and androgynous, herd their designated lists to the Mount Malapert shuttles.

Alexia has one clear sighting of the Pavilion of Eternal Light before the tram car enters the tunnel to the elevator hall. It is very much larger than she thought, a weave of spars and construction beams like a great Eiffel tower, gripping the summit of Mount Malapert, half in darkness, half in glowing light. The spear of God.

The tram arrives in the elevator hall. The young Suns steer their guests with smiles and small touches.

'Omahene Asamoah?' says a Sun escort, showing Lousika Asamoah the waiting elevator car.

'Is she taking her animals up with her?' Alexia whispers. Lousika Asamoah lifts a finger and the raccoon curls up, the parrot tucks its head under its wing, the spider turns into a ball of wire and venom and the swarm dissipates.

'Next car, our Mackenzie friends, please?'

Duncan Mackenzie leads his bright young Ozzies through the lock into the second car, newly arrived.

'Every Sun is brought here as a child to feel the power of the sun and understand the source of their power,' Lucas says to Alexia.

'House Corta?' a smiling, sexless staffer says. Elevator doors seal.

'I'm excited about this,' Alexia says as the car climbs. Through the spidery girder-work Alexia watches Shackleton crater resolve, its depths in darkness, its rim ablaze with light. Higher still and the surface furniture of Queen of South, comms towers and BALTRAN stations, power plants and docks and the long revetments of surface locks. Now she begins to make out the interlinked crater-scape of the Aitken Basin.

A colossal explosion. The elevator car is shaken as if by a fist. Alexia reels into the Taiyang worker: then she is in freefall. The lights go out. The car is dropping free. Emergency brakes engage, Alexia hits the ceiling, then the floor. Lucas is on top of her, the Taiyang kid a tangle of limbs in the corner. She can hear emergency brakes screeching: unmediated metal on metal. Impacts, loud as gunshots. Cracks. A volley of blows beat on the roof. The elevator jolts. Alexia raises herself to her elbow, the elevator glass is crazed with cracks. She doesn't know what's holding it together. Beyond the webbed glass Alexia sees a bright cloud of tumbling sparkles arcing away over the foothills of Malapert.

What?

The network is down. The elevator crawls down to dock. So slow. So killing slow. If this maze of crackled glass blows she joins the bright glinting things spinning out over Shackleton.

'The top of the tower,' Lucas says.

Alexia leans against the solidity of the elevator frame and peers up into tangled, bent, warped girders. The bright diamond, the lantern, she can't see it. Why can't she see it?

'It's gone,' Lucas says. His brown face is grey. He scrabbles for his cane. For anything that might give him security. There is no security, nothing to cling to.

'Who was up there?' Alexia asks.

'Duncan Mackenzie, Lousika Asamoah,' the Sun kid says.

Alexia swears in Portuguese. The elevator judders into the dock. The wait for the lock to seal and cycle is endless. As Alexia, Lucas and their Sun escort stumble out on to the concourse the elevator car shatters like a crystal trophy into a million glittering crumbs. Medics and bots rush to give aid and oxygen. Alexia tries to wave away the mask, the anti-shock infusions but the machines insist. She catches a glance from Lucas, his eyes above his own oxygen mask. *Look.* Lousika Asamoah sits on an upturned medical hardshell, vapour pluming from her mask. Her eyes are wide with shock, her animal retinue crouches behind her, restless. She made it down.

Dragon security arrives, pouring out of the tram cars to tangle with Sun wushis. Nelson Medeiros and his escoltas surround Lucas, check him again for medical distress. The elevator lobby thunders with shouting voices. A shriek of noise cuts into every familiar. The network is up again, and ordering everyone to be quiet. Sun Zhiyuan stands with hand upraised.

'Please. Your attention. There has been a major integrity violation. The lantern . . . the lantern has been destroyed. We don't know the details but we can confirm that people are missing.'

Voices babble, Sun Zhiyuan raises his hand again. No one wants to hear that shriek in their implants.

'VTO has dispatched a moonship from Queen of the South and we are sending rover teams to the site. The terrain . . . The terrain is difficult.' His voice falters, he is visibly sweating. Alexia has never seen a Sun flustered before. 'We will transport you and your entourages back to the Palace of Eternal Light. If you require any medical assistance, do not hesitate to make yourself known to our staff. We will update you when we have more information. At the moment, this area is structurally insecure so I would ask you all to comply with our assistants and return to the Palace.'

They have that information now, Lucas says on the private channel. *They're just trying to think how to manage it.*

'A bomb?' Alexia asks when the tram-car doors have sealed and only Cortas and escoltas can hear.

'I don't think so,' Lucas says. Nelson Medeiros nods.

'An impacter,' Nelson Medeiros says. 'Not a bomb. A shot.'

'Who has that kind of weapon?' Alexia asks.

'First thought, the people with the big space-gun.'

'The Vorontsovs?' Alexia is incredulous.

The car emerges from the tunnel and Alexia again looks up. The Pavilion of Eternal Light is shattered, its top third missing, the shaft a shivered stump of jagged beams and twisted girders, stark in the resurgent light.

'Why would they try to kill you?' Alexia continues as the tram re-enters the tunnel. 'They need you for their Moonport deal.'

Lucas and Nelson Medeiros exchange glances.

'It wasn't Lucas,' Nelson Medeiros says.

'Who then? Duncan Mackenzie?'

A nod.

'But who would . . . Fuck.'

'Fuck indeed,' Lucas says and the car slides into the platform. The Great Hall is thronged with bodies and voices and desperate activity. A dozen security squads, Sun staffers, reporters and columnists hoping to peel back the smooth skin of Taiyang corporate communications, hungry lawyers with notions of lucrative compensation cases mill and shout. Dragons and executives. The network groans under slow heavy traffic. A chime on the common channel sends every hand to every ear. Sun Zhiyuan will speak. Bodies encircle him.

'Honoured guests,' he says. 'I have more information. We can confirm that the lantern of the Pavilion of Eternal Light has been destroyed in a targeted attack. We are still examining evidence, but what we know is that the Pavilion was struck at 16.05 by an object on a ballistic trajectory. There have been at least seven casualties; Robert Mackenzie among them. Our search and rescue have turned up a number of bodies in the debris field. We have no hope of any survivors. Our thoughts go to Mackenzie Metals in the loss of its CEO and its generation of brilliant young talents. Trams will be arriving to take you back to Queen of the South. The Palace of Eternal Light is now a major incident zone and I would ask you to vacate it as quickly as possible. This is tragic time for us and for Mackenzie Metals. Thank you.'

And Amanda Sun is there, a guiding hand in the small of Lucas's back.

'I was afraid, Lucas.' She steers him towards the airlocks. Wushis in sharp suits wait at a discreet distance. 'I was so relieved when I heard you were safe. Oh, you are a sight. I wish I could offer some place for you to clean off the dust. And, Alexia, your lovely dress.' The hated frock is torn where Alexia's feet tangled with the hem, the ludicrous cinch between wrist and skirt ripped, seams split, the ivory fabric smudged with the black dust that works its way from vacuum into every part of the human moon. And her hair is a mess.

'We have facilities on the railcar,' Lucas says.

Alexia tries to hang back. She has spied Lady Sun and her protégé being hurried through the crowd in the opposite direction by a squad of suits. They are fast and determined and brook no hindrance. Neither do the Taiyang staff who move her politely but firmly towards the tram airlock. Sun security creates a space for Nelson Medeiros to move the Eagle and his Iron Hand on to the railcar.

'Remind me again,' Lucas says as the car arcs around the waist of Shackleton crater. The black sky is filled with moving lights: moonships on landing burns. Lucas counts them. Every Vorontsov ship on the moon is over the Palace of Eternal Light. 'Who wasn't at the party?'

SIXTEEN

Every day, a new handle appears in Marina's room. They start in the ensuite, at the toilet, in the shower, then they spread to her bedside, then to the closet, then around the switches and sockets, then sprout in a fungal line along the wall to the door.

'Get rid of them!' she rages and from the way Ocean and Kessie flinch she knows the responsible parties. 'I'm not a fucking gibbon in the zoo! I'm trying to learn crutches. Is all.'

She rages not because of their misplaced care, but because the hand-holds remind her too much of the tiny apartment in Bairro Alto, three rooms scooped out of raw rock and cheaply sealed. They remind her of Ariel's cableway of loops and lines strung across the ceilings; of Ariel hauling herself from her seat and swinging from room to room. Ariel, dressed and made up for the clients where the cameras could see, disreputable in borrowed leggings or track pants where she was not visible. The two of them trapped in their high exile, bitching and bickering and needing each other. Eighteen lunes, scraping and scratching. Only the foolishly optimistic or the terminally nostalgic would call that time happy. But the colours were bright, the tastes flavourful, the smells aromatic in a way that nothing is in this house. Damp, cold, softness, murk. Everything muted and hushed.

In a night, like a trial from a fairytale, the handles are gone.

Crutches are bitches. Marina can't trust her weight, her strength, her balance. Her legs are too weak, her upper body is too strong. She is too moon-shaped. She swings up and down the hall, through the room, along the porch, a sweating, swearing circuit.

On the third day she slathers up in sun block, pulls on a hat and shades and embarks on an adventure across the yard to the swing-seat. She makes it to the top porch steps, feels too tentatively with her crutches, loses her balance and goes down.

Dr Nakamura scans her on the porch lounger while Kessie makes coffee.

'You're intact,' she says. 'Use the walking frame.'

'That's for old people,' Marina says. 'I am not an old person.'

'You have the bones of a ninety-year-old.'

'I have the heart and sex life of a nineteen-year-old.'

Ocean sniggers and flees, embarrassed by her aunt.

'Sit down, will you?' Dr Nakamura says as Kessie serves the coffee.

'You have that doctor-needs-to-have-a-serious-talk tone,' Kessie says, but she closes both porch doors and sits.

'Has Weavyr said anything to you?' Dr Nakamura says.

Kessie pours coffee. Every cup is still a shot of electric joy to Marina. She inhales the aroma. If only it tasted the way it smelled.

'What about?' Kessie asks.

'In class.' Dr Nakamura's daughter Romy and Weavyr are study-mates.

'No. Nothing.'

'Romy says a lot of the other kids are picking on Weavyr. Calling her names, ganging up on her, shunning her.'

Marina takes Kessie's hand in hers.

'This is to do with you too, Marina,' Dr Nakamura says. 'They're telling her her aunt Marina's a witch, she's a spy. Your Aunt Marina is a terrorist from the moon. She's going to blow up a mall, put poison in the water, send a meteor to take out the school. They're telling Romy she shouldn't be friends with Weavyr because Weavyr is your spy.'

'Weavyr hasn't had Romy back recently,' Kessie says. 'And she won't tell me what she did in class, she won't give me any of the gossip.'

'Mean girls,' Marina says.

'It's more than that,' Dr Nakamura says. 'One of my oldest clients – the Furstenbergs – asked if I still had the Calzaghes in the practice. I said of course, Mrs Calzaghe is an important patient. They said, oh no, not her; the other one, the one who went to the moon.'

'What's it got to do with them?' Marina asks.

'Whatever it was, they've moved to the Oceanside practice. Three generations.'

'I can say something here.'

No one noticed Ocean's return, quietly opening the door, pressed against the frame half in, half out of the room.

'My social feeds?' Ocean says. 'Hate storm for the past two weeks. People I don't even know, people from the city. It's all their business that my aunt has come back from the moon, and they have something to say about that.'

'What do they say, Ocean?' Marina asks.

'The best say you should be in jail. Then it goes from that to spy to terrorist... I'm blocking them as fast as they turn up but I'm looking at closing the accounts.'

'I'm sorry,' Marina says. *They're hanging Duncan Mackenzie printouts from Sydney Harbour Bridge and burning them,* Skyler had said. She feels small and hideously alone, a solitary woman on a hostile planet. Eyes in the forests, the mountains, the airwaves and the network.

Ocean wakes. She is bright, alert, every sense sharp and she cannot think what woke her. She remembers, the swing of light across her bedroom wall.

'Time,' she says and, as the house network says, *Two thirty-eight* she hears the crunch and rumble of tyres, the whine of an engine. She dives to the window. Tail-lights turn the corner into the trees.

'What was that?' she whispers to the house.

I didn't get the licence plate, the house answers. *The car was fitted with an infra-red device to blind the cameras.*

The creak of her mother's bedroom door, a line of light under her own door. Ocean throws on the biggest hoodie and slips into the hall.

'Did you hear?'

'Go to your room, Ocean.'

Ocean follows her mother through the dark house to the door.

'Go to your room, Ocean.'

They wait behind the barricade of the front door, summoning courage.

Kessie flicks on the outside lights and heaves the door open. She can smell the paint across the yard. 'Don't come down, Ocean.'

Ocean follows her down into the yard.

'Stay there, Ocean!'

Ocean follows her mother to the attack: a white crescent with a slash through it painted on the side of the cabin, so fresh the paint still drips.

Now Marina is on the porch, leaning on her crutches.

A slashed crescent.

No moon.

'At least take the dogs with you,' Kessie says.

'I'll be all right,' Marina says.

'I don't know why you can't just settle for twice around the yard,' Kessie mutters.

'There's a whole planet out there I can walk on,' Marina says. 'You have no idea how liberating that is. I'm going up the track.'

'Take the dogs.'

Ancient Canaan furrows his creased brows and rolls to his feet; the new dog, Tenjo, who has yet to form a relationship with Canaan, strolls over to see what's going on. A walk. Exultation.

Ocean and Weavyr painted the whole cabin white over the weekend but everyone can still see the outline of the slashed moon, white in white. No matter how many weekends they paint the cabin, the affront will always be there.

The dogs follow Marina down the steps into the yard. She has the trick of it now. She has the measure and weight of gravity. The route she has planned will take her up the track, through the gate before the cattle-grid, along the part of the trail that skirts the lower edge of the forest, then left along the southern part of the river trail-turn and back to the house. Two and a half kays. It's as daunting as a marathon. There might be some late elk under the edge of the forest. That's a prize and a motivation. She longs to be among wild animals, nothing between her and them, unmediated, wild.

In yoga pants, a crop top and as many friendship bangles as she could borrow from Ocean, Marina sets out on her adventure.

'Uh oh,' Ocean says. 'Sun block.' She slathers Marina's bare belly and back in Factor 50. 'You got great definition, Mai. How did you do that?'

'Long run,' Marina says. 'And since when do you call me Mai?'

'Since Mom did,' Ocean says.

'Do you want me to come with you?' Ocean asks.

'I do not,' Marina says and sets off, crutches leaving two lines of holes in the dust. Canaan and Tenjo trot at her heel. This is not the Long Run, it can never be, but it can be a ritual of another kind, her own communion with her body and her space.

Everything that is ten times more difficult in Earth gravity is twice that with the addition of crutches. The curving slope to the concrete bridge is a descent from a sheer mountain col. The potholes are craters the size of Aristarchus. The gravel and stones on the country road turn every step into torment and she forgot to bring water.

'Tenjo, Tenjo, you're the smart dog, go and get Marina some water,' Marina puffs as she swings her way up the road. Gods, the gate is so far away.

Gods. Ariel used to say that.

Fifty steps and a rest. Fifty more steps and another rest. Cut it into pieces. Her feet hurt. Her feet hurt so much. How far has she come? On the moon she could blink up her familiar. Here it's an icon on her shades, blink blink blink blink blink before she gets into the fitness app. Half a kilometre.

Gods.

The dogs look up. Seconds later Marina hears the engine that alerted them. A car coming through the trees. She sees its dust before it makes the right-angle turn out of the trees into the open. She steps back. It's coming fast. Does it see her? She could wave a crutch. No, she would fall. It's not slowing. It must see her. It's coming at her. At her. Dust and speed and noise. At her. Marina throws herself into the ditch. As the car roars past, peppering her with stones and grit, she hears men's voices.

Fuck off back to the moon!

Winded, every bone and joint aching, Marina tries to push herself to her feet. She can't. She doesn't have the strength. She kneels on all fours in the dry ditch, panting, trying to listen over the sound of her own breathing for the car engine. Is it going on its way or has it turned round to come back for her? Listen. Oh listen.

A crunch of tyres on gravel, a squeak of brakes and the sound of wheels sliding to a stop.

Marina can't look.

'Marina?'

Bending over her is Weavyr on her bike.

'Get help!' Marina cries. 'Help me!'

*

'Hey, Mom.'

Marina pushes the wheelchair into the dark room. Night-lights glow. She hadn't noticed that the ceiling is covered in luminous stick-on stars.

'You awake?'

A grunt from the bed.

'No.'

Old family joke; maybe the oldest. Marina hears the head of the bed rise, lights come up to a soft glow.

'What happened to you?'

'A pick-up on manual drive happened to me.' Marina wheels to the space by the side of her mother's bed. Medical technology purrs and blinks, pumps hum. The perfumes of the essential oils, the herbs, the incenses are stronger in the night. 'I'm all right. Dr Nakamura thinks I must be made of teak or something.' She slaps the arms of the wheelchair. 'I'll be out of this thing in a day or two.'

'I heard,' her mother says. She lays a wire hand on the cover. Marina takes it.

'They're our fucking neighbours,' Marina says.

Her mother groans and clicks her tongue.

'Nasty saying.'

'Sorry. They wanted to run me off the road. They ran me off the road. On crutches.'

'The cabin looks nice white.'

'Mom, I have to tell you something.'

Marina squeezes her mother's hot, dry paw.

'It's not going to get any better. I don't know if you follow the news, but up there, on the moon, well, things are shaking up a little. The Suns have turned on their solar power grid... What I'm saying is, when things shake up there, they break down here. I think I'm a danger to everyone in this house.'

Her mother's mouth opens in a silent *oh* of surprise.

'And there's . . . business up there. I didn't come away clean. I broke a heart. I did the wrong thing. I need to do right.'

'But if you go back . . .'

'I can never come home again. But that's it. Mom, I love you, and Kessie, and Ocean and Weavyr are gifts from God, but this isn't home. There's no place for me here.

'Mom, I need to go back to the moon.'

SEVENTEEN

The tie is the thing. The suit was never an issue, two shades darker, two cuts sharper than the old man's signature grey. Close enough to be respectable, not so close as to mock. The shirt is simple: pure white, softened by a bias pattern. Tie. Here Darius hesitates. He wants the primrose yellow but it lacks force, presence. But the others are dull, over-patterned or so alien to him as to be painful to wear. Primrose it must be, but how to give it authority? The tie-pin will work the politics. His familiar Adelaide presents a range of variations on Australian themes. The flying kangaroo: no. Animals make Darius shudder. The Red Dog logo also, but for different reasons. It was the sigil of Robert Mackenzie. Darius wants to inherit, not usurp. A tight glitter of five jewels like a constellation of stars. This he does not recognise.

The Southern Cross, Adelaide answers. The constellation Crux, visible only in the southern hemispheres of both Earth and moon.

'Show me,' Darius says.

His vision soars out from the Palace of Eternal Light, away from the beacons and searchlights of the surface teams, whose mission has gone from rescue to investigation; high above the splinters of the Pavilion of Eternal Light, out among the stars. Darius peers to find Crux: there. Four bright stars against the shine of the galaxy, one lesser light.

'It's not very impressive.'

It features prominently on the Australian national flag.

'Print it,' Darius says. 'Real diamonds?'

I could not source them in time, Adelaide replies.

He knots the primrose-yellow tie, straightens. Checks teeth, eye make-up. Runs a comb through his hair. Last of all, he slips the Southern Cross pin through his tie three centimetres beneath the double Windsor knot.

'Okay, Adelaide. Tell them I'm ready.'

This is the Seventh Bell.

The lesson of the School of Seven Bells is that its lessons are not for the knife alone.

Be aware of the breath and when you become aware, become unaware. Over-attachment is a trap. Find your weight, your mass, understand the difference between them. Remember that we are born with our senses undifferentiated and that life is a journey away from that unity of sensation to discretion. Over-focus is an error.

Adelaide shows him the cameras. When the dot in the bottom right corner of his eye goes red, he will be live. There is Mariano Gabriel Demaria. But it is Lady Sun who commands his eye. He will not shake, he will not hesitate.

'Duncan Mackenzie is dead,' she said as she hurried him away from the melee in the Great Hall. At first he had not understood what she was saying. 'Listen to what I'm telling you, boy. Duncan Mackenzie is dead. Mackenzie Metals is headless. Bryce will try and take control now. It's why he did it.'

'Bryce destroyed the Pavilion of Eternal Light?'

They were in a moto, hurtling through tunnels cleared of traffic by executive command.

'We knew it was a BALTRAN shot before the debris hit the ground.

Bryce wanted to make it look like the Vorontsovs but he is not as clever as he thinks. He used that trick on the Cortas.'

'The method that won you this fight will kill you in the next,' Darius said.

'We must move quickly. We have a destiny for you to fulfil.'

Lady Sun inclines her head to Darius.

Countdown.

The dot turns red. The moon is watching.

'I am Darius Mackenzie. I am the last son of Robert Mackenzie and his true heir. I claim the title of Chief Executive of Mackenzie Metals.'

Lady Sun is smiling.

The Mackenzie Helium railcar slows, drifts in to the siding and comes to a halt. At the track-side is a VTO maintenance shed bermed deep with regolith, a small solar array, a comms tower and the standard lunar scrapheap of abandoned machinery. To the west the Mare Insularum curves into the horizon, to the east rise the northern outliers of the Apennines. Nothing more.

'I'm stating the obvious,' Bryce Mackenzie says, 'but this is not Hadley.'

'The situation at Hadley is changing fast,' Finn Warne says. Bryce shifts in his seat. He cannot be comfortable for more than a few minutes.

'Meaning?'

'We would not be welcomed.'

'I don't expect to be fucking welcomed. I expect to be fucking respected.'

'Hadley is hostile. I can't needlessly endanger you.'

'Hadley won't find me a coward,' Bryce spits. 'I have twenty staunch jackaroos back there.'

'Duncan put two hundred armed jackaroos on the field against the terrestrials. They never gave their guns back.'

Bryce rolls petulantly back in his seat, notices a tic on his lens. He leans painfully forward to tap the railcar porthole. 'What's this?'

'Rovers from the Wallace and Mare Vaporum extraction teams. We're going to transfer to rovers and meet up with the Imbrium and Serenetatis squads. Two hundred and twenty jackaroos. We finish this on the ground, out in the mirror field.'

'Siege?' Bryce asks.

'The siege of Hadley,' Finn Warne says. Bryce smiles. Dust plumes from the eastern horizon announcing the advent of Mackenzie Helium.

'Boss.' Bailey Dane, sergeant of the railcar security squad, calls from the rear cabin. 'Gupshup News. You got to see it.' Bryce Mackenzie despises the gossip networks and chat channels but they react faster than any other part of the lunar media. Fake news wears fast shoes. And there is Darius Mackenzie, with his quiffed-up hair, his primrose-yellow tie and Southern Cross pin in exactly the right position, claiming Mackenzie Metals. Fucking popinjay.

'Get me into that fucking rover!' Bryce Mackenzie bellows.

Thadie slides open the panel and her eyes widen.

'There's a bar in here.'

'Of course there is.' Denny Mackenzie leans back in his chair and puts his feet up on the footstool. 'Fix us something, will you?'

'What do you want?'

Denny turns back to the curve of pressure glass and the northern reach of the Apennines. The railcar is private charter, not a liveried executive-class Dragon transport but still comfortable, fast and well equipped. 'Sour. Lemon, enough to make you pucker up. A little punishment. Sweet. Syrup. Vanilla syrup. Little less than a pucker. Life is not sweet. The kick. Gin. Ice cold, of course. Four fingers. No, make that three. Gold leaf. A sprinkle. Stir, pour, consume.'

Thadie opens, prints, prepares and pours four glasses, for Denny, herself and Ji-Sung and Agneta, the two others who came down with

Denny Mackenzie from Bairro Alto. *The rest of you follow later. The Jack of Blades owes you. Understand?* The Mackenzie debt. Last in each glass is a pinch of gold dust. It settles slowly through the cold liquid. Denny takes a sip and falls back in his seat.

'Fucking magnificent. Been too long, lover. I need a name for you. Sunshine Express. No. Fucking ridiculous.' He lifts the glass to the vacuum. 'The Hero's Return!'

Moonquakes are of four types: deep, impact, thermal and shallow. These last are the most destructive and travel fastest. Within seconds of the news breaking from the Palace of Eternal Light, Meridian shook from prospket to Bairro Alto with the aftershocks of the assassination of Duncan Mackenzie. And the people of the High Town felt them, and gathered on their staircases and catwalks.

But he made you outcast.

'My dad is dead!' Denny Mackenzie roared.

Told you you were no son of his.

'I obeyed him. That's the Mackenzie way. I was staunch.'

Disinherited you.

He held up the hand he had maimed in obedience to the Mackenzie way.

'Blood says otherwise.'

What does it say, Jack of Blades?

'Go and take what's mine.'

You've no allies, no help, no bitsies.

'I'll get there if I have to fucking walk!' Denny Mackenzie shouted. 'Allies? Who of you is with me?' Thadie, Ji-Sung and Agneta dropped from their roosts and perches to stand with Denny Mackenzie. Bairro Alto cheered them all the way down the staircase but one voice said, *Who will defend us now?*

On level 85 Denny's familiar sparked back into life. Air, water, data. Money. And a message. *Meridian Main Station. From a staunch jackaroo.*

'It's a trap,' Agneta said.

'Maybe. Maybe not. But I've taken Bryce Mackenzie before, taken the best he had, his First Blade. Meantime, we take the elevator. Unless you want thigh muscles like that fucking tree in Twé.'

'You *have* got a knife,' Ji-Sung whispered down on the prospekt as the motos and bicycles zipped past.

'Two knives,' Denny Mackenzie said. And at the escalators down into the maw of Mackenzie Main Station, another message. *Private railcar reception. You won't come home like an oxygen beggar. From a jackaroo who remembers.*

The receptionist's hand had risen to summon security, then the barriers opened and Denny ushered his comrades through into thick carpets and sensitive mood lighting.

'Welcome, Mr Mackenzie. Your railcar is at stand five, departure in thirty minutes. Please enjoy our extensive facilities.'

'Showers, mates!' Denny shouted.

'We got showers,' Thadie said.

'These are hot.'

Ten minutes to Hadley, Mr Mackenzie, the railcar says.

'Come and see this.' Denny beckons his comrades forward. 'This is one of the sights of the moon.'

The railcar runs through the destroyed lands of the southern Palus; rilles graded flat, craters scraped to wrinkles in the skin of the moon, regolith worked and reworked, sifted and sifted until every atom of value has been sucked from it.

'There, see?' Denny points at the dazzling star rising slowly above the close lunar horizon. 'Hadley. We'll be coming into the mirror array any moment now. Look!' He stands up, arms outspread like a showman. Stars blaze up on either side of the track; the railcar drives on a track of shining molten steel through an array of five thousand mirrors, all focusing light on the peak of Hadley's dark pyramid. 'Fucking Taiyang thinks it controls the sun. We did it first and we do it best.'

'Den.'

'What, Thad?'

'Those other lights.' He rushes forward. Above the fixed suns of the mirror array lesser lights are falling, constellations of red and green. Sparkles of blue. Bright burns of white: one second, two seconds, again the nibs of blue flame. Thruster-fire.

'Moonships,' Denny whispers. 'Those are descent burns.'

'How many?'

'All of them. All over the fucking Palus.'

'VTO? Your mother is a Vorontsova,' Ji-Sung says. And the tip of a blade hovers over his cornea.

'My mother is Mackenzie. Say her name.'

'Apollonaire Vorontsova-Mac . . .' A squeal of fear.

'Her name?'

'Apollonaire Mackenzie.'

'Thank you.' The knife is back in its sheath. 'And if you ever disrespect my mother again, I will cut the spine from your back.'

'Denny, you should see this.' Thadie flicks the lead news item from the railcar's AI to Denny's familiar.

'Darius, you little cunt,' Denny breathes. 'It's the Suns.'

It's felt before heard, a beat conducted through the rails to the body of the railcar: a tremor. Th-th-thumm. Th-th-thumm. Denny steps into the airlock and it becomes sound: a rhythm. Doors seal, pressure equalises. The outlock door opens and the heard becomes the seen. The platform, the ramps, the stairways and overpasses, the underpasses and tunnels are thronged with jackaroos. Jackaroos in sasuits, business suits, skirt suits, sports wear and sleep-wear, high fashion and low grunge; kilts and boots and vat-grown leathers: basic issue hoodies and leggings, shorts and sleeveless T-shirts, the quintessential Mackenzie worker style from the dawn days of leaky habitats, treacherous rovers and untrustworthy surface-activity suits. All beating out a rhythm on the stone skin of Hadley. Th-th-thumm. Th-th-thumm.

Denny steps on to the platform. The pressing bodies make space for him. The rhythm stops: clean, mid-beat. Denny Mackenzie surveys the crowd.

'So, mates, did ya miss me?'

Hadley's stone corridors and shafts take the shout and, like the tubing of a vast wind instrument, turn it into roaring thunder. Hands slap his back, play punch him, tousle his hair, try to grab hold of him; voices cheer and whistle and good-on-ya! and *proper bogan, mate, proper bogan*, and *you little ripper* or just make incoherent roaring noises. Denny's comrades from Meridian are absorbed by the voices as they close behind the homecoming golden boy. Walk breaks into run; the rhythm picks up again: th-th-thumm. Th-th-thumm. Denny Mackenzie runs, grinning, between two endless lines of cheering, clapping people. Now he bursts into Hadley's central atrium; a pyramid inside the great pyramid. The floor is a flood of faces, reading his intention, parting before him. The escalator is not fast enough for him; he takes it five steps at a time and stands up on the balustrade of the level one deck.

Hadley falls silent. Faces crane up, peer down from the higher levels. Denny takes them in.

'My dad is dead,' he shouts. 'Bryce Mackenzie claims Mackenzie Metals. What do we say to him?'

Fuck him! a thousand jackaroos shout.

'Darius Sun is dropping combat bots and wushis all over the mirror array. What do we say to him?'

Fuck him too! Hadley roars.

Denny Mackenzie holds up his maimed hand, calling silence.

'What's this place called?'

The city thunders back its name. Denny shakes his head. The answer comes back redoubled.

'Hadley was my brother. First Blade of Mackenzie Metals. He should be standing here. He died in the Court of Clavius. He fought for this family. After him, I was First Blade. I fought for this family.

Fought for what this family stands for. Honour and pride, mates. Honour and pride. I did things that some thought were against the company. Yes, but never against the name. Never against what it means to be a Mackenzie. You know that too. You welcomed me like a hero. Let me tell you who I am. My name is Denny Mackenzie, I am the last and youngest son of Duncan Mackenzie and his one true heir. I claim Mackenzie Metals, I claim this city and I claim your loyalty. Are you with me?'

The answer drowns out the eternal rumble of the smelters, rings from the steel girders of the atrium.

'Are you with me?' Denny says again and again Hadley answers stronger. 'But, mates, mates. Our enemies are out there. They are strong, they are hard, they outnumber us and they will take everything we hold dear away from us. What are we going to do?'

Fuck 'em!

Denny milks the moment, cupping his ear, working the crowd, mouthing *What? What?*

'Fuck 'em!'

Balanced on the balustrade, Denny Mackenzie drinks down the adulation, arms spread wide, beseeching. *Come on.* A figure moving through the press of people on the balcony catches his eye. Apollonaire, his mother, in mourning white. He jumps from the balustrade.

'Mom!'

The open arms embrace her hard. Apollonaire smiles and bends to her son's ear.

'Welcome back, Dennis,' she whispers.

'Thanks for sending the railcar, Mom,' Denny whispers back. Apollonaire stiffens.

'What? I didn't... Good to have you back.'

'Mackenzie way or fucking what?' Over her shoulder he sees another woman in white emerge from the crowd: Anastasia, Duncan's keji-oko. More women in white step from the press: his sister Katarina, her granddaughter Kimmie-Leigh, Mykayla and Ngoc, Selma and Princesa. Cousins and out-cousins.

'Lead them right, Dennis,' Apollonaire says. 'First we have to tell you how the Mackenzie way works from now on.'

The Eagle of the Moon hands the martini glass to his Iron Hand.

'I shouldn't,' says Alexia. Lucas opens the windows on to the terrace garden.

'And you don't like gin,' Lucas says, stepping on to the terrace. 'But this isn't gin, and I want you to.'

Alexia follows him over the warm stones of the path, through the elegantly mutilated bergamot trees to the small domed pavilion perched on the precipice. It is built for two, intimate and vertiginous. Alexia sips and is ambushed by the smoke and salt of cachaca.

'What do you think?'

'Good. For the moon.'

'I try, I fail, I try again and fail better. Jorge wasn't impressed either. I thought I'd improved the recipe.' Evening descends on the hub, not a lengthening of shadows but a crimsoning of the world. In the Antares Quadra it is dawn, purple turns to blue. In Orion, it is high noon. It is beautiful and quite quite alien to Alexia. 'I find I have developed some terrible habits. This one I call "down the garden". Meetings are over, reading is finished, briefings are absorbed, I take a glass and I wander through the bergamots down the garden. The only ones who see me are my escoltas and spies.'

'And the entire hub.'

'Oh, they find me very boring,' Lucas says. 'Compared to my predecessor and his husband.'

'Bryce is refusing to back down,' Alexia says. She sets down the cachaca on the small stone table. It is shit.

'Darius will cut Bryce to pieces.'

'With any luck.' Lucas allows himself a tight, wry smile. 'Denny Mackenzie will be a different matter.'

'So how does Denny Mackenzie turn up in Hadley with half of Bairro Alto and the guns of a thousand jackaroos?'

'He was tipped off,' Lucas says. 'And bankrolled.'

'Mackenzie Metals? His mother?'

'None of those,' Lucas says. 'It was me.' He takes a sip of his down-the-garden gin. He tried cachaca once and will not make that mistake again. Pure and pristine gin of his own design, now and always. 'Don't look so surprised. You shouldn't be so expressive. They have machines reading your face, calculating your emotions. I slipped him enough money to get back to Hadley and chartered the railcar. All very discreet: untraceable.'

'Denny Mackenzie.'

'Yes.'

'In charge of Mackenzie Metals?'

'Well, that remains to be seen. Darius Sun is building a formidable force out there. Maybe he will prevail. Taiyang's pockets are bottomless. But I believe it is always good to introduce a third force into a simple binary. It sows instability and chaos. I like chaos. And the terrestrials are nervous enough about the sun-belt without Taiyang staging a hostile takeover of Mackenzie Metals. No, let Denny swagger and posture. Let him claim Hadley. I will know where he is. You always know where you are with the Mackenzies.' Lucas looks out at the deepening sunset, dropping into indigo. 'I have another bad habit, alas. I call it "back up the garden". Care to accompany me?'

They leave their glasses on the table. Subtle lighting has turned the Eyrie into a cascade of lights, pools of blue, rippling whites: a lightfall.

'One condition,' Alexia says. 'I want the gin.'

EIGHTEEN

Jesus and Mary, they're fast. Half-glimpsed flickers between the mirror pylons, using the array for cover. This is a hideous place to fight. His jackaroos are strewn across the mirror field; names, tags overlaying the visual and infra-red maps. Radar throws up five thousand false contacts. He's fighting blind. The common channel crackles.

They're too fast, the fuckers...

Rachel, where are you? Where are you?

I'm pulling back, I'm pulling back.

I can't see...

A name tag turns white.

'Fall back!' Finn Warne orders. White-outs all over his HUD and his tactical displays are blind. The enemy is radar-soft and masking its thermal signature in the heat-glow of the mirrors. Finn has helium miners, processing engineers, field surveyors, maintenance workers against sleek, fanatic Taiyang killing machines and trained wushis. Finn Warne flicks the rendezvous co-ordinates to his fighters. Jackaroos, dusters, down-on-their luck mercs. Get them under the cover of the rover-mounted chain-guns. Figures bound past him, three-metre leaps, dust pluming. Sasuits, shell-suits, a miscellany of surface-survival engineering. Workers against soldiers.

'Get the rovers closer!' Finn Warne orders, throwing out evacuation points to the AIs. 'We're being cut to pieces out here.'

A prickle on the top of his scalp: a warning from the suit haptics. He looks up to see the black sparkle with sharp blue stars, falling slowly. Thrusters.

'The fucking things are trying to cut us off!' Finn shouts on the common channel. Bots drop to the regolith, rebound on their shock absorbers. There lies their weakness. A Sun fighting drone lands in front of him. Finn Warne twists and snaps the spear into two halves. The axe-head whips out on its cable and takes two of the machine's legs out at the knee joints. Finn leaps, reverses the weapon and drives the spear-point hard through the sensory core. The thing goes down in a flail of limbs and blades. Still the bot kicks a circle of moondust around the axis of the impaling spear. Finn Warne opens the tangs and wrenches the blade from the machine's carapace in a mess of capillaries and processors. The bot is still at last.

'Where are my fucking rovers?'

He wanted guns. Gauss rifles. You need guns to take Hadley. Bryce had vetoed them: they would take too long to equip; the mirror array would be smashed to a maelstrom of flying glass.

Fuck you, Bryce, always valuing the materiel more than the meat.

Another tingle at the back of his head: he spins. Charging down on him, a blade on each wrist, is a combat shell-suit in the matt black and silver of Taiyang. Finn cracks the spear shaft, the cable whips again and drives the axe-blade through the face plate in an explosion of shivered glass and blood. He kicks the spasming body away, rips the axe free and snaps both halves of the pole-arm together again.

Nice little weapon. Some smart fucker at Huygens came up with it: easy to print, easy to use. An Information Age society that fights its wars with Bronze Age weaponry.

The rovers finally load up.

'Rachel, Quoc, with me!' Finn commands. His rearguard falls in at his side, weapons hefted, but the Taiyang bots and wushis have halted on the edge of the mirror field. They have won. They have humiliated Mackenzie Helium. There is no profit in prolonging the slaughter.

Eighty jackaroos went in. Forty-six came out.

The bots and wushis melt away into the shadow and dazzle of the mirrors, save one, which raises an armoured hand, rotates it, extends a single finger. Darius? Could be. The suit is small. Finn has only met him on rare formal visits to Crucible, spoken no more than the niceties due the son of Robert Mackenzie and Jade Sun, but he came away with the sense of a RALF. Right Arrogant Little Fucker. Darius Sun would do something like that.

Finn Warne's haptics let him appreciate the solidity and weight of the spear-axe in his hands.

Nice piece.

'Rachel, Quoc, go.'

The rovers have loaded up the survivors and fire up their traction motors.

Finn lifts the spear, finds the balance in its irregular form. He feeds power into the suit servos. He hurls it with all his amplified strength at the Sun suit's chestplate.

Weren't expecting that, were you, you little fuck?

The figure sidesteps, drops to a crouch. The hand moves faster than anything Finn Warne has ever seen and snatches the spear in mid-flight. Spins it, aims it. Finn Warne is sure he can see a smile behind that dark face plate.

'Bryce!'

No answer.

'Bryce!'

Finn Warne summons another display – the ragged wedge of rovers fleeing the bloody debacle of Palus Putridinis. There is Bryce's rover, ahead of the pack.

'No you fucking don't,' Finn swears. The combat suit calculates reserves. He has enough power for ten minutes at full speed. Enough to catch up with Bryce's executive rover, though he will be down to milliwatts and gasps.

Enough to outrun a spear aimed at his back?

He turns and kicks the suit into power run. He cries out at the agony in his joints, would fall and roll if the suit were not in control. Ten minutes. He can't take it. He has to take it.

There is the dust-line of the retreat. He sprints between the scattered rovers and their defeated cargoes: shell-suits clamped into acceleration frames, sasuited dusters clinging to struts and strapping, webbed in, lashed down, jolting to every rock and divot. Bootprints among the tyre-tracks. One set of tracks and a single dust plume now.

Power eight per cent.

He catches up with the racing rover, locks a glove around an inspection ladder. Mid-swing he slams into the ladder with an impact he can feel even through shell and pressure skin. Has he broken anything? He dangles from the back of the rover, each swing a down-tick on the power meter; then gets a boot against a bulkhead, pushes and manages to get his other hand on the ladder. From that it is a simple, agonising process to haul himself up the ladder and over the pressure hull to the life-support section.

Power two per cent.

Finn Warne uncoils the power conduit, flips up the dustcap and plugs himself in. It's like sex. Better. Air now. Fresh and sweet and so so cool. What you smell most in a shell-suit is your own mouth. He lies on his back on the top of the rover, bathing in clean, sweet air. Last, communications. He patches into the rover's common channel.

'Bryce. What you did there, running off, I didn't appreciate that.'

There is no response for a long time but Finn will not concede the weakness of having to repeat himself.

'Finn. Glad you made it.'

'No thanks to you, Bryce.'

'Finn, Finn. This was a business decision.'

'First Blades being just another fungible asset.'

No reply from inside the comfortable, air-conditioned cabin.

'I see you're taking us back to East Insularum.'

'I must get to Kingscourt.'

'Not that way you won't.'

'What do you mean?'

'VTO Moonship *Skopa* just landed at East Insularum. They're cutting off your retreat.'

Again, long silence.

'Help me, Finn.'

'What was that?'

'Help me.'

'I can do that, Bryce. I can get you back to Kingscourt in a blink. But it may not be up to your usual standards of comfort and style.'

'Just tell me the fuck where to go!'

True fear in the big man's voice. Finn Warne smiles inside his helmet. He summons co-ordinates on his suit hub and throws them through the hull to Bryce.

'Here you go.'

'A BALTRAN station.'

'It's fast and it's sure. And we have history with BALTRAN capsules.'

Finn Warne grips hard as the rover changes course at speed.

'I hold you responsible for this embarrassment,' Bryce says.

Thirty-four deaths. Good people, staunch people, gutted, dismembered, disembowelled; limbs and organs and blood sprayed across Palus Putridinis. And you call it an embarrassment.

The horns of Huygens BALTRAN rise from the horizon. *Enjoy your ride, fat man. I said I'd get you back to Kingscourt, but I lied. Two blinks, three blinks. Maybe more. You've never travelled BALTRAN before, so make the most of the experience. Tumble in your own vomit and piss and shit. I will watch you launch, then I will cycle into the rover and drink your fucking personalised vodka to thirty-four staunch jackaroos all the way to Hadley.*

I'm looking forward to the inaugural meeting of the Ex-First Blades Club.

Beauty to Jiang Ying Yue is the actinic flicker of landing thrusters over the Bradley Massif. Lights moving against higher lights. Since girlhood, Jiang Ying Yue has loved spaceships. When she first went on to the surface her class stumbled and lurched, trying to find a way of moving in the heavy rookie shell-suits, but she had jumped. Jumped and reached for the lights in the sky. Shell-suit actuators were powerful but never enough to push her right off her world to the place where the ships flew. Since that day she has been trapped, pinned to her tiny moon, looking up.

Orel is a glitter of beacons and warning lights, then it catches the sun and Jiang Ying Yue sees the moonship whole. She recognises an executive transport module in the cargo gantry. She has learned every ship, crew member, module and configuration in the Vorontsov fleet. She resents that the Vorontsovs should command such beauty. They are coarse-souled, heavy, loud; to them their ships are engineering, navigation, orbits and payloads. To her they are angels.

Then the engine burns and dust billows over her.

She walks through the dust towards the image on her HUD. The ramp is lowered, the lock opens and she cycles through. Airblades scythe the dust from her suit, revealing stripe by stripe the bright battle colours of Taiyang. Jiang Ying Yue opens her helmet and tastes the pepper spice of moondust. Beyond the lock the Suns await.

Corporate Conflict Resolution Officer Jiang, her familiar announces. She is not a Sun, she cannot wear the hexagrams of the clan. She does not need the tags her familiar adds to the gathered Suns: like Vorontsov ship design, she has learned the corporate hierarchy of Taiyang.

'So Bryce Mackenzie fled like a weeping child,' Zhiyuan says.

'By BALTRAN,' Ying Yue says. The suits suppress smirks, imagining Bryce Mackenzie bouncing like a handball inside a BALTRAN can.

'Our losses?' asks Amanda Sun. The Taiyang board sits in a semicircle of minimal, elegant chrome and faux-leather chairs. Jiang Ying Yue is very conscious that she is standing, in battle armour, leaving dusty footprints on the grey carpet.

'Heavier than I would have liked.' Her familiar sends lists and charts to the hovering hexagrams. 'The greater part of these is robotic, but we have human casualties.'

'Messy,' Sun Gian-yin says.

'Our models did not predict that the Australians would fight in the face of overwhelming odds.'

'I've never known a Mackenzie to back down from a fight,' Lady Sun says. A staffer pours a glass thimble of gin; she takes a decorous sip.

'And what do your models predict for these Australians?' Zhiyuan asks.

'We are shipping in resources to maintain the siege until we gain control over Hadley's life-support systems. At that point resistance will collapse very quickly. In the meantime, any counter-attacks by Mackenzie jackaroos will be swiftly and efficiently suppressed.'

'Denny Mackenzie is not to be underestimated,' Zhiyuan says. 'He resisted all attempts to oust him from Bairro Alto.'

'Tell me, has my great-grandson acquitted himself well?' Lady Sun asks.

'He commanded a bot squad and fought with great valour and bravery. He personally challenged Finn Warne and forced him to flee.'

'Finn Warne, who has subsequently defected to Mackenzie Metals,' Amanda Sun says. 'With first-hand knowledge of our set-up and tactics.'

'We have not experienced any significant deviation from our

model,' Ying Yue says. 'We expect Hadley to capitulate within seventy-two hours.'

'Stuck in this box for seventy-two hours?' Lady Sun hisses.

'We anticipate surrender long before then,' Ying Yue says. 'After all, it is just a transfer of management. The Mackenzies understand business.' She pauses: images on her lens, words in her ear. 'Excuse me. There has been a development.' As her helmet closes, Jiang Ying Yue says to the seated board members, 'Denny Mackenzie has come out to fight.'

There is still a memory of old dust on the air. Denny Mackenzie swipes a casual finger across a door frame. He feels the familiar prickle, the burned, spicy perfume. A soft grey smear on his fingertip. Lady Luna's deadliest weapon: moondust.

His father had done the same, when he entered this room at the very top of the pyramid to wake Hadley after decades of sleep; turn the mirrors to the sun, kindle the fire in the city's heart. He had tasted the dust.

The women stand around a tactical display: a projection shared across the lenses of everyone in the control centre. Process flows and smelter data have been replaced by a detailed schematic of the Palus Putridinis. Denny pores over the map.

'Shit.'

'The Suns have contracted the entire VTO moonship fleet,' Apollonaire Mackenzie says.

'The space-lift capacity is staggering,' says Anastasia Mackenzie, co-widow of Duncan Mackenzie.

'I thought the Vorontsovs were our mates,' Denny says. 'I had this idea that we were going into the asteroid business together?'

'A contract is a contract,' says a young, dark-skinned woman, hair piled high on her head in an elaborate, joyful ziggurat: Hadley's pyramid inverted. 'We've never been known to turn down a paying job.'

Denny Mackenzie raises an eyebrow.

'Now you, I don't know.'

'Irina Efua Vorontsova-Asamoah,' the young woman said. 'I'm to be oko to Kimmi-Leigh Mackenzie.'

'And your qualification to be here?' Denny asks.

'Her qualification is that she is the nearest thing we have to an expert on VTO,' Apollonaire says. 'And potential hostage. No offence, Irina.'

Irina inclines her head: *none taken.*

Denny studies the map again. The Suns have the numbers and the positions and more arrive every moment by moonship and BALTRAN capsule.

'How long can they stay out there?'

'As long as they want,' says Katarina Mackenzie, Denny's sister.

'Until they crack our life support,' says Magda Mackenzie, his keji-niece through Anastasia and his half-brother Yuri.

'And how long will that take?'

'Our models run at somewhere under seventy-two hours,' says Anastasia Mackenzie.

'Fuck!' Denny punches the display, punches illusion. Where there had been unity and purpose in the control room is now a crackle of fear. 'We go out there and try to duke it out . . .'

'They tear us apart,' says Deontia Mackenzie. Her mother Tara, Meridian's leading fashionista, had died in Ironfall.

'They've been testing our cyberdefences,' Irina Vorontsova-Asamoah says. 'We're fending them off. Hadley's operating system is riddled with Trojan horses. Some of them have been there since the city was built. There's ancient code in there; like fifty years old . . .' Irina stops. No one in the control room moves. Everyone looks at everyone else. Everyone has had the same idea at the same instant. Everyone except Irina.

'Trojan horses,' Denny says. 'Trojan fucking horses!'

'Remember Ironfall,' his mother says and the mantra runs around the tactical table. *Remember Ironfall.*

'We'll need a distraction,' Anastasia says. 'As soon as they see what we're doing, they'll go after the array.'

Denny grins gold and spreads his arms wide.

'Am I not the moon's number one distraction?' His call goes out through the pyroxene corridors and grey olivine halls of Hadley. *I need thirty staunch jackaroos. Fighters, gunners. Suicide mission. Airlock five. Who's with me?*

The women smile as they bend to their tasks.

'We need to hit hard,' Deontia Mackenzie says. 'We get one go at this.'

Magda Mackenzie scans the display, frowning, then zooms it and touches a finger to a glowing blue dot.

'*Orel*, just arrived from the Palace of Eternal Light. That's an executive transport pod.'

'They brought the board to watch their golden boy march in triumph through London Court,' Apollonaire says,

'Ey!' Denny shouts. 'I'm your fucking Golden Boy and don't forget it.'

'Don't get killed, Denny,' Magda Mackenzie says.

'You do your bit right, I may not even need to kill anyone,' Denny says.

'I don't understand . . .' Irina Vorontsova-Asamoah says.

'Tell me, Vorontsov, what's the Mackenzie motto?' Denny calls from the door. His fingers grip the dusty frame.

'Mackenzies repay three times,' Irina says.

'Uh uh.' Denny shakes his head. He beams a savage, golden grin.

'Seize your fallen enemy's weapon,' chorus the women of Hadley. 'And use it against them.'

'In. In. In. In. In.' Denny Mackenzie slaps each volunteer on the back as they pass into the main lock. 'You. In. You. Suit up. You . . .' His finger freezes, pointing. 'What the fuck are you doing here?'

'I defected, or didn't you hear?' Finn Warne is not imposing by lunar standards but the crowd edges away from him, leaving him in social vacuum.

'Why the fuck should I let you fight for Mackenzie Metals?'

'Because I'm the only one ever had you, Denny Mackenzie. In Schmidt crater, in that stupid gold suit. You didn't know me, I was just another jackaroo. But I got you, Jack of Blades. Left you for dead. Took a Corta to save you.'

The silent crowd waits. Denny Mackenzie jerks a thumb towards the lock.

'Get in. Suit up.'

As Finn Warne passes, Denny stops him with a hand on the shoulder and a whisper.

'You thought you had me back at Schmidt when you jumped my jackaroos and left me for dead. Got to tell you, mate, Denny Mackenzie doesn't die that easy, even if it took a Corta to save him. Understand that. And I've got a shiny new gold suit.'

The new suit is shell armour, the lacquer job still phenolic and pungent in the confined space of the suit room.

'Can't move in these fucking things,' Denny swears as the panels clamshell and seal around him. The haptic rig moves in to read his body and he feels the servos activate. The suit is power and protection but the price is speed and manoeuvrability. In the way of the knife, speed is life. Move fast, move clever, turn on a blade-tip and gut your enemy.

The shell-suit comes to life around him. A woman in space-orc armour snaps firearms from the rack and hands one to each suited fighter. Her tag reads Sonia Ngata, she is a veteran of Mackenzie Metals' assault to break the siege of Twé by the machines of the Lunar Mandate Authority.

'What's this?' Denny Mackenzie says. He holds the weapon as if it is a turd.

'Gauss rifle,' Sonia Ngata says. 'Put a slug clean through a bot from two kilometres.'

'I've fought those things,' Finn Warne says. 'The Suns have made some improvements since Twé. You don't want to see how quick they can cover two kilometres. You've got two shots, then they're on you.'

'Just give me a fucking blade,' Denny Mackenzie mutters, turning the gauss rifle over in his gauntleted hands. Sonia Ngata steps forward, slaps a release on the barrel. A bayonet snaps out. A twist and she hands the blade to Denny.

'Nice,' he says. 'Two would be nicer. Okay.' His squad fall in before him. Thirty suits. Christ on crutches. 'My friends, my dear friends. We are going to launch a diversionary attack on the Taiyang team trying to hard-hack our life-support systems. They will be defended by wushis and bots. We are outnumbered and outgunned. We shall probably die. Old men talk about death and glory and that is the oldest shittest lie there is. There is no glory in death. Death is the end of everything that is good. And I am leading you to your deaths. Our job is to buy time. And if that time is measured in lives, not seconds, then that is our mission. I don't want any of you to die, so fight like fucking demons. Fight like life itself. That's all I have to say. Thank you. You are the best of people. You are jackaroos, you are blades, yes, but every fucking one of you is a Mackenzie.'

The lock rings to cheers, then helmets seal and the pressure monitors drop towards vacuum. Green lights turn red. The outlock opens and with a roar on the common channel, Denny Mackenzie's gold armour leads the charge out on to the regolith.

Run, Jiang Ying Yue orders her suit. *This waypoint.* The battle armour answers with instant speed and power. Such superb engineering. With the suit's autonomics in control, she can devote her full attention to the counter-attack. Thirty Mackenzie Metal blades, at full suit speed, charging the Taiyang engineering team working on the hack into Hadley's main comms line. Logical. Obvious. Tactically naive. The Australians love bravado. Bravado does not win wars.

Her eyes flicker across her tactical array, identifying units. She shapes orders in her mind and her bots and wushis move to comply.

Intel is life. She zooms in on the raiding party. Her enemy is armed with Siege of Twé era shell-suits and gauss rifles. Knives of course. The Mackenzie and their knives. They are quick and determined but they have no discipline, no harmony: a loping band of brigands, battle-suits decorated in a carnival of colours and designs and patterns. Chaotic. They will fight as individuals, not a unit. Her HUD fastens on a golden shell-suit. Jiang Ying Yue allows herself a moment of surprise. Denny Mackenzie, the Golden Boy. They have sent their prince to fight. How quaint. She'll punish them for that.

She fields a distress call from the engineers.

'Hold position,' she orders. 'Reinforcements will be with you momentarily.' A touch of her will and two squads of combat bots spring into the air and light their thrusters, arcing high over the black mirrors of the furnace array.

The Australians don't stand a chance. Jiang Ying Yue relishes the thought of their defeat. She has always found them brash, arrogant people, fatally wedded to the delusion that the universe loves them.

Find Darius, she orders her suit. He flashes up on her display, running hard with Red Platoon towards the line of battle.

'Darius, return to the executive module,' Jiang Ying Yue orders. *Let the boy see blood,* Lady Sun had instructed her, but that is Denny Mackenzie at the head of a squad of hand-picked jackaroos.

'I want to face Denny Mackenzie,' Darius answers.

'Denny Mackenzie will cut you apart.'

'Denny Mackenzie hasn't trained at the School of Seven Bells.'

'Return to *Orel*. That's an order.'

'You don't order me. I am CEO of Mackenzie Metals.'

Jiang Ying Yue sighs.

'I am Corporate Conflict Resolution Officer and Field Commander with full executive authority and I can take control of your suit and make it run you back to the command module on the double.'

She hears Darius mutter coarse Mackenzie oaths. His icon on her HUD changes direction. Jiang Ying Yue sends a subtle navigation override to his suit, in case he should change his mind when he thinks he is out of line of her sight.

Yellow and Purple platoons, to my mark, she orders. Bots drop out of the sky around her and snatch up her pace. Only a few hundred metres now. Her skirmishers are already engaged.

'All units engage,' she calls on the common channel, draws her blades and leaps.

'Above you!'

Denny Mackenzie wrenches the bayonet from the central processing core of the Taiyang battle bot and looks up. The bot drops, blades down.

'Move the fuck, suit!' he yells but the haptics have read his intention and send him rolling away. Landing jets sparkle, the tip of a blade flung out at the last instant scrapes a silver line across his gold shell. Denny steps inside the blade, seizes the bot's arm and wrenches it from the carapace in spurts of black hydraulic fluid. The second blade scythes towards him and the bot's head disintegrates. It goes to the regolith in a thrash of spindly limbs and spikes.

Space-orc-armoured Sonia Ngata lowers her gauss rifle and touches a finger to her helmet.

The warning shout had been Finn Warne's.

Denny scoops up the bot blade. Two knives now. The way it should be.

Two blades, but they are down to twenty and still the bots come, wave after wave charging through the mirror field, dropping from above. The initial charge had taken them to within knife-tip of the Taiyang team working at the main comms cable; then the bots came bounding over the rovers. Blood on the regolith, much blood. They are surrounded, driven ever tighter. It will be back to back, then mate with mate, and then they will die.

'Control!' Denny yells. 'We're fucked!'

He scissors the two blades and sends a bot's sensor-head flying.

'We have target lock, Denny,' says a voice from the glowing summit of Hadley.

'Irina?'

'It is. Stand by.'

'We're dying here.'

Far out across the Palus Putridinis, an arc of mirrors suddenly blazes brighter than the sun. The clouds of battle-dust render the beam visible, almost solid. It sweeps downwards, and another section of the array catches it, throw it on to another, to another; to focus it on the furthest VTO moonship. In an instant the heat-exchange vanes glow red. There are seconds before failure, heat overload and the fuel tanks exploding.

'You dancer!' Denny Mackenzie shouts on the control channel.

The ship's crew reach a decision. Thrusters kindle, the ship lifts, the main engine burns and in a few seconds *Orel* is lights in the sky. All across the Marsh of Decay VTO ships lift clear of the mirror array on knives of blue fire.

The mirrors blaze with light and beneath them, not a human or machine moves.

'The executive module!' Finn Warne yells. 'They left the executive module! The entire board of Taiyang!'

'So they did,' Denny Mackenzie says. 'So they did.' As if every brain and AI on the battlefield has come to that realisation at the same instant, the frozen paralysis shatters. Wushis, bots, engineers, rovers explode into manic motion. Fighting machines vault through the air like heroes of sword-wielding legends. Rovers send up geysers of dark dust as they spin their wheels. Denny sees machines go down under those wheels, sees a frantic wushi try, fail to get clear. The body cartwheels high over the rover to smash into the molten heart of one of Hadley's mirror-weapons. It's a retreat to protect the board: a rout.

'Take the heat off them,' Denny says. The sudden darkness as the mirrors tilt away from the sun is so intense it is almost palpable. 'Cool heads make smarter decisions. Get me a channel to Taiyang, will you?'

'You're in, Denny.'

The blades unfold from their final stand. Eighteen. Eighteen of the thirty who roared their allegiance in Airlock Four. They form a ragged line, suits scarred and slashed, antennae lopped, face plates cracked, leaks bubbled with grey emergency sealant. Sonia Ngata rests the butt of her gauss rifle on the regolith. Finn Warne stands at Denny's shoulder.

'Taiyang: this is Denny Mackenzie.' He is broadcasting not just to the Taiyang board and army, but to his jackaroos, to the control room, to the whole of Hadley. 'I'll accept your surrender now.'

NINETEEN

'Does she wear that all the time?' Vidhya Rao asks. Luna sits at the end of the table, arms folded on the glass. Her chin rests on her arms. Her living eye glares at the economist. Her dead eye is beyond knowing.

'All the time,' Ariel says.

'It's tattooed,' Luna says.

'It's not,' Ariel says.

'I might get it tattooed,' Luna says with steel.

'You will not,' Ariel says but the victory is not assured.

'I need to talk with you,' Vidhya Rao says. 'Professionally.'

'Luna, would you like to hear this?'

Luna nods.

Vidhya Rao dips er head. The escape from Meridian and the wrath of the Suns tested the physical resources of an elderly, scholarly neutro. Small praise to the parsimonious gods of economists, e had blacked from gee-forces just before the first moonloop release. E had been unconscious the entire relay, tether to tether to tether, juggled around the moon until the final tether deposited er into the docking clamps of the Coriolis tower.

Seventy minutes is a dangerous time for a seventy-year-old to be unconscious. University crash teams extricated her from the capsule and took her to the faculty. As soon as e could move and speak, e requested a meeting with Ariel Corta. E was invited to Ariel's crater-rim apartment.

'Congratulations on turning all of Meridian on its head,' Ariel says. 'My own exodus was disappointingly mundane by comparison. An early-morning wheel down Gargarin Prospekt.'

'I had assistance,' Vidhya Rao says. 'A sub-AI on Taiyang's back-door into the Three August Ones using the persona of Lady Sun. It's complicated.'

'Three August Ones: like Fu Xi, Shennong and the Yellow Emperor?' Luna asks, swinging her legs.

'Like whatever they want to be,' Vidhya Rao says. 'I detest them. Their intelligence is so alien to ours that they can barely communicate. At best they seem eccentric; at worst deliberately obstructive. Imagine a friend who only talks in riddles, or anagrams, or quotations from a telenovela you don't watch. Perhaps they are sincerely trying to communicate, perhaps it is all games only they understand.'

'What did you ask them?' Ariel asks.

'To generate forecasts of the Lunar Bourse five, ten, fifteen and fifty years after it goes online.'

'What did they show you?' Luna asks. This is magic, bruxaria, wonder-stuff.

'Fifty years from now there is no life on the moon,' Vidhya Rao says. 'Human, animal, vegetable. The moon is a dead world run by machines making money. The cities are empty, cold and open to vacuum.'

'Me too?' Luna chirps.

'Everyone,' Vidhya Rao begins. 'Two years from now, the terrestrials introduce engineered plagues from Earth. We have no immunity, our phages are powerful but our medical facilities are overrun. This is plague upon plague upon plague. Ten years from now there are only a couple of hundred humans alive on the moon, nearside and farside. The systems are breaking down, the machines are failing, the people are ageing, there are no new children being born . . . Fifteen years from now . . .'

Luna's eyes are wide, her lips wavering, her nostrils flared.

'Enough,' Ariel says. 'You're scaring her.'

'The Three August Ones assign probabilities to their prophecies. If the LMA pursues the Lunar Bourse, the probability of the total extinction of human life on the moon within twenty years is eighty-nine per cent, within fifty years one hundred per cent.'

Luna is grey with fear.

'Ariel, is this going-to-happen or might-happen?'

'The terrestrials are scared,' Vidhya Rao says. 'The Vorontsovs want to build a network of space elevators and turn the moon into the hub of the solar system. The Mackenzies want to mine asteroids and build space habitats. Both sides need Lucas Corta to endorse them but they don't know where he stands. Then I propose my Lunar Bourse scheme. They like it. They like it very much. They like most of all that it is unimaginable wealth with no human input. They have everything they want. And I gave it to them.'

Ariel takes Luna's hand.

'Luna, anjinho, don't be scared,' Ariel says.

The girl shakes her head.

'I'm not scared. I just want to know what I can do.'

'Lucas has power, authority, the Cortas restored,' Vidhya Rao says. 'Everything but one thing.'

'Lucasinho.'

'You have what he wants. He has what you want.'

'I remember saying to you that Cortas don't do politics.'

'What you said to me was, Cortas don't do democracy.' Vidhya Rao taps a finger to the folds of er right eye. 'My external memory is flawless.'

'Then it'll remember that line came just after you told me I was some kind of Chosen One,' Ariel says.

'Our first meeting. Your first session of the Pavilion of the White Hare.'

'And you've kept turning up ever since to pronounce doom and remind me of my special status. You clambered all the way to Bairro Alto to invite me to cocktails with the Eagle of the Moon and feed me that same old Special One nonsense. Is this why you're here? Third time's the charm? Fairy stories, Vidhya. Whether it's Canopus in Aries or your Three August Ones, it's Fairy Stories. The universe doesn't have heroes.'

'Nevertheless . . .' Vidhya Rao says.

'You've always got an answer,' Ariel says. 'It's all scripted whether I want it or not. What part of the telenovela is this?'

' "Refusing the Call",' Vidhya Rao says.

'Consider it refused,' Ariel says. 'The moon stands, the moon falls: it will do it without me.'

Ariel sweeps from the room in a flurry of polka-dot jersey. Luna remains for a sustained glare, to let Vidhya Rao know the depth of her disapproval, before marching after her tia.

'But you will,' Vidhya Rao says softly to the empty room. Dust sparkles in the light from the window. 'You can't help it.'

Luna thinks she has been into every tunnel and shaft and duct in Coriolis, but Amalia Sun leads her into pipes and conduits strange to her.

'Where are you going?' Luna whispers as she peers out from a vent eight levels down in the emergency stairwell. It had been a tough climb down the zig-zagging shaft; no opportunity to drop and land; familiar-Luna showing her the position of power lines that could flash her to nothing. Amalia Sun goes through a green-painted service door and Luna has to haul herself up in a tricky ninety-degree horizontal turn into the airspace between the wall-panelling and the gas-sealed stone. She hopes the airspace runs the length of this level: she has had to double back from dead-ends or deep drops or live power relays too many times since Amalia Sun got up from her seat – always the same seat – in the common room and Luna stirred from her long watching and followed. Familiar-Luna shows her an air-vent fifty metres down the airspace. Luna scampers, hands and feet, and arrives to see Amalia waiting at the door of a freight elevator.

Where to? Luna asks Luna-familiar. Amalia Sun has switched her familiar off, but Luna's familiar can access the elevator's rudimentary AI.

Park level, Familiar-Luna says.

'Back up again.' The freight elevator is slow and arrives a long way from the park door and Luna knows a cunning short-cut.

'What are you doing?' Luna mutters to herself as she takes the service ladder three levels to Level 12. She slips out of a cleaning-bot hatch, sprints down the corridor and takes the direct elevator, the one she uses with Lucasinho on their expeditions, which will deliver her outside the park entrance even as Amalia Sun is stepping out from the sliding doors. No one on the business of good takes such a long route through nothing and nowhere. It is as if the woman is trying to avoid being seen, trying to throw as much dust over her tracks as possible.

Luna is a daily sight at the park so she can stand in the entrance and watch Amalia Sun walk towards her, nod a greeting, and walk on along the corridor towards the yellow door with the biohazard markings.

'Shitzer!' Luna swears. She doesn't have the clearance to go through that door. But there is a red door on the first cross-walk which will take her into the air-ducts, and they follow the layout of the clean room. There are only two ways out of the park-level biohazard zone, and Luna knows her prey well enough to make a good guess which Amalia Sun will take. She runs lightly along the trunking, ducks down a right into a lesser conduit and is peeping down through a vent to see Amalia Sun exit the door on to the stairwell.

'Got you!' Luna says. 'I know where you're going.'

She follows anyway, to be sure. Amalia Sun takes the staircase two levels up to the bio-fabricator level. Luna drops out of the roof to see Amalia Sun push open the door to the protein-chip printshop.

*

Dr Gebreselassie catches sight of Luna hovering in the door to her office, half in, half out. The door frame bisects her face.

'Can I come in?' says the human side of Luna's face.

'What's wrong?' Dr Gebreselassie asks.

'Why do you think something's wrong?'

'Because you never asked if you could come in before.'

Dr Gebreselassie pulls a chair out with her foot and Luna drops on to it and swings her feet.

'So tell me.'

'Okay,' Luna says. 'But first I have to ask you a technical question.'

Dr Gebreselassie has learned not to be surprised at anything Luna Corta says or does.

'Ask.'

'Technically, is it possible for someone to add memories of things that didn't happen to Lucasinho's protein chips?'

'Technically, it is,' Dr Gebreselassie says. 'Why do you ask?'

'Okay,' Luna says and tells Dr Gebreselassie about Lucasinho talking about his mother – which he never did – and when he lived in the Palace of Eternal Light – where he never lived – and all the good times he had with his Sun aunts and uncle and cousins – who he never knew. Dr Gebreselassie's face grows grave. Then Luna tells her that she is an explorer and that she knows all Coriolis's secret tunnels and corridors and walkways and how she used to them to spy on Amalia Sun and follow her strange long route through the campus all the way to the protein chip factory.

There Dr Gebreselassie holds up a hand.

'Luna, hold it there a moment.'

The door opens. Dakota Kaur Mackenzie comes into the office.

'So, Luna,' Dr Gebreselassie says. 'I'd like you to tell Dakota everything you told me.'

*

Lady Sun turns the little metal cylinder over in her hands. It is the size of her thumb, heavy, cold and slightly greasy to the touch. Her fingers sense minute markings etched into the metal.

'What is this?' she asks. She has been disturbed, in her apartment, in her solitude and contemplation. Her temper is short and not sweet.

'A note of credit from the University of Farside. Delivered by BALTRAN, to me, personally,' says Amanda Sun.

Lady Sun holds the cylinder up before her eyes, strains to make out the engraving.

'Such tiny writing,' she tuts. 'Credit for what?'

'From the University of Farside, Faculty of Biocybernetics, School of Neurotechnology to the account of Taiyang: Carbon; fifty-one thousand two hundred point eight eight grams, oxygen; sixteen thousand one and twelve point six five grams . . .' Amanda Sun says.

'The chemical constituents of a human body,' Lady Sun says and the chill of the metal invades her. She touches her hand to her chest. Her own trick of power, turned against her.

'Yes,' Amanda Sun says. 'Amalia Sun.'

Analiese Mackenzie can remember the moment she realised that music is a demon. She had completed her twelfth repetition of the twenty-third gusheh of the seventh rastgah, the Rastgah-e Mahur, and saw blood on the strings of her setar. The taut steel strings had abraded the tips of her fingers down to raw flesh. She had not noticed.

She was fourteen when the setar took blood.

She had just turned thirteen when it made her love it. Just turned thirteen and riding Equatorial One back with her mums from the new surveyings at Rimae Kopf to Crucible. Looking out of the window. Flicking the channels on her entertainment. When a spray of notes like molten silver in her ear made her sit up. Strings, notes of metallic precision, talking to her, to her alone, to no one else on this round round moon, clear and precise. She understood everything they said, every emotion they summoned – elation, peace, control, awe, fear, mystery. Everything was limned in light; everything was clear.

'Listen!' she shouted, jumping down from her seat to wake her dozing mums. 'Listen!' She flicked the music on to their familiars. 'It's like . . . it's like out there, in here.'

They listened. They didn't hear.

That silver voice was that of the setar, an instrument of classical Persia. One could be made. Anything could be made on the moon. She learned the tuning, the fingering, the gushehs that built through sayr into the dastgahs into the magnificences of the ratifs: the symmetries, the asymmetries, the free-forms: all these on a carbon setar strung with lunar steel. Later, when the setar had possessed her, she paid a stunning sum of bitsies to have one made, from wood, by hand, fretted with true silk, flown up from Earth.

She found other musicians who had been touched by this music. Not many, and they didn't see what she had seen in the music: the harsh, beautiful, austere, brilliant nature of her world. But they had been possessed by the demon, and as she met musicians in other disciplines she saw that they too were demon-ridden: devotees, ascetics, perfectionists, explorers, obsessives. Her measure of wood and wire had possessed her, harried and driven her to perfect her relationship with it, to make it the centre of her life and need. Demon.

She loves the wolf, but she is married to the demon.

It is an abusive relationship.

Analiese completes the final dastgah and lets the note fade over the closing beat of the daf. She takes a moment in the silence after sound. Nothing and everything is here but she can no more stay here than in the womb. A breath and the applause breaks over her.

It always surprises Analiese that there is an audience for her music. A sizeable audience: second and third gen Iranians and Central Asians; Moonbeams and visitors from the Islamic Republic; music lovers, musicologists, musicians of other disciplines: the demon's other lovers. On this tour, her first in over a year, she has noticed a number of terrestrials. LMA officials. Iran and the Stans have a piece of the lunar cake.

They are the most appreciative of audiences. Every concert at least one has come backstage to ask her about her instrument, her music, why a lunar Australian should be so enraptured with an alien music.

Her familiar informs her that tonight is no exception. Two men in the dressing-room corridor of the Queen's Xian Xinghai music centre. A woman and a man. Not Iranians. White Australians.

'Analiese Mackenzie?' the woman asks.

'I am.'

'A moment in your dressing room, please?'

'Were you at the concert?' Analiese asks. 'I don't remember you. Who are you?'

'Oh dear,' the woman says. The man inclines his head and Analiese feels a brief, sharp needling pain in the back of her head. She lifts a hand.

'Don't do that,' the woman says. 'No, really. There's a combat insect attached to the back of your neck. Now, can we chat?'

Analiese opens the door, conscious of the thing on the back of her neck, conscious of the man and woman following her into the room as if attached to the thing and her spine by electric nerves.

'Can I at least put the setar away?'

'Of course,' the woman says. 'It's a valuable musical instrument.'

She lays it in its case, folds the fabric over the strings, hasps shut the lid. All the time, the thing, the thing, that black thing on her neck.

'Who are you?'

'That doesn't matter,' the woman says. The dressing room is small, the woman perches on the edge of the shelf, the man on the toilet. 'There is someone would very much like to meet you. He's on his way. He'll be here very soon. We're just here to make sure you don't miss him.'

'The rest of the group . . .' Analiese says.

'You've told them you'll meet them later in the bar,' the woman says. 'And I don't think you've noticed, but we've screened off this room.'

The man pulls back his jacket to display a black box at his waist. He looks pleased with himself.

'It's quite a sophisticated piece of technology, actually,' the woman says. 'It's surprisingly difficult to isolate a person from the network. There are ten thousand eyes on us all the time.'

Movement outside the door.

'He's here. Nice meeting you. Don't touch the spider.'

The man and woman leave. Bryce Mackenzie enters. His bulk dominates the tiny dressing room. Analiese gets up from her chair.

'Sit sit,' Bryce says. 'I won't be long. And I doubt it would hold me anyway. Analiese Mackenzie. Partner of Wagner Corta. Care giver to Robson Corta. My adopted son. That's not very loyal of you.'

'It's not disloyal to live my own life,' Analiese says. 'It's not disloyal not to take sides.'

'But you have taken sides. I'll be brief. I have suffered a number of business setbacks recently. This is public knowledge. I'm in the process of reversing those. My strategy requires bargaining assets. Hostages, if you like.'

'I'm just a musician,' Analiese says. She would give anything, anything to be able to tear this black, prickling thing from her neck.

'Not you,' Bryce says. He laughs. 'Who the fuck do you think you are? No. I want Robson Corta. You have him. I want him. Give him to me.'

'Wagner . . .' Analiese stammers. 'I can't . . .'

'I wouldn't trust you to fix a martini, let alone bring me this kid. And he's a slippy little bastard. He got away from me once in Meridian. Cost me a First Blade. Then again, he did have Denny Mackenzie fighting for him. I have people for this kind of thing. What I need from you is to clear space for them. Do you understand?'

'You want me to get Wagner out of the way.'

'Yes I do. Problem is: that word trust. Frankly, you are very far from staunch. You have betrayed the family before and I find it hard to put my trust in you. So what I need isn't your loyalty, it's your obedience.'

'This . . .' Analiese hooks a thumb towards the slowly-spasming thing hooked into her skin,

'That? That's just to get your attention. I'm going to send you something.'

Her familiar whispers, *Message from Bryce Mackenzie.* Windows open in Analiese's vision: wide-angle, high viewpoint drone shots of streets, prospekts, tunnels. Each drone follows a figure: a middle-aged woman with striking long grey hair moving along a crowded prospekt, a young man taking tea with friends at a hotshop bar, a middle-aged, close-cropped woman leaning on the rail of a high balcony on one of Queen's towers, surveying her marvellous city; a young woman running, a fair pony-tail swinging.

Mom, Ryan, Mom, Rowan.

'You fuck.'

'It's agreed then?'

'Do I have a choice?'

'Of course you have a choice.' A secure contact appears on Analiese's lens. 'Arrange it, then let us know. We'll take care of the rest.' Bryce Mackenzie smiles, a thin tear in shining, straining skin. 'My business is concluded. So there's no more need for this.' He holds out a hand and the thing leaps from Analiese's neck on to his hand. He lets it run across his skin like a pet, turning his hand one way, then another to keep the vile thing in motion. It is glossy, hard and brittle and yet liquid at the same time; scurrying and intent, all legs and fangs. Analiese knows she will wake many nights, feeling the prickle of the little needle claws in her neck.

'You wouldn't have dared kill me with that thing,' Analiese says. Defiance. Defiance is something.

'I dare what I like. But correct: I wouldn't have killed you. The spider's armed with a non-lethal neurotoxin that would have fucked your nervous system so long and deep and hard you wouldn't have been able to pick up that instrument of yours, let alone get a note out of it. Goodbye. I'm glad you agreed. Your friends are expecting you in the bar. You deserve a drink.'

For a big man he moves deftly, softly. Analiese is shaking. She can't stop. She may never stop.

Demons.

As she departed, she returns, instrument in hand, the sole alightee at Theophilus's small station. And there are her men; big man, little man. Big man tight, controlled, loud with dark emotions he thinks no one but he can see. Little man sombre and serious and failing to conceal how happy he is.

She almost gets back on the train. That would be the best thing, take herself away, far away from anyone and everyone who has ever known her. Change her name, edit her identity, erase her records, smash the setar.

They would still come.

Blow the lock, blow herself and her lovely men out into vacuum, all die in each other's arms, brains burning red as each neuron guttered and was extinguished.

They would still come; by wing and wind and foot and knife-tip: Bryce Mackenzie's assassins.

There is no good in anything she does.

Wagner scoops her up and she responds as she must, but her embrace is weak, her warmth cool, her kiss thin and treacherous. He will read it. When he is this far into the wolf, he sees things humans cannot.

'Sorry, love, I'm beyond tired.'

Wagner carries her setar.

'So,' Robson says. 'We listened to you. Me and Haider.'

'What did you think?'

'It was good. I think. I don't really know if I can say anything about it because I didn't really understand it. There were a lot of notes.'

'I'll take that as a compliment.'

Wagner opens the door of the tiny apartment to a small table spread for a feast: the most intimate of celebrations: the meal in the home. There is hotshop food, and given food from friends and well-wishers, and food they have obviously made themselves. Analiese eats without thought or pleasure.

'I'm not feeling great,' she says, turning down iced ramen and white bean hummus. 'Must be true what they say about the water in Queen. Old and dirty. Would you mind if I just went to bed? Sorry.'

She lies awake in the tiny cubby, listening to her men clear up, clean up, tidy away. She listens to their voices. They speak in Portuguese, which she still barely understands, and so she can strip their words of meaning and listen to them as pure sounds, as if they were instruments. Wagner is a clarinet, fluid and sonorous, sweet and musical. Robson's voice is higher: piccolo, but she hears a crack in it, sudden drops into low notes.

She is sobbing. The bed shakes, she hopes Wagner and Robson can't feel it in the fabric of the home. She feigns sleep when Wagner comes up to join her. He slips in beside her, slides into his accustomed curl, dick pressed to her ass. She can't bear it, she can't bear the touch of his skin, his warmth, his body hair against her; the sweet wolf-reek of him.

When he is asleep she goes down to the living space. She tries entertainment but it won't out-shout the guilt. She tries alcohol but it's nauseating against the dread. She tries her music but her demon is powerless against this greater horror.

'Hey.'

She hadn't heard him get up. Wolves move softly.

'Just getting some water.'

He knows it's a lie. She knows she will never have another opportunity like this. That old Sun proverb: even the gods cannot help a woman who will not take an opportunity.

'I'm still rattling around,' Analiese says. 'I can't settle on anything, my body is wrecked but my mind is still running around shouting. I think I understand a little how you feel, when it changes.'

Wagner grimaces.

'I know I don't, fully – I can't. And this will settle down in a day or two. With you . . .'

'Don't,' Wagner says and Analiese hears him tear inside.

'It's turning light again, isn't it?' Analiese asks. She has been away for the whole time he has been in shadow. She knows his twitches, his discomforts, his small manias that build day on day as the Earth grows brighter. Shadow is turning once again to wolf.

'Go, Wagner. It will kill you. It's worse every time. I can see it. Robson can see it.'

'Don't bring Robson into this.'

'You need the pack. It's neurochemistry. You can go off the meds but it never goes away. It's who you are, Wagner, it's what you are. Go to them.'

'It's not safe!'

The sinews in his neck, the veins in his forehead betray the clenched emotion. It's not anger, not rage – nothing so simple. It's an entire other self, chained and caged and howling.

'Just for one night, two nights. Meet them halfway, even. Look at yourself, Wagner. Can you manage five years of this? Every two weeks, when the Earth is round . . .'

'I have to take care of Robson.'

'It will kill you, Wagner. But before it kills you, it will tear your body apart, it will burn every organ and fill every artery with molten steel. It will smash your mind to a smear. How will you take care of Robson?'

'I can't go to Meridian. They're looking for me.'

'Wagner, if they wanted Robson, they'd already have him. Go. I will look after him. He'll be fine. You are not. You look like death, my love.'

He shudders: the wolf within testing its chains.

'How long would you need? Would one day be enough?'

Sweat runs thickly down his neck, his arms, his inner thighs.

'It might.'

'Two days?'

He shakes his head.

'Too long.'

'One day. Go. I will take care of Robson. Do you want to tell him or shall I?'

'I will.'

'Take the meds. I can't bear to see you like this.'

'I'm scared I might not come back.'

'You'll come back.'

His arms wrap around Analiese. She can't bear it.

'Do you think you can sleep?' she asks.

'I don't think so.'

'Me neither.'

She settles on to the lounger. He settles his head in her lap. They both stare at the wall. She strokes his thick, black hair.

'You won't hurt him, will you?'

She asked that when she called the address Bryce gave her backstage at the Xian Xinghai centre. She asked it again when she was told where and when the operatives would arrive. She asks it a third time, at the door of her apartment, to the two men come to take Robson away.

'He won't be hurt, ma'am. He's a valuable asset.'

A moon man and a Jo Moonbeam. Skill and muscle. They are dressed in candy-striped suits, big lapels, wide ties, pleated pants, broad-banded fedoras, pointed shoes. They could not look more like contract thugs.

'He's asleep.'

The plan is to take him in his sleep. The Jo Moonbeam – a broad, gentle-faced Fijian – calls a box-bot into the room.

'Oh,' Analiese says. 'You're taking him out in that? I hadn't thought about how you were going to get him out.'

'We can't really carry him, can we?' the second man says. He has a Queen of the South accent.

The Jo Moonbeam opens the lid. The cargo space is generous and well padded.

'Just until we get to the railcar,' the moon man says.

They sent him off together, hugging in the airlock, waving as the locks closed, still waving as the railcar moved off though they knew that Wagner in the shuttle could not see.

Let us know when you get to Meridian.

Against right and reason, Analiese had eventually slept, the night of the betrayal. That same night Wagner must have taken the meds, for when she woke she found him prowling the kitchen area in nothing but skin, trying to find mint and glasses for tea, feral and alert, sensitive and aware in ways beyond human.

'How do you feel?'

'Howling.' He grinned. And he locked eyes with her and her heart rose and she smiled and nodded her head which was all the invitation he needed and they fucked fast and fierce on the lounger.

'Robson!' she hissed.

'He's thirteen, he'll sleep until noon,' Wagner said.

The arrangements were swiftly made. Some risks were not worth taking. He would not notify the Meridian pack until he arrived at their door. He would close down Dr Light and run a dummy familiar. He would stay one night and return on the 17:00 Equatorial Express. Communications would be kept to a minimum, except for a call to say he had arrived.

Each carefully planned stage was a nail through Analiese's elbow, wrist, knee, hip. Neck.

Robson wouldn't go to sleep, the little fuck. He generally keeled over around midnight but tonight he would not roll into bed. One o'clock. One thirty.

‘I’m getting really tired, Robson.’

‘You go to bed. I’m not ready yet.’

Two o’clock. Two thirty.

She had already sent two delaying messages to the agents. She found excuses to keep herself awake: a new piece on the historical musicological relationship of the setar and the Uighur satar, a recently released terrestrial recording of the Ensemble Chemiraani, a heated exchange on a Persian music group. She dreaded a cold war of nerves with Robson, each determined to see the other off to sleep.

Three twenty he rolled on to his back.

‘I’m off.’

Analiese waited for the first growling snore before she called the agents of Mackenzie Helium.

‘Don’t hurt him.’

‘I promise. Iloilo.’

The big Pacifican moves to the mezzanine stairs.

‘Analiese?’

He’s there in the bedroom door, sheet pulled around him. Skinny and groggy.

‘What’s going on?’

‘Fuck,’ says the moon man. He touches his cufflink. Dark motes fly up in Robson’s face. He drops the sheet, reels back and goes down in a flail of limbs.

‘Robson!’ Analiese shouts but the second kidnapper has him and carries him as light as an insect down the stairs.

‘You have the craziest dreams,’ the moon man says. ‘So I hear.’ The Fijian lays Robson gently in the cargo box, curled up in foetal position.

‘No,’ Analiese says. ‘Wait . . .’ The box, it’s a coffin. It’s death.

‘We have a contract,’ the moon man says.

The Fijian smiles and closes the lid. The bot trundles out into the corridor.

‘Oh yes,’ the moon man says. ‘One last thing.’ The blade is fast, sure and strong, punched through Analiese’s neck from one side to the other. She sprays blood, hisses, her hands flap. The knife holds her upright. 'That's for fucking a Corta.' He rips the knife free. Analiese Mackenzie falls in gouts of red heart-blood.

The moon man cleans his blade and reverently reholsters it inside his jacket. He steps back from the flood of red.

'Remember Ironfall.'

Haider takes two teas at El Gato Encantado but still no Robson. A ping to Joker comes back empty: off-net. He could be free-running: some new move or stunt. Parkour requires fierce, pure concentration: there is no place for pings and notifications a hundred metres up the heat-exchange shaft. More tea, though his mouth is as dry as if he had vaped five grams of skunk.

'Where's your little friend?' Jo-Jee asks.

Haider scowls. He has never liked Jo-Jee and his patronising comments. His money is as good as anyone else's in this hotshop. He flicks Jianyu behind the counter some bitsies and goes in search of Robson. Theophilus is not a large city and the sites where a traceur can sharpen their skills smaller still. The air-shaft, the pressurised-storage laager, the power and water ring, the purification system where they met: nothing. Last Haider visits the central core: Robson's favourite. Haider still can't watch him on the zig-zag fifty metres down to the sump: side to side to side to side, turning, flipping, spinning in the air to land and immediately kick off again. Speed is important to Robson. Surviving is to Haider.

Solveig calls Joker again. No answer.

House then.

This isn't right. Liquid from under the door. He steps back. The liquid is tacky and sticky and red on his pure white sneakers. Blood.

'Solveig! Call help!'

'Good morning, Haider,' says the door. 'You're on the welcome list. Please come in.'

The door opens.

TWENTY

The impacts rock the apartment, conversation-pit to bed-pods. Haider is out of his bed, dropping into shoes, pulling on a hoodie, transferring all his local data to network: the standard impact/moonquake/depressurisation drill. He slides down the ladder into the living space.

Max and Arjun are flapping around, scooping their precious collectables into bags.

The apartment shakes again to hammer blows. The door. Not impacters, not the Vorontsov space-gun, not a quake: there is someone outside.

'Haider! I need to talk to you.'

Max and Arjun turn to the door.

'I think it's Wagner Corta,' Haider says.

'Haider!' Fists hammer on the door again. Plastics creak and snap.

'He'll have that down,' Max says.

'Haider, go back to your room,' Arjun orders.

'I know you're in there,' Wagner calls from the other side of the door.

'Go away. Leave us in peace,' Max shouts.

'I only want to talk to Haider.'

Haider's care givers look at each other.

'He won't go away,' Haider says.

'We'll contract in security,' Max says.

'In Theophilus?' Arjun answers. The two men place themselves between Haider at the door. Arjun is short, muscular, bald-headed and bearded and works out but he is no match for a wolf when the Earth-light in hot in him.

'I can wait forever,' Wagner shouts.

'I have to talk to him,' Haider says.

'He doesn't come in,' Max says.

'I won't hurt you,' Wagner says. 'I just want to know.'

'I'll open it a crack,' Max says. 'Wagner, I'm going to open it a crack.'

'No, don't do that . . .' Arjun says and the door flies open, sending Max reeling into the conversation-pit. Arjun recovers like a cage-fighter, brow to brow with the wolf.

'I. Just. Need. To. Talk,' Wagner says. Haider has never seen him like this. Every muscle is taut as a cable. His face is pale, his eye huge and dark. He blazes with energy. He could have smashed the apartment door down one-handed.

'I won't hurt you,' he says again.

Arjun pushes Haider down on to the sofa and takes up guard on his right side. Max, bruised and shaken from the fall, sits on Haider's left. Haider loves his sweet, brave dads.

'You found her,' Wagner says. His voice is a low growl.

'I found her.' The anti-anxiety diffusers have finally halted the flood of nightmares welling up from Theophilus's deep levels. 'The door opened for me.' Blood, seeping under the door into the street. 'It opened and I went in.' On her side, limbs folded at crazy angles. Eyes wide. Hair glued into the mass of congealing blood. The knife. God, the knife, the knife through her neck. 'I called the med centre, then the zabbaleen.'

'Was there any . . . any. Sign. Of Robson?'

'I saw stuff. I couldn't make any sense of it. Broken furniture, like there'd been a fight. A sheet. The place was a mess.'

'I need you to think hard, Haider,' Wagner says. He crouches in front of Haider, presses his hands together. 'Did you see or hear anyone or anything out of the ordinary?'

Haider shakes his head.

'I'm sorry. It was the next morning when I went to the apartment. To go to El Gato Encantado. You know.'

'You're scaring him, Wagner,' Max says.

'I need to know. I need to understand what happened. I need to be able to put it together in my head. I get the call in the pack house. Analiese is dead. I think, what? And Robson is missing. I get the first train back but its still eight hours before I get there. The zabbaleen have cleaned everything. Nothing left. I need to be able to see what you saw, Haider, in my head, to get to understand it.'

'He's told you everything he knows,' Arjun says.

'I get camera footage from the network. I see the two men arrive with a box. I see the two men leave with the box. What happened in the apartment, I don't know.'

Max gets up from the lounger and crosses to the cook-space. Water boils; a few moments later he hands Wagner a glass of tea.

'Sit.'

'I'm sorry,' Wagner says. 'I can't make any sense out of this.'

'I'll try to help but I really don't know much,' Haider says. 'You don't . . . you don't think he's been kidnapped?'

Alexia pulls the quilted coat tighter around her and suppresses a shiver. Both are theatrical, psychological: Boa Vista has been at habitable temperature for ten days now but she feels the deep, endless cold of the rock around her, the memory of the vacuum ice that filled this lava tube. Plants grow, whole trees flower, small AKA-designed birds hop from rock to engineered branch to rock, but Boa Vista will always chill Alexia. It is a haunted place.

The moon has no ghosts, the saying goes.

The moon is ghosts all the way down.

Nelson Medeiros greets her in Portuguese and escorts her into the Eagle's new Eyrie. Escolta by escolta, Lucas has been replacing and reinforcing his official bodyguard with ex-Corta Hélio dusters and refugee Santinhos fled from João de Deus. She sheds the coat. Maninho shows her the way up through the machinery-cluttered corridors of Lucas's new Eyrie.

A face. She is inside the face of an orixa. Lucas's new office is inside the eyeball of Oxala. Boa Vista creeps her out. She hates the thought of Lucas permanently moving his government here.

Alexia hears a thing here she has never heard before: Lucas Corta laughing. She finds him leaning back in his chair shaking with barely suppressed giggles. He holds his hands to beg her not to speak to him while he shakes with mirth.

Lucas Corta is one of those people, naturally serious in demeanour, who are so utterly transformed by joy that they almost become another person.

'It's still the Suns, isn't it?'

Lucas nods and quivers with laughter again.

'And it will be for quite some time,' he says when he breathes.

'How much did they go for?'

'Twenty billion.'

Alexia still converts lunar bitsies into Brasilian reais. Her eyes widen.

'That's . . .'

'A fortune by your standards. Small change for the Suns. And they know it. A final, well-judged insult from Mackenzie Metals. This is all you're worth.'

Lucas indicates for Alexia to sit. He enjoys another seism of sniggering. His laughter is beginning to irritate Alexia now. It is not clean.

'So Darius has withdrawn his claim to Mackenzie Metals?'

'Denny Mackenzie is crowned king and struts around Hadley like some St Olga cage-fighter.'

Alexia goes to the window to look out over the shoots and seedlings of Boa Vista reborn.

'I don't understand. The Mackenzies killed Rafa and destroyed this place. Denny Mackenzie killed Carlinhos in cold blood.'

'My account with the Mackenzies is settled.'

'Ironfall? That's not your account, Lucas. That's my account. My account, and I will never be free from that.'

The laughter dies, the smile vanishes. This is the Lucas Corta Alexia recognises.

'The Suns are our common enemy. They set us at each other's throats. Allow me a little schadenfreude. It's a rare commodity.'

'Have you ever thought that maybe you're so scheming, so twisty, you might trip yourself up?'

'That's why I employ you, Lê. I trust you to tell me the truth. There's someone I want you to meet. He's asked for an audience.'

'This wasn't on my agenda.'

'Toquinho, have Nelson bring my guest up please.'

Three chairs. There are three chairs in Lucas's mirador. How had she not noticed?

Escoltas in cream linen suits and broad-brimmed straw planter hats guide the supplicant into Oxala's eye.

Alexia's breath catches. This short, dark, powerful man: she recognises the haunted eyes, the smoking energy coiled tight in every muscle, the bright, terrible presence in his walk, his stance, his every move. This is the wolf.

'Brother.'

'Wagner.'

The greeting is perfunctory. Lucas can barely tolerate Wagner Corta's embrace.

'Sit, sit,' Lucas says.

'I prefer to stand.' He cannot keep still; he fidgets from foot to foot, he cannot rest.

'Stand then. My Iron Hand, Alexia Corta.'

Wagner purses his fingers, dips his head to Alexia in the Corta manner. Connecting with his eyes is like gazing into the sun-heart of a fusion reactor. Alexia returns the greeting, enchanted by his dark formality. He may be the most attractive man she has ever seen.

'Senhor Corta.'

'He is not a Corta,' Lucas says.

'Bryce Mackenzie has Robson,' Wagner Corta says.

The corner of Lucas's mouth twitches. The barb has driven deep. Alexia observes that Wagner has observed it too. The wolves have strong bruxaria, she has heard. When the Earth is round, they see what others cannot, they sense beyond the human spectrum, they join together into a pack mind greater, faster than their individual intelligences. They have phenomenal sex.

'Robson was under your protection,' Lucas says.

'I was misled,' Wagner says. 'Betrayed.'

'Betrayed?'

'Analiese . . .'

'The Mackenzie woman.'

'They killed her, Lucas. Knife through the neck.'

Lucas does not flinch. Alexia can see the wolf within Wagner Corta thrash and claw. If it breaks free, all the escoltas in Lucas's bodyguard will not keep it from tearing Boa Vista apart.

'What do you want me to do?' Lucas asks.

'I need him back. I need him safe.'

'Those are two different things.' Alexia has been Mão de Ferro long enough to distinguish between Lucas indifferent and Lucas calculating. This is Lucas adding up, subtracting.

'Safe. Keep him safe.'

'You realise that my capacity to act is limited. Bryce Mackenzie's purpose in taking Robson is to have a hostage. If I move, if I show my hand, Robson dies.'

'I'll go to Queen myself. I'll make a hostage swap.'

'Wagner, you are of no value to Bryce Mackenzie.'

The true legends are the broken ones: fragments of histories, tellings, embellishments, edits and re-edits. Truth abhors a narrative. Some families have a black sheep: the Cortas have a dark wolf. Lucas has never spoken of Wagner but Alexia has picked up scraps of family mythology from staff and security: the strange child who howled at the Earth, the madrinha who wanted more than to be just a rental womb for the Cortas, the life-long hatred of Lucas Corta for a man who was an affront to his mother, to everything his family stood for. He's not a Corta.

But he is.

'Alexia.' Her name, not the apelido. 'I shall be moving my official residence to Boa Vista. I intend to taunt Bryce. He is easily provoked. He will want to move to João de Deus to show that he is in control,' Lucas says. 'Wolf: you will live here. I cannot have you running amok every time the Earth is round. Toquinho has arranged accommodation. It's in one of the construction barracks, it won't be the most comfortable. It's a laborious process, bringing Boa Vista back to its former glory. Then again, you never lived here, did you?'

'Cut, Lucas. Always the cut.'

'Thanks would be appropriate here.'

'You're not doing it for me. You're doing it for family. For Rafa. For your mother.'

'My mother.'

Alexia sees what Lucas is doing. In barbing his brother, cutting him, drawing painful blood, he is channelling the raging Earth-light inside his brother, like a rod calling lightning. Bleeding power and emotion that might lash out unchecked, that could threaten Lucas's plans.

Your child taken by a monster. Your oko, your partner, your love knifed down, alone and defenceless. These Alexia cannot imagine.

'Keep him safe, Lucas,' Wagner says.

'None of us are safe.'

Nelson Medeiros returns and Wagner understands that the meeting is concluded. When they are out of earshot, Alexia says, 'So that was the wolf.'

'Yes. Do you know why I despise him? Because he is free and has never given a second of thought to it. His condition absolves him of all responsibilities. Wolf, man; wolf, man; back and forth back and forth as the Earth grows round, and there is nothing he can do about it. It's neurobiology, see? Wonderful. He is the victim of his condition. It will always be the sole force acting on his life.'

'It's not a condition, it's an identity,' Alexia says. Lucas hisses in derision.

'That puts it beyond criticism? He's given responsibility – keep my sobrinho safe – and no sooner does the Earth shine blue than he runs off to the pack and Bryce Mackenzie takes Robson.'

'That's not fair, Lucas . . .'

Lucas waves a dismissing hand.

'I need you to go Twé. I need you to bring a consignment back to Boa Vista.'

'What is it?'

'Justice.'

Akosi the Poisoner's rings catch Alexia hard on the back of the hand.

'That hurt!'

'Do you want to die bleeding from your eyes, your ears, your shit-hole?'

'I was only looking,' Alexia says, taken by surprise, shame-faced and angry that this old woman, more wrinkle than flesh, eyes like currants folded into bags of skin, caught her out.

'Looking is not touching. Don't touch!'

She removes the set of plastic needles from the printer.

'You touched,' Alexia says.

The old woman waves her hand dismissively.

'Ach! I've been working with them so long I'm immune.'

Akosi the Poisoner lives behind a door in a tangled root mass of a strangler vine that ran away and rooted, thrived and occupied Silo 2 of Kojo Laing Agrarium after its ecosystem collapsed in the Third Great Purging and it was left to grow wild. Alexia climbed twining staircases up through the massive roots; back and forth, around and under, crossing and recrossing the light-pools of the central mirror arrays bouncing light down from the transparent cap. She was a devotee approaching a deep forest umbanda initiation. The Great Tree of Twé impressed on her the power and skill of the Asamoahs, but this two-hundred-metre cylinder of woven roots and trunks and branches was even more awe-inspiring, for magic dwelt here. Alexia imagined orixas muttering among the leaves.

And there was a door, opposite a sheer drop of eighty metres to the pool in which the Poisoner's Tree bathed its roots. She knocked.

'Who's there?' A scratch of a voice. The old woman knew well who was there. Everything had been arranged through their familiars.

'Alexia Maria de Céu Arena de Corta.' Names and titles, honorifics and qualifications played well in Twé. 'Mão de Ferro of the Eagle of the Moon.'

'Come in come in, Iron Hand.'

The door creaked wide, opened by no hand. Of course. Alexia ventured through a chain of domed rooms, bubbles blown from the pith of the great fig. In the final room she found the Poisoner.

'Part of the mystique, baa,' Akosi the Poisoner said. She was an aged woman, long and thin as famine, draped in white like a Mãe de Santo. Necklaced, bangled and be-ringed. Her dark skin, mottled, was heavily wrinkled and creased, as if she had shrunk inside her own body, 'I'm heavily branded. So, what business does the Iron Hand of the Eagle of the Moon have with the Mother of Poisons?'

Alexia told her and Akosi the Poisoner's face creased into the configuration of a grin and with a wave of her stick opened up the rooms beyond the final room; the clean and pristine and white and sterile rooms with printers and chemical synthesisers and staff – staff! – where the work was done.

'The tree isn't just scenery, baa,' Akosi the Poisoner said as the team made Alexia comfortable and served her tea which she could not bring herself to drink. 'I've engineered it to grow the feedstock for over fifty different toxins. Try not to touch your eyes or your mouth or any holes at all. And wash your hands.'

It was a process involving much tea and boredom, brewing bespoke poisons.

Akosi the Poisoner sets the needles into a second printer and coats them with plastic.

'Tagged to Robson Corta's DNA. Only he can open them.' She holds up the five plastic slivers in her fist. 'The Five Deaths, Mão de Ferro. Who are they for?'

'Just one person.'

Akosi the Poisoner hisses.

'Who does Lucas Corta hate so much he must kill them five times over?'

'I can't tell you, Mãe de Santo.'

Akosi snaps her hand shut with a small cry.

'Manners, baa, manners. The poisons must hear the name.'

Alexia takes a deep breath.

'Bryce Mackenzie.'

Akosi the Poisoner gives a high, keening cry. She pushes the container into Alexia's hands.

'Have them, baa, have them with my blessing. No charge. For the Sisters of the Lords of Now. Take them and tell me when the Brute of Boa Vista is dead. One doubt, baa.'

'What is it, Mãe?'

'Have I made enough?'

*

The dark is soft and dense, broken by dozens of tiny, dim lights that shed enough illumination for Alexia to understand that she is inside a dome, a small one; four, five paces across. The air is old, stale and carries high notes of ozone and a spicy, smoky tang at once exotic and familiar to Alexia.

'Reveillon!' Alexia says. 'It smells of New Year.'

'Moondust,' Wagner Corta says. 'Most people say it smells like gunpowder. I don't know what that is, but we say it.'

'Fireworks,' Alexia says. 'Like the morning after the party, when everyone is creeping back home hung-over and you smell all the burned-out rockets.'

The barracks where Lucas had billeted Wagner was easily found, even as the heavy contractors were moving out and the landscapers and ecological engineers moving in.

'Hey. Want to give me the wolf's tour of this place?'

He almost smiled. He took her up through the ornamental grasses and saplings, the bamboo groves and waterfalls, past the rebuilt pavilions and the miradors to an incongruous elevator door in the wall of the world.

'I kind of thought, the highlights?'

'You wanted the wolf tour.' He summoned the elevator.

At the top of that elevator is this dark, dusty dome, and Wagner saying, 'Fireworks are not a thing we have.'

'I would think so,' Alexia says.

'Dona Luna has a thousand deaths, but fire: that's the worst,' Wagner says. 'Fire burns the breath in your lungs. There was a fire at an old Corta Hélio maintenance base. When the rescue team got there, they found everything covered in black soot. The fire had burned out, but not before it consumed every molecule of oxygen in the base. Asphyxiation, or burning. You choose.'

This is a man whose partner was murdered by Bryce Mackenzie's blades, Alexia reminds herself. And the memory of Akosi the

Poisoner, and what she brought back from Twé in a sealed titanium case, and what the deaths inside can do, will not slip her mind. And she knows no better remedy than humans being with humans for such hurts.

'Dragons,' Wagner says. 'We have flying dragons. Tens – hundreds – of metres long. At New Year and Yam Festival we fly them up and down the quadras, in and out of the bridges. They're filled with lights and music.'

'Where is this place?' Alexia asks.

'Where the wolf was born,' Wagner says. A noise. Light. Shutters retract with a clatter of folding vanes and Alexia stands on the surface, under a million stars.

'This was Adriana's retreat,' Wagner says. 'She liked looking back at Earth, looking at the lights. We light the lights. That was our talisman. Or did she just want to make sure old Brasil was still there? Can you see her?' Wagner points, draws Alexia in with the gentlest of touches. She sights up his arm. Blue Earth stands in the western sky. It will pass through its phases from full to new but it will never move from that fixed point above the drab plain of Mare Fecunditatis. And there, low on the belly of the full Earth, scarred with dust storms and new deserts but still green, still blue: old Brasil. 'Old Doctor Macaraeg said I was bi-polar. Fed me pills, patches, behaviour modification drugs. The whole time I tried to tell her it's not a disease, it's more than that, but even I didn't know what it was until I learned about the wolves.'

'They're – bi-polar?'

Alexia sees Wagner wince in the Earth-light.

'More than that. We're a new neuro-ethnic identity.' Now Alexia sees him smile apologetically. 'Wolves. That's what we are. But I knew then what I was – what I'd always been. I came up here. I stood where I'm standing now. I stood naked in the Earth-light and everything was illuminated. Everything made sense. I could feel it splitting me in two, tearing me apart into two people; the wolf and the shadow. Wagner Corta died that day. I was not one person, I was two.'

He stands, eyes closed, bathing in the light. He is trembling. Every muscle, every nerve is burning.

'Is the light hurting you?' Alexia says.

'Hurting me? No, never. But yes – it hurts.'

'Wagner. Listen to me. Analiese betrayed you.'

'Why would she do that?'

'I don't know.' Alexia has a guess but she will not say it here.

'They stabbed a knife through her neck. Through her neck. Why did they do that?'

Wagner looks on the edge of collapse.

'All I know is that she let Bryce's blades walk in and take Robson. She betrayed you, Wagner.'

'Bryce Mackenzie dies for this,' Wagner hisses.

'He will,' Alexia says. 'Oh he will. Lucas may be slow, he may be subtle, he may take the long way around, but he never misses.'

'It should be mine,' Wagner says.

'Let Lucas take it,' Alexia says. 'You're too close.'

Wagner turns on her. Alexia steps back: here is the wolf, jaws wide, fangs bared, alien light burning in its eyes. *Wagner Corta is dead,* he said. *There is only the wolf and the shadow.*

'You don't say that to me. This is for the Cortas.'

After the shock of the abrupt lycanthropy, Alexia meets Wagner's darkness.

'I am a Corta.'

The Earth-madness shatters.

'Yes. Of course.' Wagner's hand moves, the shutters snap back into place. The blackness is blinding. The soft white lights emerge like stars over Barra. 'We should go now.'

'Are you all right?'

'No. But I never am.' Wagner summons the elevator. The door

opens and floods the dark, dusty observatory with a cool blue glow. 'I'm sorry, Alexia.'

'The wolf.'

'Yes. Too much light.' Wagner closes the elevator door. 'I love him, you know. Robson. Like he was my own. I would do anything for that kid.'

Alexia touches his hand. His skin is hot, she can feel the tremor of muscles fading.

'You already have.'

'Last of all, the death of the senses.'

Alexia places the final set of five plastic needles on Lucas's desk behind the eye of Oxala. Red, green, blue, yellow, white. Black. The final darkness.

First death: the death of the bowels. The victim shall piss and shite themself as the linings of stomach, intestines, bladder slough off and liquefy.

The second death: the death of the blood. Blood shall spurt from eyes, ears, nose, every orifice of the human body.

The third death: the death of the soul. The mind shall be cast into a hell of hallucinations; endlessly replicating demons, fiery pits, falling through larger and larger universes.

The fourth death: the death of the self. The body shall reject its own organs, vessels and architecture through a massive immune system failure. Even the skin shall blister and slough off in bloody sheets.

The fifth death, the final death: the shutting off of the senses from the sights, sounds, smells of the other four deaths at their work. It is no mercy: the mind is trapped, sightless and soundless and helpless. The only sense that survives to the end is pain.

'Good work,' Lucas Corta says. He does not flinch, he makes no comment as Alexia lays out the toxins. He is still and cold and merciless as his poisons. That same deadly chill Alexia remembers when she felt his assassin fly stroke her neck in the suite in the Copa Palace Hotel. If he had had any doubt he would have killed her: cold, merciless, without lifting a hand. 'Fine work.'

'The Mother of Poisons waived her fee,' Alexia says. 'Because of . . .'

'Bryce,' Lucas says. 'Why are you afraid to say it?'

The poison must hear the name of its victim. Else how will it know?

'I have a problem,' Lucas says. 'All this beautiful justice is so much junk unless I can deliver it to its target.'

Lucas Corta stymied. For a moment Alexia is nonplussed, then a name comes to her. She sees it, whole and entire and beautiful. And cold and ruthless and exploitative, and the only thing that will work.

'I've a suggestion,' Alexia says.

The care givers are good simple academic folk – he a selenologist, he a professor of poetry, and despite Lucas's best intentions they are terrified. They sit side by side on the lounger, upright in readiness for flight, nostrils wide, eyes wider, touching often and gentle.

Lucas sits almost knee to knee, leaning forward, keeping his head lower than theirs to signal intimacy. Many hand gestures, some touches. They flinch from each touch.

Alexia can't blame them. Even operating minimal security there are still escoltas at every door for a hundred metres up and down the ring. Theophilus has been invaded. The kid, though; the kid is something different.

Haider sits opposite Alexia, hunched over in the chair, feet splayed, hands between his knees. Lanky and awkward. White hoodie and leggings. The whitest skin she has seen on the moon; black hair falling over one eye. *Makes you look cute but you know that,* Alexia observes. Boys can be cute and sweet and vulnerable. Then puberty makes them horrid.

She tries not to think of Caio, up there in high Brasil.

She flicks up her briefing. Lucas's intelligence is thorough. Maninho knows things about Haider that his CGs don't. That he is a kid of words, of stories. The stories he has written and given reluctantly to people. The stories he has written and does not give anyone. The stories he will never let anyone read: the ones about his BBFF Robson and Haider's little boycrush.

'What is it you want him to take, Senhor Corta?' the selenologist, Arjun, asks.

'I won't lie to you,' Lucas says. 'Poison to kill Bryce Mackenzie.'

Arjun and Max, the poetry professor, make small cries of consternation.

'Political assassination?' Max asks. He is the taller of Haider's two care givers, with a poetry professor's salt-and-pepper beard.

'Robson will not be safe until Bryce Mackenzie is dead,' Lucas says. 'And because I am here – because Wagner came to you – you will not be safe until Bryce Mackenzie is dead. You are part of it now, I am afraid.'

'I never asked . . .' Max begins, then stops speaking as he realises the futility of his argument.

'I will protect you,' Lucas says. 'For as long as is necessary.'

'And Haider? What about him? You are asking our son to carry deadly poisons into the very heart of Mackenzie Metals,' Max says.

'I'm asking him to visit his best friend,' Lucas says. 'There will be no issue, he will visit at the behest of the Lunar Mandate Authority. There will be no danger.'

Max snorts with pained contempt.

'So you say, but what about your nephew? You were supposed to keep him safe. This places Robson in deadly danger,' Arjun says.

'Robson already is in deadly danger. You are aware of Bryce Mackenzie's reputation. There are some things worse than death.'

'I'll do it.' Haider's voice fills the tiny room. He looks out fierce and resolved from behind his fringe. 'I'll go. For Robson.'

'We forbid it!' Max says.

'Let him speak,' Lucas says.

'Nothing to say,' Haider says. 'Except I'll do it. It has to be done. No one else can do it.'

'We are your care givers,' Max says. 'Your parents.'

Arjun rests a hand on his oko's.

'We have no power here. He can do whatever he wants.'

'I'm glad you see it my way,' Lucas says. 'Be assured that he won't be alone. Haider will be accompanied – as far as possible – by an office bearer of the Lunar Mandate Authority. My own Mão de Ferro.'

'Ancillary staff here, on hand.' Lucas leads the LMA executives across the bridge of the nose to the north eyeball. His cane clicks loudly on the polished stone floor. 'Your committee room. For those times when network conferencing will not suffice. Discreet. Secure.' He points out through the pupil-window with the tip of his cane to the stone face across the chasm. 'My own office. Eye to eye, so to speak.'

'Oxala, Lord of Light and Beginning,' Anselmo Reyes says. 'And we are to be stationed in Omolu; orixa of Death and Disease.'

'Also orixa of healing,' Lucas says. 'And keeper of the graveyards.'

Wang Yongqing purses her lips in displeasure.

'It is inefficient to split and duplicate our efforts between Meridian and Boa Vista.'

'I anticipate moving the entire LMA to Boa Vista. There is much to be said for separating the capital from the largest city. Much practised on Earth, though not in any of your nations. Boa Vista would be your own private city.'

'*Your* own private city,' Wang Yongqing says. 'With the LMA as your hostages.'

'That's an unfriendly expression, Madam Wang.'

'But one with much currency on the moon. Senhor Corta, the LMA is concerned.'

Birds call among the saplings. A blue morpho butterfly sweeps heavily past Omolu's north eye. A thought to Toquinho and escoltas bring seats. Everything is prepared, everything is choreographed and Lucas will allow no deviations from his script.

'We've approved and accredited your assistant,' says Monique Bertin.

'My Mão de Ferro,' Lucas says. The terrestrials loathe the title. It sounds medieval, atavistic to their ears. Therefore Lucas delights in using it.

'And the boy,' Anselmo Reyes adds. 'And provided a small escort.'

'Thank you,' Lucas says.

'We have not asked your interest in this,' Wang Yongqing says. Her hands are folded in her lap. Lucas's staff erect a table, serve tea. 'This is not a favour. Ours is a business enterprise with commercial goals.'

'I am a man of business,' Lucas says.

Wang Yongqing regards him for a cold moment.

'I'm not sure you are, Senhor Corta. Not as we understand it. Of late you have been sending missions, holding meetings – doing deals – without our endorsement.'

'I have to wheel and deal, Madam Wang.'

'We are concerned,' Anselmo Reyes says.

'Earth is concerned,' Monique Bertin says. 'You recently sent your personal assistant to St Olga to set up a supply and confidence deal with the Vorontsovs.'

'The Moonport space elevator system,' Anselmo Reyes says. 'I know that we have relied on VTO's mass-driver as the bargaining position of last resort, but coupled with a monopoly over access to trans-lunar space – Earth cannot agree to that.'

'The price of our favour is this,' Wang Yongqing says. 'VTO has asked for a vote in council. You will veto it. This is not a democracy. Are we clear on that?'

'My position could not be clearer,' Lucas Corta says.

TWENTY-ONE

The car has been behind her for some time now, matching her pace as she swings along the track on her crutches. Crisp crackle of gravel, the pop of stones under the tyres. Marina feels it like a gun barrel pressed against the back of her neck.

'I know it's you, Kess,' Marina shouts. 'Just go past me!'

She hears the car pull up alongside. Kessie rolls down the window to shout.

'Are you all right?'

Marina sets her jaw and her determination. Rhythm and swing. Timing is everything. Break the rhythm and you go down. You are a quadruped, remember. Quadrupedal.

'I'm all right. Go away.'

The pick-up rolls along beside her. Kessie still leans on the window. Marina still swings along the dirt road to the cattle-grid that marks the edge of the world.

'What do you want, Kess?' Marina shouts.

'Thought you might like to see the eagle nest down on the river trail.'

Crutch step, crutch step.

'The North Campsite nest?' That eyrie has lodged in the dying pine as long as Marina can remember, a rickety slum of river-washed branches stacked year upon year, clutch upon clutch.

'There's a second hatching.'

'Goodie for them.'

'They're still feeding the hatchlings.'

Marina stops, leans into her crutches.

'What is you want, Kess?'

Her sister opens the pick-up door. Marina slings her crutches into the back of the pick-up and slides into the seat. Kessie turns neatly in the track and drives back past the house, past the white-painted cabin, past the barely stirring dogs on to the river track.

'Dr Nakamura told you to rest up. Your bones are weak.'

'My bones are my bones.'

The river track is a series of zig-zags down the steep western bank. The tyres kick up heavy, fragrant dust. It settles quickly. Moondust falls slow and brilliant: glitter and moonbows. Marina remembers the trails of dust thrown up from the wheels of the moonbikes by her and Carlinhos on their mad, wonderful ride to claim Mare Anguis for Corta Hélio. Their tracks would have been visible from space. That telescope on the back porch would have picked them up, two tiny scars across the upper shoulder of a full moon.

Kessie bowls the pick-up along a suggestion of track; tyre-tread in a dried-out puddle, snapped twigs, flattened grass. Marina feels every rock and rut. Kessie parks the pick-up a respectful distance from the nest-tree. The eyrie is enormous, a second crown to the dying pine tree. Some of the really old eyries weigh up to a ton. The desiccated grass beneath is spattered with droppings. The river finds new words among the stones and gravel.

'Really; what do you want?' Marina asks.

'Are you going back?' Kessie says. 'And before you deny it, Mom told me.'

Marina tries to find comfort in the battered seat. She is never comfortable now. She has no comfort on this world. This chuckle of water, this seasoning of road dust, this high clear sky and somewhere, turning in it, the eagle, seem thin and translucent. Overlit, colours too bright. Lies. The tree is flat, insubstantial, paint on film. Set hand to that mountain and her fingers would go through it. The moon is ugly and the moon is cruel and the moon is unforgiving but she is only alive there.

'It's changed me, Kess. Not just physically. The moon knows a thousand ways to kill you. I've seen terrible things. I've seen people die. Horrific, stupid, pointless deaths. The moon doesn't forgive, but Kess: life there, it's so intense, so precious. They know how to live. Kids here, you turn seventeen, eighteen, you get the car, get drunk, throw a party. Kids there, you run bare-ass naked across ten metres of hard vacuum. They live every second of those ten metres.'

'If you go back—'

'I can't ever leave.'

A space for river-talk and the click and creak of the wind in the fabric of the eagles' nest.

'Can you go back?' Kessie won't look at her. The two women sit in adjacent seats, worlds apart. 'When you went up on the shuttle you said you felt like you were going to turn to lead and die. To do it again—'

'I don't know,' Marina says. 'If Lucas Corta could do it—' She chokes on the memory, sudden and sharp as a bone in the throat, of Lucas Corta: trim, dapper, his beard neat, his hair brilliantined, his nails polished and his suit sharp as a Corta blade. Lucas Corta as she first saw him in Boa Vista, at the Moonrun party when she got the hosting job that had saved her from the slow suffocation of being unable to pay her Four Elementals. Late-capitalist asphyxiation. Go back to that, to not knowing who was paying for your next breath. Yes, more than anything. A dark speck turns circles in the sky: dead cells in the humour of her eye or an eagle?

'You told me it almost killed Lucas Corta,' Kessie says.

‘It did kill Lucas Corta,’ Marina says. ‘He came back. Lucas Corta is unkillable.’

‘You’re not.’

‘No, but I’m Earth-born. I’ve got the physiology. Train myself up.’

‘Is that what you were doing when you got run into the ditch?’ Kessie asks. ‘Is that why you were out today? Training?’

It is a bird, spiralling, wing-tips wide-feathered, feeling a path down through the air.

‘I hadn’t decided then.’

The eagle turns up where the river bends and glides in down the valley.

‘You’ve decided?’

‘I decided the moment I touched down. It’s ugly and its cruel and I was scared all the time and I was more alive in those twenty-four lunes than all my life before. This is shadows and fog, Kess.’

The eagle ghosts in, pulls up into a stall, feathers unfurled and drops on to the lip of the nest, scales and gore clenched in her claws.

‘Look,’ Kessie whispers. Heads appear over the eyrie’s rim, the eagle tears pale bleeding chunks from the fish for the open maws.

The hiking sticks are surer and more subtle than the crutches but Marina still takes the companionway to the fore-deck one fumbling step at time. Kessie is already at the rail. It’s a family ritual, to catch first sight of the Space Needle as the ferry rounds Bainbridge. It is never warm on the sound; Marina pulls her light jacket tight round her. In her years away the bland towers have shouldered in around the landmark building like bodyguards, even spread across Elliot Bay to West Seattle. An automated container ship negotiates passage out towards the strait and the ocean beyond; a cliff-face of moving metal. The ferry bobs across its wake and Kessie raises the cry.

‘She’s out!’

House Calzaghe had taken the ferry to the city at most twice a year – sometimes whole years had passed with them coming to

Seattle and, though the first glimpse of the towers had been beacon of arrival, the sight of Mount Rainier had been the welcome. The long trips had become more frequent when Mom had been in hospital; sighting the mountain had become an oracle. If she stood high and clear, her snow-cap higher than any imagining, then all would be well. If clouds covered her, if it was raining, then prepare for setbacks and disappointments. But always: she. Rainier was a drowsing goddess, sitting head bowed over her city and islands.

'She's clear,' Marina says but even over two years she can see that snows have melted deeper, the glaciers retreated higher. She can't bear the thought of a snowless Rainier: a crownless queen.

The ferry swings in to the terminal and the passengers stream towards vehicles and exits. Kessie clears a path for Marina through the swarm of foot passengers but Marina finds the close press of bodies in the narrow walkway reassuring. The moon was people, all people, only people, all the way down.

The moto whirls them up between the dark towers. Every other pedestrian or cyclist seems to be wearing a breath-mask now. Another new and lethal bacterial evolution. Every moon-dweller's great fear was of a new terrestrial disease arriving in the moon's sealed cities and passing lung to lung through Meridian's quadras, up Queen of the South's high towers before medical resources could be mobilised against it. Plague on the moon.

VTO's office is a glass and aluminium trinket in a prime site on the shore of Lake Union. Float-planes land and take off beside full-wall animations of cyclers over earth-rises.

'Give me a hand here.'

Kessie holds Marina's sticks while she shrugs off the jacket. Proud in her Corta Hélio T-shirt she hikes past the aspirant Jo Moonbeams in the lobby. Eyes catch, heads turn.

'I've an appointment at the med centre,' Marina says to the receptionist.

'Marina Calzaghe,' the receptionist says. He's the definition of a

VTO boy; tall, glossy, killing cheekbones. He squirts a location to Marina's data assistant. 'Welcome back. We don't get much repeat traffic.' As she grips her sticks he adds, 'Like the retro shirt.'

The waiting area is busy. There will always be people ready to seek their fortune on the moon. Young people of all colours and nations, nervous and excited. The tests are psychological as well as physiological. Not everyone can tolerate the moon's tight, claustrophobic society. Hopes will be crushed as well as elevated behind those white doors.

'Corta Hélio.' The young woman in the row in front of Marina and Kessie turned to take in her potential launch-mates and read the shirt.

'Used to work for them,' Marina says.

'Which office?'

Marina jerks a thumb at the ceiling panels.

'Head office. I was a duster.'

'You worked up there?'

'Two years. The maximum.'

'So, I have a question,' the woman says.

'Ask away,' Marina says.

'If you went there, why did you ever come back?'

A white door opens.

'Marina Calzaghe?'

The arms curl their fingers and fold into the cracks in the white walls. The panels close and seal leaving pure, sheer surface. Marina swings from the scanner couch. She left her hiking sticks by the door. It looks a longer walk back to them than from them.

'Am I good, Doctor?'

Dr Jaime Gutierrez blinks back the reader lens over his eye.

'Eighty-eight per cent probability of surviving launch,' he says. 'Maximum gee to orbit is two gees, effectively twelve gees lunar. It'll not be comfortable but you've got good muscle armouring. You've been working out.'

'The Long Run,' Marina says, knowing that the doctor won't understand and is too incurious to ask.

The doctor blinks his lens away.

'One question: why?'

'Is this part of the psychiatric assessment?'

'I've never seen anyone go back. I've seen tourists and executives and university researchers and LMA staff on six months up, three months down rotation. But someone who's worked the full two years? No. Once they're down, they stay down.'

'Maybe I shouldn't have come down,' Marina says.

'There's someone, isn't there?' Dr Gutierrez says.

'There is,' Marina says. 'But I had to come here to see it clear.'

'Expensive moment of clarity,' Dr Gutierrez says.

'It's only money,' Marina says.

Dr Gutierrez smiles and Marina thinks she may have misjudged him. The door opens and Melinda is in the white room. Marina hasn't given thought to her rehabilitation liaison since her tail-lights turned the corner of the dirt road and vanished behind the trees.

'Are you finished, Jaime?'

'She's good to fly,' Dr Gutierrez says.

'I need a word, Marina.'

Marina follows her up the corridor, the tips of her hiking poles tick-tacking on the wood.

'Coffee?' Melinda asks as Marina settles herself carefully in to the sofa in the small, bright room with high views over Lake Union. Low sofas are upholstered fly-traps to moonwomen. You can get in but you can't get out.

Coffee arrives with a woman in a suit that reads *government*. She pours two cups of coffee.

'Thank you, Melinda.'

She slides the cup across the low table to Marina.

'My name is Stella Oshoala. I work for the Defence Intelligence Agency.'

'I thought it might be something like that.'

Stella Oshoala stirs two sugars into her coffee and takes a sip.

'You've been experiencing some hostility in the neighbourhood.'

'Do you keep tabs on all the returnees?'

'We do. Many returnees find assimilating back into the terrestrial lifestyle challenging. The moon often gives rise to unorthodox political ideas. Extreme libertarianism, a yearning for utopian communities, anarcho-syndicalism. Alternate takes on the legal system.'

'All I was trying to do was fit in. Make a new life for myself.'

'But that's not true, is it, Marina?' Stella Oshoala sets down her cup. 'You're going back. That's unprecedented.'

Marina's coffee no longer tastes of wonder and nostalgia.

'What do you want?'

'I want to pay for your mother's healthcare.'

'I pay for her healthcare and you don't talk about Mom.'

'You can pay for your Mom's care or you can go back to the moon. You can't afford both.'

'You've been into my accounts?'

'You applied for a Earth-moon transit loan. Of course we're going to be interested in that.'

The government woman is right. The figures don't add up. Marina hadn't calculated on moonflight costs rising, medical care costs spiralling. Now, as when Marina first came to this lakeside office for her pre-flight assessments, VTO was prepared to advance loans to potential moon-workers. Now as then, filled in the application in the dark, private heart of night. She was fearful of exposing her secret: moonworker Marina, long the pillar of the Calzaghes, might not be as rich as she thought.

'All I want to do is cover all my responsibilities.'

Stella Oshoala looks at her shoes. Her mouth twitches.

'You need to know that your loan application is unlikely to be approved.'

Marina feels gravity reach out and pull down every strong thing in her. The room swims. The floor looms at her.

'What?'

'VTO has not approved your loan.'

'It's only a hundred K.'

'Hundred K or a hundred thousand, the answer would be the same,' Stella Oshoala says. She takes a sip from her cup but the coffee has turned cold and stale.

'I don't understand,' Marina stammers. Her world has imploded. Her every hope is falling into that hole in her heart.

'A returnee who wants to go Jo Moonbeam again isn't VTO's idea of a safe and stable investment.'

Stella Oshoala makes eye contact.

'I want you to do some work for us, Marina. For which you will be paid. Enough to cover your shortfall. More.'

And out of that hole comes anger.

'You told VTO to turn down my loan, didn't you?'

Stella Oshoala sighs.

'You are in a unique position that my organisation would be negligent not to exploit.'

'You want me to spy.'

Stella Oshoala grimaces.

'That's not a word we use, Marina. We're interested in information. Updates. Insights. Our government is not one of the major players in the LMA. What's happening up there is important but all we're thrown by the Russians and Chinese is bird feed.'

'Are you telling me it's my patriotic duty?'

'Those aren't words we use either, Marina.'

Marina feels trapped in the deep, swallowing sofa.

'Spy on my friends.' The anger is red and hot and oh so joyful but she must keep it controlled. She bites back the words *spy on my loves.*

'Your mother will receive the best of care,' Stella Oshoala says.

Now the hot anger gives Marina the strength to push herself out of the suffocating sofa, across the room to her hiking poles.

'We look after our own,' Marina says as she slips her wrists through the loops and takes the grips.

'I'll leave it with you,' Stella Oshoala calls, a parting shot as Marina stalks down the corridor. Tick-tack, tick-tack. A spy. A tout, a traitor. How dare she? The hurt and humiliation is doubly hot because the woman was right. She can afford to go to the moon or look after Mom. Or betray the family that took her in, raised her up from the dust, placed their trust and confidence – placed their lives – in her.

'Good?' Kessie asks as Marina swings past the lines of hopefuls with eyes full of moon, towards the car pulling in under the porch. 'You were gone a long time.'

'Sound in wind and limb,' Marina says. 'Give me a hand with this. will you?' Kessie holds the sticks while Marina struggles into her jacket. It's too small and too hot for the city but her proud Corta Hélio T-shirt feels like a brand of treachery.

Cloud has drawn in around Rainier. Fickle goddess. Marina turns her back on the mountain, on the Space Needle, on the thuggish towers of Elliott Bay. Traitor town. She grips the rail and looks across bay and sound to the mountains of her homeland. She zips the jacket up to her throat. Always cold on the sound. A good jacket won't let you down.

The ferry has rounded the southern point of Bainbridge Island before Kessie says, 'You are in one hell of a mood, sister of mine. Did something happen back there?'

Jellyfish tumble through indigo water, bouquets of blubber and poison.

'I need you to lend me one hundred thousand dollars.'

'That's what it was about.'

'What is was about, Kessie,' Marina says, her knuckles white against the dark wooden rail, 'what it was actually about, was the Defence Intelligence Agency trying to turn me into a spy.'

Wooden houses line each stony shore, dapper and wealthy. Beyond them rise the trees.

'They don't call it spying. I'd be an information feed. Feed them the Cortas and they'll pay for Mom's care.'

The engine pitch changes as the ferry lines up on Bremerton pier. Kessie shifts uncomfortably at the rail.

'I have to ask—'

'The Cortas are the most egocentric, narcissist, arrogant – outright weird – pack of fucks I have ever met,' Marina says. 'And every second I am away from them, it kills me.'

Docking announcements blare on the speaker system. The ferry shudders as the bow thrusters open up. Dark waves lap high up the concrete piles and rubber buffers of the pier.

'I don't know, Marina.'

'I have to move fast on this, Kess.'

'Marina, I don't know.'

The off-ramp scrapes up the concrete of the dock. Marina is the last one at the rail. She can clearly make out Kessie's car in the lot, that will soon take them back between the mountains and the water to the house under the eaves of the forest.

TWENTY-TWO

Haider frowns, eyes flicking in concentration, nostrils flared.

Alexia understands that when you are scared, when you are headed into the worst thing in the world with no escape, no adjournment, you find deep engagement in your trivia. Your music, your chat, your beloved shows. But Gods, how many games of Dragon Run can one thirteen-year-old play?

The LMA rail car drives east from Hypatia Junction across the smooth black glasslands of the sun-belt. A landscape to drive the soul inward, to dark reflection and self-examination. Gods. She prefaced the thought: *Gods*. The lunar way. Gods and saints and orixas, the whole a crazed feijoada melding into something strange, something new, something more. And she is part of this melting, mixing, melding. How long since she thought of home, of the green and blue of Barra, of the people of Ocean Tower who cheered and toasted her up into space, of gorgeous, vain Norton, of Marisa and Caio? Days of forgetting slip into lunes and one day you find years have turned and you cannot go back again.

'Haider.'

No answer.

'Haider.'

He looks out, focuses from game to Alexia.

'Are they safe?'

Haider opens his mouth wide. Alexia sees nibs of colour under his tongue, in his cheeks. Red, green, blue, yellow, white. The black she can't see, concealed in the darkness within the human body. It's there, the last death of all.

'Fuck's sake, Haider!'

He spits the vials out into his hand.

'Just trying it out. You never noticed me put them in, did you? I picked up some of Robson's tricks. I've got this thought out. Can't hide them up my ass because I'd never get them out without everyone seeing. This way, I slip them in when we get there, I slip them out again when I see Robson. All I got to do is keep my mouth shut.'

'What if you swallow?'

'They're coded to Robson's DNA. Only he can open them. They just go right through me.'

And you trust that?

'How long to João de Deus?'

'Ten minutes.'

'Enough time.' Haider settles in his seat, refocuses his eyes back into his game. Strange boy. Deliberately awkward, challenging others to come to him. She tried to talk, to engage him, to understand him on the rail ride from Theophilus. He rejected every approach. The quietness, the inwardness repel Alexia. She would never have him as a friend, but she is not thirteen, she is not a boy, she is not Robson Corta and to know a friendship you must see both parts of it. But he is a friend, the greatest and bravest friend Alexia has ever seen.

The railcar slows. The deceleration jogs Haider from his game. The LMA honour guard take up positions, swaying as the railcar takes the points on to the branchline to João de Deus. Four of the best non-Corta mercenaries Nelson Medeiros could recuit. They'll last forty seconds if it comes to a real fight. They know it. The railcar is in the tunnel now, lights strobing, slowing as it brakes into the station.

'Okay, Haider.'

No answer.

'Haider?'

When Alexia looks back Haider's hand is empty.

Alexia hates João de Deus. She hates the thick, rebreathed air, she hates the stench of cooking oil rubbed deep into the porous stone, the reek of piss and poorly managed sewage. She hates the taste of dust and the soft scrape of it under the soles of her Bonwit Teller shoes. She hates the meanness of the streets, the judging loom of the overhanging levels, the claustrophobia of the too-close sunline – she can read the individual cells of the false sky. She hates the eyes that glance as they pass, or from the alleys and ladeiras, or look down from crosswalks. The eyes that glance and turn away when she looks back. She knows what they say. *Mão de Ferro? There has only ever been one Mão de Ferro: the woman who built this place, who built a helium empire on regolith exhausted of all other value. Adriana Corta.*

Her wards and charms are immaculate: she and Haider were greeted at the station by Hossam El Ibrashy, Mackenzie Helium's new First Blade. Finn Warne, his predecessor, was now First Blade at Hadley.

Fifty Mackenzie blades landed on these two platforms, overwhelmed Corta Hélio defenders and attacked up Kondakova Prospekt, Maninho informed her as the LMA railcar drew into João de Deus Station. *On your right, first level, highlighted is Lucas Corta's erstwhile apartment. His sound-room was the finest in the two worlds.* She can't refuse to look: she sees smoke-stained windows, charred interiors, imagines she still smells burned woods, melted organics. Hossam El Ibrashy makes charming small talk, the two Mackenzie Helium blades are tight and discreet and Maninho whispers the other story. Every centimetre of the city is embossed with a history of Mackenzie perfidies: every door, every alley overlain with the memory of wrongs. *Estádio da Luz: home of João de Deus Jaguars, formerly Gatinhas and Mocos.*

'Hold on a minute.'

Maninho highlights the Boa Vista tram stop, shuttered and sealed, but here is something not written in its histories. A semicircle of biolights flickers at the foot of the wall – red, green gold. Among them, cheap printed figurines loll and slump or wobble on unsteady bases.

'A moment please.' Alexia breaks away from her escort to crouch before the biolights. Haider joins her. Icons have been hung on the pressure seal: elderly women in white and beads like old Baianas. Mães de Santo, holy women, the Sisters of the Lords of Now, arranged around a broken triangle of portraits. Two men, a woman at the centre; a gap where one has been removed; the adhesive pads still tacky to the touch. That picture lies face down among the votives. Alexia touches each picture in turn. So this is Rafa. Golden son. Smiling, popular, but Alexia reads demons behind his eyes. And this is Carlinhos, the fighter. He is beautiful. Alexia regrets she will never meet him. And this: a strong-featured, dark-skinned woman, dark hair flecked with radiation-grey, looking out with eyes of empire: this can only be Adriana Corta. The Iron Hand that dug a dynasty out of the regolith. The Iron Hand would not hire criminals to bring justice to the men who damaged her beloved brother. The Iron Hand forges and delivers her own justice.

Alexia doesn't need to turn the fallen portrait face up. She knows who it is. Iron Hand, charmer, fighter. Traitor. You'll see, João de Deus.

'Senhora Corta, we need to move on.'

'Of course.'

She squeezes Haider's hand. He glances at her, startled and she regrets the gesture: too big a startle and he might choke on the deaths hidden in his mouth.

Almost there, she says on their private channel.

Mackenzie Helium has appropriated a half-kilometre of prospekt-front offices. The logo is worked out in neon, three levels high. Heavy security. Alexia can tell the Santinho recruits by their furtive glances of guilt and hope.

'If you please, Senhora Corta, this is as far as you go.'

She nods to Haider. This was expected but he is afraid now.

'You go on, Haider. It'll be all right.'

Seats are provided, tea is brought by bright staff in neat Mackenzie Helium uniforms. Hossam El Ibrashy touches Haider lightly on the arm and escorts him through the sliding doors.

The room is white, bright, upholstered ivory faux-leather. No windows. Haider blinks against the hard brilliance. Robson is a spirit in white shorts and sleeveless T. His skin and hair stand stark against the white white white.

'I'll leave you alone,' Hossam El Ibrashy says. 'Five minutes.'

The door closes. Now is the part you cannot practise, that has to be right. Now is where the friendship is tested on the edge of the knife, where Robson has to accept and understand without a whisper or a flinch. Now is the trick.

'Hey.'

'Ola.'

Haider hugs Robson to him. He still feels like a sack of bones and cables. Pulls him close.

Now.

Kisses him. On the mouth. Pushes the first death with his tongue against Robson's lips. Quick quick please be quick. Cameras are watching. AIs are scanning up and down the private frequencies. Quantum processors stand by, ready to crack encryptions like an infant's skull. Robson hesitates, then Haider feels his body relax. Robson opens his mouth. Haider locks his fingers behind Robson, turns his head to make the kiss deeper, longer, more passionate. Death by death, he slides the poisons into Robson's mouth.

'You're okay, you're okay, I'm so happy,' Haider babbles, still clinched boy to boy. It's cover, and it's pure nervous relief. 'Are you all right? Are they treating you good? Is the food okay? Do they let you move around? Wagner says to give you his love – they wouldn't let him come. Do you know about… about, what happened?'

Robson nods solemnly, eyes wide.

'I'm okay. I'm okay.'

Will an AI hear the change in his voice? Will machines read what lies behind the awkwardness? Are these all imaginings?

'Do you want some horchata?' Robson says. 'I got a kitchen. Sort of.'

It's hard to talk. Conversation is as heavy as lead. Words are rough and uncomfortable. Haider drinks the horchata. It is how he likes it. His eyes widen as he sees Robson take a sip. Nothing. Cool and controlled as if he were taking a saut de bras off the Level 5 water tank. That's clever, so clever. He's drinking horchata so there can't be anything in his mouth. They forget that Robson knows both the trick and the misdirection.

'Got a gym, want to see it?' Robson says. Robson has more rooms in his João de Deus prison than entire sectors in Theophilus. 'I'm supposed to work out.' Robson shows Haider the free weights, the running track, the step and swivel trainer. 'There's a lot of stuff for working on my ass here.' He pauses. Frowns. ''Scuse me. Bathroom. Be right back.'

And this is where the switch is done. From mouth to another hiding place. Not in the bathroom; they'll surely search that. The ass, probably. Robson can work it so even if there are cameras in there – and Haider wouldn't put it past Bryce Mackenzie – they will never see it.

'Sorry about that. This has been happening. The water here is weird.'

The door opens.

'Sorry, but it's time,' Hossam El Ibrashy says.

'Kiss me again,' Robson says. Of course. The kiss seals the trick. *Thank you,* Robson mouths, and kisses Haider. *Wagner says, you aren't alone,* Haider mouths back. The trick is done. Robson takes Haider's face in his hands. Big eyes, freckles. Haider's heart could burst.

'Now kiss me goodbye,' Robson says and he kisses Haider like the world will break, like it's the last thing he will ever do.

The mud is dense and grey, with a lustrous mica-sparkle where its laps and folds catch the light. It is a highly sophisticated ecology of mineral supplements, dermal nutrients, scrubs and emollients, anti-fungals, anti-bacterials and phage suspensions against the most troublesome of the resistant diseases coming up from Earth, and it fills a pool in the floor of Mackenzie Helium's presidential suite.

Bryce Mackenzie lolls back in a wave of grey mud, scoops up fistfuls of ooze and massages them into his pendulous breasts. The ignominies of the Battle of Hadley slip away like dead skin cells.

'Bliss,' he whispers. 'Bliss.'

The mud was transported from Kingscourt by BALTRAN and was waiting, body-warm and unguent for Bryce's arrival. Travel is ache and inconvenience, discomfort and dyspepsia. Over the past two years, Bryce has spent more and more hours in his mud-pool.

'Have him brought to me,' Bryce commands.

'How prepared?' Hossam El Ibrashy says.

'The swimwear.' Bryce's voice is hoarse and coagulated with want. Hossam El Ibrashy dips the head and leaves. Bryce props himself up against the side of his pool. Mud slides from the mounds of his belly and breasts. Mud twinkles in the folds of his neck, the creases of his chins. He has smeared streaks of it on his cheekbones, like war-paint. His breathing is heavy but regular, his heart a tight clench of angina. Good for a hundred thousand beats yet, his doctors assure him. The people of João de Deus had better bet the doctors are right. He feels his penis stir against the warm, heavy mud.

'Bryce.'

Hossam El Ibrashy stands behind the boy, one hand on his shoulder.

'Thank you, Hossam.' Bryce scrutinises Robson Corta. The trunks are minute, pure white. No footwear: he has never been able to achieve orgasm with anyone wearing any kind of covering of the feet. 'Well, step forward, step forward, let's take a look at you.' He hears the pumping want in his voice. This is where he takes everything from Lucas Corta.

'I thought I told you to put on some muscle. You're skinny as a fucking girl.'

No answer. Defiance in the eyes, the lips. Good. Sullen is cute. Sullen is fun to break.

'Well, it'll have to do I suppose. Right. Take those off.'

'What?'

'It speaks. Wonder of wonders. The Speedos. Take them off.'

Pretty consternation on his face. A hit, a solid hit. More will come; hit upon hit upon hit.

'Oh for fuck's sake, boy, what did you think was going to happen? Get naked.'

'Um, do you mind?' The boy flicks his fingers – *look away, look away*. Now it is Bryce's turn for the incredulous *what?* 'I need not to be seen.'

'What you need, boy, is to get those Speedos off.'

'Yes, yes, I will, but . . .'

'Oh for fuck's sake.'

Bryce rolls away. He'll make the Corta boy pay for that later. Mackenzie. Was, is, always will be: Mackenzie. His.

'Then get in here with me.'

When he heard Bryce order him to strip naked, Robson thought his heart would stop. It had been easy magic to hide the deaths in the tiny white trunks. He slid the bare needles through the stretchy white weave – bare needles because Robson knew when it came to the deaths he would never have time to unlock the plastic containers.

Bare needles, next to his skin. Move with care and precision. No move a traceur, a magician, makes is ever careless or imprecise.

The plan had not involved him leaving his weapons on the floor of Bryce's spa.

He must be quick he must be sure and he must be safe. Haste, incaution, inattention and it will be him vomiting, haemorrhaging, shitting his organs over the rubber matting. One at a time, make it safe, on to the next. He slips the first death, the red death, from his trunks, weaves it into his hair. Remember where it is; burn it in with body memory. You cannot afford to miss. The blue death, the green.

'Almost ready,' he says. The white and the black; woven into his 'fro. 'Ready now.'

He has never felt more naked, more exposed, more raw. He is skin, he is meat, he is nothing. He kneels by the side of the mud pool. He cannot bear to touch the mud. It is pollution. Touch the mud and he will never be clean again. The man lolling in it, smiling, he cannot even look at. It is beyond pollution. It is corruption.

'Now isn't that better?' Bryce slides in under Robson, smiles up at him. He puckers his fleshy lips. 'Now kiss me like you kissed that fucking fag-friend of yours.'

Robson leans close.

'No I won't.'

He reaches up. The body memory is perfect. He takes the Red Death and stabs it down into Bryce's left eyeball.

'That's from Rafa,' he shouts as Bryce bucks in agony, the needle throbbing in his bleeding eyeball. The cry dies on Bryce's lips as his body convulses, a slick of reeking liquid diarrhoea rising to the surface of the pond. The second death is in Robson's fingers. He drives it clean and deep into Bryce's right eye.

'This is from Carlinhos.'

Bryce's hands flap wildly, blindly. It is easy for Robson to restrain one as he slides the next death out of his hair. Blood runs down Robson's wrist: Bryce is bleeding from his cuticles. Cuticles, ears, tear-ducts, the corners of his flapping mouth. Blood runs down his shivering jowls on to the heaving surface of the mud. His bowels and bladder still pump their contents into the pool.

The third death, the death of the soul, goes into the left eyeball beside the first death.

'This is from the Queen of the South traceurs.' Robson is bawling now, hysterical.

A tiny voice squeaks a long, keening wail. Bryce's eyes would roll up but the needles pin them in place.

'This is from Hoang.' Roaring, half-blinded with tears, every muscle tight to hold the discipline; Robson drives home the fourth death: the death of self.

The hands no longer reach for Robson; they shake, beseech. Bryce's throat convulses: a wave of bloody vomit spews from his bleeding lips, rolls down his greasy breasts. The mud spa is a putrid swamp of piss, shit, blood, vomit, liquefying organs. Robson's sure fingers slide the final death out of his 'fro. He holds up the black needle in front of Bryce's blind eyes.

'And this is from me.'

He stabs the needle deep into Bryce's left eyeball. Somehow, somewhere, a tiny voice pushes past the hells of the hallucination and pain and sensory shutdown.

'Fucking. Corta. The bombs. City is wired. To my heart. Bombs!'

Robson freezes. The door to the spa bursts open. Robson turns on Hossam El Ibrashy charging, two knives raised. Robson scrambles away, then there is a whistling hiss, something wraps itself around Hossam's throat. Cubes of raw rock spin in, accelerating, and crush his head like a mango.

A Mackenzie Helium blade rushes the room, buries a knife through Hossam, vertebrae to lung, but the improvised bola has done its work.

'You okay?' Portuguese. *Wagner says, you aren't alone.*

'The place is bombed,' Robson whispers. His strength is gone.

Bryce Mackenzie slides, smiling, into the vile sewage of his death.

The blade is offering a hand. There are bombs, bombs, everyone must get out, and she offers a hand?

'The bombs are wired to Bryce's heart! If he dies . . .'

The blade hauls Robson to his feet. The mud closes over Bryce Mackenzie's face, pours into his open mouth.

'Oh those.' She has a Santinho accent. And does Robson now hear voices, shouts, the noise of battle? 'We found and took care of those lunes ago.' Robson takes a tottering step. The blade slips off her jacket and slides Robson's arms into the sleeves. He is shivering now; tremendous, racking full-body seisms. 'Come on, Corta,' the blade says. She helps him on with the trunks. She wraps his arm around her neck and they hobble to the door.

'Corta,' Robson whispers. The world is both very large and very small, very near and infinitely distant and he can't stop shivering. 'Corta.' He collapses into shuddering sobs. He can't stop. The fury is spent and the ashes are cold and dead.

'Let's get you some nice hot tea,' the blade says.

'Horchata,' Robson bawls through the tears. 'I drink horchata!'

Wagner Corta has never given thought to the zabbaleen. They are the Fifth Elemental; the strippers and recyclers, the cleaners and de-boners, the hewers of flesh and the renderers of fat. Life, memory, reduced to chemical elements.

All end this way; as a spreadsheet of carbon, oxygen, nitrogen, calcium; traces. The carbon of the dead becomes the feedstock for the three-D printers of the living.

He too will end this way; a ration, an apportioning, someone's party dress, someone's pull-toy, someone's killing blade.

The zabbaleen are discreet and the zabbaleen are assiduous. Not one spot of blood, one skin cell is left in the apartment. No trace that there was a murder here. A murder and a kidnapping. Wagner imagines the smell of blood, of murder, of knives must meld with the walls, the floors. The zabbaleen are good: the apartment smells of citrus tinged with the ever-present electric scent of moondust.

The apartment.

Their apartment.

He's glad the zabbaleen have cleared all the furniture, stripped the place down to bare architecture.

Haider found her by the door. Here. Wagner stands on the spot. He thinks of her fingers, her so clever fingers that could call the most wonderful music from warped wood and stretched wire. Those fingers trying to staunch the terrible wound, fingers fluttering, failing, soaked red to the knuckles, to the palms, to the wrists.

He can't think too long and deep on that image.

No one deserves a death like that.

Whoever did it, whichever of Bryce's blades or mercenaries, he hopes they tasted some of what they dealt to Analiese when João de Deus rose.

He needs to get out of this apartment. Wagner's attention catches on a fold of paper on a shelf. There is no way that would have escaped the zabbaleen unless it was not for their attention. A note, folded four times.

I'm sorry Wagner. I can't ever be forgiven. I've betrayed you, I've betrayed Robson. They would have hurt my family.

Family first. Family always.

The words of the betraying are handwritten, archaic marks on expensive paper.

Words like musical notes, the work of her fingers.

Robson crumples the note. He would throw it across the aparment – an affront to perfection of the zabbaleen – but for all her betrayal, she should not be left lying for strangers to find.

Bryce Mackenzie is dead. Robson is safe. Now he can close the door behind him, go on the BALTRAN and return to his family and city.

TWENTY-THREE

I'm not a fighter, he says in the rover from the BALTRAN terminal.

I'm a wolf, he says as the rovers roll down into João de Deus Lock 4.

I'm not really a Corta, he says as the guillotine gates of the outlock close and the pressure equalises.

You're a Corta, they say and put a knife in his right hand and a knife in his left hand.

I'm not a leader, he says as the inlock opens. *I'm not the Iron Hand.*

You lead, says the Iron Hand. *This is your fight.*

And I've got you, Nelson Medeiros whispers at Wagner's shoulder. *You'll just get yourself stupidly killed.*

Then the wolf breathes deep of the reek and perfume of João de Deus and with a cry he leads the escoltas on to Kondakova Prospekt. The liberation of João de Deus is fast and overwhelming. Rover-borne Corta squads seize the city's surface locks; mercenaries arrive from Twé on a chartered train. Pods of materiel drop into the electromagnetic hands of the BALTRAN relay; VTO track-queens on day-hire contracts feed it to the assault teams down on the prospekts. But there is no battle here. João de Deus has liberated itself. Lucas's dusters and sleeper agents inside Mackenzie Helium moved to secure the city's air, power and water. Santinhos left their work and schools and homes and mobbed the public printers to print up knives and body armour. João de Deus rose: Mackenzie Helium blades sheathed their knives. There is no profit in pointless death. The board fled at the first rumour that Bryce Mackenzie was dead at the hands of a Corta; senior management turned in their resignations and quit their offices.

Kondakova Prospekt is filled wall to wall with escoltas, dusters, Santinhos. Cheers and whistles and applause snow down from the levels and crosswalks as Wagner leads the liberating army. More join every minute. By the time he reaches the smashed doors of Mackenzie Helium's headquarters all of João de Deus is behind him. He raises a hand. The army halts. The voices fall silent. The neon MH sign flickers on the edge of death, most of its tubes taken out by slingshots and quick-printed stonebows.

Through the broken doors come two figures: a blade and a boy. The woman still shelters Robson under her arm. He is bruised, blood-stained, broken. The woman whispers to him. He looks up. Light fills his eyes.

The blades fall from Wagner's hands. He runs to Robson and scoops the skinny, wrecked boy up in his arms.

'Oh you,' he gasps. Tears stream down his face. 'Oh you you you.'

João de Deus answers with a shout.

Revolution is so untidy. He walks through the detritus of the liberation: water bottles, knives, pieces of door frames and window surrounds for clubs; chunks of hacked-loose sinter for missiles. Placards. Items of clothing. A shoe. Two bodies. Lucas regrets those. He had intended this to be a bloodless acquisition. Bloodless, save for those whose blood had to be shed. Ahead he can still hear the singing and chanting of the crowd. An ugly town, João de Deus. He never recognised its ugliness when he lived here. The eye of the conqueror sees the cost of the conquest.

Conqueror. Salve Lucas Imperator. Lucas smiles at his presumption.

He kicks a lump of stone up the prospekt. The roar of the crowd is closer, louder, rising and falling in waves. The wolf knows how to work a crowd. The bastard did well. Mustn't let the people love him too much. After the reconstruction, after the zabbaleen have crept out of their digs and tunnels to clear away the wreckage, he must rotate Wagner back to Meridian. Some role in the civil service. Not too demanding. Plenty of time to fuck his wolf friends.

The kid: when it came to it, he had the Iron Hand.

Lucas isn't sure he could have done what Robson Corta did.

Toquinho is ready at the edge of Lucas's consciousness with a highlight, but Lucas does not need the hint. He knows where and when to look up. The empty windows, the smoke-blackened walls, the caved-in doors have no power any more. The best sound room in the two worlds. He made Jorge unpack his guitar in the living room so that the shape of the case would not affect the sonic landscape. Gone. He won't rebuild it. Pointless to live in a museum. Boa Vista is his home now and he will rebuild this mean city as it should have been; tough, energetic, chaotic, celebratory. And do something – something – about the João de Deus reek.

Denny Mackenzie hung Carlinhos by his heels from this bridge. Slung a cable through his Achilles tendons. Blood from his throat ran down his arms and dripped from his fingers to the paving: here. They said he fought like a demon; killed twenty Mackenzie blades before Denny took him down and cut his throat through to the bone. As Alexia pointed out, that same Denny Mackenzie Lucas helped install in Hadley.

The old moon is dead. It died at his first meeting with the financiers, the government representatives, the military advisers, down on the hell of Earth. The new moon is not yet born. The piece is not played through.

Duncan and Bryce Mackenzie are dead. Denny Mackenzie is the flash and dash of the old, buccaneering spirit of Robert Mackenzie while quietly competent women build a new Mackenzie Metals. The

Vorontsovs reach for the worlds beyond. The Suns are humiliated, yet prepare for all-out economic war with their ancient enemies on Earth. The university stirs from its long sleep. The Asamoahs: who knows what they plan and scheme? And the Cortas? The Helium Age is over. Corta Hélio will not return.

It was never about Corta Hélio.

'Family first,' Lucas says. 'Family always.' In the corner of his eye, a new thing, strange to his memory of João de Deus. He walks to the wall of shuttering over the old Boa Vista tram station. A shrine to the Sisters who sacrificed themselves to free Lucasinho from the hands of Bryce Mackenzie. More: to the Cortas. To his family. The golden triangle. Rafa. Honest, straight Carlinhos. Lucas never told his younger brother, but he always admired Carlinhos. Carlinhos knew what had to be done and did it. No doubt, no question. In the centre, his mother. The image is from the old wild-catting days, when Lucas was the strangely silent, frowning baby in the berçario.

'Mamãe.'

One portrait missing. Of course. The whole moon saw him as the traitor when he threw Jonathon Kayode down from his Eyrie and took the high seat of the Eagle of the Moon. Lucas crouches, brushes dust from his pants, picks up his image. So solemn, so serious. He presses it against the wall until the adhesive fixers bind. He tips his hat forward.

'Well, I'm back,' he says.

Two shell-suits, one blue and white, one pink and purple. The suits stand on an elevator platform, holding hands. The elevator climbs slowly up the airless shaft of Coriolis's West Rim lock.

Blue and white are the colours of the University of Farside. Pink and purple are the colours that Lucasinho Corta picked out of the row in the lock's suit-room.

'Are you okay about this?' Luna Corta said as the haptic rig enclosed Lucasinho in its silken web.

'It tickles,' Lucasinho said.

'Only for a minute,' Luna said. She was an old hand at the haptic rig, at the whole shell-suit thing now. A true duster. 'If you feel weird, we can stop.'

'I don't want to stop,' Lucasinho said. His face twitched. Still the spasms and tics as the protein chips forge new pathways in his brain. 'Luna, if I do . . .'

'I'll be right there.'

He looked nervous as the suit began to seal up around him; legs, hips, torso. Arms, shoulder: he gave a small cry as the helmet folded around him.

'You all right?' Luna asked on the common channel. Lucasinho's right glove formed an 'O' with thumb and forefinger: the ancient pressure-suit sign that everything was all right. But on the far side of the lock, on the elevator platform, he took a clunking step closer to Luna and held out a hand. She took his armoured gauntlet in hers. Shell-suits are all the same size; it is the bodies and hearts inside that differ.

The elevator climbs, the two suits emerge into the surface clutter and debris of Coriolis's crater-rim.

'On top of the world!' Luna says as the platform stops and locks. The view is stupendous, far far over the too-close horizon, across an endless panoply of craters, craters within craters, rilles and broken rim-walls, strongly shadowed in the light of a sun halfway to the zenith. Beyond, on the far edge of seeing, the mountains of Farside.

'You okay?' Luna asks. She squeezes Lucasinho's hand. The haptics will turn it into reassurance.

'I'm okay.'

'Let's try a walk,' Luna says. She leads Lucasinho a few paces off the elevator on to the rim. The crater-top is an undulating upland curving almost imperceptibly on either side of them. Comms dishes occupy the higher summits. The shadow of the eastern rim lies long across the crater floor: Luna points out Equatorial One, the station, the magic-box glimmer of the cable-cars spinning down from Coriolis's campuses and districts. Lucasinho is spellbound. Luna squeezes his hand again.

'Look up.'

'Up?'

'Look up.'

She sees his helmet tilt back. There is a long silence, then a longer, amazed, sighing breath.

'Nothing but stars!'

From Rozhdestvenskiy to Schrodinger, from Mare Orientale to Mare Smythii, in the biology labs of Mandelshtam and the antennae arrays of Muscoviense, Farside is in uproar. A muted, unrushed, considered uproar, but Ariel has dwelt in the halls of the university long enough to read the upswing in conference calls, the bustle of senior academics and facultarians through Farside train stations, the recall and dispatch of ghazis. A political impacter of world-breaking mass has struck Nearside and the moon is ringing like a terreiro bell. A seism greater even than the War of Mackenzie Succession.

She likes that term. She might have Beija Flor flick it over to the history faculty at Mare Ingenii.

Vidhya Rao, Beija Flor announces.

'Fuck.'

State-of-the-planet surveys are best taken from the perspective of one's own bed. Ariel swings out from beneath the sheet and summons clothes.

Vidhya Rao has now been waiting for ten minutes, Beija Flor announces as Ariel dresses.

'Face first,' Ariel says.

By the time she is dressed and faced, she knows exactly what has hit the world.

'Clever, clever boy,' she whispers as she adjusts the sit of her hat.

'Did your August Sages foresee that one?' Ariel asks as she sweeps into her drawing room.

'I no longer have access to the Three August Sages,' Vidhya Rao says. 'Lunar politics has entered a critical stage.'

'Most people would look at it as a robust change of management.'

'The Eagle of the Moon is independent, impartial and does not involve themself in corporate politics.'

'Jonathon Kayode was an enthusiastic meddler in corporate politics. He was married to a Mackenzie, for gods' sake.'

'There is a difference between dropping hints and slipping information, and assassinating your rival and taking his corporate headquarters.'

' "Slipped information" about the Mare Anguis licence sparked the Corta-Mackenzie war,' Ariel says.

'He also suggested the Corta-Mackenzie marriage to end the bloodshed.'

'Knowing full well that it would never happen. Knowing full well that the repercussions would lead to war. Your point?'

'It's started. What I saw. Those futures, with the cities full of skulls; they begin with the death of Bryce Mackenzie and Lucas paralysed politically by the LMA. He has been ordered to refuse the Vorontsovs' Moonport proposal. He will side for the terrestrials against the Dragons. He will sanction the Lunar Bourse proposal and the genocide as the terrestrials *rationalise the market*.'

'Vidhya. I ask this every time you wedge yourself into my life. Why are you here?'

'To ask you to stop him. Because you're the only one who can. He needs to step away from the Eyrie, but he can't because the terrestrials will seize power. He needs an heir he can trust, Ariel.'

'Leave me,' Ariel orders. 'Go.' The sudden verbal aggression rocks Vidhya Rao. *Never seen this before, have you? Never considered I could be anything other than composed, calculating, courtroom. But it's in me, it always has been in me, years deep, like geology. The layers warp, the stresses build. The surface cracks. Marina saw this me. Abena saw this me. Now you see it.* 'Enough of your shit. Enough. My family are not your dolls to push around your playhouse. Out!'

Gods she would love a martini. Good and pure and the most marvellous thing in the universe. Outside the slit window, the gondolas swing up and down their cables. Carnival lights, festive lives. She should apologise to Vidhya Rao. She will apologise to Vidhya Rao. Not yet. Let er suffer in er sanctimony for a little longer. E was right. Ariel has always known that the final battle would be between her and Lucas. Sister and brother. Two reefs of human wreckage, ruined by family.

'Lime spritzer,' she orders Beija Flor. 'In a martini glass.' It looks good in her hand. It feels good, right. Here is clarity and precision. She has known what she must do for a long time. Now she has the idea of how to do it. She looks out over the Coriolis crater and sips from her martini glass and ideas flow to her.

It is insane. Only insanity will work now.

'Beija Flor, get me Dakota Kaur Mackenzie.'

The ghazi is on Ariel's lens in a heartbeat.

'What can I do for you?'

Ariel smiles.

'Issue a challenge.'

A subtle shift in the air conditioning. A door is open.

'Luna?'

'Tia.'

'Come on in, anjinho.'

'I heard you shouting.'

'Were you spying?'

A pause. A small *yes.*

'Do you have tunnels everywhere?'

'Yes.'

The girl is at her side. Ariel runs fingers through Luna's hair.

'I thought you were going to clean that stuff off your face when Lucasinho was safe.'

'He's not safe yet.'

Ariel laughs small.

'True. But he will be. Very soon.'

The girl parts the curtain of streamers and leads the ghazi by the hand into the carnival. The musics of a dozen sound systems assail them: old school samba from the station plaza faces off funk from the First Street Bridge; deep bass shouts bravado across the prospket to the impudent house foro on Second East; neo-Tropicalia blasts horn stabs from a pulpit at the Primeiro Serviço intersection while a waggon pushed by devotees blowing handball whistles circles it, laying down a bombardment of baile. Everywhere: the drums the drums the drums. Hand in hand girl and ghazi flit through rhythm and beats: they slip between the marching ranks of a batteria of drummers, close as the stick to the drumskin, completely unseen. Where music plays, humans dance. João de Deus is a working town, not a dancing town: all the better to party. It dances with delight and without inhibition. To each music its dancers. The smash and crush of bodies in booty-shorts and glitter around the baile-funk systems; old-school samba squads in body-paint and feathers and the stuttering hip-flick of the marching dance. The sweet sway of couples to the syncopations of bossa and jazz Brasiliera. The stomp and sashay of the batterias. Sweat and perfume. Hair flying; legs wide, feet planted. Shaking it, shaking it. Eyes wide, pupils dilated, tongues protruding; bodies leaning in, taking the rhythm of each other, swaying back and forth. Almost but never touching. Through them all ghost the girl and ghazi. The prospekt is ankle deep in paper streamers, street-food wrappers and discarded cocktail glasses. The girl kicks them away, kicks through.

And the voices the voices the voices. Shouting over the beats, shouting into each other's faces, laughing, yelling. The girl cannot make herself heard to the ghazi: they communicate by flickers of familiar-to-familiar traffic, by look and touch and intent.

Inflatable icons of João's heroes bob over the heads of the revellers: handball stars, musicians, telenovela actors, dustbike racers, gupshup channel celebrities; legends of old Earth: Ayrton Senna, Capita Brasil with his fists on his hips, Pele, Maria Funk Fujiwara, one-legged Saci Perere with his hat and pipe. The orixas: fierce Xango, gracious Yemenja. More than any of the others, there is an armoured fist, clenched. The Iron Hand. A Capita Brasil breaks loose, unmoored by children. It wallows up to the sunline to join the cumulus of escaped balloons. Up on the Level Four crosswalk kids open up on it with slingshots.

The girl halts as a dragon loops its coils around Third Bridge, swoops, hovers a moment before her, eyes glowing, daring her to pass, then arcs up and away, sweeping its hundred-metre length past her. It glowers at her from the top of the city, then undulates down the prospekt.

And the food! Oh, the food! The city's hotshops have taken in their tables and seating – this is carnival! – and rattle twenty cuisines over their counters. Here are tacos, there noodle boxes. Dumplings and salads. Soup for those as must; doces and baklavas, flatbreads and tofu kofta. The biggest crowds are around the churrascarias. Smoke plumes from their electric grills filling the air with the illicit perfume of danger and burning flesh. There is meat here. Real meat!

The girl's step falters – she last ate half a world away, and she loves the doces. The ghazi squeezes her hand and she remembers: she is on a mission. They press on, towards the great knot of bodies and lights at the heart of the carnival

What is food without drink? João boasts a thousand duster bars and each one of them has spilt on to the street in impromptu barzinhos: a folding table, a door across two trestles, the back of a misplaced rover. With furious concentration, the bar staff mix, muddle, macerate. They pour from height, they drizzle over ice, they add fruit and decorations. But this is carnival for them too and even as they stir, shake, serve they nod to the beat, sway and murmur lyrics.

The girl keeps a distance from the bars. She leads the ghazi a long way around, up a level, along a higher street. She has seen what alcohol does to people. It makes them not people any more. The girl knows this city, but the high streets do not feel comfortable either. The people here wear body-paint and masks and look at her and the ghazi as they speed past. The eyes behind the masks are filled with wants. Up here everyone is looking: something new from the narco-DJs, a partner, quick sex; everyone is weighing and assaying. A wolf-face appears in front of her. She stops with a small cry.

'Your face.' The wolf-mask moves closer, inspecting her. A man's voice: he is naked apart from a thong. His body is painted grey like the wolf. Highlights glow along the contours of his muscles as he crouches down to the girl's level. 'What are you?'

The ghazi steps forward.

'Death,' she says. The wolf leaps back, hands held up in supplication.

'Sorry, sorry... didn't mean to... Fuck. That's not a costume.'

'No,' says the ghazi.

'Let's go down again as soon as we can,' the girl declares. A ladeira brings them down within a hundred metres of their destination but here, around the old Mackenzie Helium offices, the crowds are at their most dense. The girl gives a small cry of exasperation.

'We'll never get through this,' she says.

'We will,' the ghazi says and steps forward.

The girl has brought baggage to carnival: a long, flat case slung across her back from a strap. The ghazi turns back to offer a hand, the girl accepts. The music is loud, the voices are stupefying and the crowd is terrifyingly close, but they part before a ghazi. The girl follows footstep close; she smells sweat, vodka, cheap perfumes, then she is in the lobby. She has never seen this place when it was the headquarters of Mackenzie Helium, so she does not know that the neon letters recently had different shapes, that logos and branding have been hastily removed from doors and walls and glass. She looks up at the pulsing neon: C. H. C. H. Yellow green. Yellow green.

Escoltas in sharp suits move to block entrance.

'There is a dress code,' says a sharp suit to the ghazi. 'And an age limit.'

'Do you know who you are speaking to?' the ghazi says.

'They do now,' the girl says. Her familiar has flashed the escoltas her identity.

'Apologies, Senhora Corta. You are welcome.'

'Dakota is my personal bodyguard,' Luna says.

'I'm not your bodyguard,' Dakota Kaur Mackenzie hisses as they cross the decorporatised lobby to the grand staircase. Beyond the doors the thunder of carnival give way to voices, glass chiming, bossa nova. The dress code is 1940s movie-star glamour. White tie and tails for the men, spats and top hats, canes and gloves. White teeth and pencil-line moustaches. The women glide in ballgowns and cocktail dresses; sweeping, sumptuous, caressing close, flaring out into folds and flounces. The field of vision seethes with a luminous host of familiars. Luna Corta freezes, very much the Farside parochial in her grey dress and very sensible boots. Dakota Mackenzie, in pragmatic riding breeches, boots and check print, stops dead. A young woman, her dark skin glowing against her ivory gown, stoops to wonder and smile at Luna.

'Fabulous face art,' she murmurs, then sees beneath the art and jerks upright in astonishment. Her surprise ripples across the room. Glasses halt at lips, conversations evaporate in puffs of gossip. The band puts up its instruments and stops playing.

'I think you got them, chiseller,' Dakota says.

Then someone runs out from among the frozen socialites and snatches her hard into his arms and throws her up in the air and as she comes down she sees hair, she sees Mackenzie green eyes, she sees freckles. She sees Robson. Luna squeals and laughs and he catches her and holds her so close she can feel his heartbeat, feel his breath tremble, feel him shake and now they are both shaking and crying and laughing. The party erupts into cheering and applause, the band picks up instruments and plays something loud and joyful. Robson steps away, elegant and awkward at the same time in his white shirt and tails. He looks to Luna as if every bone has been broken and reset out of true. A pale, dark-haired boy comes to him, stands with him.

Faces from her memory push through the crowd.

She sees Alexia the Iron Hand in a long, tight dress and opera gloves. She sees the wolf, the dark legend that haunted the edge of her life, the tio she never really knew. She sees a raccoon push its masked face between immaculately trousered ankles. A bird swoops over her head: she sees her mother, a sunburst in gold. Her swarm forms a halo around her elaborate hair-sculpt.

She sees her Tio Lucas. He is not the uncle she last saw at the wedding at the Eyrie, dapper and composed, joking with her father. Years have fallen on him; his body is broad and bulky with muscle but it weighs him down; he is stiff and bent, leaning on a cane, his face drawn down, his eyes dark.

Sorry to piss on your happy reunion, Dakota says on Luna's private channel, *but we have business here.*

'Tio Lucas,' Luna declares. 'Listen.'

'I am Dakota Kaur Mackenzie, Ghazi of the Faculty of Biocybernetics, School of Neurotechnology of the University of Farside,' Dakota announces. 'Before these witnesses, I am charged to deliver this formal challenge to you. In final settlement of the custody case of Lucas Corta Junior, in a mutually acceptable court and legislation at a time not exceeding one hundred and twenty hours, Ariel Corta will meet you in trial by combat.'

The music ceases, mid-beat. Lucas Corta is smiling.

'I accept,' Lucas says.

Gasps. Glasses drop from hands. Luna slips the case from her shoulder and presents it in her two hands to Lucas.

'You will need this.'

Lucas accepts the gift. Luna observes that it is heavier than he thought.

'Careful,' Luna says as Lucas opens the case. He holds up the knife of meteoric steel. It glitters in the mirror-ball party-light. His breath catches.

'Carlinhos's knife.'

'Mãe de Santo Odunlade gave me the battle-knives of the Cortas. She said they could only be used by a Corta who is bold, great-hearted, without avarice or cowardice, who will fight for the family and defend it bravely.'

Lucas turns the blade in the light, fascinated by its vicious beauty, then lays it across the palm of a hand and offers it back to Luna.

'I am not worthy of this blade.'

Luna pushes his hand away.

'Take it. You will need it.'

TWENTY-FOUR

The rule is this: women of a particular status, in their ninth decade, do not hurry. They do not scurry. A fussy bustle is permissible but it is the limit. A lady never rushes.

Lady Sun rushes, heels clip-clopping in an undignified trot down the palace's curving corridors. Caught between walk and run, her entourage struggles to keep pace with her. The message on Amanda's secure channel had ordered her to come at once. Her granddaughter's suite is too near for a moto to arrive in time, too far to avoid the shame of haste. A palanquin, like the dowagers of old China. That would be the very thing. Like the Vorontsovs use to gad around St Olga, powered by Earth-muscle and youthful enthusiasm. Perfidious Vorontsovs. Lady Sun will not soon forgive the humiliation of the Battle of Hadley. Marooned by VTO, taken in an upholstered cage to Hadley. The smirking politeness of the Mackenzies. Denny Mackenzie grinning his ghastly gold teeth. Grin while you can, golden boy. The power rests elsewhere and when you have served their purpose, the women of Hadley will arrange a boardroom coup, and it will cost you more than your finger. The ransom was insultingly low; Taiyang will recoup it through the breach of contract case against VTO, but it is another unforgivable offence. Fucking Australians.

Lady Sun instructs her sharp young women and men to wait

outside Amanda Sun's apartment. Zhiyuan is present, Tamsin. The whole board. The surprise is Mariano Gabriel Demaria.

'Is it Darius?' Lady Sun asks at once. 'What has happened to him?'

'Darius is well,' Zhiyuan says. 'Mariano brings information about the Eagle of the Moon.'

'Lady Sun.' Mariano dips his head in respect. 'Now that I have the board in full, I can deliver my information. Lucas Corta serves Amanda Sun, plaintiff in the case of Corta versus Corta, Sun and Luna Corta as an Academic Ward of the University of Farside, with a summons to satisfaction at the Court of Clavius. The time and location of this satisfaction to be mutually agreed, but within one hundred and twenty hours.'

'Satisfaction?' Amanda Sun says.

'Trial by combat,' Lady Sun says.

'I know what it means,' Amanda Sun snaps.

'Ridiculous,' Zhiyuan says. 'There hasn't been a satisfaction by combat since . . .'

'Since Carlinhos Corta opened up Hadley Mackenzie balls to voicebox,' Amanda Sun says. She twists open a vape, inhales deep, exhales slow. 'The Cortas have form here.'

'He knows he was a weak case,' Lady Sun says.

'Or he needs to settle quickly,' says Tamsin Sun. 'Within five days.'

'Obviously, he has been served with his own challenge to trial,' Lady Sun says.

'The only one with skin in the game is his sister,' Amanda Sun says.

'I see no legal advantage in Ariel Corta issuing a challenge,' Zhiyuan says.

'You didn't see Ariel Corta putting her nephew on the witness stand at the preliminary,' Tamsin Sun says. 'To her eminent advantage.'

'Get yourself a zashitnik, girl,' Lady Sun says to her granddaughter.

'I've already summoned Jiang Ying Yue.'

'Jiang Ying Yue, who surrendered her blade to Denny Mackenzie and twenty grubby jackaroos,' Lady Sun says. 'You have the greatest knife-fighter on the moon, Nearside or Farside, sitting right in front of you. Write him a contract, pay him five million bitsies and post it on the Court Listings and Lucas Corta and whatever back-stabber he's persuaded to step into the arena for him will fold.'

Again, Mariano Gabriel Demaria dips his head respectfully.

'You honour me, Lady Sun, but I am unable to accept your contract. I am already contracted as zashitnik in this case.'

Consternation on the luxurious upholstery. Zhiyuan is on his feet; Tamsin's familiar is calling security. With a whim Lady Sun could summon her entourage from the corridor but what would it avail but pointless blood? If Mariano Gabriel Demaria intended mayhem no force in this room, in the Palace of Eternal Light, could prevent him.

'Whatever Lucas Corta is paying, I pay you five times,' Amanda Sun says.

'Ridiculous,' Lady Sun says. 'He doesn't need your money. This is personal. He was Carlinhos Corta's second in the Mackenzie duel. He taught Carlinhos Corta the path of the Seven Bells. Old loyalties die hard.' Lady Sun adds, with venom, 'Though, it seems, not to his current pupil.'

'I shall dedicate myself to Darius's training,' Mariano Gabriel Demaria says. 'If Darius wishes to continue.'

'He does not,' Lady Sun snaps. 'We too take personal loyalty seriously in the Palace of Eternal Light. You have earned my enmity. The enmity of the Suns. Please leave us.'

A bow to all and Mariano Gabriel Demaria is gone.

'Lucas Corta intends to frighten us off,' Lady Sun says.

'I propose we don't give the satisfaction,' Zhiyuan says.

'I concur,' Amanda Sun says. 'We will face him in court. This family will not run again.'

'He will cut us apart,' Tamsin Sun says.

'Of course he will,' Lady Sun says. 'We have no defence. But you of anyone should know that one hundred and twenty hours is a long time in law. Perhaps Lucas Corta is lying. Perhaps he is bluffing. Perhaps Mariano Gabriel Demaria's legend greatly outshines his ability. And perhaps Lucas Corta will never go to trial at all.'

'What do you mean?' Tamsin Sun says. Sun Zhiyuan nods. He understands.

'Lucas Corta has an important vote in the LMA,' he says.

'Precisely.' Lady Sun finds she is reaching for her flask. How good, how triumphant, how affirming and reassuring a sip of her gin would be now. No. This too is a rule. Dowagers of exalted houses, in their ninth decade, do not drink in the street. 'Now, I must go and talk to the Three August Ones.'

Again, the voices beyond the stone doors. Again, the tap of heels, the click of cane on the smooth stone. Again, the flutter in the belly, the bladder, that makes Alexia press her fingers to the tightly buttoned waist of her two-piece Chanel suit. She could throw up.

'Do you want me to announce you?'

Lucas Corta shakes his head.

'I want you up in the seats. I want you to read the room and report to me.'

'Report what?'

'Anything that takes your attention.'

This is the day of the vote. The day when the future of the moon is decided. The Lunar Mandate Authority is in full session. The Dragons have arrived from their cities and palaces in their full panoply. The terrestrials in their poor suits and unfashionable shoes have ridden down from their mid-level executive apartments. They know, but have yet to understand, the lunar way; that the higher the status, the further from radiation it lives. To the Earth-born, status is always altitude. Legal counsels and advisers have been retained. The university, for half a century loathe to involve itself in the moon's politics, has sent observers.

'You hesitate?' Lucas asks.

Alexia grimaces.

'Denny Mackenzie will be there.'

'Denny Mackenzie will be everywhere from now on,' Lucas says. 'This is a small world. You will meet the same faces over and over again for the rest of my life. Love them hate them fuck them kill them. Again and again.'

Alexia takes the staircase to the upper tiers.

You hear me? she says on the secure channel.

I hear you very well, Lucas answers.

It's a hell of a show, Alexia says. Lousika Asamoah has left her ward-animals outside the council chamber but she and her party fill their seats with colour and spectacle. Kente robes, staffs of authority, extraordinary hair arrangements: wings, inverted pyramids, cascades of braids, plaited loops. Yevgeny Vorontsov occupies his traditional ring-side seat while his young controllers jostle and brood in the high tiers, groomed to molecular perfection and so so easy on the eye. Yevgeny is flanked by two avatars; humanoid bots with pixel skins carrying the images of the two other aspects of VTO: Sergei Vorontsov, two seconds out of sync, for VTO Earth and Valery Vorontsov for VTO Space. Alexia has never seen Sergei Vorontsov before: he is less distinctive, less theatrical than the other two patriarchs. Burdened. Eroded by politics and gravity. Valery Vorontsov in avatar form is even more of a horror than when Alexia met him in his cylindrical forest in the core of *Saints Peter and Paul.* His attenuated limbs, his weak, spindly neck, his deceptively broad chest turn him into a puppet from nightmare, controlled by strings from orbit. That his feet don't touch the ground compounds the horror.

The Mackenzies command an entire sector of the council room. Gone are the grey men of Duncan Mackenzie's reign. The White Women of Hadley stake their claim to the Council Chamber and the future of Mackenzie Metals. In the heart of the white dresses and suits is a bright yolk: Denny Mackenzie, in a very good suit of russet-gold synthetic tweed. Alexia's attention snags on the woman at his side, ivory dress contrasting with dark skin. Irina. Irina Efua Vorontsova-Asamoah, of St Olga, who had come to her in tears and melodrama when she was to marry Kimmie-Leigh Mackenzie. And now looks well in with the Golden Boy of Hadley, from the way his smile displays his gold tooth when she whispers in his ear.

Alexia knows that smile very well.

Irina notices eyes on her, then notices whose eyes. Her face lifts in recognition. Alexia exchanges the briefest of smiles. But she won't bet on an invitation to that dynastic wedding.

The murmur begins by the main door and circles the council chamber. The Suns are here. Not creeping, not shame-faced, not their single token delegate, but as Dragons. First a coterie of aides and assistants, girls and boys and others of a beauty to match the Vorontsov kids, a style that rivals the Mackenzies and hairstyles – sculpted, gelled, engineered, fighting gravity and inertia – that challenge the Asamoahs. Then, the advisers and legal representatives, impeccable, professional, diamond-bright. Last of all, the delegates from the Palace of Eternal Light. The murmur turns into a rumble and Alexia calls Lucas.

Lucas, Taiyang just rolled up like a rock show. Your ex the Queen of Mean.

The Suns overflow their assigned seats; Team Taiyang spills up into the top tiers, aides jostling Vorontsov bravos.

Amanda Sun places herself in the seat directly beneath Alexia. She turns, smiles like murder.

'Mão de Ferro. I know you're in contact with Lucas. Tell him that unless he drops the court action against me, Taiyang will abstain in the vote.'

'You're bluffing. You'll hand victory to the terrestrials.'

'We will have all the victory we need when the sun-belt contracts start coming in. As for emasculating the Vorontsovs and Mackenzie dreams of space, can you blame us? We have nothing to lose here.'

Alexia summarises to Lucas. Their familiars have made the mathematics clear to them, and the consequences of Lucas's choice. The Suns abstain, the proposal fails. Lucas votes for the proposal, he declares war against the terrestrials. Lucas votes against, he makes himself the enemy of the Vorontsovs and Mackenzies. Lucas abstains, everyone draws blades against him.

The VTO presentation team is in position, engineers and designer briefed and ready.

What will you do? Alexia asks.

The answer comes back at once.

'Lucas says, see you in court.'

The bafflement, becoming confusion, becoming fury on Amanda Sun's perfectly made-up face is a pleasure to Alexia Corta. Lady Sun, seated at Amanda's side, turns to Alexia.

'You filthy little favelado whore,' she whispers. 'Sitting there in your suit imagining you're quality. You are nothing but a ridiculous clown, a thief in stolen silks. You see this room? Everyone in this room laughs at you. Everyone in this room knows you are a joke. Iron Hand. Vainglory from the mouth of a four-year-old. Childish. Vain. Like all you Cortas. You are dirt and I will see you return to dirt. My only regret is that those fucking Australians did not finish the job, from that preening cretin of a CEO to his mewling brat.'

'Sers,' the public address announces, cutting short Lady Sun's bile. 'The Eagle has landed.'

Lucas Corta crosses the floor to his seat. Every eye follows him, every body leans forward, rapt. The council chamber is as tense, as charged, as energised as a fusion containment vessel. Lucas waits for the growl of voices to subside. He stands, one hand on his cane.

'Sers. I have reviewed my position as chair and president of the Lunar Mandate Authority and find that I have been compromised in my duty to conduct myself equably and impartially. Our legal system recognises bias and prejudice, but these must be evaluated and compensated for. I subject myself to evaluation pending compensation and therefore I must suspend myself temporarily from the functions and duties of the Eagle of the Moon and adjourn this vote.'

He turns and clicks out of the Pavilion of the New Moon... Thunderstruck silence, then the tension fractures and the council chamber rises in shouting voices and yelled questions. Delegates are on their feet, jabbing accusing fingers but Lucas Corta is gone.

Meet me, Lucas says.

Hell yes, Alexia replies.

Alexia scoops up her bag and bends close to Lady Sun's ear.

'Fuck you, old woman. We beat you, and we will beat you again, and again and again and then you will die beaten like a street dog.'

Escoltas meet Alexia in the lobby and transfer her to the Eyrie where Lucas waits in his office, at his desk. Two glasses, a flask of his private gin in a cooler. He pours and pushes one glass across the desk to Alexia.

'I know you don't like it but drink.'

She raises the glass.

'Congratulations. A malandro move if I ever saw one.'

'I bought a little time, nothing more. If I am to be saved by a malandro move, it must come from my sister, I think.'

'I don't understand.' Alexia takes a polite sip from the glass. Neat gin. Flowery, astringent stuff.

'The trial. Ariel issued the challenge, and she knows I have retained Mariano Demaria. Even if she replaces the zashitnik Abena hired for the preliminary hearing with Dakota Kaur Mackenzie, she still cannot beat my man. She has another move, one I have not foreseen and I cannot work out what it is.'

'As long as you can push the vote back to after the trial...'

'I've made sure of it. We go to court in forty-eight hours.'

'Gods.' Again, that invocation. 'Are you ready?'

'Can anyone ever be ready? Lê, I have no idea what's going to happen. I find that liberating.'

An entropic chill grips Alexia's spine. It is a sobering realisation, the mark of adulthood: people in power are making it up as they go along. Alexia reaches across the table to take the flask of gin. It is deep frozen crystal, purifying and cold. Alexia tops up Lucas's glass.

'So what do we do?'

'We wait. We listen to bossa nova.' Lucas takes a sip, hisses in pleasure at the bite. 'We drink gin.'

Ariel smells it before she sees it: the electrifying blend of perfume, sweat, dust, printer-fresh fabric, hair products, make-up and shaving gels that can only be generated by one thing: a crowd. Her smile widens to a delighted grin as she rides the escalator up from Meridian's private railcar station. The city has turned out for her.

The impatient murmur becomes a rumble harmonised to the hum of camera drones as the ones at the front catch sight of the faux-feathers of Ariel's Adele List hat, then an excited chatter, then exultation as she steps off the moving staircase.

No handball team ever ran out to a reception like this. The station plaza is solid with bodies, pushing and craning to catch sight of the celebrity story of the year. Voices call her name, Ariel pauses at the top of the staircase to strike a pose. A thousand lenses capture her, a heartbeat later Ariel Corta in her Charles James suit, Ferragamo shoes, Guccio Gucci bag and deadly lipstick tops a million news feeds.

'Get out of the fucking way,' Dakota Kaur Mackenzie hisses, narrowly avoiding being pushed by the moving stairs into Ariel.

Voices bay her name, craving a smile, a look, even a quantum of attention. Questions fall in barrages: Ariel pouts, smiles, lifts a gloved hand and snaps out a titanium vaper. There is a collective gasp, then rapturous applause as she takes a long draw and exhales plumes of fragrant vapour. Ariel Corta is back.

'Isn't it fabulous?' Ariel whispers behind the smokescreen.

'Your transport should be here by now,' Dakota grumbles.

A surge in the commotion: now Luna has reached the top of the stairs. The same beseeching voices call her name. A shout of 'Show us the knife, Luna,' is taken up with gusto. The knife, the knife! Luna clutches the case tight to her and moves to safety beside her madrinha.

Silence sudden as depressurisation falls on Station Plaza.

He is coming.

Lucasinho steps off the moving staircase. He hesitates a moment, stunned by the size of the crowd. The crowd holds its breath. He is hospital-pale and thin, his hair is patchy from the treatments but he has shaved chevrons and concentric circles into the dark stubble. His eyes are dark and his cheekbones can shred dreams. He wears his old Moonrun pin on the lapel of his jacket. He stands surveying the crowd. He looks uncertain. He smiles. He waves. The crowd explodes. Ariel beckons him to stand by her side. The drones swoop, the crowd surges forward; security moves to protect Team Lucasinho. Voices shouting, faces looming, bodies shoving: questions questions questions.

'Gods!' Ariel shouts into the bedlam. 'I've missed this!'

Dakota harrumphs her way through the Han Ying hotel's prospekt-level Armstrong suite. She frowns at the office, sniffs at the deep sofas and wide armchairs. Growls at the private spa with its sauna and five-person whirlpool. Rolls her eyes at the beds she can walk all the way around. Purses her lips at the personalised printer in every room. Sneers at the personal butler with such disdain that he flees.

'This had better not be on the faculty account,' she says to Ariel.

'I booked it,' Abena Maanu Asamoah says from the depths of an armchair the size of a rover.

'Class is as class acts,' Ariel says. 'Perception is half the battle.' She taps Dakota lightly on the wrist with the tip of her vaper. 'And don't worry about your academic budget; the gupshup channels are paying for all this. In return for exclusive content.'

Ariel trickles two plumes of vapour from her nostrils.

'I'm going to stick that thing up your hole,' Dakota mutters. 'And don't vape in here. It's antisocial.' She puts herself between Ariel and the balcony. 'And don't go out there either. There could be a dozen drones waiting.' To Abena, 'And while you are congratulating yourself on your PR coup, have you had this place swept for security?' She jerks a thumb at Rosario de Tsiolkovski, diligently working her way through the kitchen space in search of something to eat. 'This is what you hired?'

'Hey!' Rosario de Tsiolkovski rounds on Dakota. 'I'm the contracted zashitnik.'

'You're a ghazi-school drop-out,' Dakota says. 'The university wouldn't have you.'

'Don't wave your doctorate at me,' Rosario says defiantly. 'I can take you.'

'You?'

'Speed and skill takes size and pomposity every time.' Rosario swaggers from the kitchen space. The two women face off. The zashitnik is a head shorter than the ghazi, but she radiates punk ferocity.

'Girls,' Ariel says. 'Rosario remains Team Corta's zashitnik.'

'You do know Mariano Gabriel Demaria will carve her up on the fighting floor,' says Dakota Kaur Mackenzie.

'Mariano Gabriel Demaria will carve both of you up on the fighting floor,' Ariel says. 'Unless you fight clever. Now go and get tea someplace. I've got my first interview in five minutes and I need to get the smell of testosterone out of the soft furnishings. Everyone except Lucasinho and Abena. You too, Luna.' The girl scowls. 'Elis, take Luna.'

Madrinha Elis takes Luna's hand and coaxes her towards the door.

'Hey.' In the corridor Rosario crouches at Luna-height. 'Is that the knife box? Can I see the knife? I mean, like hold it?'

Ariel hears Luna say, 'No,' and the bickering between ghazi and zashitnik moves lobby-wards.

Dakota has heard of these fantastic creatures but she has never seen one until now. The wolf and his son are two pools of darkness in the hotel lobby. Guests and staff alike avoid them as if they glow with radiation.

Of course Wagner Corta is not a wolf. He is a man with a specialised social structure for a neurological condition. And Robson Corta is not his son, though from what Dakota has heard Wagner has been more a father and mother to him than Rafa Corta and Rachel Mackenzie ever were. But they can be nothing other than the wolf and his son.

The wolf burns with a tightly constrained intensity: Dakota's trained perceptions show her a sharp insightfulness and honed faculties even she cannot match. He is in his light aspect, then. The boy: she has never seen a child more damaged. Torn in two and whip-stitched together, the sutures barely holding. Her heart goes out to them both, the wolf and his son.

'I am Dakota Kaur Mackenzie. Ariel is very happy that you've come. Please follow me.'

The glances of the other guests are brief, the whispers hushed but not so that Dakota can't make them out. *That's him . . . the boy who killed Bryce Mackenzie. Needles in his eyes. His eyes . . .*

They move well, the wolf and his son. Like assassins.

Wagner is taken aback by the intensity of the greeting. Dakota can see that he has not expected everyone to be there. Luna. Lucasinho. His sister.

'Irmão.'

'Irmana.'

From the hesitations, the flinchings, the small moments of

discomfort and unfamiliarity, Dakota fills in the gaps of the family history. Wagner was made the outcast, Ariel made herself the outcast.

'The last time we met you were in a bed in the med centre in João de Deus,' Wagner says to Ariel.

Dakota raises an eyebrow. Weird family. Mackenzies are straightforward, to the face, speak your mind and your heart. Cortas, you never know where you are with them. One moment they love, the next they are radioactive ice. Resentments brood for years, for generations. She watches Robson embrace Lucasinho: these boys are beautiful and damaged and aliens to each other.

Dakota slips close to whisper to Rosario.

'A word. On the balcony.'

Dakota closes the windows and breathes in Meridian's unique fragrance. The noise of the prospekt beyond the screen of shrubs is warm and human.

'Keep an eye on the wolf and the boy.'

'That's not my job,' Rosario starts.

'You won't have a job if your employer is assassinated.'

'Wagner and Robson?'

'The kid killed Bryce Mackenzie. Smuggled the Five Deaths of Twé right into Bryce's private slime pit bare-ass naked. When they found him there wasn't a bone or organ in his body. Just a skin full of liquefying fat.'

'They're family...'

'The people most likely to kill you are your family. Keep an eye open and a hand on the hilt.'

What is a Blue Moon? Alexia asks and the bar-keep makes her one. The conical ice-cold glass, the house gin (fifteen botanicals), the slow pour of the blue curacao over the back of the spoon and the tendrils dropping slowly, monstrously into the spirit, twining and dissolving into sky blue; sunline blue; the globe of orange peel.

She sips it, doesn't like it.

'I don't get it.'

'The Cortas are back,' the bar-keep says.

Alexia still doesn't get it, but he's late so she finishes it and he's still late so she orders another and doesn't get it any more than the first. She'll give him until the bottom of this glass and then fold up the courage she flew to ask him for a drink and walk away.

Nelson Medeiros recommended the bar and his taste is sure: low enough for swank, high enough for bairro-alto raw. The music hit her and she smiled: beats, rhythms she could move to. Feet to tap and head to nod. She took a seat at the bar and asked for the signature cocktail.

He arrives with half a centimetre of Blue Moon left. Heads lean together: *That's him. Then who's she?*

He slips on to the seat beside her. He's different. Changed. She can't put her finger on details, only generalities. Impressions. Deeper rather than wider. Slower but more profound. Present not restless.

He winces at the music.

'We can go somewhere else if you don't like the music.'

'I don't like any music right now,' he says, jerking a thumb roofwards. Beyond the sunline, through two hundred metres of stone, an Earth five days past full stood high over the Sinus Medii. This was the liminal place between the wolf and the shadow. 'It passes.'

Wagner Corta died that day, he said up in Boa Vista's dusty observatory. *I am not one person, I am two.*

'Sorry,' he says, getting up from the chair and stepping back. 'Let's do this right.' He kisses Alexia on each cheek, the formal way. He indicates the seat.

'Please,' Alexia says and he sits again.

'I apologise for being late. Robson wanted to stay later with Luna.'

'Is he...'

'Back in the hotel.'

'You're not with...'

'The pack? No, that doesn't work for him.'

'I was going to say with Lucas.'

'That doesn't work for Lucas.'

He smiles differently; guarded, rationing the emotion.

'Robson wanted to go and meet up with some of his old traceur friends, from when he lived up in Bairro Alto. I told the escoltas not to let him out of the house.'

'You have escoltas?'

'The accessory of the moment. I would like a drink, Alexia Corta.' In the abruptness is an echo of the swift bright wolf.

'I've been drinking Blue Moons,' Alexia says.

'I've never got on with those,' Wagner says and orders a caipiroshka. Alexia joins him: glasses clink and the music is a comfortable, pregnant pulse in her stomach. Conversation is lubricated by vodka but there are still long pauses while Wagner considers a question, odd asides and non sequiturs and intense picking apart of casual remarks. In the spaces, Alexia wonders if it is possible to love both the shadow and the wolf. If she had to choose one, which Wagner Corta would it be? Can anyone but a wolf love the wolf? Then she realises that another woman asked that same question and reached an answer. A woman he loved, who betrayed him and paid a hideous price. And now Alexia Corta turns these compromises and accommodations over in her mind.

He's looking at her. His eyes are wide and uncomfortable.

'Sorry, mind wandering.' He won't let that go. 'Just thinking about tomorrow.' Get him talking. 'You've been, haven't you?'

'I was in the Court of Clavius when Bryce challenged Lucas.'

'Do you mind? Can you tell me? What it's like.'

Wagner goes into himself for dark moments.

'Fast,' he says. 'Faster than you can think. I'm fast – when it's the other me – but not as fast as knives. Knives are faster than conscious thought. One mistake, one lapse of concentration and you are dead. There is nothing clean or honourable about it.'

'Did you see... the result?'

'The death? That's the result. That's always the result. Knives are drawn, someone dies. I saw Carlinhos drive a knife through Hadley Mackenzie's throat and kick his blood up in his mother's face. I saw him take the knife and become something I didn't recognise.'

'How can your law allow a thing like that?'

'I've thought much about this. I'm not a lawyer, but our law prohibits nothing and permits anything, as long as it is agreed. If the law says you can't fight to the blood to settle a case, then there is a thing that can't be agreed and the law is nothing. But I think there is a deeper lesson, which is that the law allows violence to settle disputes to show that violence never settles anything. Violence comes back again and again, down years and decades and centuries and so many lives.'

Four caipis down and Alexia no longer has any taste for a fifth. The bar is crowded with shadows.

'We've a day of it tomorrow,' Alexia says. Wagner reads her true.

'We do.'

'One question: where will you sit?'

'Robson will be with Haider. I will be with you and Lucas.'

'Lucas asked me to be second. I don't know what that means.'

'Hold the knives, check your zashitnik complies with the judges' rules. Arrange for the zabbaleen to take the body away, if necessary.'

'Shit.'

'The judges will guide you.'

Alexia hesitates.

'Wagner. When this is done – whatever happens, can we, you know?'

'Meet again?'

'Yes.'

'I'd like that.'

'I'd like that too.'

*

Ariel intercepts Abena at the bar. Touches two fingers lightly to the back of her wrist.

'Before you go to Lucasinho, I need a word.'

Between Team Corta and ghazis the suite is low on private places but Ariel takes Abena to the spa room. They perch on the edge of the pool. Blue light, swirl-shadows and the prickle of ozone.

'This humidity is wrecking my hair,' Abena starts and then sees a look on Ariel's face that she has never witnessed before. Gone is the arch knowingness, the swagger and the artifice, the affected cynicism. Abena sees caution, even fear.

'Tomorrow, in the court: whatever happens, don't stop me.'

'What are you going to do?' Now Abena is alarmed. This is not Ariel's voice, these are not Ariel's words.

'The greatest malandragem is that you play on yourself,' Ariel says. 'You asked me once, back in Coriolis, if I was having maternal feelings, Lucasinho and Luna tucked away under my wings. You asked that of the wrong person, I think.

'You see, Abena Maanu Asamoah, I have been a self-centred, arrogant monster all my life. I knew it. I always knew it. I pretended I loved the monster. I convinced enough people I did. But it took me to drive away the one person who stood with me, who supported me when we were broken, who loved me, to start to convince myself.'

'Marina,' Abena says. 'I was there when you tried to stop her going to Earth.'

'She went to Earth because I drove her away. And I would do anything for her not to have gone. But no one comes back from Earth.'

'Lucas did.'

Ariel smiles.

'That he did. Just to repeat; tomorrow, whatever happens . . .'

'Don't try and stop you.'

'And if you try and give me any of that redemptive shit, I will have Dakota gut you. Cortas don't do redemption.'

'I thought Cortas didn't do politics.'

'History, I think, will show that we do. Now go to pretty boy and cover him with kisses and tell him you love him.'

Ariel opens the spa room door.

'And your hair does look like a train wreck.'

He doesn't taste the same.

Lucasinho was always sweet to the lips. When Abena licked the sweat from his biceps, the small of his back, it tasted of honey. His skin was soft and scented of herbs and sugar.

He doesn't taste the same, he doesn't smell the same, he doesn't feel the same. Abena holds him tight and she feels a stiffening, a pulling in and away, as if this is their first embrace. As if he has never embraced before. Abena knows how the university rebuilt his personality: she is the Abena Asamoah of snapshots, network comments, sharings and postings. Does he remember when he was the lost boy in Twé, bored and frustrated under the Asamoah's protection, does he remember when he cheated on her with Adelaja Oladele and made up to her with cake and sex? Does he remember anointing her chakras with cream and them laughing and laughing as he licked it off, Anahita to Muladhara? Does he remember when they were apart and she skinned his avatar as a fabulous futanari, and he found it thrilling? How can he trust anything he thinks he remembers?

He doesn't look the same. Those ripe lips, those haughty cheekbones, those long eyelashes will always break boys' and girls' hearts but his deep beauty was his eyes and it is there that the changes lie deepest. Those eyes have been dead. They've seen the nothing.

He doesn't act the same.

'There's a few of us from my colloquium up in a bar on Twenty-Two,' she says. 'Sneak away from this?' He looks uncertain. She runs a finger down his nose, over his lips, his chin to his throat. 'Just a few. Not too many.' No, not uncertain. Scared.

'Would it be okay . . .'

'Whatever you want.' He would have stormed that party, crashed that party if he wasn't on the list, climbed twenty-two levels of Meridian straight up to get to that party. Before. Abena's Tumi calls her friends, waiting with banners and streamers and narco-poppers. *He doesn't want to come.* 'So, what about I just take you out to a hotshop for a quiet glass of tea?' She sees him shudder. 'Or even just a walk? I'm sure you want to get out of this place. It would be good to get some fresher air.' He glances over his shoulder to the balcony of his state room and the city beyond. The voices and sounds of the prospket tempt him. He shakes his head.

'Dakota says it's not safe.'

'We'll take Rosario. She's as good as Dakota. You won't even know she's there. And my aunt has given me some extra protection. Asamoah-style.' She taps a large-jewelled bracelet on her wrist. Lucasinho's resolve wavers, then Abena sees the fear refreeze in his eyes.

'Maybe some other time. I'm really tired. I think I should sleep.' He hesitates. Abena knows that pause. Her breath catches. It's sweet. 'I'm a bit . . . scared.' He bites his lower lip. It's adorable. 'I know we were, you know. Back in Twé.' He looks up through those long lashes. 'I don't want to be alone. I've been alone too much. Would it be okay for you to sleep with me?' Abena's breath catches. Her heart is a thing of light and movement, fleet as a festival flier. In this moment she is not the brightest star of her political science generation; Ariel Corta's legal agent, the advocate who took down Amanda Sun and the Eagle of the Moon, the shining scion of the Golden Stool; she is a young woman with a boy she adores, whom she has adored since she pushed the vouch-safe of the Asamoahs through his earlobe on the evening of his Moonrun party. Moondust to moondust, vacuum to vacuum.

'Yes,' she says. 'Yes I will.'

TWENTY-FIVE

Marina wakes with a cry from a dream of crushing: roof-fall, avalanche, the ceiling of Meridian bearing down on her like a kill-box in an action movie. Light. She blinks scintillas out of her vision. Her optic nerves ache. She clamps her eyes shut. The light is so bright, so sudden she can see the veins in her eyelids.

'Mai?'

'Kess?'

Marina squints through barely open eyes. The door is a dark rectangle, the shadow beside it is her sister.

'I've been calling for five minutes.'

'What's wrong?'

The shadow moves. Marina can risk opening one eye fully.

'Come and have a cup of tea.'

Marina opens the other eye.

'It's—' Once her familiar would have told her the time even as she framed the question, would have woken her with a whispered warning that her sister wanted to take tea at three twenty-seven in the morning. 'Let me throw something on.'

The kettle is boiling by the time Marina pads barefoot into the kitchen. Illumination is from the status lights of network-connected kitchen devices. The room smells of herbal teas, flowers and small fruit. Kessie sets down two mugs. Marina dunks her tea-bag: a hot baptism.

'I've done something I hope I don't regret,' Kessie says. She slides a print-out across the table to Marina. Marina squints in the blue gloaming. It's a notification of the transfer of one hundred thousand dollars to her Whitacre Goddard bank account in Meridian.

'I raided a few old accounts,' Kessie says.

'You'll get it back, as soon as I start earning,' Marina says. 'Every cent.'

'As long as it's before Ocean starts college.' The two mugs of herbal brew steam, untouched. 'I put it in your lunar account because you said the DIA was watching your US bank. I think you do need to move fast on this.'

'I can transfer it to VTO right away. Thank you, Kess, thank you.'

Kessie holds up a hand.

'I think you also need to leave pretty soon too. As soon as they see the payment go through to VTO, they'll guess what's happened.'

'You think like a Corta.' And now there is a break in her voice and her eyes are full and her words are tangled and knotted.

'I've been thinking,' Kessie says. 'Canada. VTO has a launch site in Ontario. I know it's not like making an airline booking, but you launch from there, soon as you can.'

Kessie speaks fast, words running into each other. Marina understands: if she slows down, she too will trip and break into tears.

'They'll be watching the border,' Marina says.

'That's why you have to move fast. Tomorrow.'

'Tomorrow?'

'You take the fast ferry to Victoria. Once you're in Canada, you're safe. You can take your own sweet time to wander over to Ontario. But you need to be in Canada before you buy your ticket, because that's the trigger.'

'Tomorrow?'

Rain has started, a soft hissing on the shingles. Marina hears every drop with the numb shock of knowing that this is the last time she will ever hear it. No time for the rituals of leave-taking. This is the last rain, the last sussurus of the wind through the trees, the last notes from the wind-chimes. This the last time at this table, in her bed, under this roof. She can't go. It's too soon. She needs time to fold all her memories and put them away.

'What's tomorrow?' Ocean stands in the doorway in an oversized T-shirt, dogs at her heel. 'I heard voices. I thought it might be, you know, bad people.'

'I'm going back to the moon.' The spell is broken. The rain was just a shower passing down the valley.

'Tomorrow?'

'It's complicated,' Marina says.

'But if you go back, you'll have to stay there,' Ocean says.

'Yes.' Marina says. 'I will miss you. So so badly. But there's someone I love up there. I heard a story once about the Irish, that when someone left Ireland to come to the States, everyone knew they would never see them again, so they held a wake for them, just as if they were dead. New York wakes, they used to call them. You won't see me again, so let's have a new moon wake. Let's have a proper Calzaghe party. Ocean: lights. Kess, get some music in here, and I'll do the catering.' Marina pushes herself up from the table and rolls to the refrigerator. She loads the contents on to the table: pickles, cheese, bread, yoghurts, ham, everything in a glorious buffet of randomness. Marina uncaps wine, pours generous glasses. The dogs circle, tails wagging, ears pricked.

'What's going on?' Now Weavyr takes the between-place in the doorway.

'I'm having a going-away party!' Marina says. 'Weavyr, Kess, go and get Mom up and put her in her chair and get her in here.'

Marina has filled the kitchen with candles by the time her mother is wheeled over the lintel. Flames glint from wine glasses, there is old dancing music and a table heaped with good things. The women eat and drink and the dogs weave happy through the table legs and glasses are raised to the moon! Donna Luna! until grey light fills up the windows.

The Victoria ferry is a trim, fleet twin-hull, shimmying high-pluming white wakes from a cheeky, Union-Jack-painted stern. The strait is choppy today; a westerly, funnelled between the peninsula and Vancouver Island, drives the wave-train in towards the sound and the boat skips and bounces against the run of the white caps. Most of the passengers are outside, clinging to the rail and trying not to remind each other of their nausea. Marina is the sole passenger in the forward lounge. She sits hands in pockets head sunk to chest. She wants bulkheads between her and what is behind her in the curdling wake.

Everyone came down to the ferry, dogs and mothers included. Kessie brought Mom in the pick-up, Ocean brought Weavyr in the runaround. Kessie was too hung-over and Ocean too young so the cars decided among themselves to do the driving. The kitchen was still strewn with empty glasses, empty bottles, empty fried-food packaging. It was a glorious day which is the worst kind of day for leave-taking. The plan called for Marina to arrive late, buy her ticket last minute with cash and board directly. She was happy to keep the goodbyes brief and sharp. All farewells should be sudden.

Weavyr was stoical but Ocean collapsed into tears and broke Weavyr's resolve. Mom was semi-coherent and mumbling but Marina saw a dark glow in the back of her eyes, shifting and lustrous like mercury, that told her that her mother understood and approved.

Then there was Kessie.

'I'm scared,' Marina said. They held each other in the long embrace, holding each other's forearms.

'What's to be scared about? We've got it all rehearsed. You clear immigration in Canada and the transfer goes through to VTO Earth.'

'That I'll fly away and they'll come for you.'

'They won't,' Kessie said.

'But if they do?'

'Moon-money buys good lawyers.'

'They could tie you up for years. They're vindictive.'

'Then we follow you.' Kessie nodded towards the pier where the ferry was warping in.

'The moon?' Marina says. Her mind is curdled from the night wine and the suddenness of her departure. Kessie laughs.

'Well, Canada first.' She steps back from her sister. 'Go. The boat's here. Go now.'

Now the speakers are delivering customs and immigration instructions and the passengers are filing in from the deck, dumping their coffee cups, hunting for their documentation.

Now.

Marina slips out on to the deck and moves against the current of people to the rear of the boat. Across the dark water rise the mountains of her home. She can't bear it. She knew she could not bear it so she left this until the moment before her exile is made permanent. Marina slips the hiking poles from her wrists and spears them one, two, out into the white water. Wake-riding gulls dive, then see that this is nothing they can use and pull up with resentful cries. The boat rolls as it crosses the bar into the dock. Marina wavers, might pitch against the bulkhead or the rail, then finds her balance. She walks upright and confident towards the companionway. Easy.

Now Marina is in a car being driven through a forest. She has been driven through forest for hours now on a long straight road that has sent her nodding and drooling into sleep half a dozen times. The boreal forest of north-west Ontario is one of the planet's few remaining continuous tree-belts and out in it somewhere is a launch facility.

Dirt crunches under tyres. She hasn't seen a vehicle since the VTO bus twenty minutes back.

The car pulls over and stops.

'What's this?'

An event is about to occur that you might want to witness.

'An event?' Marina has never heard of a car going insane but there is a first for everything under the sun and moon. From Victoria she took another ferry to Vancouver where she spent three days booking with VTO Canada, then three weeks in Toronto in pre-flight training. It can't end here, marooned in the great Canadian wilderness by a mad AI, found years later – if ever – her bones gnawed by wolverines. The door opens.

You will have the best view if you disembark, the car says. Marina steps out but keeps one hand on the handle. She can swing herself in at the first treacherous movement. *Face directly down the road.*

'What—' Marina begins. Then she hears it, a far thunder, a rumble under a roar diffracted by a million trees and as she begins to realise what she is hearing, she sees a tower of flame and smoke climb above the tree-line. A ship has launched: a pillar of cloud and fire, climbing high over her and higher still, up beyond the edge of the world. Now the vapour trail begins to disperse on the westerly wind but she can still see the ship, a cold brilliant diamond, reaching away, reaching up to the moon.

TWENTY-SIX

The machines have worked all night, painstakingly polishing the ten-metre disc of green olivine into the perfect killing floor. Dust-bots swarm the squat Doric pillars, the contours and crevices of the raw-rock roof, the arcs of benches, the staircases; their electrostatic wands glittering with treacherous moondust. Over forty hours, heating elements have brought the chamber up to skin-warmth. Recessed lights switch on, throwing pools of illumination and shadow across the seating tiers. Banks of powerful floods stab brilliance on to the fighting floor. Vents open, the polishing bots scamper for the darkness. An imperceptible hiss becomes a whistle, becomes a shriek: the room repressurising.

Clavius Courtroom Five is an amphitheatre hacked from the dermis of Lady Luna; a rough-hewn cavern disciplined by Classical Greek architectural features. It was designed to represent the contradictions of the law: the raw and the constrained, the deliberate and the deadly. It has never been used. It has been kept dark, vacuum-sealed. Until this day.

The last of the dust-bots vanishes into its service conduit as the stone doors unseal and open.

Ariel Corta walks slowly down the steps. Her fingers brush the stone seats, trace the flutings of the pillars. She walks to the centre of the killing floor, shades her eyes to study the seating banks, the lighting. She climbs the three steps to the bench and runs the palm of her hand along the curve of the judges' desk. She sits in the middle of the three judges' seats, surveys the court. Next she crosses and recrosses the seats, pausing to take in the angle, the ambiance.

A floor section retracts; Dakota Kaur Mackenzie comes up concealed steps from the darkness into the light. She ventures on to the fighting floor.

'Good thing I wore sensible shoes,' she says.

'What's it like down there?' Ariel asks from the topmost ring of seats.

'Too small,' Dakota says. 'Do you do this every trial?'

'I need to walk the stage,' Ariel says. 'I need to know the sight-lines, the acoustics, how far my voice will reach, how many strides wide this is, how many deep that is, how many steps up or down. I need to see what the judges see.'

'This is not a stage,' Dakota says.

'It isn't?' Ariel works her way down through the seats again and sets her bag on the second space from the right of the left floor-level tier. 'Front and centre is a rookie error. You want to be the speck in their peripheral vision. You want them distracted, looking over all the time to see what you've just done that they've missed.'

'And what will that be?' Dakota perches on the edge of the judges' table, swinging her booted feet.

'What do you mean?'

'That smart thing that makes the judges look around. What will that be? I'm no expert on the law, but even a ghazi knows that a legal team needs a strategy. Even a decent argument. All I'm getting is, "I've challenged my brother to trial by combat, he's hired the self-proclaimed greatest blade on the moon but hey! I've got good sight-lines".'

Ariel takes out her compact and checks her lips, her eyes. She snaps the little case shut and slips it into her bag.

'You're right.'

'So?'

'You're not a lawyer. What you are is a woman in the most need of a siririca I have ever seen. Take yourself off. Flick the bean. Enjoy. Make noise. I did. Best preparation for a trial there is. Are all you ghazis this uptight?'

Dakota's mouth is still open when the doors open and Abena peeps through.

'Am I late?'

'We're immorally early,' Ariel says.

Rosario Salgado de Tsiolkovski follows Abena down the stairs, frowning at the court architecture.

'It had to be a man designed this. A man not getting any sex.'

She slides a foot on to the mirror-bright fighting floor.

'What the fuck?'

'It's not a floor problem, it's a footwear problem,' Dakota says.

'My footwear is always non-problematic,' Rosario says.

Ariel indicates for Abena to sit on her left.

Tell me what we're doing here, she says on the private channel to Ariel. *Rosario is so jacked up on enhancers she could fight all of Meridian but she doesn't seem to realise she could get killed here.*

Rosario will not get killed, Ariel answers through Beija Flor. *Nor the ghazi, who's itching for a fight.* Aloud, she says, 'And Luna and Lucasinho?'

'On their way. The judges approved Madrinha Elis as an appropriate adult.'

'I want them in last,' Ariel says. 'And Luna with us.'

'You're bringing the kid here?' Dakota says.

'She has the knife,' Abena says.

Dakota Kaur Mackenzie shakes her head.

'You people,' she says. 'You fucking people.'

'Heads up,' Ariel says. 'Court-faces.'

*

Tamsin Sun and her legal team are waiting outside the court. Amanda Sun has had her turn in the spotlight and she was bested by an Asamoah brat. The professionals will take this. A junior advocate extends a hand to help Lady Sun from the moto. The Court of Clavius has restricted personal security to prevent the violence in the arena spilling into the city but there is no limit on legal aides so Tamsin Sun has rebadged Taiyang's wushis as junior advocates. The court of argument has failed; this is the court of knives. The forecourt is solid with spectators and socialites. The quasi-legals move to clear a path to the lobby. Cries and yells: Tamsin Sun's aides are unyielding and quick with hands and shock-staves.

The final moto arrives and Lady Sun waits for the last member of the Taiyang team to step from the plastic petals.

'Lady Sun . . .' Jiang Ying Yue begins. Lady Sun lifts a hand.

'Not now.'

Lady Sun pauses to admire Court Five. The lowering bare-rock roof, seeming on the point of collapse; the short, ugly columns and seating tiers; the dazzling circle of the fighting floor: there is nowhere to hide here. This is intimidation architecture. It succeeds with Jiang Ying Yue, who leans in to Lady Sun.

'I understood we would not enter actual combat,' she whispers. 'Why am I here?'

'We cannot be seen without a zashitnik,' Lady Sun hisses. 'This family has endured humiliation enough. We will not look like we have already surrendered.'

She takes a seat in the second tier beside Amanda Sun. Tamsin Sun indicates to Jiang Ying Yue that she should join her on the courtside benches. Legals to the fore. Lady Sun nods across the arena to Ariel Corta. A sharp move, arriving first: she has her pick of the pitches. There must be a compelling reason for placing herself on the margin of the court. The Asamoah girl is with her – Lady Sun will not greet her. A ghazi of the University of Farside. Impressive, but she cannot be Ariel Corta's zashitnik. The university does not involve itself in

Nearside politics. That Bairro Alto tramp, then. They are putting their trust in that?

Tamsin Sun turns in her seat to Amanda and Lady Sun.

'Lucas has arrived.'

Alexia sees him baulk at the size and noise of the crowd. His eyes widen with fear, his stomach muscles tighten, his brow breaks pearls of stress perspiration.

She twines her fingers with Wagner's. A moment of reassurance that he is not alone against the mob. He squeezes her hand and they part before the gossip spotters and their cameras catch them. They have a more flamboyant spectacle to occupy them: word ripples in an instant from the front to the back of the crowd. *Mariano Gabriel Demaria. Lucas Corta has contracted Mariano Gabriel Demaria.*

The legend of the greatest blade parts the crowd. Lucas follows, elegant but sober in the grey micro-brocade suit he wore to the eclipse party; then Alexia and Wagner. No lawyers, human or AI. Robson is at the Eyrie, with Haider and Haider's care givers, whom Lucas has brought from Theophilus.

Robson and Alexia's arguments had raged through the Eyrie's terraces and mezzanines.

'You're not coming.'

'He's my primo!' Robson yelled back.

'Lucas doesn't want you there.'

'I want to be there.'

In the end she talked Haider, Max and Arjun into pleading for her and to be extra sure, had the Eyrie's security team hack Joker, Robson's familiar. His money wouldn't work, his network was closed down and if he tried to free-run his way up the walls of the Eyrie and along the sunline Nelson Medeiros would have him cuffed and kicking within thirty seconds.

It was a weak case to argue. Robson had seen and done worse than anything he would see on the floor of Court Five. Alexia would gladly have changed places. But the Eagle of the Moon must have his Iron Hand two steps behind him. And his shadow.

Wagner takes a seat at the top of steps. Without looking, Lucas tips his cane: *With me.* Alexia links fingers again with Wagner. She saw. Fuck it. Ariel Corta saw her.

Lucas indicates that Alexia should take the row behind him. He nods to his one-time wife, to his sister. A nod. The Suns occupy an entire section of the court, Ariel and her entourage a couple of tiers but none are as small and compact as Eagle Team. Lucas turns to Alexia.

'Show me.'

Alexia lifts the small valise. She has carried it from the Eyrie to the court. It is anonymous, innocuous, impact-proof carbon fibre and titanium, the kind routinely carried in legal cases even in this age of AI documentation. It has been designed to pass unregarded. It carries the meteoric-iron battle blade of the Cortas.

'Keep it close.'

Alexia sets the case on the bench beside her.

Every head goes up. Every back straightens. The news on the court network is that Lucasinho Corta has arrived.

First Luna, the two halves of her face set fierce, the fighting knife slung across her shoulder. Next Lucasinho, the object, the prize. Groomed, hair quiffed to an insouciance only possible in lunar gravity, shaved and shod, Moonrun badge. Yet Abena sees him hesitate and look down before he commits to the steep steps. Behind him, Madrinha Elis also notices the uncertainty. Hands folded demurely in the sleeves of her robe slip free to support, to catch. Abena's heart is in her mouth. Lucasinho takes a breath and descends the staircase.

Luna takes her seat at Abena's side. Lucasinho continues to the furthest right section where court zashitniks emerge from a slot in the floor to form an escort around him. Abena catches his eye; makes him smile.

The throb of noise in the lobby becomes a roar as the court is opened to the public. Eager spectators cling to each other as they totter down the treacherous steps, jostle and shove in the narrow aisles as they fight for seats. By the time the doors are closed the crowd is squatting on the steps, standing five deep at the back. Court Five beats like a drum: then there is silence. The judges have entered.

Preceded by their zashitniks, Judge Rieko Ngai, Judge Valentina Arce and Judge Kweko Kumah take their seats at the bench. Judge Rieko surveys the packed court.

'Court of Clavius in final settlement of Sun versus Corta versus Corta,' she says. 'All parties are present or represented?'

Mumbles from the three respondents and Madrinha Elis.

'Case to be tried under the mutually agreed judgement of Nagai, Arce and Kumah?' Judge Arce asks. Ayes, nods of the head. The spectators take breath. The informality shocks them: ninety per cent of them have never been inside a court, even to agree a marriage-nikah.

'And it is also agreed this is to be settled by combat,' Judge Kumah says.

The spectators exhale. A rumble of assent.

'The bench is compelled to note that this is not the first time that the Cortas have settled a case by violence, and deplores it,' Judge Rieko says. 'It is atavistic and demeaning and the Court of Clavius is disappointed that a family with as noble a history as the Suns have been drawn into this monstrosity. However, the legalities have been observed, we as judges are tied by our contract, so it will be settled the old-fashioned way.'

A tense purr runs through the spectators. It's on. No retreat, no escape. Knives out. Blood on the stones.

'I believe the Sun/Corta case will resolve first?' Judge Arce says. 'Who represents Lucas Corta?'

Mariano Gabriel Demario rises from the bench. The purr becomes a murmur. All Nearside knows the legend of the School of Seven Bells. The incongruous gripshoes beneath his neatly turned-up pant cuffs tell that he is dressed for fight.

'Tamsin Sun?'

'Amanda Sun has indicated . . .' Tamsin Sun begins. Lady Sun's claw hand descends on her shoulder, grips like famine.

'Jiang Ying Yue will represent Amanda Sun,' she says.

Tamsin Sun snaps around in her seat. Her face is hollow with incomprehension. *We agreed to withdraw*, she says on the private channel. The public, sensing a departure from the script, mutters and chatters.

'It was agreed that we would . . .' Jiang Ying Yue begins.

Lady Sun raises a hand and a sheathed knife is passed down the tiers of legal assistants, hand to hand to hand to Jiang Ying Yue's hand.

'Lady Sun . . .'

'You have a question?'

'Lady Sun, with respect, I am no match for Demario.'

'You failed my family at Hadley,' Lady Sun hisses. 'You humiliated us before the Mackenzies. You must correct that fault. You will show the world that there is honour and courage still in the Palace of Eternal Light.'

'Madam Sun, what are your intentions?' Judge Arce asks from the bench.

'We are ready,' Tamsin Sun says.

Fear hardens to resolution on Jiang Ying Yue's face. She returns the knife to Lady Sun, for zashitniks by long tradition do not carry their own weapons down to the pens, and steps down into the arena. The courtroom floor opens and she descends into the dark. Court Five is thick with silence.

'Seconds,' Judge Kumah says. Lady Sun hands the blade to Amanda.

'Do your duty.'

'Die in screaming agony, you withered crone.' Amanda Sun snatches the blade and crosses the floor boldly to the judge's bench. Knives must be examined by the judges for any non-negotiated toxins.

Across the arena Lucas Corta nods to his Iron Hand. Alexia lifts the valise. As she turns on to the steps she catches Wagner's eye. He cannot look.

Alexia's heart pounds as she crosses the fighting floor. Gods but it's treacherous. This whole Colosseum is treacherous. Every one and every thing is on trial in the Court of Clavius. Some petty infraction, some oversight or offence to an injured party and the knives would sing out of their sheaths and serve justice on her.

She sets the valise on the judges' desk. The locks click loud. A strange sound, part gasp, part moan, goes up from the arena as she lifts the knife and presents it to the judges. Light gleams along the edge of the blade as they pass it from hand to hand, pretending to examine it. Clever machinery embedded in the desk does the sniffing and tasting and analysing.

'Meteoric iron,' Judge Kumah says.

'Where is its twin?' Judge Arce asks.

'This is an unclean thing,' Judge Rieko says. She almost tosses the knife to Alexia in her haste to get it away from her skin. 'It reeks of blood.'

Maninho guides Alexia to her second's position. She glances across to Amanda Sun. She could vomit. She could weep with fear. She has never hated anything more than standing here in a Coco Chanel suit with a knife in her hands. Yet she stands. The floor opens, the fighters emerge. The crowd rises in thunder.

Wagner's head is bowed, face in hands.

Jiang Ying Yue takes the knife from Amanda Sun, tries it for heft and balance. She is fit, leanly muscled, athletic in capri leggings, crop top and squeaky, fresh-printed gripsoles. Alexia can see at once that she knows nothing of the way of the knife.

Mariano Gabriel Demaria has stripped down to black shorts and gripsoles. His body is the way of the knife incarnate, sinews and knots, wires and scars. He carries himself with the easy grace of the fanatically competent.

He turns dark eyes to Alexia, she offers the valise. He lifts the Corta blade. A voice cries out. A child's voice.

Luna Corta marches on to the fighting floor.

'You don't touch my knife!'

'I'm sorry?'

Luna is small and exposed and utterly defiant and there is not a note of condescension in Mariano Demaria's voice.

'That knife can only be used by a Corta.'

Mariano looks to Lucas. A nod. The zashitnik returns the blade to Alexia. The crowd exhales slowly. A sheathed blade slides across the fighting ring; Mariano scoops it up, unsheathes it. He holds it, inspects it in the hot hard light beating down on to the arena. He dips his head in a small bow. From the far side of the arena, the hidden side, Dakota Kaur Mackenzie returns the courtesy.

'With your permission?'

'I have no objection,' Tamsin Sun says.

The judges' appraisal is perfunctory.

'We have endured enough interruptions and theatrics,' Judge Rieko says. 'If this type of justice is necessary, it is best done swiftly. Proceed.'

Alexia's heart skips. It's blades now and nothing but blades will decide this. There will be blood on the stone. And she realises that she is a coward. When the Gularte's left Caio for dead in a drainage channel in Barra, when they broke his future, she swore justice. She went to Seu Osvaldo; had him visit terrible deaths on the brothers. She was satisfied, she did right, and she was no different from the bloody justice she condemns here.

'Seconds out,' Judge Arce says

Alexia returns to her seat. No: there is a difference. All the difference. She did not have the courage to deliver that justice with her own hands.

'Approach,' Judge Kumah says.

Mariano Gabriel Demaria and Jiang Ying Yue move to the centre of the fighting floor. They raise blades before their eyes in salute.

'Fight,' Judge Rieko says.

Blades blur, bodies dance at sex-close distances. Blood sprays, Ying Yue's blade slides across the shimmering stone. She stands, shivering with shock, breath fluttering, blood streaming from her bicep across her wrist to drop from her spasming fingers.

The crowd is silent. This is not what they expected. They are not entertained.

Beija Flor pings. Dakota Kaur Mackenzie, private channel.

He will leave the de Tsiolkovksi woman in steaming chunks on the floor.

Yes, Ariel answers.

Fire her. Hire me.

No.

Dakota Kaur Mackenzie leans forward.

'Do you have any idea what you're doing?'

Ariel looks over at Lucasinho, ash-faced, terrified among the court zashitniks. Wagner's face is buried in his hands. Alexia is pale with dread. Madrinha Elis has pulled her hood low to conceal her features.

'Always.'

Ying Yue staggers across the fighting floor towards her knife.

'Leave it,' Mariano says. Ying Yue picks up the knife in her left hand, launches herself across the killing floor at Mariano Gabriel Demaria. He sidesteps easily. With a despairing cry, Ying Yue swings at him. He sways away from the knife like thought. Quicker than thought. Like instinct.

'Stop this,' he says.

Slipping in the pooling, thickening blood, Ying Yue stumbles towards Mariano Gabriel Demario, slashing wildly.

'Enough.'

Mariano drops his knife, steps inside Ying Yue's guard and snaps her wrist. The crack rings from the stern pillars, the lowering, chaotic ceiling.

'Do you have satisfaction?' he says to Tamsin Sun. He is not sweating. There is no trace of any distress, much less exertion in his body. 'Are you satisfied?' Tamsin Sun glances at Lady Sun. The old woman shakes her head.

'I am satisfied!' Amanda Sun's shout carries from the killing floor to the stone gates of Court Five. 'I am the complainant, not my legal advisers, not my grandmother. And I have satisfaction.'

'Then by the contract entered into by the combatant parties, I dismiss Amanda Sun's claim to custody of Lucas Corta Junior,' Judge Rieko says. A stuttering moan of consternation goes up from the spectators, echoed and redoubled moments later by the crowds outside; pulsing through Meridian's quadras, taken up in turn in hotshops and bars and offices and homes, in trains and rovers and on private suit-helmet feeds from Rozhdestvenskiy to Queen of the South, St Olga to João de Deus.

The Suns have lost.

Medics converge on Jiang Ying Yue, standing bloody and shaking, arms crippled, on the fighting floor. Patches take away the pain, staples staunch the blood loss, tubes and lines counteract the shock. Taiyang medics escort the bot-gurney into the undercroft of the Court of Clavius.

'Can we agree a thirty-minute recess to clear up this mess?' Judge Rieko says with clear distaste. Ariel is on her feet.

'If parties concur, I would like to move to final resolution immediately.'

Now comes the gasp. Abena opens a private channel: Tumi to Beija-flor.

What are you doing?

Follow me, Ariel says. *No questions, no hesitations. Can you do this?*

I can do this.

'Senhor Corta?'

Lucas gets to his feet. The babbling gossip ceases.

'If Mariano is fit to fight?'

'I am,' the zashitnik declares.

The judges are still for a moment, conferring on their private channels.

'If both parties agree, we would not disagree,' Judge Kumah says. 'Senhor Corta, I take it you will keep the same representative?'

'I will.'

Judge Arce turns to Ariel's team.

'Who represents you?'

A long pause, then Rosario stands.

'I am Rosario Salgado O'Hanlon de Tsiolkovski, contracted zashitnik of this party.'

'Step forward please.'

'Not so fast.'

Ariel steps to the edge of the ring.

'Who represents is one thing. Who fights is another. Luna.'

The girl has been cued. She skips down the steps to Ariel's side.

'If you please.'

Luna unwraps the ritual blade. Ariel snatches it up, there is an audible hiss as the edge cuts the air.

'By the legends of my family, this knife may only be borne by a Corta who is bold, great-hearted, without avarice or cowardice, who will fight for the family and defend it bravely. I am that Corta, and I will fight you, Mariano Gabriel Demaria.'

Court Five explodes.

*

Alexia suspects her mouth is open. She feels her eyes are wide and her heart is hammering and there is a high-pitched noise in her ears. Like everyone else in Court Five.

You clever, clever woman. If Lucas refuses the fight, he surrenders the case. If he fights, he sets the moon's greatest blade against a disabled woman who barely knows which side cuts. His own sister. With the whole of the moon looking on.

'Senhor Corta?'

'Mão de Ferro,' Lucas says. He holds out his hand. 'The blade.'

Alexia sets the knife reverently in Lucas's palm. No questions, no hesitation, no explanations. He orders, she obeys. Leaning on his cane, Lucas gets to his feet.

'Bold, great-hearted, without avarice or cowardice,' Lucas says. 'A Corta who will fight for the family and defend it bravely. Stand down Senhor Demaria. It is time for me to take the blade.'

He levels the blade at the judges.

'Are we agreed?'

'The bench has no objection,' Judge Rieko says.

'Sister?'

Ariel is smiling. Has she planned this? Did she know the only way out of the trap was for Lucas to take up the blade? A long exhale: Alexia realises she has been unconsciously holding her breath. Her and all of Court Five. This has stepped from insanity into mythology.

'I will fight you, Lucas,' Ariel says.

'Best get to it then,' Lucas says. 'Second.'

And Alexia is again on the killing floor with Lucas handing her his jacket, his suspenders, his tie and his shirt. He undresses neatly, folds his clothes before passing them to Alexia. Across the ring, Ariel has seconded the ghazi. She takes off her Adele List hat, kicks off her Ferragamo shoes, shucks her Charles James jacket, lets the skirt fall. Beneath the fashion suit is the timeless uniform of the fighter: short trunks, a crop top. A hiss passes over the court: the spinal link; the smooth plastic, the puckered livid scar tissue. Lucas tests the fighting surface, then slips off his own Oxfords. He is an unwieldy wedge of old muscle softening into mass. Bulk in the wrong places: massive thighs and calf muscles to kick against terrestrial gravity; muscles banded around his spine to hold him upright. This is what Earth does to a moon-born body and what the moon does with that when that body returns to its proper environment. The build of a superhero, walking with a cane to protect his eroded knee joints.

'Please.' Lucas passes the cane to Alexia. He studies the knife. 'Have you any idea what to do with this?' he asks his sister.

'You try to kill me with me it,' Ariel says.

The judges hurry through the formalities. Lucas and Ariel raise their blades in salute, step back, circle each other.

'We are ridiculous,' Lucas says. 'Human wreckage playing with knives.'

'Someone has to make the first move,' Ariel says.

'Yes,' Lucas says. 'They do.' He drops to a crouch and with all his strength drives the Corta blade into the fighting floor. Polished olivine cracks and chips; meteoric steel shatters halfway to the hilt. A flying shard lays Lucas's cheek open. Ariel dips her head to him in salute; reverses her grip on her blade and stabs it into adamant stone. The tip snaps, flies; the stone stars. And Court Five is on its feet.

'Let's talk,' Ariel shouts through the babel of voices; ecstatic, abusive, enraged, thrilled, non-comprehending.

'No,' Lucas shouts back. 'Let's deal.'

The bots and drones have been less than scrupulous cleaning the zashitnik stables underneath the court. The rooms are small and dusty, the air stale. Lucas Corta perches on the edge of a stone dressing-shelf. Ariel has the sole chair. Alexia has thrown Lucas his shirt and he buttons it with the care and respect of a man who understands clothes. He is still barefoot. The court above is still in uproar, the noise a sonic ceiling to the tiny room.

'A telenovela could not have played it more melodramatically,' Lucas Corta says.

'Thank you.'

'You took the mother of risks.'

'There was never any risk. Family first...'

'Family always. What's your deal?'

Ariel is still dressed in her fighting garb. As one who spent lunes remapping his body in the gymnasium of the *Saints Peter and Paul*, Lucas appreciates the definition of her arms and upper body. The last time he saw her she was in a wheelchair. Before that, in the dark time, she had only that Jo Moonbeam to help her – what was her name? He can't remember. She had a closet up in Bairro Alto, strung with lines so she could swing herself from room to room.

That's discipline.

That is the politics of the body.

'You're staring.'

'I'm sorry.' Lucas had not been aware that his eyes had strayed to her spinal link and remained there. 'I can't get used to it.'

'Would you have preferred the old prosthetics?'

Lucas sees again the hideous, clicking things; servos and actuators picking and tapping. He sees again his sister in the bed in the João de Deus med centre, pushing herself upright in her trauma bed to berate him for attempting to negotiate his son's nikah.

'Is this...'

'Permanent? Unless I can find six spare lunes for the university to regenerate the nerve tissue.'

'I would have aimed for it,' Lucas says. 'If it had come to blades.'

'It's the logical target.'

'Your deal?'

'Let's not fool ourselves here. Lucasinho can walk and smile and charm every heart in Meridian but he is a long way from legal independence,' Ariel says. 'I have something you want. You have something you don't want.'

'The Eyrie?'

'The Eyrie.'

'You don't want the Eyrie.'

'No. I don't. I know what you've been forced to do by the LMA to get to Bryce Mackenzie. You've kicked it down the road but it will always be there. I can't say that I won't make a worse job of it than you. But I'll be able to try. You never could, not with Lucasinho. You would always have been afraid for him. I have no children, no lovers, no ties. I'm made of iron.'

'What will you do?'

'Act for the people of the moon. We're not an industrial outpost, we're not an Earth colony.'

'Ariel Corta, independence fighter.'

'If I had my vaper, I'd blow smoke rings at you, brother. Here's the deal. You take Lucasinho and whoever else you want home to Boa Vista. You build whatever kind of empire you want out there in the Mare Fecunditatis. I take the title, honours and responsibilities of the Eagle of the Moon. Straight swap.'

'Is this legal?'

'There's no law against it,' Ariel says. 'This is the moon.'

'Everything is negotiable,' Lucas says. 'One rider.'

'Try me.'

'Take Alexia.'

'Your Mão de Ferro?'

'You'll need help. She knows the business. Deal?'

'Deal.'

In the cramped, dusty pen under the killing floor of Court Five, Lucas Corta and Ariel Corta shake hands. They embrace briefly. Ariel moistens a wipe under the faucet and dabs clean the cut on Lucas's cheek where the blade fragment grazed him. Blood has run down his neck, his chest, trickling to the waistband of his pants.

'There ought to be a first aid kit down here,' Ariel grumbles.

'The kind of wounds you get here are not amenable to first aid,'

Lucas says. They look at each other. Faces crease. Choked mirth bubbles into giggles, into aching, breathless laughter. Malandragem. The flyest of fly moves. The Cortas are back. Lucas wipes his eyes.

'Shall we keep them waiting a little longer?'

'Oh, I think so,' says the Eagle of the Moon.

TWENTY-SEVEN

These are the images from Corta versus Corta that will endure as long as the moon hangs in the sky.

Broken knives on cracked polished stone.

Judges on their feet, trying to shout over a courtroom in uproar.

A hovering sphere, half black, half silver, unfolding wings, drinking colour out of the air, becoming green Luna moth.

A nine-year-old girl wiping skull-paint from her face.

A father hugging his son to him, oblivious to everything else.

'I recall saying that the next time you tried to pull a trick like that in my court, I would order the zashitniks to gut you.' The counsel chamber is one of the hive of ancillary rooms and corridors beneath Court Five and as small, dusty and cramped as the fighters' stable. Judge Rieko Nagai perches on the edge of the basin as Ariel Corta strips off her sweat-stained fighting garb and drops it into the de-printer. Ariel slips into the shower for thirty seconds of pre-programmed hot water.

'I'd've taken them,' Ariel shouts through the gush.

'You broke your knife,' Rieko says.

'The ghazi would have taken them.'

'She probably would.'

The drier buffets Ariel; she throws back her head, letting her dark hair fall out, runs her fingers through it, flounces it, fluffs it up to the hot air. Then into the robe extruding from the printer.

'I also remember last time I gave you one of these.'

Judge Rieko takes a small bottle of ten-botanical gin from her purse.

'Thank you, but I don't any more,' Ariel says. 'You brought that to court, didn't you?'

'I knew you would pull some piece of gratuitous malandragem.'

'And if I hadn't?'

'I'd've toasted your memory.' Judge Rieko's tone darkens. 'The terrestrials are in panic. They've filed over five hundred writs already. Court of Clavius AIs are winnowing them out but you might want to keep that ghazi on a retainer.'

'They can't stop me. And they can't count on the Vorontsovs' space-artillery.'

'They have fifteen thousand combat bots deployable in seconds.'

'Do they?' Ariel says with a sly smile.

One last thing, Lucas said as they prepared to go up on to the fighting floor and shake the moon in its orbit. *You'll need this.*

Beija Flor logged a file transfer.

What is this?

The word for the terrestrials' bots. I did a deal with Amanda Sun.

What does it do?

Whatever you want fifteen thousand combat bots to do.

Ariel said, as the roof slid open, throwing a lengthening box of light into the zashitnik pen, *Your own private Ironfall.*

'You have those courtroom eyes again,' Judge Rieko says. 'You scare me when you look like that.'

'We need to grow up,' Ariel says. 'All of us. Rule of law, not rule of the blade.' The printer is at work again.

'That's your first decree?'

'My second.' Ariel holds up the print-wet Pierre Balmain dress. 'The fifties are back.'

*

The elevator seizes the moto and lifts it high above Gargarin Prospekt. Ariel takes her vaper from her purse and snaps it out to its full decadent length.

'Do you mind?'

'Yes,' Lucas Corta says.

Ariel vapes up and cracks open the roof.

'There.'

She leans back and exhales a ribbon of pale fumes.

'That doesn't help.'

The crowds outside the court show no signs of dispersing; numbers have doubled and redoubled in size and noise. Gargarin Prospekt is solid with bodies, wall to wall. Half of Meridian waits with questions, demands, concerns, fears, opinions for the new order that emerges from Court Five.

The Cortas and their retainers depart from the service entrance in a flotilla of chartered motos, and immediately take to the heights. Each vehicle follows a different route. Not to the Eyrie. The Eyrie is the first place the terrestrials will send their bots. Not even to the station: the gupshup channels' bots are already swarming there. The transports will rendezvous at the VTO moonship dock, where Nik Vorontsov has *Orel* fuelled, crewed and ready to lift for Boa Vista.

The moto bearing the former and current Eagles of the Moon runs the high streets, ascending and descending, crossing and recrossing as soon as it senses gossip-drones closing in. Bossa nova and vaper fumes fill the bauble of titanium and carbon fibre. A sudden stop and turn and the moto drives on to the cargo deck of a cable car and swings out into two kilometres of sheer airspace.

LMA bots closing in, Beija Flor and Toquinho announce.

'It's time to give you this,' Lucas Corta says as the moto reels through the glittering void.

Beija Flor lights up with a massive data transfer. Information, codes, privileges and accesses, every thing the Eagle of the Moon requires to administer, coming so fast Beija Flor sags under the torrent.

'You've made me God,' Ariel says. Vapour leaks from the corners of her mouth as she takes in the enormity of the powers she has been granted. 'All that time I was in the White Hare, advising Jonathon Kayode, and he could do all this . . .'

'The thing about God is that there can only be one,' Lucas says. 'It's a failing of monotheism. Take this.'

A final transfer.

'What does it do?'

'Shuts anyone but you out of the executive powers.'

Ariel grimaces.

'What's keeping you?' Lucas asks. He closes his eyes, breathes deep. Aguas do Marco.

'It feels very final.'

'It's supposed to. Do it.'

Toquinho chimes a guitar chord and says, *Executive authorisations erasing*. Lucas calls up a visualisation and watches his powers dissolve in slow detonating puffballs of dying code. Elis Regina sings a plangent, melancholy soundtrack. Saudade.

'How do you feel?' Ariel asks.

'Do you mean, am I like some kind of superhero who loses his powers? No. Not that. Not that at all.' He does not tell his sister his feelings: he is filled with light and lightness like a New Year balloon. He could weep tears of release rich as pearls. He understands what it is to be blessed.

The cradle docks, the moto turns towards the Sixty-Third West upramp.

'I regret that Jonathon Kayode died,' Lucas says. 'Adrian Mackenzie fought like the very devil. I think my abiding sin may be underestimating my enemies.'

The moto takes the freight elevator to the moonship dock. *Orel* stands gleaming under spotlights, a fantastic beast of fuel tanks, thruster nodes, struts and spars and comms dishes, solar and radiator panels nearly folded. An environment pod stands open, ramp lowered. Everyone is there: the ghazi, Ariel's Bairro Alto zashitnik, Abena Maanu Asamoah. Madrinha Elis. The wolf. Luna. The Iron Hand. Lucasinho.

'Get in get in!' Nik Vorontsov, still rebelling against taste and fashion in his aggressively blue-collar shorts and T-shirt and dock boots comes down the ramp to escort Ariel and Lucas. 'Standing around like a wedding photograph. We have a launch window!'

The inlock gate stirs. *Orel*'s dock is a massive airlock, the outlock overhead, opening to the surface; the inlock opening to the city. And the inlock is grinding open.

'Bots!' Nik Vorontsov yells. Dozens of them, swarming behind the slowly opening gate, blades unfolding and closing with a terrifying snicker-click.

'I've got the word for these,' Ariel says and orders Beija Flor to run Lucas's patch.

Bots force legs and blades through the widening gap.

'Lucas...' Ariel says.

'I hacked fifteen thousand Type 33a combat bots...' Lucas begins.

'Those aren't 33as,' Dakota Kaur Mackenzie says. 'Those are old Type Three basics from the initial assault at Twé.'

'How many old type are left?' Ariel asks.

'This discussion for later,' Nik Vrontsov shouts. 'Everybody onboard now!' As he closes the pod door, multiple-barrel guns unfold from the ship's superstructure.

'What the hell?' Lucas says.

'We stole it from Mackenzie Helium,' Nik Vorontsov shouts. The dock is a clicking-clatter of racing stiletto-tip bot feet. 'If they could shoot one of our ships to hell, we can shoot them back. Sorry, kid, if that brings back bad memories.'

'I don't have any memories of Twé,' Lucasinho says.

'I do,' Luna says.

Five loud reports in quick succession.

'One shot one bot,' Nik Vorontsov says. 'There's a lot of delicate equipment in here. We can only shoot if we have a clear firing solution. Buckle in.'

'How many are there?' Ariel asks, fastening the harness of her acceleration chair.

'More than five,' Nik Vorontsov says. A rattle of shots, so fast they blur into one. Silence.

Launch sequence initiated, says *Orel*'s AI. *Outlock opening.*

'They're up there!' a human voice interrupts on the common channel. 'The surface is crawling with them.'

'Get us some clear space!' Nik Vorontsov bellows, strapped in between Luna and Lucasinho.

'We have a new launch solution,' says the VTO captain. 'Stand by.'

The countdown appears on everyone's lens. Nik Vorontsov takes Luna and Lucasinho's hands.

'It's good to yell,' he says and never finishes the sentence as *Orel* blasts off. The passenger pod roars with full-throated voices. Audible over the cacophony of shots and the thunder of rockets is the crack, crack, crack of the miniguns. The ship shakes, the seats shake, the air shakes, every cell in the passengers' bodies shakes.

Lucas sees the fear and the pain on the faces of the people he loves. You fear it will end too soon and you will crash out of the sky, then you fear that it will end in an instant in a huge explosion. Last, you fear that it will not end at all.

Counting down to main engine shut off, Orel says. *Standby for freefall in three, two, One.*

It ends. Lucas feels his stomach lurch, his weight vanishes. Seeing the distress on Abena Asamoah's face, Nik Vorontsov snaps free from his harness and drifts over to her with a vomit bag. In the silence after the retching and the mumbled apology, everyone clearly hears the sound of clicking coming from the bulkhead. Tip-tap, tip-tapping towards the ramp.

'Fuck,' Nik Vorontsov says. 'They're on the hull.'

'How?' Ariel asks.

'They must have jumped while we were launching. They're under the guns' firing arc so we can't hit them,' Nik Vorontsov says.

'Can they open the door?' Lucasinho asks.

'They could wreck enough systems that we can't land safely.'

'You mean crash,' Luna Corta says.

'I mean crash.'

'How do we get rid of them?' Alexia Corta asks.

'Someone will have to go out there and take them out,' Dakota Kaur Mackenzie says.

'There are suits?' Alexia asks.

'There are two SE suits,' Dakota Mackenzie says. 'Isn't it good someone checks these things?' She unclips her harness, pushes herself up out of her seat towards the ceiling lock to the control centre. She slaps Rosario de Tsiolkovski softly on the back of the head as she flies past. 'Come on, fighter. Two suits. Let's see if you've still got the ghazi spirit in you.'

Sasuit. Surface Activity suit. A tight-fitting sealed pressure-skin with helmet and recycling life-support pack, designed to allow freedom of movement and environmental protection for up to forty-eight hours.

SE suit. Short Excursion suit. A stretch-fabric unitard, sufficiently tight to supplement the human skin's natural pressure resistance and prevent liquid loss. White to reflect heat. Combined helmet-respirator glued to the suit, only as airtight as the suit-wearer is careful with the glue strips. Designed for no more than fifteen minutes activity in vacuum.

On average, moonship ballistic flights last fifteen minutes. If a problem can't be solved in the lifespan of a SE suit, it won't be.

The service lock is so small Rosario and Dakota must curl around each other like twins in a womb.

'Tether tether tether,' Captain Xenia says as she seals the EVA lock.

'Fifteen minutes,' Dakota Mackenzie says on the suit channel. Rosario clips her weapon to her, herself to the carabiner inside the lock. An axe and three flares, to battle combat bots that can unfold into a hundred knives.

The lock opens. Rosario pulls herself on to the hull. Immediately she is disoriented. Head down, the sun-belt a band of black so profound the silver moon could have been cut in two. She cries out, grips hard: fear of falling. No, the moon is not down, nor is it above her, there is no up or down, there is only motion. Yes, she is falling, everything is falling. She checks the carabiner again: it would be all too easy for an over-aggressive move to launch her away from the moonship.

Mare Tranquilitatis races beneath her. Her stomach lurches.

Fourteen minutes.

The SE suit HUD is rudimentary but carries enough detail to locate the enemy: two bots on the opposite side of the hull, among the fuel tanks. *Orel* is a free-fall climbing frame; struts and construction beams make easy handholds to climb. Not climbing; climbing implies gravity against which to climb; this is another form of movement. Clambering. Rosario clambers across the surface of the moonship. The tether reels out behind her.

'You need to move,' Captain Xenia interrupts. 'We're down a fuel pump already.'

No need for the HUD now. The enemy is in sight, two bots sawing at a fuel line. Moonships and bicycles wear their engineering on the outside. Rosario pulls a flare, Dakota readies the axe.

'How do we do this?' Rosario asks. The question answers itself as the bots register threat. Synthetic muscles flex, artificial sinews tighten, the carapace splits into sections and realigns for action. A bot strikes, Rosario bats away the killing thrust, jerks the arm and snaps the joints. Spraying lubricant hazes her visor but she has no time to clear it. She twists the cap of the flare; the chemicals mix and ignite. She jabs it into the sensor array. The bot reels, throws arms between its many many eyes and the flare. The flare gutters, oxidiser spent, and flickers out. The bot uncoils in a leap. A needle leg grazes Rosario's belly and lays open the thin skin of her SE suit. A free hand reaches for a grip to swing around for the killing lunge. And the axe, flying true with all Dakota Kaur Mackenzie's strength behind it, takes the bot full in the core and sends it spinning into orbit.

'Shit,' Rosario says, feeling the precision slash across her suit-skin. 'Shit, I'm bleeding. Shit shit shit shit shit.'

'Never mind that,' Dakota says. 'That was the axe. We have one bot, and two flares.'

The second bot, as if reaching this same conclusion, extricates itself from the moonship's engineering. It is like a vile hatching, long limbs extricating, pulling free, reaching for purchase. Rosario sets her jaw against the pain. Fuck, this hurts. Hurt hurts hurts hurts. How long can the human body survive in vacuum? Her helmet seal is good but with the pressure skin ruptured her body is effectively naked. She wears a belt of free-floating blood droplets, smearing against the white of her suit as she moves.

She has seconds before the second bot is ready to strike.

Rosario throws a flare to Dakota.

'When I say, stab it in the fucking face.'

'What are you . . .'

War in freefall is the territory of unanswered questions. Rosario throws herself headlong at the bot. She ignites the flare, twists past the unfurling blades as the bot locates her through the glare and heat and stops herself hard, painfully against a heat-exchange panel.

'Now!'

Dakota Kaur Mackenzie attacks with fire and fury. She is fast, almost as fast as the bot, dodging, parrying with the flare, always coming back with the flare stabbing at the machine's round, glittering eyes.

In the glare and the blindness, Rosario unhooks her tether and clips it through one of the bot's knee joints. The bot kicks out, Rosario tumbles away, head over heels, one hand in a death-grip on a landing gear strut. *Orel* arcs high over the diggings and revetments of Twé, almost at the apex of its ballistic flight.

And that is how Rosario Salgado O'Hanlon de Tsiolkovski wins.

'Dakota, catch me!'

She launches herself towards the ghazi. Flying free. Flying untethered. If she misjudges, if Dakota mistimes her move, if the bot recovers too quickly from its disorientation, she flies into her own partial orbit. She won't have to worry about the life-support limits of her ruined SE suit. Impacting East Tranquillity at two point seven-five kilometres per second will decide everything. She'll be a crater. They might even name it after her.

And Dakota Kaur Mackenzie has her forearm tucked through Rosario's belt. She's worked it out. She hits the tether reel and flings the guttering flare at the bot as the winch snatches them away from a dismembering slash.

'Xenia,' Rosario shouts. 'Spin the ship!'

'We're not at turnaround,' Captain Xenia begins. Dakota shouts over her.

'Do what she says! Three-sixty her!'

A pause. The bot scrambles towards them, blades held aloft like some many-armed deity of knives. Rosario hauls herself towards the lock, the latch, the carabiner at the other end of the tether.

'Hold tight,' Captain Xenia says. And the world wheels. Acceleration tears Rosario's fingers from their grip. Dakota has her. Dakota has her. Moon stars sun spin around her. Don't look. Don't look, you'll throw up in your helmet. She has to look. One glance over her shoulder is enough: the bot has lost its grip and is snapped by centripetal acceleration to the full extent of the tether. In a moment it will haul itself in. *Orel* tumbles across the lunar sky, a carnival of sputtering blue attitude jets. Rosario climbs up Dakota's body to the edge of the airlock. She unsnaps the carabiner. It whips from her fingers. The bot flies free, following its own, helpless ballistic trajectory. They'll name no craters after you, thing.

It's all physics. It's all momentum tether engineering.

'Fuck off you old-school Type 3 bot,' Rosario whispers. On comms she says, 'Hostiles eliminated, Captain.'

'Good work. Thank you,' Captain Xenia says. 'Now get in here.'

'Good one, ghazi,' Dakota Mackenzie says as the two women squeeze themselves into the lock. At that moment, in that place, those are the greatest words Rosario has ever heard. She knows the horror stories about vomiting inside a helmet in free fall. Are there any such legends about tears?

Gravity kicks, kicks again, attitude jets turning *Orel* into descent mode. Foetus-curled, bawling from strain and relief, smeared with a starburst of her own blood, Rosario Salgado O'Hanlon de Tsiolkovski falls towards the Sea of Fecundity.

Ariel sniffs at the administrative suites. She raises an eyebrow at the stale, windowless offices and looks askance at the refurbished boardroom. When she comes to Lucas's eyeball-sanctum she can hide her disdain no longer.

'Now I remember why I left this shit-hole.'

She whisks on, leaving a vaper trail to disperse slowly in the sluggish air conditioning.

'Stone stone stone stone stone,' Ariel complains as she descends the grand staircase to ground level.

'Exit through the mouth,' Alexia hints. Ariel rolls her eyes. On Oxala's lip, Ariel stops, touches Alexia on the arm.

'What is that?'

It takes Alexia a few peering moments to make out the object of Ariel's interest. The accelerated-growth trees are in full leaf now, and the cupola half-glimpsed through the slow-stirring leaves is like an image from a dream. Old, perilous gods live here.

'Take me there.'

Beija Flor could rez up a map of Boa Vista but Ariel enjoys setting small tasks, tests and traps in Alexia's path. Iron Hand? Maybe to my brother, but Ariel Corta is not so easily swayed. As Alexia finds a path of stone flags winding through the bamboo, Ariel takes a long draw on her vaper. Marina killed an assassin with this vaper's predecessor, stabbed him up through the jaw, drove the point out through the top of his skull. Jo Moonbeam strength. Strength enough to kill for love, strength enough to keep her through the dark time but not enough to stay. Since taking the Eyrie, Ariel's thoughts have more and more gone to Marina. How do you find Earth? How does Earth find you? Does the light in the night sky fill you with longing, like a wolf? Do you look up and think of me?

What is your strength, Alexia who calls herself Mão de Ferro, and what in this world will break it? For something will.

The turning path ends at a pavilion; plinth, pillars, a dome. Water runs around the base of the plinth. Ariel climbs the steps. The air is fresh, made sweet by running water, the sunline is blue and the artificial wind rustles the bamboo. The canes screen the pavilion from the gaze of the orixas; it is an encircled, private place. Ariel walks the circle, stroking her fingers across the columns. Warm stone.

'This is the place,' Ariel declares. 'I'll need a desk, three chairs, one comfortable, the others not so. Beverages on demand. Can you arrange that?'

'I have people on it now. Lucas has requested a private meeting.'

Ariel savours the moment.

'Of course. Let him know where he can find me.'

Ariel hears his stick on the stones before she sees him emerge from the bamboo maze.

Human wreckage, meeting in the circle.

'Our mother's favourite place,' Lucas says. 'In the latter days she would come here to talk with Mãe de Santo Odunlade. Her confessor, Mamãe called her.'

'Is there anything left of the Sisterhood?' Ariel asks.

'The madrinhas. The shrine in João. Legends,' Lucas says. He leans into his cane. 'Is that enough? I don't know. I'm not a person of faith. This will be your office?'

'Until I can move back to Meridian.'

'There's a thing I need to do first. Lucas, I can't let you get away with it.'

Lucas smiles wryly, sags on his stick,

'I thought this would come. I used to have dreams: burning, gasping for air. Drowning in molten metal. Horrific dreams.'

'You did a horrific thing.'

'I did it for Rafa, Carlinhos, our mother. You.'

'Our debts are settled.'

'They are now.'

'You'll retire gracefully,' Ariel says. 'Cultivate your garden. Become the two worlds' greatest expert on bossa nova. Get into sports – you have your own handball team now. Learn politics, comment with insight and pungency. Raise your son.'

Ariel sees old pain tighten Lucas's face.

'It seems a light sentence.'

'Is it?' Ariel says. 'Why did you want to see me, irmão?'

'Why did you do it? Cortas don't do politics. And here we are, a convocation of Eagles.'

'Vidhya Rao showed me the future.'

For a moment Lucas can't place the name.

'The economist. Whitacre Goddard. Did er computers prophesy for you? What is it e calls them?'

'The Three August Sages. No, e told me about a conversation e had with Wang Yongqing, Anselmo Reyes and Monique Bertin. E proposed er Lunar Bourse idea.'

'I saw er present it.'

'Were you there at the meeting where the terrestrials proposed funding it, on the basis that it needed no human input?'

'What do you mean?' Lucas shifts uncomfortably on his stick.

'Vidhya Rao asked her computers to construct likely futures. They all foresaw a moon depopulated by disease. Plagues, Lucas. The terrestrials' plan for us. A dark machine, grinding out value. I was the only one in a position to act. I had a clear path to the power to stop them.'

'Use the codes.'

A command – and Beija Flor has laid them all out in plain vision, the options and powers of the Eagle of the Moon – and she could put every terrestrial to the blade.

'We have to be better than them, Lucas.'

She will not commit another Ironfall.

'They wouldn't hesitate.'

She surveys the virtual array of commands, edicts and executive functions. There. The work of a thought.

'I won't do that, Lucas.'

'So be it.' He purses thumb and fingers in the Corta salutation. 'I will retire, but not gracefully. I intend to be as irritating and vexatious as I can be. Someone needs to hold you to account, sister.'

'Lucas.'

He turns on the top step.

'That thing I told you about. The one I needed to do first. I just did it.'

At Leeuwenhoek a VTO track-queen plugs her suit into the diagnostic port of the broken-down freight hauler.

Out on the glass-fields south of Abul Wafa a glasser sends his maintenance bots scurrying out in search of cracks.

In the helium-fields of Mare Anguis a duster uncaps a vac-pen and scrawls *Corta Hélio* across the Mackenzie Helium logo.

In Meridian in the Seven Funk hotshop on Tereshkova Prospekt the star noodle-maker twirls and stretches and pulls the fine dough while the customers gossip about the shocks and surprises of Corta versus Corta.

In Twé a horticulturist checks grow-tower availability and cross-indexes it with AKA seed banks. She has heard there is to be a society wedding; Mackenzie-Vorontsova-Asamoah. Someone will have to supply the flowers.

In the eighty-seventh level of Queen of the South's Perth Tower, a schoolkid glances away from her networked classmates to look out of the apartment window: what was that flicker in her bottom right corner of her eye? A flyer? She loves flyers.

In the bottom right corner of each of those eyes, of every eye, for all life and memory, there have been four tiny icons. Air, water, data, carbon: the Four Fundamentals.

And all at once, everywhere, those little lights go out.

First the panic. In half a century, those lights that spell life and health and wealth have never failed.

Then the whole moon holds its breath. Holds it, not knowing if there will be another one. Holds it until the eye bulge, the brain seethes red, the heart screams. Until it cannot be held any longer.

The moon exhales.

And inhales. No charge. No tick of bitsies in the little golden icon, no price notifications. Priceless. The second breath, and the third, and the one after that and the one after that. Breathing free.

Ariel Corta has abolished the Four Fundamentals.

The young man is very good-looking in that lunar way; tall, brown skin, soft brown eyes, dark hair, close-shaved to quantum levels. Tall of course and pleasingly put together. When she first came to the moon she had found the moon people unsightly; their proportions disproportionate, top heavy, limbs too long, joints subtly out of place. She has learned to see them by their own aesthetics, and by those, this man is most easy on the eye. And outside are five equally handsome compatriots, ready to storm the apartment should she conjure some opposition to him. A middle-aged functionary of the Lunar Mandate Authority, against a fit young Brasilian.

She wonders where he keeps the knife in that suit.

The fashion has changed again. She could never understand the lunar fascination with historical styles and retro fads. She knows they think her dowdy in her modest, political suit. She thinks them effete and reactionary.

'Senhora Wang? My name is Nelson Medeiros. I have been sent by the Eagle of the Moon. If you please?'

He indicates the door.

The bots would have cut that sharp suit from around this cocksure puppy, then taken him to pieces. When the bots went into sleep and could not be made to obey, she knew this visit was inevitable.

'So which is it to be?' Wang Yongqing asks. 'Out the airlock, or a blade through the cervical vertebrae?'

'Senhora,' Nelson Medeiros says. 'You hurt my pride. That may be how you do things down there, but up here we are civilised people.'

The escoltas she imagined are waiting outside, with Monique and Anselmo, and a flock of motos waits.

'We're going to the station?' Wang Yongqing asks. Anselmo and Monique never learned Meridian's three-dimensional cartography, but she grew up in the sky-scraper towers of Guizhou and can read the levels and ramps and elevators like the corridors and crosswalks and overpasses of her childhood.

'A railcar is waiting for you,' Nelson Medeiros says. 'You will be taken to a secure site, when you will remain in safety and comfort during the political transition.'

'Hostages,' Wang Yongqing says.

'Hostages is an old-fashioned word,' the Primo Escolta says. 'This is a different moon. You are our guests.'

'Guests who can't check out.'

'That depends on how eager your governments are to negotiate. But it will be six-star luxury.'

'Where are you taking us?'

The young man's smile is like a sky full of stars.

'Boa Vista.'

'So do I pass?'

'You're the Eagle of the Moon,' Alexia Corta says.

Ariel Corta tuts in exasperation.

'What did my brother ever see in you? *Pass.*' She sweeps a theatrical hand down the front of her attire.

Dress; Cristobal Balenciaga 1953, Maninho says. Alexia knows nothing and cares less than nothing about 1950s couture. *Black unlined wool trimmed with finely ribbed silk satin. Hat by Aage Thaarup, shoes by Roger Vivier, bag and gloves by Cabrelli.*

Alexia adjusts the set of the Thaarup cartwheel hat.

'Perfect.'

'You're a shit liar, Mão de Ferro. And are you going to introduce me in that?'

How many times has Alexia attended here, in the antechamber to the Pavilion of the New Moon, fussing over the lie of his cufflinks, the set of his tie, the drape of his jacket, with Lucas? Habits and superstitions that quickly became rituals.

'I like this look,' Alexia says. She has only just learned how to wear 1940s style. She likes the forties. She can rock the forties.

'You like to look like a refugee,' Ariel says.

'How did anyone ever work with you?' Alexia says.

Ariel beams at the defiance.

'Because they adored me, darling. Well, that'll have to wait. Impatient Dragons are irritable Dragons. Now, I want you to go in and give me the kind of introduction a god would envy.'

'Lucas had a . . . thing.'

'Thing?'

'From the old days. The first days. "Sers: the Eagle has Landed".'

Ariel hisses in distaste.

'That's ridiculous, darling. My name, my title, and a bit of swish time.'

'Okay, senhora.'

Ariel's smile is genuine now.

'I'm fucking terrified, you know,' she confides.

'You faced down Lucas in the Court of Clavius,' Alexia says.

'That was my territory. My domain. Here I have no idea what I'm doing.'

'If it's any help, Lucas didn't either,' Alexia says.

'I sat on the other side of the floor when Jonathon Kayode abolished the LDC,' Ariel says. 'He didn't know either. No one does.'

'You're a hero. You abolished the Four Fundamentals, you arrested the terrestrials...'

'Gave them to Lucas to look after,' Ariel says brightly. 'You make me laugh, Mão. Right. Show time.'

As Alexia opens the door to the council chamber floor she catches Ariel de-correcting her correction to the tilt of the Thaarup hat. Alexia steps into the light. The familiar council murmur falls silent. Through the glare she can see the tiers reserved for the Dragons and great families filled, the sector kept for the terrestrials empty. Arrayed along the gallery at the rear are academics, heads of faculties, deans from the University of Farside.

'Sers,' she says. 'Ariel Corta, the Eagle of the Moon.'

Ariel takes Alexia's place under the spotlights. Her face is hidden beneath the wide brim of her hat. The silence is total. She looks up, smiles, throws wide her arms. And the Pavilion of the Full Moon thunders with voices.

'You call me the moment you get in, you hear?'

Robson rolls his eyes and tries to drift away across the station's thronged concourse to the escalators down to the platforms but the

Earth is bright and Wagner Corta has the eyes and reactions of a wolf and he moves effortlessly to follow the boy.

'Okay okay, the moment I get in.'

Wagner knows he is being overprotective. He signed the co-parenting agreement with Max and Arjun; Robson will live with Haider when the Earth is round and Wagner goes back to the pack. They are honest, they are kind, they are loving and they are trustworthy to the extent that they have changed jobs and moved to Hypatia to break the link with Theophilus. Robson will be safe and happy and cared for. But who can blame Wagner for being overprotective, after the horrors of Theophilus and the assassination of Bryce Mackenzie at João de Deus?

Assassination. A thirteen-year-old kid drove five poison needles into Bryce Mackenzie's eyeballs. One would have killed him sure as stone. Five was to advertise to the whole moon that this was the slow justice of the Cortas. Poison needles procured by that kid's uncle, brought to him by his best friend. Poison needles he hid in his hair, because Bryce wanted him naked and vulnerable.

Wagner can't think of that. In the bright of the Earth, emotions burn hotter and more fiercely and Wagner cannot look too long at the failure and weakness and inadequacy he feels when he thinks of Robson a hostage. A toy.

Lucas had done what he could not. Lucas had wrought the revenge. Not out of any senze of loyalty to his own brother – to his nephew – but for the name of Corta. Family first. Family always.

It was for family that Analiese had betrayed Robson. He loathes her but he can't blame her. The Five Deaths of the Asamoahs were not enough for Bryce Mackenzie.

The train is in, the crowd move towards the stairs. Wagner and Robson ride down, side by side. Gods. The kid is getting big. It seems only hours since they escaped this city under the protection of a Mackenzie debt, and Robson had been a cute kid sleeping on his shoulder as the train ran east towards the Sea of Tranquillity.

'You don't have to come with me to the lock,' Robson says as they step off the escalator. The train waits beyond the pressure glass, a big double-decker Equatorial Express. Meridian is still giddy and disbelieving, almost hung-over after Ariel's abolition of the Four Elementals. A pillar of life, knocked away, and yet the roof of the world stands. The quadras glitter with excitement. What next? Abolish the Court of Clavius and have laws? An election? Politics? The contagion of enthusiasm has spread even to the crowds boarding the Equatorial Express: there are smiles, people give way to others, there is laughing and chat and a sense of leisure that comes when every breath is no longer an entry in a profit and loss account.

Robson stands obdurately between Wagner and the lock, making it as clear as he can that this is the place of parting.

'I'll see you in João,' Wagner says. He takes up the new position as soon as the Earth diminishes. Corta Hélio is back, but it will never be what it was. The Helium Age is over, a new age is beginning. The Suns empower, the Mackenzies mine, the Asamoahs grow and the Vorontsovs fly. What do the Cortas do now?

The Cortas do politics.

Wagner and Robson embrace long and close. There is still nothing to the boy; he is wire and bone.

'See you in João,' Robson says. He turns at the lock. 'Pãe . . .'

Wagner heart turns over.

'What did you say?'

Robson blushes, then looks up, fierce and determined.

'Pãe!'

'What, filho?'

'Look after yourself.'

Then he turns and passes through the lock into the great train and Wagner turns, his heart burning, his breath catching, his throat tight and rides the escalators up into the light of Meridian and the high, blue Earth and the place where the wolves are waiting.

*

In one, two, three steps Robson is twenty metres up in the roof-world. New city, new infrastructure to run. Hypatia is a much larger city than Theophilus and its secret traceur geography very much more exciting. Here are dark shafts so deep they return echoes, vaults so high they have their own weather. Piping runs from which he can spy, unsuspected, on whole districts. Gantries and ducts, ladders and handholds. Older too: Robson's early explorings deep into the inner city found names and dates from the last century. Thick dust. These old, virgin places drew him. His church, his healing place.

Robson understands why Max and Arjun had brought him and Haider straight from Meridian to this new city. Theophilus would always smell of blood and fear to Robson. But Haider had found Analiese.

I see it, Haider said. *I see her every day. In the corner of my eye, something moves and I look and she's there.*

He came back every day to the Church of Dust until he found the footprint. A gripsole, small. Pace long. A traceur's tread. The perfection was defiled so he added his own prints to the trail as he tracked the runner's course through the dust and a tic-tac up between two pipes to a duct node.

Another runner. He was not alone.

At first he felt a knotted, resentful anger.

Anger is good, his therapist said, *anger is right. It's where the anger takes you.*

Driving poison needles into Bryce Mackenzie's eyes, that's where, he wanted to say every session. Wanted to say, but never said. He saved that anger for the dust, where he could take it out and look at it and ask it to lead him across the pristine dust to somewhere new. Until someone else ran the dust before him. That is a different anger, one that half-lifed quickly into a different emotion: curiosity, excitement. Another runner.

He loves Haider, Haider is half of his soul, but he is not and never can be a runner and the thing between runners can't be explained to anyone who is not a runner.

He's not alone.

'Ey-ho.'

That is Haider. Robson vaults a thick water-pipe on to a narrow gantry and sits, legs dangling into the drop. There is Haider, looking up, the only dark on him the flop of hair over his eye.

'I wish you wouldn't do that, it makes me sick,' he calls up.

'Then come on up,' Robson says.

Haider makes an obscene gesture.

'You cut your therapist again.'

After Theophilus, after what Lucas Corta made them do in the name of family, after João de Deus, Robson and Haider have been prescribed therapy. *It will be months of work*, the doctors said. *Maybe years.*

'Mine's human,' Robson says.

Haider grimaces as if he had tasted sick.

'Since when?'

'Since I started being obstructive with the AI.'

' "Being obstructive"?'

'That's what Damien calls it.'

'Your therapist is called Damien?'

'He's called Damien and he smiles too much.'

'Maybe,' Haider says, 'it's easier if you just talked to the AI.'

'I like it here.'

'It will work.'

'Everything works. Nothing works.'

'Something for you.' Haider holds up a hand. In his palm is a small package wrapped in exquisite fabric. It sits eaily, comfortably. Robson's breath catches.

'Where did you get that?'

'It was delivered to Max and Arjun,' Haider calls. 'It's from the Palace of Eternal Light. Do you think it's . . .'

Robson pushes himself off the crosswalk. Haider's eyes go wide but twenty metres is nothing to someone who once fell three thousand metres. And got up and walked. A few steps. He puts out his arms to let his baggy shirt parachute and break the fall. Robson Corta lands coiled, elastic on his feet. He shakes out his high-piled hair.

'... Safe?' Haider concludes.

'Safe now,' Robson says and takes the small pack, and unwraps the beautiful fabric. Half a deck of cards. As he suspected. 'Thank you, Darius,' Robson whispers.

'Darius?' Haider asks. 'Like, that Darius?'

Robson takes his cards from the pocket of his parkour-shorts, lays the half-deck on top, riffles, shuffles. Together again. Whole.

'That Darius. I'll explain. Not now. Hey, I've found a new hotshop to try out.'

'Might give that a go,' Haider says. A kid's hotshop is important. More important than therapy. It's the heart of their social life. It's where your friends are.

'Okay,' Robson says. 'Let's check out the horchata in this town.'

Wang Yongqing has requested another meeting; her fifth since arriving in Boa Vista.

'What is it this time?' Lucas Corta asks Toquinho.

Access to printers, his familiar replies. *Some of the financial delegates have had to wear the same clothes three days in a row.*

Lucas sighs. He turns in his chair to look out over the lush green leafscapes of his kingdom. He had dreamed of wildness. Instead he is warden of a gilded jail. It's a poetic punishment.

'My schedule?' Toquinho shows him an array of slots. 'Postpone Naomi Allain; standard apologies. Move Senhora Wang into her slot.' There is little Lucas can do; resources are stretched and it is more politic for any new printers to be sent to João de Deus. Wang Yongqing will make her protest, standing as ever. He will issue more standard apologies and then he will invite her to sit and they will talk. She is a good conversationalist. Art, politics, the ways of two worlds. Jazz. She is an aficionado. She is too intelligent ever to make the mistake of assuming that they have an enemy in common. Family first. Family always.

Still, they pass the time, these small exchanges.

The conversation will be especially good today. In her inaugural address to the new Lunar Assembly, Ariel gave name to the thing that has haunted every imagination since the ecstasy at the ending of the Four Fundamentals wore off. Euphoria has a short half-life. *Independence.* Ariel can be relied on for a rhetorical flourish but Lucas, in his internal exile, routinely intercepts the communications between Earth and its representatives on the moon and the words are darkening, the tone hardening, the attitudes turning to stone.

He could be here for a long time if Ariel decides to hold the terrestrials as guarantors of Earth not nuking Meridian and Queen of the South. He does not doubt that there would be one warhead with *João de Deus* vacuum-markered on the side. Wang Yongqing will have the most wonderful horror stories to chill him over their tea and modal jazz.

It won't happen. The terrestrials think they are tough and can cut a shrewd deal but they haven't grown up negotiating every breath of air, every sip of water, every scrap of shelter scratched from the rock. They haven't argued for their lives with Dona Luna. Ariel will always pull the malandragem move.

It will be a hard-won independence. The moon-kind are small in number, their weapons few and their enemies great as the number of stars in the sky. But they hold the high place. That, Lucas Corta thinks, will be enough.

Toquinho chimes. *Your delivery from Queen of the South.*

He has not seen this escolta before. Wagner sends them over from João on rapid rotation. It would not do for security to become too familiar with the secured. The wolf is working well in João: the de-Mackenzie-isation is straightforward. Revenge attacks are few though there is still friction between Santinhos and former Mackenzie Helium dusters who have contracted to the resurgent Corta Hélio. Disrespects, cold shoulders, glances and looks. 'This is a Brasilian city, speak Portuguese!' Squarings-up, facings-off; flash-fire fights. As long as the helium flows. Wagner, who has worked on the glass, understands that the future of fusibles lies in space, not on Earth.

The delivery is a long, shallow impact-case. Lucas trusts it has not been sent by BALTRAN. Where everything is printed, shipping hand-made goods is a vanishing skill. The delivery sits in his desk but Lucas hesitates to unseal it. To open it is to accept the challenge within; to let it test his courage and commitment. Yet he aches to snap the locks and hold the thing inside in his hands, press it against his body, explore its curves and contours.

Robson is with Haider in Theophilus. The adoption will be straightforward and Wagner is the only one who can begin to heal the wounds driven deep into that boy. Lucas's hand made some of those wounds. He almost believes that all he did was enable the kid's rage but self-delusion has never been Lucas Corta's sin. He wielded Robson like a blade of meteoric iron.

Luna is with her mother in Twé. Eldritch child. Her painted face, half living, half skull, has become lunar legend; the symbol of hope, persistence and justice. Lucas cannot shake the notion that it will always be there, within her skin.

Lucasinho is preparing for his first independent visit. He is going to Meridian to see Abena Asamoah. Lucas argued firmly against it – not that the journey might be too much for Lucasinho, but that Abena Asamoah would eat him alive. Dangerous, ambitious, hungry young woman. The spaces and sinuses of Oxala had rung to shouting voices. The strength of Lucasinho's resistance was what had convinced Lucas to let him go. That zashitnik will be going with him. Lucas can't remember her name, but she was handy on the flight of the *Orel*. He might offer her a permanent contract.

What wreckage we are, each and every one of us.

But the family is away and he has nothing but a day of meetings and a special delivery from Queen of the South.

'Toquinho, cancel my ten thirty.' He opens the locks, removes the lid. 'And my eleven and eleven thirty.'

He lifts out the guitar case and sets it on his desk. Every instinct is to open it at once but that would rush the experience. Everything has its pleasures and perfections. Lucas Corta runs his fingers over the true leather, the bright brass hasps and hinges. Then he snaps the catches and opens the case.

What strikes him first is the perfume. Wood, priceless organic varnishes, natural resins and polishes; Lucas almost reels at the aroma. Then he sees the colours, sungolds and ambers, dark mahogany, mother-of-pearl lozenges hand-cut from Twé-farmed shellfish between the frets, the halo of marquetry around the sound-hole. He picks it up like a newborn. It is light and muscular and filled with life. He sits down carefully but the guitar tells him how to hold it, where to place it, how to meet its body with his.

He wants it to speak, to welcome its first vowels, to hear its tone and voice, but his fingers hesitate over the strings.

He knows nothing. Less than nothing.

That is the beginning of any relationship: strangers drawn to each other.

Can he do it? He has the time, the dedication, the discipline to learn hard things, but is there more? What if, after years of study and practice and learning, he realises he will never be able to make those strings whisper and laugh like João Gilberto?

It will still have been a journey worth taking. Perhaps only João Gilberto could be João Gilberto, and all that is necessary is for Lucas Corta to be Lucas Corta. Still, some day, some year; it will be good to duet with Jorge Mauro.

His fingers strike the strings. It is out of tune. Irrational to have expected concert pitch to survive the trip from Queen of the South.

So, tuning then. The first thing that he will perform every day of his playing life.

All good work is the work of a lifetime.

Flour, sugar, butter, eggs.

The four fundamentals of cake.

The connections between his reforged memories still surprise Lucasinho Corta. Think of Abena Maanu Asamoah and his memory says, *Cake.*

'I made cake?' he asked Jinji.

You were famous for it, Jinji says and throws up a montage of images of parties, surprises, gifts, culminating in him anointing Abena Asamoah's chakras with real cow-cream from his strawberry gateau.

'I'm bringing cake,' Lucasinho says.

Jinji calls up recipes but none of them are worthy of Abena.

'Is there a thing called coffee cake?' Lucasinho asks.

There is, Jinji says and shows him how to make it. The ingredients are rare – one unobtainable in the political climate, but printers can synthesise a coffee flavouring that will pass for anyone who has never tasted the true bean – and the equipment dauntingly technical.

I can requisition a catering microwave oven, Jinji says.

'Will it make a difference?'

As much as the synthetic coffee.

Flour. Lucasinho frowns at the white powder. He sticks a finger into it. Surprised by the silky liquidity, he pushes his hand into the bowl, feels it flow over his skin, through his fingers.

Sugar. He sniffs the crystals, moistens a fingertip, dips, tastes. Images flood through him, a torrent of sense-memories so vivid and poignant he reels back against the cook-room wall.

Butter. Congealed cow-fat. He takes the pat, squeezes it through his fingers, enjoys the greasy unctuousness. He rubs a smear along each cheekbone. It feels dirty and sexy.

Eggs. He holds each one up before him, marvels at its perfect completeness. It is a universe in the palm of his hand. Yet it came out of a living creature. He shakes his head.

From such unpromising materials, he must work magic.

Coffee cake says, I would move the Earth in the sky to make you happy. He remembers he said that, somewhere, to someone. Luna. On the dark walk.

The bowls, the bakeware, the implements, the flavourings and decorations are to hand. Something is missing. Something is not right. Lucasinho takes a deep breath. Then he kicks off his shoes, slips his shirt over his head. He draws in his belly muscles, unfastens his pants and lets them fall. He steps out of them, kicks them away.

Naked, he stands ready for cake.

He cracks his fingers, lifts the butter and begins. Above him, beyond the curved brow of Oxala, beyond the artificial sky of Boa Vista, the bare, airless, radiation-blasted surface of the Sea of Fecundity stretches beyond the edge of seeing.

GLOSSARY

Many languages are spoken on the moon and the vocabulary cheerfully borrows words from Chinese, Portuguese, Russian, Yoruba, Spanish, Arabic, Akan.

Pronunciation guide: in Portuguese, nh is pronounced like a Spanish ñ. Lucasinho is approximately 'Lucasi*nyo*'. The diphthongs *ãe* and *ão* are nasal, almost an 'n' sound.

A: common contraction for asexual.
Abusua: group of people who share a common maternal ancestor. AKA maintains them and their marriage taboos to preserve genetic diversity.
Adinkra: Akan visual symbols that represent concepts or aphorisms.
Afilhada: goddaughter.
Amor: lover/partner.
Amory: polyamorys, one of the moon's many forms of partnering and marriage.
Anjinho: little angel. Corta term of endearment.
Auriverde: the Brasilian flag.
Banya: Russian sauna and steam bath.
Beija Flor: Hummingbird.

Blackstar: AKA surface worker (derived from the nickname of the Ghana national football team).

Boceta: Brasilian slang for vagina.

Bogan: Australian slang for a vulgar person of low status.

Bruxa/Bruxaria: witch/craft.

Chib: a small virtual pane in an interactive contact lens that shows the state of an individual's accounts for the Four Elementals.

Coracão: my heart. A term of endearment.

Cunhada: sister-in-law.

Escolta: bodyguard.

Feijoada: a Rio de Janeiro bean and meat stew. An icon of the city.

Four Elementals: air, water, carbon and data: the basic commodities of lunar existence, paid for daily by the chib system.

Gatinha: kitten/young woman.

Globo: a simplified form of English, the lingua franca of the moon, with a codified pronunciation comprehensible by machines.

Ghazi: Arabic knight-of-the-faith. On the moon, a warrior-scholar of the University of Farside.

Gupshup: the main gossip channel on the lunar social network.

Humpy: Western Australian slang for a rough shack.

Irmã/Irmão: sister/brother.

Jackaroo: Mackenzie Metals slang for a surface worker, from an Australian word for a male apprentice sheep-station hand.

Jo/Joe Moonbeam: new arrival on the moon.

Keji-oko: second spouse.

Kotoko: AKA council, of rotating memberships.

Kuozhao: dust-mask.

Ladeira: a staircase or ramp from one level of a quadra to another.

Laoda: boss of a Taiyang surface squad.

Maame: Mom in Akan. The standard Asamoah term of maternal endearment.

Madrinha: surrogate mother. Literally 'Godmother'.

Mãe de Santo: Mother of the Saint, abbess of the Sisterhood of the Lords of Now.

Malandragem: the art of the trickster, bad-assery.

Mamãe/Mae, Papai/pai: Mother/Mom, Father/Dad.

Mirador: a viewpoint or lookout.

Moto: three-wheel automated cab.

Nana: Ashanti term of respect to an elder.

Nikah: a marriage contract. The term comes from Arabic.

Oko: spouse in marriage.

Okrana: VTO private security.

Omahene: CEO of AKA, on an eight-year rotation.

Orixa: deities and saints in the syncretistic Afro-Brasilian umbanda religion.

Oware: Asante strategy game of the pit-and-pebble type.

Primo: cousin

Santinhos: 'Little Saints'; slang name for residents of João de Deus.

Sasuit: surface-activity suit.

Saudade: homesick melancholy. A sophisticated and essential element of bossa nova music.

Sobrinha/o: niece/nephew

Terreiro: meeting place for Afro-Brasilian religions.

Tia/Tio: aunt/uncle.

Wushi: Taiyang security.

Zabbaleen: freelance organics recyclers, who then sell on to the LDC which owns all organic material.

Zashitnik: a hired fighter in trial by combat; literally defender, advocate.

Zhongqiu: the second most important lunar festival after New Year.

Dramatis Personae

CORTA

Lucas Corta: Eagle of the Moon.
Lucasinho Corta: only son of Lucas Corta.
Ariel Corta: former lawyer in the Court of Clavius.
Wagner Corta: estranged brother of Lucas Corta, moon-wolf.
Robson Corta: son of Rafa Corta and Rachel Mackenzie, under the protection of Wagner Corta.
Luna Corta: daughter of Rafa Corta and Lousika Asamoah.
Alexia Corta: Earth-born Iron Hand of Lucas Corta.
Elis: madrinha of Luna Corta.
Marina Calzaghe: former PA and bodyguard to Ariel Corta, returned to Earth.
Jorge Mauro: musician and one-time amor of Lucas Corta.
Nelson Medeiros: chief escolta to Lucas Corta.

TAIYANG

Lady Sun: the Dowager of Shackleton, grandmother of the CEO of Taiyang.

Darius Mackenzie-Sun: late son of Jade and Robert Mackenzie, protégé of Lady Sun.
Sun Zhiyuan: CEO of Taiyang.
Amanda Sun: ex-oko of Lucas Corta.
Tamsin Sun: Head of Legal Services.
Jaden Sun: board member and owner of Tigers of the Sun handball team.
Amalia Sun: Amanda Sun's agent to the University of Farside.
Jiang Ying Yue: Taiyang Head of Security.

MACKENZIE METALS

Duncan Mackenzie: oldest son of Robert and Alyssa Mackenzie, CEO of Mackenzie Metals.
Anastasia Vorontsova: oko of Duncan Mackenzie.
Apollonaire Vorontsova: keji-oko of Duncan Mackenzie.
Denny Mackenzie: youngest son of Duncan and Apollonaire; disinherited by Duncan Mackenzie for treachery.
Kimmie-Leigh Mackenzie: (briefly) betrothed to Irina Efua Vorontsova-Asamoah.

MACKENZIE HELIUM

Bryce Mackenzie: brother of Duncan Mackenzie, CEO Mackenzie Helium.
Finn Warne: First Blade of Mackenzie Helium.
Hossam El Ibrashy: First Blade of Mackenzie Helium.
Rowan Solveig-Mackenzie, Alfonso Pereztrejo, Jaime Hernandez-Mackenzie: executives Mackenzie Metals.
Analiese Mackenzie: dark-amor of Wagner Corta in his dark aspect.

AKA

Lousika Asamoah: Omahene of the Golden Stool.

Abena Asamoah: political science student at the Cabochon colloquium and legal assistant to Ariel Corta.

VTO

Valery Vorontsov: CEO VTO Space.

Yevgeny Vorontsov: CEO of VTO Moon.

Sergei Vorontsov: CEO VTO Earth.

Irina Efua Vorontsova-Asamoah: ecologist and daughter of a dynastic Asamoah/Vorontsov marriage.

LUNAR MANDATE AUTHORITY

Wang Yongqing: Chinese delegate to the LMA.

Anselmo Reyes: delegate from the Davenant Venture Capital fund.

Monique Bertin: European Union delegate to the LMA.

UNIVERSITY OF FARSIDE

Dakota Kaur Mackenzie: ghazi of the Faculty of Biocybernetics.

Dr Gebreselassie: physician to Lucasinho Corta.

Rosario Salgado O'Hanlon de Tsiolkovski: failed ghazi, zashitnik to Ariel Corta.

Vidhya Rao: economist and mathematician, former banker with Whitacre Goddard.

EARTH

Marina Calzaghe: former PA TO Ariel Corta.
Kessie: sister.
Ocean: niece.
Weavyr: niece.
Skyler: brother.

OTHERS

Mariano Gabriel Demaria: director of the School of Seven Bells, an assassin's college.
Haider: Robson Corta's best friend.
Max and Arjun: Haider's care givers.

Lunar Calendar

The Lunar Calendar is divided into twelve lunes named after the signs of the Zodiac: Aries, Taurus, Gemini, Cancer, Leo, Virgo, Libra, Scorpio, Sagittarius, Capricorn, Aquarius, Pisces, plus a New Year's Day.

The days of each lune are derived from the Hawaiian system of naming each day after a different moon-phase. Thus the lune has 30 days and no weeks.

1: Hilo
2: Hoaka
3: Ku Kahi
4: Ku Lua
5: Ku Kolu
6: Ku Pau
7: Ole Ku Kahi
8: Ole Ku Lua
9: Ole Ku Kolu
10: Ole Ku Pau
11: Huna
12: Mohalu
13: Hua

14: Akua
15: Hoku
16: Mahealani
17: Kulua
18: Lā'au Kū Kahi
19: Lā'au Kuū Lua
20: Lā'au Pau
21: 'Ole Kū Kahi
22: 'Ole Kū Lua
23: 'Ole Pau
24: Kāloa Kū Kahi
25: Kāloa Kū Lua
26: Kāloa Pau
27: Kāne
28: Lono
29: Mauli
30: Muku

Additionally, the larger cities (with the exception of Queen of the South) operate a three-shift system: mañana, tarde, noche. Each shift is eight hours apart. Noon in mañana is 8 p.m. in tarde and 4 a.m. in noche.